WITHDRAWN
FOR SALE

5ºp

Heaven, Hell & MADEMOISELLE

Heaven, Hell & MADEMOISELLE

Harold Carlton

First published in Great Britain in 2010 by Orion Books,
an imprint of The Orion Publishing Group Ltd
Orion House, 5 Upper Saint Martin's Lane
London WC2H 9EA

An Hachette UK Company

1 3 5 7 9 10 8 6 4 2

Most   any
reseml   ntal.

A CIP catalogue record for this book is
available from the British Library.

ISBN (Hardback) 978 1 4091 1517 5
ISBN (Trade Paperback) 978 1 4091 1518 2

Typeset at The Spartan Press Ltd,
Lymington, Hants

Printed and bound in Great Britain by
Clays Ltd, St Ives plc

The Orion Publishing Group's policy is to use papers that
are natural, renewable and recyclable products and made
from wood grown in sustainable forests. The logging and
manufacturing processes are expected to conform to the
environmental regulations of the country of origin.

www.orionbooks.co.uk

For Joan Marquès

One

Monique Far

Chanel's glass doors swung open at precisely ten o'clock in the morning. Two demure young girls in grey dresses stepped on to the pavement. They held huge flacons of perfume which they began to spray up and down the Rue Cambon. The aroma floated across to the other side of the narrow Paris street where a young woman stood watching, her round dark eyes wide in disbelief. Monique's nostrils flared as she breathed in the heady scent of Chanel No. 5. Perfuming the street could only be a preparation for the arrival of the most successful, most respected woman in fashion: Mademoiselle Gabrielle Chanel, the woman for whom she hoped to work.

The girls disappeared back into the Chanel building, taking their flacons with them. Monique waited, neat in a grey tweed suit she had tailored herself to flatter her matronly figure. Her breath escaped visibly in the crisp, September air. She stared at the doors that would lead to her first haute couture interview. 31 Rue Cambon. The significance of that address, engraved on her brain since she was fifteen, could only be appreciated by another fashion-addict. She had always dreamed of working there. And now here she was, early for her interview because she had been told that she might glimpse Mademoiselle Chanel herself, crossing the street from her home at the Ritz Hotel. Monique had dressed down for today, still with the ridiculous (she knew) notion that make-up made a girl seem cheap.

'Kiss me, Papa!' she heard her eight-year-old voice demand.

1

Why did her mind choose to flash back to her childhood? Was it because her entire life seemed to have led up to this very moment?

'Kiss me,' the little girl repeated, and she saw herself leaning her face close to her father's, lips pursed in a child's idea of a kiss. She was playing in the living-room of their modest Angers house, a doctor's home with its heavy mahogany furniture and Oriental rugs beaten once a year in the garden, then spread on parquet floors. A living-room 'too good' to be used too often.

Her father dutifully pecked her cheek.

'*Not* like that!' she cried disappointedly. 'On the *lips*! The way the prince kisses the Sleeping Beauty!'

She remembered closing her eyes, expecting her father to comply, as he always did with her commands. But the game was suddenly cut off by a stinging slap across her face.

'Little girls don't kiss their fathers on the lips!' her mother screamed.

Monique had been too astonished to cry. It was the first time anyone had hit her. The slap hurt, her cheek turned red. She gave her mother an incredulous, hate-filled look before running upstairs to her room, slamming the door and throwing herself face down on the bed.

Moments later, a soft knock on the door preceded her father carefully sitting beside her on the bed.

'I'm so sorry. *Maman* shouldn't have slapped you, darling. But you see, fathers cannot kiss their little girls on the lips.'

'*Why?*'

'They just don't. But aren't I lucky to be loved by two such pretty women? You are my special little girl, you know.'

Monique considered this. 'Am I really pretty? *Maman* is, but I don't think I am.'

'But of course you are, my darling. All my women are beautiful . . .'

Two years later, Monique's sister was born. Caterine resembled her mother and Monique took after her father. Monique wasn't in the least jealous of her pretty sister. She saw her as a kind of doll to dress and play with.

Angers parents liked to fetch their children from school. The girls would run screaming from school at the end of each day, Monique shouting as lustily as the others, looking for the familiar face of her papa.

One afternoon, a group of mothers were huddled around someone lying in the street. Monique stopped, frowning. It was a man. Some women parted to allow her through. It was Papa. He looked as if he were sleeping. She bent over him and tugged at his arm, crying, 'Papa! Papa!'

A mother knelt to place her arm around Monique, whispering, 'Poor little thing.'

Monique shook her father. Surely, he would sit up and tell her this was a joke? But he did not move.

A woman held her powder-compact mirror at his mouth, waiting.

'He's dead,' she said.

An ambulance arrived and her father was carefully lifted onto a stretcher and taken away.

Monique was twelve. After a large funeral, which showed how respected her father had been, there was a terrible gap in her life. She missed the warm hand holding hers, the feeling of being loved when he had hugged her. She could never convince herself that his death had not somehow been her fault. After all, he had come to fetch her from school.

She filled the gap by visiting Madame Denise, the woman who made her mother's clothes. Here she found a welcome and a warmth that was missing from her home. The dressmaker liked her and allowed her to pore over the latest copies of *Vogue* or *Jardin des Modes*. She was showing Monique how to perform little tasks for her, hemming a skirt or preparing a garment. Madame Denise's establishment became her escape into a different world and when she was praised for her perfect sewing, she felt the glowing pride of being very good at something: fashion! Fashion would be her greatest love. Not designing it, *making* it. Later, the idea came to her that it might be possible to work for a world-renowned Paris house, like Chanel.

Chanel! A small figure emerged from the Ritz's back entrance into the Rue Cambon, jerking Monique back to the present. The silhouette of this woman, hands thrust in jacket pockets, cigarette between lips, tweed boater set jauntily on her head, projected a defiant chic. Monique stared at her for a moment: there was no doubt who she was. Without even thinking, Monique found herself walking right up to her.

'Yes?' a hoarse voice barked.

Monique looked into impatient coal-black eyes set in a rather bitter face, criss-crossed with lines.

'Excuse me for introducing myself, Mademoiselle,' Monique began. 'I am Monique Far. I have an interview today with your staff manager for a job as seamstress. You are my idol. I love your clothes!'

The impatient eyes flashed at this interruption of her morning routine of crossing the road to work, but the girl staring adoringly at her seemed so sincere that her expression softened a little.

'Well, what a way to introduce yourself,' she said. 'In the street. What did you say your name was?'

'Monique Far, Mademoiselle. I have always loved your style.'

Her idol wore the first genuine Chanel suit Monique had ever seen. There was a freshness about the pink tweed. Looking closer, she saw the flecks of lavender and blue. It was so Chanel it took all of Monique's control not to reach out and touch it. But finally, she was unable to resist grazing it with her fingertips. Mademoiselle, following Monique's gaze, seemed to regard this touch as normal.

'Woven in Ireland especially for me,' she murmured.

Navy silk braid trimming pockets and cuffs, chunky gold buttons embossed with intertwined Cs, the cut and swing of the garment, the way ropes of pearls and chains tumbled carelessly over it, all combined to give Monique her first, unforgettable look at haute couture. The heady perfume wafting down the street propelled her into the world of fashion she had always wished to be in. Overwhelmed, she burst into tears.

Mademoiselle regarded her, puzzled. 'But what are you crying about?' She grasped Monique's arm, more to steady herself than to be friendly. They crossed the street together.

'It's just that . . .' Monique dabbed her eyes, 'I never dreamed I would meet you, Mademoiselle.'

'Where are you from?'

'From Angers, Mademoiselle. It's a small town just outside—'

'I know exactly where it is.'

Through her tears, Monique tried to return the penetrating stare.

'It is just such a great honour, Mademoiselle,' she whispered.

Mademoiselle dismissed 'honour' with a brusque gesture.

'This jacket.' She plucked at Monique's sleeve. 'Did you make it?'

Monique glanced down, having forgotten what she was wearing, 'Yes, I did.'

Without warning, the old lady pulled it open, bending to peer at the lining.

'Nicely finished.' She nodded at the blue and white cotton gingham. 'Silk linings pull on easier but it's the right idea, the inside must be as attractive as the outside . . .' She flashed her own jacket lining – a floral silk in pinks, blues and mauves, pretty enough to make up into a dress. She was famous for these touches of luxury which only the wearer saw. 'Well.' She raised pencilled eyebrows. 'The person you see will decide whether you suit our needs. If you are taken on, no doubt we shall meet again. Now I must get to work myself. Good luck.'

She walked towards the glass doors of Chanel, which magically opened as she approached, as if sensing her arrival. Monique stared after her, breathless, worshipful.

Sophie Antoine

Perched on a gilt chair at the back of the Hotel Druout auction-rooms, Sophie Antoine tried to look inconspicuous. She usually projected a smouldering sensual presence, but tonight she wished to keep very much to herself. The Cartier necklace her father had given her for her twenty-first birthday was about to come up for sale. She wanted to watch the proceedings through spread fingers, like a child watching a frightening film. Instead, she hid behind her sale catalogue. Her small face with its tiny tilted nose and lush rosebud mouth was exquisite. Petite and shapely, she wore a Burberry mackintosh over a black sweater and slacks, in contrast to most of the other women's little black dresses.

She was surprised that her necklace had ended up in such an important sale, the first of the autumn season, a special evening event where people gathered to witness jewels sell at record prices, hoping some of the glamour might rub off on them.

She looked over the elegant crowd. The women addicted to jewellery sat alongside their reluctant husbands, then there were the dealers, and the usual assortment of oglers seeking vicarious excitement.

This evening was the climax to events which had begun a few months ago when she had told her best friend Ines: 'I hate my life. The Sorbonne, the lessons, the work . . . I would do anything to run away, to rent my own little flat.'

They were sprawled on the tiny lawn of her parents' garden at the back of the Ecole Militaire house. It was the last warm autumn day. They both wore short filmy summer dresses with cardigans. A tray of tea sat between them.

'What's stopping you?' Ines looked directly at her.

'Lack of money,' Sophie had said.

'Sell that necklace your father gave you,' Ines suggested. 'You'll never wear it. It's worth plenty.'

'Papa would be furious,' Sophie said.

'Papa doesn't need to know,' Ines said.

'It belonged to his mother,' Sophie told her. 'He wanted it kept in the family.'

'But he gave it to you. It is *yours*. And you know how "in" art deco jewellery is at the moment?'

'Are you trying to get me into trouble, Ines?' Sophie had asked her. Ines often goaded her into being more daring than she actually was.

'You're twenty-three. Don't act like a little girl of thirteen. It's *your* life. And it's *your* necklace. Selling it isn't illegal.'

'Just immoral?'

Ines made a face. But she had sown the seed of an idea. Sophie had taken the necklace to the auctioneer's and, from the moment they had seized on it, assuring her a high price, she had felt trapped, half-wanting, half-dreading the chain of events she had set in motion.

'The Cartier diamond necklace,' the auctioneer announced now, making Sophie's pulse quicken. 'Art deco styled, containing five very good three-carat diamonds. We have had several written bids . . .'

Unsure whether to watch the proceedings, Sophie settled for shielding her eyes. Suddenly, an elegant hand snaked around her catalogue. A wave of perfume engulfed her.

'It *is* you!' Ghislaine de Rives, a celebrated socialite and friend of her mother's, smiled triumphantly. 'I thought I recognised that necklace.' Around forty, one of the most elegant women in Paris, Ghislaine wore a little black Chanel dress, her dark silky straight hair swept back by a wide black grosgrain ribbon.

She frowned. 'Do your parents know about this, Sophie?'

Sophie looked at her guiltily. 'Please don't say anything, Ghislaine.'

'Oh, Sophie.' Ghislaine gave a doubtful frown and returned to her seat.

'Shall we start at fifteen thousand francs?' the auctioneer suggested.

Sophie gasped: fifteen thousand was more than her wildest dreams.

'Sixteen? Seventeen, eighteen from over there? Twenty? Thirty? Fifty?'

Ever-growing sums of money were hurled around the auction-room as Sophie's eyes widened: this was like a dream!

'Telephone bid for one hundred thousand francs.' The auction-eer nodded to the blonde, chignonned assistant on the phone.

Sophie almost lost consciousness for a few moments. She was revived by the gavel smashing down with the cry, '*Sold!* At one hundred and twenty thousand francs!'

Ghislaine twisted around to look at her, goggling her eyes. It was an amazing amount of money. It represented freedom! Head lowered, Sophie hurried out of the auction-rooms.

She almost fell onto the red banquette of a nearby café and ordered a *vin blanc*. She lit a Gauloise, took a long puff, leaned back and closed her eyes. Now she was in trouble, her parents would be furious, but it was done and she must continue with her plan. She shrugged, her way of discarding all the petty irritations of life . . . parents, money, men, career. Long ago, she had assumed the pose that she simply didn't care. About anything. But, of course deep inside she did care, very much.

A man at the bar stared at her. So many men stared that she only noticed the men who did not stare. She ignored this one. She was very good at looking through men as if they were transparent. Her green eyes could flash from wickedly sexy to deceptively innocent, depending on how she aimed them at a man. The wild red hair framing her face gave her an incongruous halo. Her attractiveness and her magnetism were two things she took completely for granted.

The wine arrived and she sipped at it, relaxing. She had done it, she had set the wheels in motion. It was the culmination of a childhood and adolescent rebellion against most things her parents thought she should do. She had tried to believe that she was a lucky little girl: a lovely house, pretty clothes made for her, an exclusive girls' school, family holidays in Deauville or Nice. And yet there had always been that feeling of being very unlike her sisters, Francine and Isabelle, who were obedient, toed the line and did what their parents wanted them to do.

'Why can't you be like your sisters?' she remembered hearing so many times.

'Because I am not like them!' she would reply defiantly. She was the one who did not fit in. Why? Had she been the unwanted third daughter? Had her parents expected a son? Was this why she felt so different?

She remembered nothing before their elegant Ecole Militaire town-house, a corner one, grown over with glossy, dark green ivy. Yet she had always had the feeling that she had not been born there. In her imagination, she had been born far, far away.

Her mother was a formidable woman with intensely blue eyes set like sapphires in sculpted cheeks. Her hair had turned pure white early and she was lucky in that a short, feathery cut suited her and made her blue gaze even more dramatic. Her perfectly shaped head was like an oval Brancusi sculpture. She was known as 'Madame Antoine'. Sophie was a little afraid of her. Throughout her childhood, her mother and her father, a French Minister, Laurent Antoine, ran the chicest *salon* in Paris, where Paris's top people met on Sunday evenings to swap gossip, sip cocktails, nibble canapes and 'ooh and ah' over the hostess's perfectly behaved children. Sophie had rebelled against all this.

Madame Antoine was quite small and whilst not exactly slim she wore clothes in a way which made designers crave her presence and need her approval, especially when they designed their collections. She become a muse to famous designers. Christian Dior had doted on her. Finally, she ended up as *directrice* of the house of Chanel. A *directrice* – an elegant, well-connected woman who smooths things between clients, sales-ladies and designer – acts as a kind of 'image' for the house and wears only the designer's clothes. Madame Antoine considered Chanel the peak of her career.

Sophie grew up, developing perfect breasts, a slim body, and a height of about five feet four. She was precociously aware of her allure to men and enjoyed their frankly lustful glances at the cocktail parties her parents gave.

She carved imaginary notches on her bedpost of all the men who had desired her that day. She tested her powers: flirting, teasing, knowing men wanted her. At sixteen, she allowed a particularly handsome man to enter her bedroom, and shortly after that, enter her. She found the experience extremely enjoyable, almost guiltily so, though she felt little guilt. She kept the incident, and many subsequent ones, to herself. She was a modern young girl who enjoyed sex. The endless supply of admiring men just two floors below her bedroom was too convenient and exciting to resist. She grew addicted to the power and confidence sex gave her. The magazines she read so avidly were starting to say that there was nothing wrong in sex as long as one took precautions. The Pill became available. She continued her seductions but she rarely slept with any man more than once.

Once, she became besotted with a very attractive married man. Breaking her own rule, she enticed him three times into her bedroom. She suffered for that when he finally told her there was no future for their love. How difficult it was to cut a man out of your heart, and your mind, when you found yourself loving him. She vowed never to fall in love again, at least, not with a married man.

With *Maman*, she had visited the *maisons de couture* since childhood, sitting wide-eyed through the collections, the mannequins and their fantastic make-ups fascinating her even more than the clothes. Luxurious velvets, wools, crêpes, silk jerseys swished by as cooing women reached out to finger the fabrics and make notes of the dresses they wished to try on. She enjoyed watching the models shrug off their barbaric furs and carelessly drag them behind them on the floor as they walked.

She adored the cool, grey salons full of elegant women who left a breeze of perfume in their wake. She envied the girl apprentices who did little more than retrieve pins from fitting-room carpets and spray perfume throughout the *salons*. She longed to be part of this magical scented world.

Fashion was a way out from the endless political discussions at the dinner table. Politics was her father's life. By the time she was twenty-one and enrolled at the Sorbonne, Paris's most prestigious university, politics was all her fellow students talked about, too. If you didn't protest the Vietnam War alongside them, you were not accepted as '*au courant*' or 'happening'.

She broke a few hearts, sleeping with boys and discarding them.

In her parents' house, she continued her flirtations with older men, usually married ones. She liked leading them on, all the way to her bedroom door, which she would shut firmly in their faces.

She was a tease, yes, she knew that, but she could not resist a compulsion to test her powers. She soon realised they were considerable. If men seemed ready to make fools of themselves, surely that was their problem?

Fashion was a way out of the serious life being forced on her. Fashion was frivolous and sexy. She never believed women who said they dressed for other women – fashion was to seduce, surely? Sophie liked clothing which revealed the body and fabrics which clung to her and showed off her breasts and legs. She finished her outfits off with the highest heels she could find, even though her parents forbade them as 'tarty'. She hid them in her handbag to smuggle into the Passy teenage discotheques, slipping them on in cloakrooms. She was always surrounded by boys.

Staring out at the street, she thought about her busy father. He would see her in his library on Saturday morning at eleven thirty. *Maman* would be supervising the cook in the kitchen as people were expected for lunch that day. People were always expected for lunch. She would tell him that she had sold the necklace. She would also tell him that in her opinion education was wasted on her so she was quitting university. She hoped he would order her out of the house.

Christopher Hutchins

The young man with the face of a mischievous angel sat on the morning Air France London–Paris flight, forehead pressed to the window as he stared down at the clouds. Was this a terrible mistake? Would he achieve his dream of becoming the first English designer to succeed in Paris, or would he fail and have to return home to his father's derision and his mother's disappointment? He shook the thought of failure from his head. He had talent and someone in Paris would recognise it and employ him.

His regular features, shock of tousled blond hair, startlingly blue eyes and full lips couldn't hurt his progress, surely. Or would they work against him? He had heard enough gossip about predatory fashion males to make him a little worried. He hugged his secret closely to himself: that although dressing women was his obsession, he also looked forward to undressing them. He was heterosexual. Did that disqualify him from Paris haute couture? Or did it make him unique?

A real man does not design women's clothes.

A real man is not that interested in what women wear.

A man who thinks only of fashion must be gay.

These thoughts had churned in Christopher Hutchins' mind since he was fourteen.

Now that it was nineteen sixty-seven, less emphasis was placed on a man being macho. 'Unisex' clothes had blurred the line between the sexes. Many pop stars had continued to blur it.

Christopher contracted the fashion bug when his Uncle David, a suburban tailor, paid him to help in his workshop at weekends and school holidays. Christopher found the fabric swatches, the subtle weaves and tweeds, the very making of a suit, fascinating. He enjoyed the different stages, the tacking, the inter-linings, fitting the client, and, finally, the last fitting of a finished, perfect jacket. He tried to sew, carefully hiding this from his friends, who would laugh at him and call him a 'poof'. He knew, from the way his body reacted to women, that he was not gay. But 'Fashion' was still a tricky subject between men and had to be handled carefully, secretly.

After 'Mod' paper suits for 'dolls' of football players, he graduated to cutting out women from his mother's magazines and making paper clothes for them, too.

His uncle did not laugh at him when, very shyly, Christopher showed his paper dolls. Instead, he peered carefully at Christopher's 'clothing'.

'We have the makings of a designer here,' he said. 'Is that what you want to be, Christopher?'

'Oh God, yeah!'

'Then why have you enrolled in accountancy school?'

'Because Dad wanted me to.'

Uncle David was his mother's brother, married but without children. Christopher had acted as a kind of son to this man who seemed so different to his father. His father had always been cold and gruff. His uncle showed Christopher that a man did not have to act tough. Had the clothes, the fabrics and the sewing softened his uncle into a kinder, more understanding man, or had he been born that way?

The profession of tailor was perfectly respectable and had no connotations of effeminacy. Even so, Christopher did not have the courage to state his ambitions to his father and obediently began training to be an accountant, the profession his father had chosen for him.

After a year of studying, Christopher had desired enough girls, and enjoyed fumbled sex with a few, to feel no doubts about his sexuality. Women's clothes were more exciting than men's: he felt an undeniable urge to design them. Gradually his defensive excuses crumbled. He was free to dare to become a designer.

His first year of accountancy studies reached its end: Christopher felt he had reached the end, too.

'I don't want to spend my life organising other people's money,' he told his mother as they sat at the pine table in the green-tiled kitchen sharing a cup of tea and biscuits one evening. 'Remember those paper dolls, Mum? I really want to design clothes,' he confided.

'Men's suits, like Uncle David?' she asked.

'No! Women's clothes. Fashion!'

They exchanged meaningful looks. She stared at him, thoughtfully.

'If you're really keen about it, ask your dad if you can leave accountancy school for art school. I'll back you up!'

The following evening he plucked up the courage to speak to his father. They were in the sitting room, watching the television news end. A long silence was broken only by the evening paper rustling as his father pretended to read. His mother hovered nearby, listening.

'The plan was for you to be an accountant,' his father finally said.

'Dad, I really want to go to art school. I've submitted a folio of designs and drawings. If they accept me—'

13

'You've completed a year of accountancy. And you're doing well.'

'I can't go on there, Dad. I only agreed because I didn't have the guts to disagree. I wanted to please you, but I won't be the first to leave accountancy school. People change their minds! I know now that I want to be a designer. I just didn't dare tell you before. I'm sorry, but now I want to study art.'

'His art teacher always said he had talent, Joe,' his mother put in.

His father put aside his paper and stared at him.

'I'm not supporting you through any art school,' he said. 'In a year you may change your mind again.'

'I won't,' Christopher assured him. 'But Uncle David says he'll support me . . .'

His father glanced at his mother. 'He'll have to come and tell me that himself.'

Uncle David visited the next evening.

'You're interfering with my plans for my son,' Mr Hutchins said.

His brother-in-law stared at him. 'What about *his* plans?'

Christopher looked from one to the other, like a Wimbledon spectator, as they argued about his destiny.

'Forcing a boy into a profession he doesn't like . . .' Uncle David ended. 'Well, he'll always resent it. Chris wants to be a designer. I guarantee you, he will succeed.'

Under his brother-in-law's relentless pushing, his father eventually gave in. Christopher tried not to show his excitement.

'Mum?' He looked into the kitchen later that night, to find his mother sitting sipping tea. He placed his arms around her. 'I'm sorry . . .' he told her.

'Don't apologise, love,' she said. 'You always had an artistic side. I should have encouraged it.' She shot him a pleading look. 'I've stood up against your dad for you, I'll look pretty stupid if you let me down.'

'Don't worry, Mum,' he promised. 'I won't let you down.'

*

He chose Saint Martins School of Art 'Dress Design' course, because he had heard it was the best. The school was in Charing Cross Road, on the borders of Soho. Here he learned to draw, to cut patterns, to sew, to design. Fashion meant dressing women and the idea of dressing a woman seemed erotic to him. Fashion gave him the power to decide what a woman looked like. Whether waists drop a couple of inches, elongating the torso, or inch up to the bosom, forming an Empire line. Whether coats stayed slim and snug or suddenly swirled out at the hem like a trapeze. As he studied the old fashion magazines, he saw how a great designer must know exactly when to instigate such changes. They cannot be too sudden, hems must creep up or down over several seasons, as mood or climate decrees. And a designer must be a little ahead of mood and climate.

He was aware that two other boys in the course, a Chinese boy named Ling, and the London boy, George, were gay, Ling quite effeminate. Christopher preferred a softly rounded bosom to the flat-chested boyish look, and was drawn to designing clothes for 'real' sensual women. After all not all women were skinny or flat.

Christopher developed into a typical London cheeky chappie, his full lips and mischievous blue eyes making him almost irresistible to women. 'OK, I'm on the small side, but not where it counts!' he would assure girls, with a wink. He was three inches shorter than his imagined height. According to his detractors he was a little 'too full of himself'.

He was greatly in demand, and in the freer climate of the sixties, many girls pulled him into the cloakroom for 'a quickie'. He started to regard his desire for the female body as an asset, since few designers desired the bodies they dressed. He loved fitting his clothes on a real live girl. It was a sensual, exciting experience, providing a good excuse for touching her in intimate places. Just taking a bust measurement, stretching the tape measure across the nipples, made him hard!

His obvious appreciation of women helped his social life at the school. He usually shared a coffee-break with two or three girls, but work always came first.

At the end of the three-year course, he won his Design

Diploma. As his colleagues chased jobs at Marks and Spencer, Wallis Shops and Jaeger, Christopher was thinking of Paris haute couture, the very pinnacle of fashion. He yearned to work at the top end of the market, not in manufactured clothing, which everyone said was the future of fashion.

How ambitious did he dare be? Was it possible that if he went to Paris, he might make some contacts and find a job in a real fashion house like Dior or Givenchy? Could a name as English as 'Hutchins' ever be welcomed amongst a group with names like Yves Saint Laurent or Balenciaga?

His uncle promised one more year's support. If a person is ambitious and has hopes and dreams, he needs only one person to believe in him. Christopher had two: his mother and his uncle.

Now on this half-empty Air France flight, a big smile on his face, a proud Brit began his one-man invasion of Paris haute couture. His best designs, mounted on thick card, were in the hold of the plane in a large black leather portfolio his uncle had bought him from Reeves art supply shop in Charing Cross Road. He would lug them around every fashion house in Paris, working downward from Balenciaga.

He would polish up his rough edges, style his long hair, practise his grammar-school French, meet as many girls as he could, wear his London boots, frilly shirts and elephant-legged trousers with flair, think and breathe fashion. He would give this his very best shot, he promised as the plane landed. If you wanted something enough you could get it, he assured himself.

He stepped off the plane and took a deep breath of Gauloise smoke, garlic and perfume mixed with airport petrol fumes. He was in Paris. It was 17 September 1967, a date he would never forget.

Samantha Lipstaadt

Samantha Lipstaadt stood in a hotel conference room amidst chattering women dressed, exactly like her, in pink tweed cardigan-suits with matching boaters, white camelias perched on the brims. Two-toned shoes and black leather quilted shoulder-bags completed The Look.

'I declare The Samantha Lipstaadt Chanel Addiction Treatment Centre open!' she said.

She strode down the centre aisle to a dais, grabbed a microphone and looked into a sea of perfectly made-up faces.

'I'm Samantha,' she began hesitantly.

'Hello, Samantha,' the women trilled.

'And I am a . . .' she faltered, then quietly added, 'I *was* a Chanel-junkie.'

There was applause.

'Night sweats, dilated eyes, trembling hands . . .' she continued. 'Coco-dependency makes life hell. I had to cross to the other side of the street if I passed a Chanel window. But together we can beat the four Cs. Coco, Chanel, credit cards and camelias!' More applause and a few whoops. 'Together we *can* kick our habits. Together we can go cold Coco turkey!'

The room errupted in cheers. Samantha beamed: her Treatment Centre was up and running!

She woke with a start, eyes blinking open.

'Weird dream,' she said aloud. Suddenly it all flooded back to her. She was in Paris! Since last night! She jumped out of bed to throw apart the shutters of her apartment overlooking (if you leaned out) the Seine. It was a little small, a tad shabby, but God, *so* Parisienne. If she leaned further out, she could see the Eiffel Tower. An old man wearing a beret cycled by on a rickety old bicycle, a baguette under one arm.

'Typically French,' Samantha breathed. She caught the whiff of a strong cigarette and a tinge of garlic.

If an accordian played '*La Vie en Rose*', I could be in a French movie, she thought. I *will* be in my own French movie! she vowed. Something romantic like *Un Homme et Une Femme*, or sexy like *Belle de Jour*! She had nagged Daddy for years to subsidize a year here. And she intended to make the most of it: by locating a good dry-cleaner's *immédiatement*.

Her image of France, created entirely from the romantic films she had seen and re-seen, had so far proved surprisingly accurate. Her favourites were *A Man and a Woman* and, somewhat older, *Funny Face.*

A Man and a Woman was filmed with such circling, hand-held camera-work that Samantha was surprised to see that France was not in a state of constant movement.

As for *Funny Face*, she remembered Audrey Hepburn prancing around Montmartre, perching at café tables to philosophise with wise old men and crying '*Bonjour!*' to everyone on the Champs-Elysées. She could hardly wait to get out there and '*Bonjour!*' a few people herself.

But it was only six thirty so she returned to bed and was soon in her back-up dream: the Beverly Hills High School 1975 ten-year reunion. She arrives, dressed entirely in Chanel, to the gasps of her friends. ('Friends' in inverted commas, she thought, for Beverly Hills High girls were super-bitchy.)

In this dream, Gloria DeFries and Shelley Goldenblatt (both enemies) sidle up to ask: 'What are *you* doing now, Samantha?' Both smugly sure she'll answer, 'Nothing much . . .'

Instead, she replies, oh so cooly: 'I run Chanel. I'm head of the Paris couture house. I inherited it from Mademoiselle Chanel.'

Suddenly, they realise that her suit, purse, belt, two-tone shoes, camellia and sunglasses, emblazoned with intertwined Cs, are *not* copies! Their jaws drop, revealing perfectly capped teeth. They exchange looks.

'I am *totally* lost for words,' Shelley gasps.

Samantha's eyes blinked open to reality. Eight o'clock. She got out of bed wearily, more tired than the first time she'd woken, and peered into the dressing-table mirror to study her Aztec mask of a face: the high cheek-bones, slanted eyes, long jaw, thick lips. Where did you begin with a face like hers? No one had ever figured out where this face came from. Some strange ancestor had

18

left her some very strange genes. Men guessed Oriental, Magyar, or a unique combination of different influences.

For years, she had thought of herself as ugly and played down her dramatic features. In Paris, she hoped to become *jolie laide*, that useful French term for a woman not conventionally beautiful.

' "*Jolie*" means pretty and "*laide*" ugly . . .' she would spell out to people. 'Not "pretty ugly", it's "pretty *slash* ugly": a girl so striking and unusual that not even her mirror can decide!'

Eye-liner, blush-on, mascara, lip pencil, tons of Max Factor pan-cake and sheer will-power. A publicity genius rubs a little of this genius on herself each morning in order to hold her head up high, she assured herself as she left the apartment. She would personally drag Paris into the next century because she felt fashion so intensely and knew how to promote it. She had watched her father closely as he created successful women's clothing firms in Los Angeles during the nineteen fifties. When she was eighteen, they had moved to Manhattan where Daddy began his domination of the New York garment centre. Today publicity was the magic ingredient in any fashion success. Would publicity be enough to keep Chanel at the very top? she wondered.

It had only ever been Chanel. An unrequited love, for she was madly in love with Chanel and Chanel did not even know she was alive. Samantha strolled down the street, towering above the Parisiennes, thinking hard. In New York, she'd bought anything with a Chanel label, paying with one of the first credit cards, American Express, given to her by her father.

At twenty-one, she had begged to change her name to 'Chanel Lipstaadt'.

'The Lipstaadts don't have funny names,' Daddy had maintained.

Her mother's untimely death when Samantha was fourteen had caused her father to spoil her. Well, to say her father had spoiled her was like saying that the Arctic is a little cool. Samantha was used to getting what she wanted. Now Mademoiselle Chanel would know she was alive, for she was determined to work for the most prestigious fashion house on the planet.

I can *sell*, she thought, walking along. I know how to make things sell. That's what fashion is all about. Otherwise we'd all be wearing the same sackcloth dress . . .

After locating a promising-looking dry-cleaner's, she paused, giddy with desire, before a delectable display of pastries in a window. Was it a *patisserie* or a jeweller's? The glazed strawberries and blackberries, on their little pastry beds, shone like rubies, the rich cake was gold, the *mille-feuilles* delicate works of art. She went in and pointed at four. They were wrapped in wisps of tissue and placed in a square white box like precious jewels. Tied with twine and a loop knotted, the sweet jewels dangled from her finger: brunch!

Tucking a *Herald-Tribune* from a nearby news-stand under her arm, she hurried back to her apartment, becoming Audrey Hepburn on the way.

'*Bonjour*,' she greeted each old man carrying a baguette under his arm. Even their berets are basic black, she thought.

She was aiming her Instamatic at the third old man when she realised he was making an obscene gesture with his baguette.

'*Oh!*' She dropped the camera. No one had done this to Audrey Hepburn.

She chose the chic accessory of the thinnest baguette at a *boulangerie* near home. It was called a *ficelle*. She tucked it under her arm like a real Parisian, hoping it wouldn't taste of deodorant.

At home, she devoured the pastries with two strong black coffees. At eleven thirty, high on sugar and caffeine, she began dialling the numbers on the list she had compiled in New York. Every friend of a friend who might lead to a job was on her list. Her aim was Chanel, but she would accept a position any-where.

She left messages if they were out. By the end of the afternoon she had five lunches scribbled in her diary, three drinks parties and two interviews. She sat back with a sigh. A year to make her mark on Paris fashion. A year to find a man. The two goals were somehow connected.

Lights blazed on the top floor of 31 Rue Cambon. It was eleven o'clock at night. Gabrielle Sidonie Chanel hunched over a jacket, cigarette in mouth, pinning a sleeve into an armhole, turning it this way and that in her arthritic hands. How many sleeves had she eased into armholes? Thousands? Tens of thousands? And had one ever been exactly right?

Mademoiselle Chanel shrugged, ash from her cigarette dropping onto her tweed skirt, her beady dark eyes concentrating fiercely through the strong lenses and smoke.

She had been unable to resist crossing the Rue Cambon from the Ritz after dinner for one more go at setting in this damned sleeve. The suit was for a very important client and it had been a long time since she had actually sewn any clothes. That night she wanted to see if she still had the talent, the craft, to set in one perfect sleeve. Of course, the open-weaved, airy tweed did not exactly make things easier. She consoled herself with the thought that if she made a mess of it, Monsieur Guy, her very best tailor, would put matters right the next morning.

Carefully, she eased the fullness of the sleeve into the armhole, spacing it out, gently allowing the '*ampleur*', which would give that rounded 'set in' appearance only couture sleeves have. The smooth ridge at the shoulder had to be perfect. Neat as a pin. Tailored! A beautiful word, she thought. Although set high under the arm, there must be enough fullness to allow the arm to move. The woman would need to raise her arms, wouldn't she? If she was French, she would need to gesticulate.

She lit another cigarette, her lower lip turned down in a kind of rictus of misery. How alone she was. And yet being alone in her own fashion-house, with a jacket in her hands, with scissors, thread and pins, was not really being alone. It was *working*! And work had always kept her mind off her life.

'Mademoiselle?' a voice enquired.

She looked up at the concerned face of her loyal porter, Louis. He kept guard at Chanel throughout the night. They were old friends.

'Shouldn't Mademoiselle be asleep?' he asked.

She laughed a grim laugh. 'Could I sleep knowing there is a pucker in this sleeve, Louis? Don't you know me by now?'

'Yes, I know Mademoiselle.' He nodded. 'I also know we all need our sleep.'

'I'll sleep very well when this sleeve is *perfect*. I am sewing again, Louis, the way I did when I first began. I have come full circle. Now go downstairs and do whatever it is that you do . . . guard the house. Protect me! I like to feel protected.'

Nutty old girl, he thought, leaving her. But he was very fond of her and he did worry about her health. She was old, possibly pushing ninety? Even Mademoiselle Chanel could not live for ever, although she gave all the signs of doing so.

She left the house when she was satisfied that the sleeve had been set in as well as anyone alive could do it. If she could accomplish one small piece of beautiful, perfect work, she still had a use, her life still meant something.

In the chill air outside, Louis took her arm as they crossed the cobbled street. He escorted her into the Ritz Hotel. There, a porter took over and accompanied her to the lift. The liftman took her up to her floor and wished her good night.

She walked slowly down the corridor. To reach the age of eighty-four and retire to one's bed alone! A kind of failure, wasn't it? Even a widow had the comfort of memories of a husband. She had never married. She was still 'Mademoiselle' at eighty-four.

She knocked on the door. The small suite was modest. A room in which to read, a room to bathe in, a room to sleep in, that was all. Her maid, Jeanne, awaited to put her to bed. Like a child, she thought wryly. Full circle. Except – her mouth twisted down as the door opened and she remembered the orphanage – no one had ever put her to bed as a child.

Two

When Monique finally met Chanel's harassed *Chef du Personnel*, the woman barely glanced at her, but she did take a close look at the *Chambre Syndicale* diploma certificate before pushing a form at her.

Monique was told to begin work the next day. Evidently there was a backlist of suit orders and they could not find enough qualified seamstresses. She stumbled out onto the Rue Cambon, hardly able to contain her joy. A weak sun had pushed its way through the Paris clouds. She decided to walk back to her lodgings, buying some wine on the way to celebrate her new job that evening.

On the long walk back to Châtelet, her mind again returned to her childhood. Her sister Caterine had grown prettier, far prettier than her. People blurted out: 'You can't possibly be sisters!' She knew exactly what that meant.

Monique had applied herself diligently to helping Madame Denise with sewing and cutting. She soon learned that there was only one woman for whom she wanted to work: Mademoiselle Chanel. When it came to her craft, Monique lost her timidity. She had, Madame Denise assured her, the special touch, which produced exquisite work. Chanel would need her, she just knew it.

When she was twenty-one, she announced she was leaving for Paris, using the money her father had left her. Caterine knocked softly on her door the night before she left.

'Take me with you. Don't leave me with her,' she begged.

Monique stared at her. 'But you must stay at school. And you love *Maman*, don't you?'

'I love you more,' Caterine blurted. 'Now, I will be alone with her.'

Monique hugged her.

'When you finish your studies you will visit me in Paris,' she promised.

Although Monique had never heard a mean word from Caterine, the distance between them would remove a small weight from her shoulders: she would no longer need to try to compete or stifle any envy when Caterine attracted admiring glances.

On the train to Paris, her round eyes had widened at the thought of life in such a big city.

The train chanted: 'Get a new life! Get a new life!' and she promised herself she would do just that.

That slap from her mother all those years before had made Monique wary of men. She had never again asked a man to kiss her. So far, no one had tried to. Would any man find her attractive? She was so self-conscious about not being slim that she overlooked her flawless complexion, her kind, maternal aspect, her pretty hair and smile. Her natural tendency was to lower her eyes when a man's gaze met hers.

In Paris, she promised herself she would re-invent and re-design herself. She might never be classically beautiful but at least she could use her love of clothes and create well-cut outfits for herself. The new, tailored, chic Monique striding down a Paris boulevard might not turn men's heads but *women* would notice her clothes and wonder where she had found them. Fashion would fill her entire life, leaving no room for a husband. She could love no man more than her father so why bother to find a replacement? If she was dedicated to her craft with nothing to distract her, surely she had every chance of becoming a great couturier? The train stopped with a jerk in the Gare du Nord – her adventure had begun.

*

24

Since then, Monique had lived for two years in Châtelet, the only lodgings her mother had allowed her to consider. An unmarried girl from Angers, if not fantastically beautiful, could become a nun, be a teacher or escape to *Paris* and the Catroux sisters. Here no one thought of her as 'the plain sister', and she was spared the pitying looks.

The Catroux sisters – Odette and Sandrine, so alike she could hardly tell them apart – had given her a warm welcome. They had worked in Paris for many years, installed on their attic floor near Le Châtelet making hats. They farmed out hats to freelance workers and were soon in demand by the smaller couture houses without their own millinery workrooms. They had slowly bought up the other attic-rooms on their floor, renting them out to young, unmarried girls. Exactly as she remembered them from their Christmas visits to Angers, old-maidish and giggly, their fantasies had been diverted into hats. And why not? Extremely skilled craftswomen, they had succeeded through talent and sheer hard work. And they seemed to enjoy the company of the six girls who lodged with them.

Monique had a small, clean room with a circular window framing some Paris rooftops. Whitewashed walls, bookcase, framed photograph of Caterine, chest of drawers, armchair, floral curtains and matching bedspread completed her decor. The narrow bed was too small for two, even if a man could be smuggled in. She had shaken that thought from her head on her very first day as she hung up her clothes.

Although she had rejected religion when her father died, there was something devotional and nun-like about a dedication to fashion. She found the craft, the workmanship, the search for perfection, almost holy. Her gods could be Balenciaga and Chanel. She might not pray to them but she could aspire to them. Perhaps the point was to get as *close* to perfection as humanly possible?

She enrolled in a two-year course at the dressmaking school of the *Chambre Syndicale de la Couture*.

On her way home from the school each evening, Monique would glimpse elegant women on the Faubourg Saint-Honoré or around La Place de la Madeleine, leaving Aux Trois Quartiers or queuing at Fauchon for a kilo of delicious *amuse-bouches* to serve at that evening's 'drinks'. The styles were changing. On the Left Bank, the young wore skimpy or hippie fashions. Here on the Right Bank, ladies were still elegant in the classic style Monique admired. They were her inspiration, although she had no ambitions to be a lady herself, doubting she could carry off the grand style. She had an inexhaustible supply of ideas for what women could wear, and tried to be original and modern and classy. Like Chanel.

She worked through the long hot month of August, when Parisians deserted the city and so many bakeries closed that there were long queues for bread. It was the haute couture's busy time, showing their new autumn collections.

The sisters taught Monique to make silk flowers, sew linings and long strips of what she called 'silk spaghetti', which was looped into decorations or trimming. Sewing for the Catroux sisters, she earned enough to pay her fare back to Angers to see her family at Christmas.

Now she entered the huge emporium of Aux Bonne Marché to choose four bottles of good red wine for the sisters and the girls that night.

At dinner, they celebrated Monique's new position at Chanel, the sisters and the girls genuinely pleased for her. Dinners in Châtelet were always copious and well-cooked, the huge work-table covered with a white lacy cloth, the meal eaten amidst giggles and gossip, especially that night when extra wine celebrated a special occasion. The girls were a cut above the average seamstress, from middle-class families all over France, drawn to the capital through their love of fashion and because their skills were needed there. The conversation ranged from fashion (of course) to affairs of the day, the social changes taking place, the students' protests, and sometimes, when the sisters were out of the room, sexual liberation and how best to pursue it. The Catroux sisters served good old-fashioned French food, including *escalopes à la crème*, their speciality. There was no time to be bored or lonely. Monique enjoyed her new life and her new 'family'.

The moment she fell into bed at midnight, she slept, her dreams compensating for the lack of romance in her life. And her dream was usually the same: she was being held in the warm protective arms of a man. Although she could not see his face, she somehow knew he was an older, comforting man. She awoke to the loss of this man, almost crying.

'A dream is a wish your heart makes', a song said: where and when would she find the man in this dream?

After some flea-bitten nights in a dingy St Germain des Prés pension, Christopher answered a *Paris Soir* advertisement to share a bargain-priced street-level flat near L'Opera with Klaus Mueller, a struggling young German fashion photographer.

Klaus was tall, bearded and friendly. He was the house photographer for Jean Patou and did as much extra freelance work as he could find. He loved black-and-white film and was just a little arty. He considered himself a hippy. The decor of the flat he rented was a mixture of student-hippy (bean bags and cardboard boxes) and the reproduction French Provencial furniture left by his landlady.

'I pay five hundred francs a month. That would be two hundred and fifty each,' Klaus said.

They became room-mates, two young men in the fashion game. It crossed Christopher's mind that Klaus might be gay, but this was the Peace and Love era so did it really matter?

'What are the girls like here?' he asked, giving Klaus two hundred and fifty francs.

'Oh, Christopher . . .' Klaus blew out his lips. 'When you work with pretty girls every single day . . .' He pulled a face. 'You need something a little different.'

'You . . . don't like girls?' Christopher tried to sound casual.

'Yes, I like them a lot. Just not too pretty.'

27

Christopher laughed. 'Well, would you mind passing on the too-pretty ones to me?'

'You'll find your own girls,' Klaus said. 'English guys are *très 'à la mode'* at the moment.'

'In pop music,' Christopher agreed, 'maybe not in haute couture?'

The winter of 1967 was just the right time to arrive in Paris from London. Thanks to pop groups and actors like Sean Connery and Terence Stamp, the French suddenly found British men desirable. Brits were 'in'. The other British things crossing the Channel – boots, Vidal Sassoon haircuts, models like Twiggy and Jean Shrimpton – changed the dowdy image of *les Anglais* for ever.

Christopher spent his first day of sharing Klaus's apartment exploring that area of Paris. Passing the Café de la Paix, near l'Opera, on a cold day he got a whiff of briny '*crustaces*' – great platters of sea creatures complete with spiky *oursins*, oysters and mussels, served with lemon wedges and flourishes by white-gloved waiters on the café's heated terrace.

The chicest Paris cafés were Café de Flore and Les Deux Magots, where clients kept their eyes peeled for glimpses of Alain Delon or Catherine Deneuve. Anouk Aimée had been seen late at night in the cavernous La Coupole on the Boulevard Montparnasse.

It was chic to slum it in St Germain des Prés. 'Protest' was hip and fashionable: being seen on the Left Bank was a way of protesting the bourgoisie on the Right Bank.

Fashion was being ripped apart, splitting into 'elegant and expensive', or 'retro and hippie'. 'Hippie' involved trailing scarves, Indian kaftans, flowers and ropes of beads, often accompanied by a whiff of marijuana.

Right Bank ladies still wore couture at its most formal. The contrast between these two different lifestyles sparked Paris's excitement.

Christopher wandered around the city, the background music Edith Piaf's voice floating from café jukeboxes.

He began showing his folio of designs. The two most influential designers, Balenciaga and Chanel, declined to see him. At Nina Ricci, Pierre Cardin and Guy Laroche, he was fobbed off by young studio-assistants who flicked through his designs and politely thanked him. At another house, a man leaned towards him intimately and Christopher snapped his folio shut and walked out.

'It would have been just as bad if it had been a woman,' he told Klaus over spaghetti in their kitchen that night. 'I'm not a prostitute.'

'Chris, it is not called "prostitution" in Paris,' Klaus sighed, putting down his wooden spoon and looking at him. 'Here, we call it "charm and flirtation". And it's part of the job. You should be happy that people find you attractive.'

Sophie did not see her father alone until Saturday morning, nearly ten days after the auction. She knocked on his library door and was admitted. The room was furnished classically with an antique desk boasting exquisite marquetry, shelves of rare leather-bound books behind glass-fronted cabinet doors and two navy velvet-covered armchairs. A floral needlepoint rug on the floor and thick velvet curtains muffled noise from the street. Sophie found it suffocating but this is where her father loved to work.

She perched on an armchair, smiling as he poured her orange juice, not realising that she usually diluted it with plenty of vodka. He was so what the Americans termed 'square'.

She took the glass and sipped at the juice.

'I have not been getting on with *Maman*,' she began.

He shook his head. 'Sophie, all young people are going through this phase of not wanting to do what their parents advise . . . it's called "rebellion". It's very fashionable, I know.'

'I am not trying to be fashionable, Papa,' she cut him off. 'I really don't like studying law. I want to work in fashion. It would be so easy for mother to introduce me into Chanel, even just for an apprenticeship in a workroom. She owes me at least that and I would prove my worth after six months.'

Her father's expression became grim. 'Sophie, nobody "owes" you anything,' he said, 'except perhaps a good education. Fashion

29

is not what your mother and I expect for you,' he went on. 'We think you are capable of more.'

'*Maman* has enjoyed a fashion career,' she pointed out.

He shook his head. 'Employment prospects for women are much wider today. Only a formal education can—'

'Please, Papa, I'm really unhappy. And I have a way to get what I want. I'm starting to feel desperate!'

'What do you mean?' he asked.

She took a deep breath. 'I am quitting the Sorbonne,' she told him.

'After all I did to get you in?'

'That's just what I mean: I don't really belong there. You pushed me in.'

'And what do you plan to do?' He raised his eyebrows.

'Rent a flat and live alone, for a start.'

'And who will pay your rent, food and expenses?'

'I am independently wealthy.'

'Oh? May I ask how you reached this enviable state?'

'I sold the necklace you gave me for my birthday.'

'*No!*' Laurent Antoine's eyes widened in disbelief. 'You didn't sell the necklace? But, Sophie, I gave it to you so it would stay in the family. It was my mother's. It was extremely valuable, too.'

'Don't worry, it got a good price at Druout's. And it *was* mine, wasn't it?' she asked. 'I just want a tiny attic to live my own life in and an introduction to Chanel. I won't disgrace you.'

He stared at her for a long moment.

'You have already disgraced me,' he said quietly, his dignified face collapsed in puzzlement. He shook his head. 'I give you the most valuable thing I possess, something beautiful I often saw my mother wear. And you *sell* it? Didn't you realise it was a family heirloom?' He stared at her incredulously. 'A daughter simply does not do this to a father.'

Sophie did not know what to reply. She remained silent.

'I am very disappointed in you, Sophie,' he said, finally. 'I must discuss this with your mother. We'll talk again tomorrow.'

'There's nothing to talk about,' she retorted, leaving the room. 'I'm leaving and you can't stop me.'

No house seemed interested in employing Christopher or he was offered 'apprenticeships' with no salary. He was about to give up and look for a job as a cleaner when on an impulse he tried an old house on the Rue de la Paix called Delange. With perfect timing he arrived just after an assistant was fired, and was offered an interview with the formidable Camille Delange. This house dressed grand old ladies who couldn't quite afford Chanel or Dior. Camille's heyday had been in the nineteen thirties. She had not made many *Vogue* covers lately. She had not appeared inside *Vogue* lately, either.

Camille received him rather grandly in her pure art deco office. He was startled by the Marcelled hair in tight, flat waves, the rouged cheeks and cupid's bow red mouth. The 'tea-dress' she wore, fitted to her thin body, was perfect, he thought, if the year had been nineteen thirty.

'You're very young,' she said, peering through his designs and whispering '*épatant!*' – French for 'ripping'. 'You design with a younger cliental than mine in mind? Perhaps the daughters or granddaughters of present clients? You do take clients' fittings?' she asked sharply.

'I won my diploma at Saint Martins School of Art,' Christopher replied. It sounded better than 'I've never tried'.

As she examined him, a tiny twinkle appeared in her watery blue eyes.

'My clients might enjoy being fitted by you,' she decided.

He was offered a six-month contract as 'assistant designer' with a small salary. Camille Delange left him in no doubt that she was doing him a great favour by allowing him to work for her. But she did officially produce haute couture and this was Paris: of course he accepted.

That night, Klaus took him to La Coupole, a huge Montparnasse café, to celebrate. It was thronged with 'happening' Parisians, young, fashionable and animated. Klaus impulsively ordered champagne. A happy evening.

*

On his first morning at Delange, he was told to take a fitting for a Madame Gervaise, a large lady of around sixty. She awaited him in the mirrored *cabine* wearing her ecru slip. One glance and he estimated her measurements: 40, 41, 42. *Inches!*

'Excuse me one moment, Madame,' he said, leaving.

He peered into the office of Madame Genevieve, the snooty *directrice* of the salon.

'The client has no waist,' he complained.

Madame Genevieve looked up with a frown. 'Give her one.'

'I'm not a doctor, Madame Genevieve.'

Madame Genevieve's eyes narrowed. 'A client who orders ten outfits a year deserves to be given a waist, don't you think?'

'I don't understand.' Christopher frowned. 'You show the collection on slim young models?'

Her eyes widened. 'Should we show them on old fat models?'

'But—' he stopped, as the first bit of fashion reality sank in. 'Your clients imagine they'll look as young and slim as the models?' he asked.

Madame Genevieve made an impatient face.

'Christopher, fashion is about dreams,' she reminded him.

'Dreams, not fashion!' Christopher told Klaus in their flat that night as he attempted to make a salad for dinner.

They had an understanding that they would try to cook dinner together each night. It was usually spaghetti, which Klaus was quite good at.

'I didn't come here to design "dreams", Klaus,' he said, rinsing lettuce. 'I want to design clothes! If all the clients are old and fat, I may as well work at an upholsterers recovering large armchairs.'

Klaus dunked the spaghetti into the simmering tomato sauce. The minimal decor of the flat suggested two students more than two fashion-people. Recently they had found a huge carton which had housed a television set. Covered by a cloth, it made a groovy dining table.

'This Camille Delange.' Klaus pronounced her name ironically. 'She must be eighty, huh?'

'She only fits one or two old valued clients. You can hear them screaming as she sticks pins into them. Mostly she acts as a figurehead, like a mermaid on the prow of a ship.'

'Yes, a washed-up old shipwreck?' Klaus laughed. He poured them some wine. 'You have arrived in Paris at an exciting time. There is a lot of unrest and protest amongst the students.'

'Really?' Christopher sipped his wine. 'Protest at what?'

'Everything!' Klaus said with relish. 'They wish to bring about a new order. I am with them all the way.'

'Well, perhaps I'll join them.' Christopher nodded. 'But I shall be protesting the age of couture clients!'

Delange's classic scent, *Ballerina*, brought in the money that allowed three workrooms to employ thirty seamstresses. The couture operation probably broke even, Christopher guessed, kept alive to keep Camille happy while *she* remained alive. Camille's famous draped evening dresses, inspired by Greek columns, were revived for nearly every collection and had sometimes been 'rediscovered' by young fashion editors and become fashionable again. Some loyal old clients ordered new dresses, almost out of habit, but there was no fashion pulse. Christopher began to feel that he might be the ideal young designer to rescue the house if Camille ever retired.

He pored over the old archives, sheaves of fashion drawings hand-coloured in water colour. There were albums of yellowing press-cuttings and endless anecdotes from the old tailors happy to reminisce to an eager young Englishman.

Jacques, the milliner, took a shine to Christopher and explained the art of making hats. Christopher lapped it up, wanting to learn everything he could about Paris, the couture, fashion.

When he could, Christopher perched at the end of the dressing-table in the models' *cabine*, soaking up the gossip and watching them make up. He found the girls fascinating and erotic and was careful not to stare too much at their slim bodies beneath white overalls which had a habit of falling open.

Designers were not always good artists and Christopher knew

his designs would look much better if he could draw elegant women instead of gorillas. In his folio, he was obliged to leave out faces, hands and feet, suggesting shoulders or legs with a few deft lines.

He enrolled for evening drawing classes at the *Chambre Syndicale* school. They sketched five-minute poses of a young girl, clothed.

During the first session, his gaze was drawn to a pretty fellow-student in a skinny white sweater, which hugged her perfect body. Her mini-skirt revealed slim legs. Her tousled red hair was pinned on top of her head to look careless, as if she had not secretly arranged every escaping tendril. She returned his look with an expression so frankly sexual that he felt his body react. At the end of the evening he asked her name and invited his new friend Sophie for a drink at a nearby café.

'I just quit my course at the Sorbonne . . .' she sat on a red leatherette banquette, lighting a cigarette. 'I could not take it any more. I must do fashion.'

'What kind of clothes do you design?' he asked, sipping his wine.

'Elegant, but modern . . .' She lit a cigarette. 'And you?'

'Clothes for tomorrow,' he said proudly.

'But you work for Delange?' she said with a frown. 'Aren't they yesterday?'

He pulled a face. 'It was the only job I could get. I'm English, remember. And the haute couture is French.'

She nodded, exhaling smoke. 'That could be an advantage if you have talent.'

'Do *you* have talent?' he asked, gazing into her eyes.

'I hope so,' she shrugged. 'You would have to see my clothes. So far, only I wear them. And one friend, Ines.'

'Wear something of yours the next time you come here?' he suggested.

'When I get my own apartment I'll model them for you.'

'When will that be?'

'Well, we shall see.' She gave him another inviting smile that instantly aroused him again. Unconsciously he adjusted his tight hipsters. Sophie, glancing down, giggled.

'It's funny,' he looked intently at her, 'I feel as if I've known you before?'

'On another planet or in another life?' she responded in true Sixties' mystical fashion.

'Well, I'm not sure I believe in that stuff,' he laughed. 'But I do feel as if I've always known you.'

He walked home strangely shaken.

'Can you just luck into the only woman on the planet for you, on your first month in Paris?' he asked Klaus later.

'The only woman on the planet?' Klaus laughed. 'Don't you mean the only sexy girl in the art class? Come on, Chris! You cannot afford to be that naive.'

On the following Sunday, her father called Sophie into the library.

This time her mother was at his side, her calm, icy manner more menacing than any rage.

'Sophie,' she said quietly, to say that we are disappointed . . .' She made a helpless gesture. 'That a child we brought up with love and care could do such a thing! And it cannot be undone, your father has called Druout: it's over a week since the auction and they say the necklace went to Switzerland. How *could* you sell a family heirloom?'

Sophie groaned '*Everything* in this house is a family heirloom.'

She looked around the room's heavy drapes and antiques. 'It's like living in a museum. The necklace was mine. You gave it to me. You're acting as if I stole it.'

Her father spoke. 'I gave it to you thinking you would cherish it for life. As for everything being a family heirloom, what is wrong with that? It is a beautiful thing, to be a family. Do you know how privileged you are to be part of one?'

'You did something thoughtless and ungrateful just to get what you want, with no thought for anyone's feelings . . .' her mother said. 'If you want to leave so much, we won't insist on your living here with us. Sophie must have what Sophie wants, *n'est ce pas?*

You wish to labour in a Chanel workroom? Fine, I'll get you into one if that is what you want. I hope you will be very happy there. You want to forget that you were ever part of this family?'

The blue eyes looked at her so coldly that Sophie almost began to cry.

'I never felt part of it, anyway!' she burst out, standing up.

'Was that our fault?' her mother asked. 'Or yours?'

'Wait, Sophie!' her father cried as she made for the door. 'You didn't feel part of this family because you are *not* part of it!'

Sophie stopped, staring at him.

'Laurent!' Madame Antoine held his arm. 'Please don't say any more!' He shook off his wife's arm, staring at Sophie.

'We adopted you!' he went on, unable to stop. 'We have tried to do our very best for you but—' He broke off, shaking his head.

'*Adopted*?' Sophie heard only that word. And suddenly everything clicked into place: all her rebellious feelings, all her different attitudes, all her criticism of her sisters.

'We said we'd never tell her,' Madame Antoine said quietly, levelling a disappointed look at her husband.

'Perhaps it's time she knew,' he said. He turned to Sophie. 'We adopted you when you were four years old. Isabelle and Francine have never known. And I have no wish to tell them what kind of person we have treated as a loved daughter and they as a loved sister for nineteen years.'

Madame Antoine came over to her.

'We wanted to give you a loving home and family. In time you will realise how wrong your behaviour has been. I hope you will regret it.'

Sophie stared at them helplessly. 'It was my necklace,' she repeated. 'You gave it to me. I did nothing wrong.'

'You may go now,' Laurent Antoine dismissed her.

She closed the door, leaning back on it, dizzy. She left the house, throwing on a sheepskin coat. She needed to think, she needed to walk around Paris aimlessly, lost in thought, trying to understand this idea that *Maman* and *Papa* were not her parents, that Isabelle and Francine were not her sisters. Once that had somewhat sunk in, the next thought was: who had her real parents been? Were they dead? Surely they had died? No one would just give away a child, would they? That thought was too painful to think.

She drifted towards St Germain des Prés and window-shopped the new clothes, not really seeing them, then people-watched from a café terrace, not really seeing the people.

She arrived home at around eight o'clock. To go from the thronging youth of the Boulevard St Michel to one of the prettiest, calmest streets in the Ecole Militaire district was always a jolt. She looked up at the four storeys cloaked in glossy dark green ivy. The dining-room windows were lit in preparation for their usual, formal dinner with their usual, formal friends, a dinner Sophie now realised she could not possibly share, not tonight.

For once, she was unable to summon up her usual shrug. She gave a great sigh instead and entered the house. That's all it was, now, just a house, no longer her home. She would sneak an apple from the kitchen and go to her room.

Two weeks later, after signing for a small attic flat in the Avenue Kléber, the agent handed Sophie the keys. She went up to the top floor and let herself in to her new home. It was nicer than she remembered from the first viewing: a delightful two-room attic looking out over Paris. What could be better? She stood at the window, staring out over rooftops, feeling absolutely empty. So this was adult life? You could get what you wanted but there would always be a big 'if'. She gave a huge sigh. The flat was semi-furnished with the essentials. She would scour the flea markets to find bits and pieces to make it a home. How would 'men' fit in to this new life? She could entertain them now, instead of merely teasing them. She shook her head at this thought. Suddenly men did not seem that interesting. But already she felt lonely. Perhaps she would buy a little dog?

Three

'Adopted.'

Sophie was back in her cafe the following Saturday morning.

'Adopted.' No matter how many times she repeated that word, it still refused to take on any real meaning.

'*Well?*' a voice broke in upon her reverie.

Sophie looked up. Her friend Ines leaned to kiss her. She sat down and lit a cigarette, looking at Sophie with her wide fake-eyelashed eyes. She was dressed exactly like Sophie in skinny sweater and jeans, a denim jacket thrown around her shoulders.

'How much?' she asked.

Sophie shrugged. 'About ten times what they expected.'

Ines's eyes widened a little more. 'And your parents? Furious?'

'Shocked.' Sophie gave her a long, meaningful stare. 'Antoine jewellery is always kept in the family . . .' She mocked her father's grave tone.

'What did you expect?' Ines blew out smoke.

'I got the apartment,' Sophie said. 'But it turns out that Laurent Antoine is not my father, after all. And the perfect Madame Antoine is not my mother.'

'What are you talking about?' Ines frowned.

'I am adopted, Ines,' Sophie said. 'My sisters are not my sisters.'

'He told you that? You believe him? Maybe he was just so angry that—'

'He was too angry to *stop* himself from telling me.'

'Well, how does that news feel? You're so pale.' Ines stared at her friend with concern.

'It hasn't sunk in. I'd like to know who my real parents were,' Sophie said.

'They must know.'

'She says she doesn't.'

'Ha!' Ines burst out. 'People like them don't just pop into an orphanage and choose any child.'

The waiter brought Ines a *café crème*.

As she stirred sugar into it, she regarded her friend admiringly, shaking her head. 'You sell a necklace for a fortune, your parents aren't your parents, and you move to your own apartment. Anything else? You're so calm!'

'You think I'm calm?' Sophie stubbed out her cigarette. 'No, Ines, I'm numb. But meanwhile I enrolled in the *Chambre Syndicale* school's evening classes. I met a very attractive English boy there. I plan to show him my new apartment. Then I have an interview at Chanel next week. It is only a formality, they will take me.'

Ines sat back. 'Your life is perfect.'

Sophie stared at her. 'I thought it would be, but I feel very odd. I hate what I have done. I hate what they told me. If you had seen that man's face, you would know how I feel.'

'Oh!' Ines shook her head, laughing. 'I am so sorry for you, Sophie. You poor little rich girl.'

Men! Samantha thought several times a day. If only life could be lived without them! But that would be as impossible as living without pastries, hair-lacquer or a good dry-cleaner's. She had not found 'Mr Right' in New York, maybe she would run into '*Monsieur* Right' in Paris?

In Paris, *les hommes* posed a new problem, one of size. There seemed to be lots of tiny little Frenchmen scurrying around the fashion industry.

She had made a new friend, a very pretty house model at

Nina Ricci. They had been introduced during Samantha's visit to Ricci's publicist, a flamboyant man who had politely turned down Samantha's offer to assist him.

'Audrey here is from New York, too,' Percy had said.

Samantha had stared at Audrey in full make-up of doe-eyes and lashes, white overall just covering her slim body.

They had gone downstairs to a Rue des Capucines café for coffee and croissants, Audrey still in her white overall over underwear. Samantha could not stop staring, hypnotised and envious, at Audrey's sleek dark hair, perfect nose and full lips. Everyone in the cafe was staring, too.

'I can't date tiny men,' she told Audrey, dunking her croissant into coffee. 'I'm nearly six feet, I need to be held in the arms of a six foot, five inch footballer type.'

Audrey frowned. 'Not many of *them* became fashion designers.'

'Is it hard to meet men here?' Samantha asked.

'I'm not trying to meet any,' Audrey said. 'I'm unofficially engaged to my high school sweetheart, back in New York. He's a dentist.'

'Oh, you're so *lucky!*' Samantha sighed.

'Maybe you need a gay *visagiste*,' Audrey suggested.

'What's a *visagiste*?'

'*Visage* is face. A *visagiste* redesigns faces,' Audrey said. 'Y'know, improves them.'

'Does he *have* to be gay?'

Audrey frowned. 'They sure *tend* to be. Jean-Jacques Batiste is *the* makeover man. He specialises in *jolie-laide*. You go in *laide*, you come out *jolie*.'

'So I am *jolie-laide*?' Samantha wailed. 'I mean, it's like, official?'

Audrey nodded encouragingly. 'Honey, in Paris that's a *good* thing.'

'Does my face need redesigning, Audrey?' Samantha whispered.

'A *visagiste* makes the best of your assets,' Audrey declared, 'Why don't I ask Jean-Jacques if he can squeeze you in?'

Samantha nodded.

She parted company with Audrey, begging her to keep in touch. Audrey was so beautiful that Samantha couldn't help believing whatever she said. She walked towards a metro, exhausted from her rounds. All these friends of friends she had been assured would help her seemed, now that she was in Paris, not that helpful. Her energy and charm had won her a little group of 'friends'. She had been to a few discotheques, given out her phone number to a few men who had not called her and grown a tiny bit discouraged.

Maybe a *visagiste* was the answer?

Monique's first day at Chanel was spent in the workroom of Madame Michelle, a sad little woman with a faint moustache who seemed on the verge of tears, which she sniffed back throughout the day. She introduced Monique to the other girls then indicated a wooden stool at the end of the work-table.

Monique was taken aback at the bare workroom facing a bleak courtyard. It was serviceable and clean, with two long work-tables seating fifteen girls at hard, wooden stools.

'She's not the best,' the girls told her when Madame Michelle was called to the *salon* for a fitting. 'But if you do well here, you'll get sent to the best.'

'Who is the best?' Monique asked breathlessly.

'Monsieur Guy, the head tailor,' the girls all said together.

Monique nodded. She began working on her first assignment: a silk lining for a jacket. A dull task, but this was not any old lining, she reminded herself, it was a lining for a *Chanel* jacket. If she made it the best lining ever sewn, perhaps she would be promoted to Monsieur Guy's workroom. She began to sew. Halfway through the morning, a ray of sunshine slowly worked its way through the dusty windows and diagonally across the work-table. Monique welcomed this sunray each morning as if it were a new friend, the spirit of the couture keeping an eye on her. She worked diligently. She put herself into her work. And it showed . . . very quickly it was remarked upon. She was moved higher up the work-table to actual jackets, and it was soon obvious that she was probably the best seamstress in the workroom.

Jean-Jacques, her *visagiste*-to-be, turned out to be a very serious man, and, yes, he was tiny, Samantha noted, encased in tight black leather which somehow made him even tinier. He should be dangling from a rear-view mirror, Samantha thought. She used the confidence-booster of head-to-toe Chanel for their first meeting in his St Germain des Prés studio, choosing a cream bouclé tweed suit and tying back her thick hair with a scarf. His '*studio de maquillage*' turned out to be a small apartment in the Rue de Bac with a big dressing-table outlined in lightbulbs. Here, he studied Samantha, asking for a list of all her faults, imaginary and real. As she listed them, she began to cry.

'I feel naked,' she sobbed.

'What is wrong with being naked?' Jean-Jacques whispered, proffering a box of Kleenex. 'Tell me,' he urged softly, 'who do you want to be?'

'Jackie Kennedy?' she sobbed. 'Veruschka?'

'Hmmmm . . .' Jean-Jacques frowned, reaching for his make-up box. '*I* see a Jewish Sophia Loren.'

He peered at the blank canvas of her face. Carefully, he began to transform all the 'imaginary' (he said) faults she had spent her life trying to disguise.

Better than a shrink, Samantha thought. Shrinks don't apply make-up.

'I don't disguise, I *exaggerate*,' he explained. 'A striking girl shouldn't apologise.'

'*Striking?*' Samantha sniffed. She blew her nose loudly. Her new *visagiste* began to paint his canvas. He had a solution for everything. Her thick lips? Outline them in brown pencil and colour-in with bright scarlet lipstick. Her impossible hair? 'Don't tie it back to get it out of the way, make it bigger. Make it an *asset*.' He gave her a mane. He even back-combed.

'I'm too tall,' she wailed.

'Then don't stoop as if it embarrasses you; wear even higher platform soles and walk tall,' Jean-Jacques urged.

'Platform soles don't go with Chanel!' she corrected. 'She shows everything with two-toned slingbacks.'

He worked hard on her. Later that night she finally became what he wanted her to be.

She frowned into the mirror. 'Teh!' she exclaimed, her own personal expression of surprise. 'I don't look like Jackie Kennedy *or* Sophia Loren!'

'No,' Jean-Jacques agreed, satisfied. 'You are more like a larger-than-life, white version of Josephine Baker.'

'How do I live up to *that*?' she asked.

'We will see on Saturday,' Jean-Jacques said. 'I will take my Fashion Frankenstein into the city.'

Another evening bent over another jacket. By focusing on work, I can still function, Mademoiselle thought. But there was more to life than easing a sleeve into an armhole. It has been reduced to this, she told herself. She was bored with anything that wasn't work. The magic had left her fingers and she no longer sewed well. Seeing that young girl from Angers (what was her name?) had shown up rather cruelly that she could no longer perform those perfect little stitches, nor manoeuvre the needle like some magician's wand. In many ways that girl had reminded Mademoiselle of herself at that age.

Later, she walked down the Ritz corridor to her suite. Jeanne, her maid, opened the door to her and helped undress her, getting her ready for bed. She let Jeanne do this, lifting her arms, turning when required. The wonderful life she tried so hard not to constantly relive now seemed to have belonged to someone else. It had been so exciting, so heady! Those sparkling weekend parties she had hostessed at her jewel of a house on the Côte d'Azur, where Picasso and Stravinsky and Diaghilev (not 'people', *geniuses*!) had gathered to discuss their exciting arts. Had that hostess really been her? Well, yes, she frowned, staring at the white ceiling. Everything had been fresh and original. The way she'd dressed, wide slacks, pearls swung over a striped fisherman's sweater, even the kind of food served at her buffet lunches. All so casual and elegant. She had photographs of it all, but it hurt too much to study them and see all the people she had loved, now dead, to remember beloved furniture now stored in Switzerland, and, above all, to see her own face, alive and happy.

Friends. People who had experienced much of her life with her. Who did she have now? A few duty visits from people who felt they should be seeing her? Old friends, yes, but when they visited her, she found she could not stop talking. This scared them off.

Young people visited her because they needed her help. Sporty American girls – clients' daughters – who wore her clothes so beautifully, but preferred to wear jeans and T-shirts. Or, worse, jeans and T-shirt under a Chanel jacket. Their healthy tanned skin, lithe bodies and white teeth brought her great pleasure but it was mixed with pain, for it reminded her how old she was.

The people she saw most often were the Ritz waiters who served her, twice a day, with the same dishes from the same menu. Never had she imagined she might suffer from the deadliest sin of all: boredom. Chanel, bored? That was a contradiction in terms, surely? She needed a new circle of friends. People with lots to look forward to in their lives. Young people who fell in love and wished to succeed. She could introduce them to each other, play matchmaker. She'd help them to succeed – if they deserved success. She could play with her living dolls and change their lives. Where could she find these new friends?

The following Saturday, Jean-Jacques ushered his newest creation onto a bus. Samantha had forsaken Chanel just for one day and wore a mid-calf-length embroidered Afghan coat over jeans and boots, to blend in with the hippies she expected to see.

'Paris is two cities,' he began.

'Oh?' Samantha gazed around them. 'Where's the other one?'

'We go to it now. I teach you a little about Paris.'

It was so nice to be accompanied by a man, even a tiny, leather-clad man. Even though she towered over Jean-Jacques, she felt happy.

He paid their fares with a *carnet* and they stood on the outside platform at the back, clinging to the hand-rail as the bus whizzed across the Pont Neuf.

'A Parisian never says "Let's cross the Seine",' he told her. 'We say: "Let's visit the Left Bank." *Le Rive Gauche* is where it is "all happening", as you Americans say. All the quirky, new things start here. Like the Village in New York, or London's Chelsea. Creativity begins here!'

The bus reached the other side and they clambered off.

'You see how different it feels?' He waved at the leafy streets.

'Yeah!' Samantha stared around her. 'There's a kind of intimacy that the Right Bank doesn't have.'

'The Left Bank is also politically left,' Jean-Jacques told her, as they strolled. 'The bourgeoisie stay on their Right Bank. The young adventure-seekers escape to the Left.'

They strolled the Boulevard St Germain.

'People are more aware of who they are here, it *does* feel kind of different,' Samantha enthused, looking around.

Jean-Jacques indicated a shop window. 'Here are the cheaper, younger clothes. The students are here. "Boul Mich" is the short name for Boulevard St Michel, which leads to The Sorbonne. It's always full of students.'

Samantha gazed around, taking it all in. Book and record stores jostled clothing stores selling jeans and shirts. People looked younger, hipper.

They visited the chic boutiques which had sprung up in St Germain, L'Odeon and Saint Sulpice, showing eccentric clothing for the more daring fashion-junkies.

'Maybe we'll see Sartre or de Beauvoir discussing philosophy and smoking like chimneys!' Jean-Jacques said, guiding her towards Le Flore.

'I'm not an intellectual, Jean-Jacques,' Samantha warned him.

He nodded. 'I realise that, but these two cafés . . .' he indicated

Les Deux Magots, opposite, 'have been adopted by the fashion crowd. So now they are fashion-intellectual!'

He ordered *les Welsh Rarebits* – a Flore speciality – wonderful melted cheese mixed with mustard and wine, poured over bread then grilled. Samantha got through two *café crèmes*. This would be her place!

She made a note in her notebook; *Café de Flore, corner of Blvd St Germain and Rue St Benoit.* Jean-Jacques was very pleased.

In Montparnasse, which they reached at *l'heure du thé*, he showed her the cavernous La Coupole. Because it had been the artists' quarter, they had sometimes allowed poor artists to settle their bills by painting colourful murals on pillars and walls.

'I *love* the *Rive Gauche!*' Samanatha enthused. 'It'll be my hangout. I'll always come here.'

She loved the charming little squares which usually enclosed several shops – milliners, *boulangeries*, rare books – clustered around a few trees, some old lamp-posts and a tiny water fountain in the centre.

'Like a cartoon of Paris,' Samantha exclaimed, gazing around.

During the following nights, they hit the discotheques, Samantha acting as a kind of living calling-card for Jean-Jacques' work. The hippest was Regine's, where Jean-Jacques was always waved in. Sometimes they danced, he at waist-level as she writhed opposite him, not touching. Samantha leaned backward and swayed, an expression of ecstasy on her face.

Other *jolie-laide* girls begged to be redesigned.

'We've got close,' she confessed to Audrey over lunch at the Champs-Elysées Drugstore. 'Like analyst and patient.'

Audrey raised her perfect eyebrows.

'I call him every night to tell him what I did that day. He's like my diary. I could be a tiny bit in love with him,' Samantha confessed. 'And he wears that groovy black leather so tight! The way he stares at me really turns me on!'

Audrey pursed her perfect lips. 'He stares at you as a *visagiste*, Samantha, not as a man.'

'Audrey,' Samantha began, if I relax *my* rule of "no men under five feet eight", surely he can relax *his* rule of "no women"?'

Audrey frowned, thinking hard.

'Y'know something, Sam?' she said. 'I think you're barking up the wrong tree.'

But one night, after three Kir Royals at La Coupole, Samantha got to thinking that it simply wasn't natural for two people of the opposite sex to see so much of each other without one of them making a pass. She placed her hand on Jean-Jacques' black leathered behind as he refreshed her make-up halfway through the evening. Jean-Jacques delicately removed her hand, making it very clear he preferred her to sit passively as he glued fake lashes and painted his canvas.

Samantha threw her Kir in his face and stalked out.

They did not speak to each other for a week. Samantha had overstepped the sexual mark. It became a test of wills. She found herself missing him so much that she knew she must mend the tiff. Jean-Jacques might never give great sex but he gave great phone, and she could not face Paris life without that nightly confession.

She called, begging him to meet her at the Café de Flore the following Saturday evening.

Jean-Jacques turned up ten minutes late, encased in his trademark black leather, dark glasses covering his eyes. Samantha awaited him patiently. This was evidently the *prix* one paid for touching the ass of one's *visagiste*. He sat stiffly on the bench alongside her at the best table on the terrace, the one nearest the entrance, back to the glass windows.

'Perhaps we needed this little argument to cement our friendship?' she suggested with pleading eyes. She had donned a Sonia Rykiel knit suit in a pretty blue, with lower heels. Jean-Jacques sat immobile for three minutes then turned, pushing his dark glasses up into his hair.

'Samantha, I consider you one of my greatest creations,' he said, making her feel more like Frankenstein than ever. 'But I don't need the stress of your expected sexual relations,' he added

47

curtly. 'You should have guessed by now that I never touch a woman except to make her up.'

'I dig it.' She nodded seriously. 'So . . . be my gay confidant? Every girl needs one, y'know.' She leaned to peck his cheek, pointing out: 'That was a sisterly kiss!'

Jean-Jacques nodded.

'I love you, Jean-Jacques!' Samantha told him, a tear running down her cheek. 'I've missed our nightly phone calls.'

He watched her warily. 'I like them, too,' he finally admitted, smiling.

'OK, so tell me about sex?' she urged. 'How do I go about getting some in Paris?'

'Well, there are two types of person,' he told her, narrowing his eyes. 'The one who hangs around a bar or disco all night, shyly glancing at people, and the type who approaches anyone in sight and asks, "Hey, baby, you want sex?"'

'No kidding?' Samantha breathed, staring at him hypnotised.

'Nineteen out of twenty people run away when you ask this question,' he told her. 'But the twentieth says yes. *That* is how you get sex!'

'Fascinating . . .' Samantha nodded seriously, staring at Jean-Jacques' leather-clad body, wondering if he ever shed this shiny black skin. It was hard to imagine *him* having sex with any-one.

'Hey, baby, you want sex?' she practised. 'Am I saying it right?' she asked.

He shrugged.

She shook her head. 'It's so with-it, the way you French shrug all the time!' she told him. 'Just like New Yorkers saying "no big deal!"'

They were friends again. And, secretly, Jean-Jacques had to admit he had never known anyone quite like Samantha. He could hardly wait to hear how she would get on with his technique.

Christopher watched Camille Delange begin to put together her rather dowdy spring collection. She was going to stay fiercely loyal to her palette of beiges, browns and greys. The pile of 'young' sketches he had hopefully submitted were politely ignored. There was not a hint of youth in the suits and gowns.

'It's "Camille's greatest hits",' he confided dolefully to Klaus over omelettes at home. 'It's just not possible that "fashion" can be this dull.'

'You have to shake up that old girl!' Klaus grunted.

'How? We're on different planets.'

Four

Three weeks, no work, and Samantha played her trump card: *Daddy!* Rich, powerful, a brash young Hungarian immigrant to Los Angeles in the nineteen forties, he had cornered the Californian market in sportswear clothing, building up a sizeable fortune as the state's fashion industry grew.

Sandor Lipstaadt founded several dress firms and become the American licensee of Delange perfume. By clever marketing, including Mother's Day gift packs, he sold several million dollars' worth of their scent annually. Now he was 'launching' Samantha onto the fashion scene. With contract-renewal time coming along, Samantha suggested that he suggest to the Delanges that they find her a position in their Paris house. Or else.

Thus the minor Paris fashion house, Delange, was forced to hire a publicist. They had never had a publicist. The Delange directors rolled their eyes and accepted the condition as the price for making more million-dollar American sales.

They quickly changed a store-cupboard into an office for her and tacked together a position: *Directrice* of Image & Promotion. It was supposed to be a fake title for a fake job, but they reckoned without Samantha's ambition and creative powers.

On her first morning, she called a meeting. She wore Chanel, one hundred per cent. Perhaps that was a mistake, she thought later. The directors of Delange were mostly haughty daughters, nieces and cousins of Camille Delange. Slim, blonde, chic, Parisienne, they were everything she wasn't. Samantha smiled brightly as they glared at her, knowing she must make an immediate impact. She felt a little woozy on the heavy-duty New York tranquilliser she had taken to calm her down.

'*Bonjour*,' she began. Before she could continue, the most aggressive of the women interrupted her.

'You're *American*!' she cried out, almost like an accusation.

'So?' Samantha countered.

'What makes you think you can tell us about fashion?' the woman asked.

'How to *sell* fashion,' Samantha corrected her. 'You do want this house to make money, don't you?' she asked bluntly. When she was nervous, she was blunt.

The women exchanged glances and Samantha felt that horrible feeling she had felt at Beverly High, being judged and found wanting by the hip girls.

They continued to watch her, frozen with contempt, as she held up a huge roll of paper on which she had written a short list:

1) SEX
2) SEX
3) **SEX**!!!!!

They stared, silent.

'Why all this sex?' Chantal Delange, the youngest niece at around thirty-five, finally asked with undisguised contempt. 'For French people, sex is a *plaisir*, not a sales tool!'

'Sex sells clothes . . .' Samantha explained patiently. '*And* perfume. *And* cosmetics. And sunglasses. And shoes. And handbags. And . . .'

They continued to stare.

'Get the picture?' She smiled.

'How do you know this?' A Delange woman asked her. 'How do you seem so sure?'

'I was *born* knowing this,' Samantha assured her sincerely.

'And where do we put all this sex?'

'Into the advertising,' Samantha announced. She began to outline her plan to revitalise the staid image of Delange.

'My *office*,' she snorted to her father from a street phone-box later, 'is smaller than my New York shoe-closet. And my first morning at Delange was heavy-duty scary.'

'They should be scared of *you*,' he said. 'Are you Sandor Lipstaadt's daughter, or what?'

'It wasn't easy walking into a room with all those skinny little Delange women *glaring* at me, Daddy,' she whispered into the phone. 'They have this . . . Parisian expression, as if someone's shoved some ripe Camembert up their nostrils. I wore head-to-toe Chanel and I don't think they appreciated it.' She laughed.

'Aren't you as good as them?' he grunted.

'I think the French hate Americans, Daddy . . .' she whispered.

'Oh yeah? They don't hate our dollars, do they?'

'I'm planning to make a lot more money for them. OK, I gotta go, Daddy. I'm starving and my *centimes* are running out. Call you tomorrow. I love you.'

The next day at Delange, she royally received, one by one, all the important members of the staff.

'Delange is such a wonderful *sound*,' she told them. 'Like some delicious raspberry sorbet. We must make young girls everywhere want it. With fabulous new advertising, we'll sell oodles of scent.'

She had not been hired to change their advertising but she seemed so sure, her enthusiasm so contagious, that suddenly the staff felt Delange had a future, not just a past. She was determined to milk the Camille Delange name and reputation for all it was worth, perhaps a little more.

'Just one thing, Samantha.' Chantal Delange stopped her as she left her cupboard one morning. 'Should a Delange employee be wearing Chanel?'

She stared at Samantha with an expectant expression.

'But . . . this is all I have!' Samantha wailed.

'In the interest of self-promotion, I suggest you take advantage of our cost-price clothing for staff,' Chantal snapped.

Samantha was very reluctantly fitted for the least dowdy suit she could choose from the current collection.

At the end of November, Madame Michelle's workroom stopped working on private orders to prepare for the new Spring '68 collection, to be shown in January.

People in the house said that Mademoiselle became impossible. She did not sketch but arrived at her designs by draping fabric directly onto a living model, cutting as she worked. A cutter would take away the pinned jacket or skirt and bring it back the following day to fit again. They fitted and re-fitted until Mademoiselle was satisfied. Except that Mademoiselle was never satisfied.

One afternoon, Madame Michelle returned to the workroom from a fitting, tears streaming down her face, holding a torn-apart jacket. She placed the jacket on the cutting-table as if it were an almost-drowned child, indicating the furious slashes Mademoiselle had made, the chalk marks, the ripped seams. How to revive it?

The girls muttered that Mademoiselle automatically destroyed the first fittings, barely glancing at them. Because her fingers had become painfully arthritic, she seemed to be taking out her frustration on the seamstresses, making them re-do a jacket or set in a sleeve over and over again. It was, they sighed, the price for working *chez* Chanel.

Madame Michelle's tragic sniffs punctuated the day. At intervals, she pulled the stopper from a flacon of No. 5, shook a few drops on her handkerchief and mopped her brow and face with it. Monique wondered whether it promoted moustache growth?

The collection was finished just in time, but nobody from the workroom saw either the rehearsal or the actual showing. During the following season, Monique graduated to making actual suits. The clients told the *vendeuses* who told Madame Antoine who told Mademoiselle Chanel that it was the best work they had ever seen.

*

Samantha gradually met everyone who worked for Delange. But only with Christopher did she feel something in common.

'It's because we can speak English together,' she told him. 'I mean, speaking French is fun because I don't care what I say, but speaking in English is the only *real* way to communicate.'

She invited him on a Sunday visit to the Marché aux Puces, an antique market. They took the metro to Porte de Clignancourt, pushing through the crowds to find a real local hang-out for lunch, a modest café complete with elderly three-piece band.

'It's like the soundtrack of a foreign movie,' Samantha marvelled as they were whisked to a table with accordion music swirling around them. She wore her more democratic Afghan coat for the occasion, slipping it off onto the chairback to reveal a hugging scarlet ribbed sweater over matching scarlet trousers.

'Christopher, why do they hate me?' she wailed, after ordering Kirs.

'They hate anyone who isn't French,' he reminded her. 'We just have to work around it.'

'But they admire *you*,' Samantha pouted. 'They adore *le style Anglais. Le thé, le Shetland, le cashmere, le Tartan*, all that stuff. They just *resent* me.' She sipped her drink, frowning. 'But I'll turn this Delange job into something much better. Did you see that movie *Belle de Jour*? Catherine Deneuve plays this rich woman who works as a prostitute in the afternoons. It's so wonderful to have a job you really love.'

They ordered the *steak frites* that everyone else seemed to be ordering and tucked into their food when it came. Samantha demanded ketchup, which got raised eyebrows.

'An American in Paris can do anything because people think you're crazy anyway,' she said, shaking ketchup over her fries. 'I was once laughed out of a café for ordering hot chocolate with a tuna-fish sandwich.'

Christopher watched her, fascinated. He stared at her long angular face and gawky movements, her six feet of statuesque height balanced on platform soles, her high cheek-bones and generous lips.

54

'You are the most extraordinary person I think I've ever met,' he said.

Samantha shrugged. 'I bet you've never met a JAP before?'

'What is it, exactly?'

'Jewish American Princess.' She traced the capital letters in the air with her finger. 'JAP Get it? And not only that, I'm bi-coastal! Daddy and I lived in Beverly Hills *and* New York!'

Christopher frowned. 'Is there also something . . . oriental in your background?'

'Oh no, this is *jolie-laide*,' she said.

When their plates were removed, she stared in dismay at the desserts listed on the menu.

'Why does everything have to be in *French*?' she whined.

'It *is* their national language,' Christopher explained gently.

She shot him a hurt look. 'Well, it sure makes things harder for me.'

She chose a cake. 'If we're really going to be friends, we must tell each other *everything*, right? You're gay, of course?' She nodded knowledgeably.

'Actually, no, I'm not,' Christopher said.

'But I thought all guys in fashion were?' Samantha's knee immediately wedged itself between his legs.

'I have a girlfriend,' he lied quickly.

'Oh?' She made a face, removing her knee. She brightened instantly. 'You got a brother?'

Four months after Monique had started at Chanel, Mademoiselle's assistant came to the workroom and asked for her. No one in that workroom, aside from Madame Michelle, had ever been personally summoned by Mademoiselle. The other girls looked up in awe as Monique stood, blushing, to follow the assistant.

Chanel's tiny suite at the Ritz Hotel was reputed to be surprisingly modest. She used a larger, more luxurious suite on the top floor of the house as her living-room, to rest or read in, or in which to receive visitors.

Life-sized blackamoor statues guarded a honey-coloured soft

suede sofa. Exquisite Chinese coromandel screens proved excellent substitutes for paintings. Leather-bound books lined an entire wall. Mademoiselle's room had the air of an intellectual woman who loved luxury.

Perched on the sofa, Mademoiselle pored over a suit Monique had just finished for an important client, a fabulously rich widow named Madame D'Aubigné who ordered at least six outfits each season.

Mademoiselle looked up. 'I thought it was you. You're the girl from Angers who waylaid me in the street, aren't you?' she said. 'If I could find fifty people like you, I could retire.' She sighed. 'Remind me of your name . . . Monique? Well I know treasure when I find it. You will be transferred to our best workroom.'

Monique tried to take in what she was being told: a rise in salary, a position with the best tailor at Chanel, Monsieur Guy, the master tailor she had heard about but never seen.

'Guy always has a waiting-list of clients,' Chanel told her. 'We only allow our most valued clients to order suits or coats from his workroom. You will be happier working there.'

'Thank you, Mademoiselle.' Monique was close to tears.

'Please, don't cry again. I want you to be happy in my house.'

Dismissed, Monique descended Chanel's famous mirrored staircase in a dream, hardly daring to look at the multiple images of herself walking alongside her. So many photographs had been taken on this stairway, the slivers of mirror set at different angles, magically reflecting back women as more glamorous than they really were.

It took a certain amount of flair to use this staircase: Monique admired the models who sailed down it with great chic. During collection showings, it was the ultimate status symbol for the front-row overflow to be allowed to sit on these stairs to watch the collection. It was the place from which Mademoiselle herself viewed her collection, judging from its reception whether or not she would appear at the end for the applause. Monique averted her gaze from the faceted reflections pointing up how far she was from being a model; her face too plump, eyes too wide and trusting, body too rounded to ever be truly elegant.

She might not be a glamour girl, but she would be a *Premiere Main* in Chanel's top workroom. What would it be like to work for Monsieur Guy? She had heard he liked the ladies. Would he like her?

The Delange directors developed a grudging respect for Samantha. For the Christmas season, she had replaced their staid advertisements with a new, sexy campaign, after fighting everyone on the board to get it. Her conviction had convinced them. They had changed their advertising agency, and sales of Delange perfume had soared.

'They're starting to think I know how to sell,' she told Christopher on a coffee-break at the café downstairs. 'I changed their image. Parisians *want* bronzed musclemen grinning down from street billboards clutching Delange perfume between their thighs!'

The advertisements – just as Samantha described them – were not only on street billboards but splashed across *Elle*'s pages, on the back cover of French *Vogue* and over entire pages in newspapers.

'*Ohhhhhhhh Delange . . .*' said the ads.

Sales continued to climb and Samantha got a bigger office. Her professional life underway, it was time to tackle her next problem: men.

Sophie missed a few drawing classes, but, when she reappeared, Christopher sought her out and sat next to her.

'Still designing your own clothes?' he asked her.

She gave him a brilliant smile. 'Yes, and making them. And now I have my own place to live in.'

'Where is it?'

'In the centre of Paris. Near Etoile.' She shot him a look. 'Perhaps you would like to see some of my clothes on Saturday, around noon? I could make lunch afterwards?'

This was the most exciting invitation Christopher had ever received.

The workroom received a shot of magic if an exquisitely made-up model ran in, naked under her white overall, to gossip with Madame Michelle. Although there was a huge social gap between rich clients and poor seamstresses, Monique felt at ease in the lush *salons*. Madame Michelle began asking her to take down garments or fetch them after fittings.

Monique loved pushing open the door on the second floor's backstairs. The other side of the door was mirrored. As it swung open, the poor surroundings magically vanished. She stepped from worn floorboards onto thick grey carpet. The salon was hung with long grey velvet curtains which muffled the noise and the air was heady with Chanel No. 5.

She hurried to a *cabine* to pass a jacket inside to the *vendeuse*. Then back through the mirrored door to the shabby workrooms. Backstage, she thought of it, because the brilliantly lit salons suggested a theatre, a stage.

A humble seamstress earned a pittance yet there was no shortage of uneducated girls happy to accept it. In letters to her mother and sister Monique made it sound like an accolade to have been accepted into the prestigious house of Chanel, a place where she could improve her craft and advance to a better-paid position.

Each morning, she was first to arrive in the workroom. The silence, the day-to-day drudge of neat sewing, made her life resemble a sacrifice.

Her favourite place was the store room where fabrics in tightly rolled bolts were kept. It was called the *manutention*, an Aladdin's cave of fresh, bewitching tweeds and wools in fat rolls, stacked up. Gorgeous silk chiffons, (much of it black, for the famous little black dresses), rolls of ribbons, braids and trimmings, feathers, embroidered panels, fake jewels . . . all patiently awaiting their transformation into Chanel suits or dresses. Monique touched them wonderingly, wishing she could be left alone to play with them. But the keeper of this room, Elvira, a strict woman with a 1940s upswept hairdo, guarded her treasures fiercely, doling out carefully measured lengths to the workrooms.

*

The following Saturday morning, Christopher took the longest shower of his life. Just in case. Klaus watched as Christopher ate a hearty breakfast, becoming quite curious.

'Someone has a hot date?' he laughed.

Christopher winked at Klaus, as he left the flat. It was sunny but crisp outside. He decided to walk to the Avenue Kleber, quite a distance but it would distract him because he felt slightly nervous.

Halfway up the Champs-Elysées, he bought a tiny bouquet from a flower stall. The flowers, packed tightly into a circular mosaic of colour, were wrapped in a wisp of paper. Suddenly, he realised how wonderful it was to be in Paris, to be visiting a beautiful girl and probably making love to her. He strode up the wide avenue with renewed vigour. He stopped at Le Drugstore, to leaf through American magazines and stare covetously at the latest sunglasses. It was the 'in' place for young Parisians and he caught the eye of several pretty girls before remembering his rendezvous was with a much prettier one.

He reached Sophie's address five minutes before noon: it would not be cool to arrive too early so he walked slowly around the block twice before pressing the old porcelain bell at three minutes past. The heavy door sprang open and he took the lift to the top floor.

Sophie finally answered the door wearing a carelessly wrapped bathrobe, its whiteness making her skin pink. Flashes of her body showed as she moved.

'*Bonjour*, Sophie,' Christopher said. He kept his eyes on her face.

She was wearing more eye-liner and shadow than she wore in the art classes. She seemed more sophisticated, sure of herself. He felt awkward, and dropped the bouquet as he presented it to her, mock gallant.

'Oh, thanks. Something to drink?' she offered.

'No, thanks. I just had coffee.'

A dog ran out into the small hallway, barking and jumping up.

'He is very jealous,' Sophie warned. 'Very possessive.'

59

The dog finally accepted his caresses. 'At least your dog likes me,' he tried.

She smiled. 'Don't be so modest. All the girls in the school are in love with you.'

Christopher laughed. 'Really? They have a funny way of showing it.'

She gazed at him knowingly. 'Women don't like to show men what they think . . .' she informed him. She gestured to her robe. 'I kept this on because I will be modelling my clothes for you.'

'Oh, yes.' He nodded, businesslike.

In her *salon*, some pretty antique chairs had been re-covered in blue and white gingham, lengths of gauzy white fabric draped across the tops of windows, a table covered in droopy white lace . . . it suggested the set of some romantic play. And Christopher felt like the player who did not know his lines. Fashion magazines and books were stacked in piles on the floor. A stand on a white-painted sideboard sported a large straw hat trailing coloured ribbons. It looked as though she had just moved in. Outside, the clouded Paris sky was grey and golden at once.

'You are a little shy?' Sophie approached to whisper in his ear. He tried to swallow but his throat was too dry. Clearing his throat, he said, 'I think I *would* like something to drink, if you don't mind. Water is fine. I suppose it's too early for lunch?'

'Yes, it is much too early,' Sophie giggled, close. 'What do you usually eat for lunch?'

'Mmm, don't know really. Maybe beans on toast?'

'That sounds *very* English,' she shuddered. 'Now, Christopher . . .' she said soothingly. 'I should like to guess your fantasies. We all have fantasies, every man and woman, no?'

She was so near that they were almost touching. 'But we women hug them to ourselves . . . picturing them only as you make love to us. What is *your* fantasy?'

'Well . . . it's hard to say,' he croaked.

He was amazed that now, the nearest he had come to real unrushed intimacy with a beautiful girl, it was suddenly the last thing he felt like doing.

'Perhaps it is connected to fashion?' Sophie asked. 'Fashion is sensual – touching women's bodies, here . . . and here . . .' She slipped her hand beneath her robe, as he watched.

'Touching their breasts and between their legs . . .' she went on, taking his hand. 'Imagine! In some tiny *cabine* a girl like me, standing, legs apart, as you feel her all over?' She shot him a triumphant look. He was as hard as he'd ever been.

'How they will enjoy your hands on them,' she murmured, placing his hands on the sides of her body. She moved and the robe parted. 'Now, how about fitting me?' She rubbed against him like a purring cat. 'In the *cabines*, Monsieur Christophe.' She jerked her head towards the bedroom. 'Will you fit my new dress?'

She disappeared into her bedroom leaving the door ajar. Through the gap, shadows moved on the white walls inside. Christopher heard the swish of a curtain being pulled. He was usually confident, if not cocky, but now he felt out of his league. He could not compare Sophie to the suburban art-school girls he had fumbled with in the cloakrooms. They had not treated sex like this. This sophisticated, beautiful Parisian girl had a very grown-up attitude to sex, taking it to new heights of erotica.

Christopher took a deep breath. This would be nothing less than his first real sexual experience. It would be terrifying if it weren't so exciting. He stepped into her room.

Five

Four panels of gauzy fabric hung from the ceiling of Sophie's bedroom, enclosing and silhouetting her body. A full-length mirror rested at an angle against one wall. Was this *'cabine'* always in her bedroom or had she erected it solely for today? She had sprayed scent around, casting an atmospheric spell. Christopher drew back one filmy panel to see her pose, half-fashion, half pin-up, one leg invitingly bent, her arms stretched upward in an almost Hollywood attitude, eyes half-closed, moistened lips shiny. The pose took her out of everyday life and into a world of pretence, of sex.

The mirror reflected her entire body down to the small feet with their scarlet toenails. She shrugged off the robe. Christopher stared at her small, perfect, upward-pointing breasts. She slipped on a transparent straight sheath which came to her knees, handing him a tape measure.

'Give me a fitting,' she said.

He joined in the game, stretching the tape behind her back then gently across her breasts. The nipples strained against the fabric as he brushed them with his fingertips. They were hard.

'It must fit tight to my body,' she whispered.

She slipped a pin-cushion on an elastic band over his wrist.

Using the long pins on the flimsy material, he pinned the sheath tightly, as if imprisoning her slim body, her breasts crushed against the restraining fabric. Why was it more erotic to see the almost-transparent fabric holding her than to see her naked?

While he considered this, she quickly unfastened his trousers and reached inside.

She giggled. 'Nothing to be ashamed of in that department!'

Her expression was questioning, slightly surprised.

'Some women get wet between their legs . . .' she told him. 'Others have nipples which become painfully stiff, like mine are now. Touch them tenderly please, Monsieur.'

He brushed his fingertips across the tips of her breasts. She bit on her lower lip. 'You surely noticed how the models' breasts push their pretty silk brassieres?' She smiled. 'How their nipples jut out against them?'

With each word, he became harder. He felt as if he were about to explode.

'Divide the skirt between my legs,' Sophie whispered. 'Like *culottes*. Fit me there.'

As he attempted to pin the thin cloth, she parted her legs, allowing him to feel the heat of her there.

'Further up . . .' she urged.

He removed the last flimsy barrier and found himself grazing the softest skin he had ever touched. Velvet, finest suede, the furled petals of a fuchsia – he was reminded of all these. As she crouched down, she made his fingertips disappear inside her, as if dipping into melting silk. He gasped at the moist softness, hearing her long deep sigh. Her eyes closed blissfully, mouth pursed in enjoyment.

She broke away to stretch out on the broderie-anglaise-covered bed. He looked down at her. During his hurried, often drunken lovemaking, there had never been time to examine a woman's body. Now he viewed the most beautiful, intricate piece of workmanship, a couturier's masterpiece: a series of pockets or purses, each leading to the next, brown welted seams outlining and revealing a deep pink, as if a woman's body was fully lined in rose satin. The edges, shirred and blushed, made a welcoming entrance, beckoning him in.

He removed her dress, shucking his jeans. His desire was evident, making him feel ridiculous.

'Continue the tight, tight fitting . . .' she murmured. She held out her arms.

He stretched between her legs and she suddenly twisted away, laughing.

'Are you just teasing me?' he asked.

'Yes!' she said.

Then she rolled back to him and guided him into her so smoothly that the sensation, as he slid up to the very hilt of his body, was quite overwhelming.

She clasped him tightly and he realised she would be milking the pleasure from him and he would be unable to hold back. He had moved into the world of the mirrored reflection, the crystal gaze, the female body he had studied and stared at so often but never experienced so fully as now.

Pressing his mouth to hers, he nibbled on her lower lip as if trying to locate love. One thing he knew he was good at was kissing. He had had plenty of experience at art school, in the cinema, even in the street. He showed off all his well-practised techniques, until their mouths formed a vacuum filled with thrashing, thrusting tongues. When he kissed, all his yearning for love showed. She had never had a man kiss her quite like this before and it excited her.

Christopher groaned. He could not hold back much longer. The sensations building up in him demanded release. The act of love should last much longer, he knew, and he felt that he was somehow failing her, but now it was too late. Shutting his eyes against the bliss as if to postpone it, he felt a series of sparks ignite and he was unable to stop their progress. He clutched Sophie's shoulders tightly, each finger leaving a faint bruise. Lips still pressed to his, she swung her legs up behind him, forcing him deeper inside her and with a roar of surprise, the last sensation broke loose and there was a rush of pleasure. The most unexpected, concentrated bliss he had ever experienced swept him, the echoes sounding in his body almost as intense as the pleasure itself. He collapsed onto her pale, smooth breast, face pressed against her heart.

He was about to tell her he thought he loved her when she blew out a resigned sigh: 'You will learn.'

A Paris breeze billowed out the gauzy curtain, shrouding the young couple in white transparency. It was sucked back to unfurl outside the window. Christopher watched its dance. Sophie lit a cigarette, thinking hard. Torn between wanting to throw out this gauche young *Anglais* and hugging him, she solved the dilemma by smoking.

'The female body must have been designed by a master couturier . . .' he said, running his hands over her shoulders.

She laughed. 'You're an expert on the female body?'

He nodded. 'A designer has to be. It's obviously been designed to give the maximum pleasure possible to a man.'

'Not the designers I know,' she laughed.

'That's where I'm different,' he said.

'Was this your first time?' she asked.

He gave a rather hollow laugh. 'My first time? Are you kidding?'

Something in him was shaken real time. 'Why, was I that bad?' he asked.

Sophie smiled. 'Not bad exactly, just . . . quick.' She took another puff. 'But with a few lessons, you could be the best lover in Paris.'

She stubbed out the cigarette.

'OK, you see here . . .' she indicated a secret place. 'Kiss me here the way you kissed my mouth. Using your tongue. You were very good at *that*!'

He felt a thrill of excitement at being told what to do. As if he were following her commands.

'I am your slave, . . .' he said, kneeling down before her.

She relaxed back on the bed. She was always determined to achieve her pleasure when with a man for the first time. And somehow it added to the excitement if she told herself it would be the first and *only* time. Was she perverse? Why did she find it so difficult to trust a man?

She told him how she needed his tongue to be hard and regular and how he must keep on doing what he was doing for as long as she needed it. And within minutes she felt a wave of pleasure building up in her until she began to gasp and cry 'Don't stop! Don't stop! Don't stop!' her rhythmic cries matching his regular tongue-thrusts.

Pleasure began to sneak up on her from everywhere because his hands stretched to gently pinch her nipples, the two sensations driving her wild. More intense than the pleasure she usually enjoyed with a man, it built up to a wave that threatened to overcome her. She grasped a handful of his thick blond hair and her entire body sang and swooned as pleasure suffused it, her back arching as if to take in more. Their movements slowed until they were both still and Sophie fell back on the pillows.

'You see how easy it is to give pleasure to a woman?' she murmured, her eyes closed.

He joined her, taking her in his arms, feeling a thrill of triumph at having pleased her.

'I'll be a very keen pupil,' he said. 'I'll do my homework. Make me the best lover in Paris.'

'Why should I do this?' Sophie suddenly sat up, indignant. 'So you can give pleasure to all the other sluts in Paris?'

'Sophie!' He broke away, frowning at her, puzzled. 'Do you have to be so tough? Has somebody hurt you? Can't you just relax and be nice?'

'Relax and be nice?' She seemed surprised at the suggestion. 'Perhaps. And . . . yes, someone has hurt me.'

'A man?'

'Yes, but not in the way you think.'

'Then how?'

'He pretended to be my father.'

It was the last thing she had meant to blurt out. She fumbled for a cigarette to cover her confusion.

Christopher frowned. 'How do you pretend to be someone's father?'

Sophie lit the cigarette, glancing at him as she inhaled.

'You adopt them,' she said.

66

Something stopped him from asking more. Or from telling her he could easily fall in love with her. If she was just playing with him, he would play it cool, too. So he dressed, kissed her, and casually asked, 'When can we meet again? Tomorrow?'

'Tomorrow I have plans,' she said quickly.

'Oh!' he blurted. 'And after tomorrow?'

'I don't know. Call me.'

He had not been looking for love, but this fragile, tough girl was definitely as near as he had yet come to it. He bent to kiss her again.

'Well, thanks for lunch.'

He left with the feeling that he might never see her again.

Sophie remained on the bed for some time after he'd left, a tear escaping one eye. Why had she told him about being adopted? Who had the right to know about that? Nobody. She was furious at herself. This fantasy she had always nurtured, of a sweet, somewhat innocent boy who would give her adoring love, how she wanted it. In one way. And yet now she felt disappointed at herself. She had always been so in control with the men she had seduced in her parents' house, pretending they had seduced her. She had enjoyed their admiration, their lust, but she had always had the upper hand. They had wanted to see her again and she had refused them. One time only, she had stipulated. But this boy, so obviously inexperienced and so obviously sincere, had somehow got through a little chink in her emotional armour.

He could only hurt her. You can get hurt if you allow yourself to be loved, she reminded herself. Yes, this boy had an effect on her: he made her feel weak. She must be very wary, not allow anyone to hurt her, not now.

When Christopher and Klaus found a secret back door to Chez Regine, their social life improved considerably. Getting to that door involved clambering over dustbins, then sneaking in and picking up unfinished drinks to nurse, saving the twenty-five-francs cover-charge which they could not afford.

Entering Regine's by this method one weeknight, they glanced around at *le beau monde*. Discotheque style was predominant – tiny dresses, coloured tights, big plastic earrings against the dark suits of the men.

'You are so lucky, Chris: women *and* men look at you,' Klaus told him. 'You get *two* chances to make it big. If I could wean myself to bisexuality, *I* would have two chances, too.'

'But I don't *want* two chances, Klaus.' Christopher made a face. 'I'm friendly with guys, I have nothing against them, but if a guy tried anything . . . forget it.'

Klaus shrugged. 'The next time a guy comes on to me, perhaps I should try it just to see what it's like. It can't be worse than some chicks I've been with?'

'I'm turned on by slim, chic girls . . .' Christopher mused. 'Usually models. But only if they are very attracted to me! Does that make me a narcissist, Klaus? Perhaps my partner's desire ignites my desire?'

'I will accept any desire, Chris. Mine, theirs, hers, his – all is good for my career.'

'You still believe in the myth of sleeping your way to the top?'

'It's no myth, Christopher. It happens all the time. And with photographers, I mean who are we kidding? It is not that difficult to take a photograph. You need someone powerful behind you.'

Christopher looked intently at Klaus.

'To reach Fashion Immortality,' he began, 'I have to deliver new, desirable clothing that women will kill for.'

'Or at least kill their husbands for,' Klaus added.

The new song '*Je t'aime, moi non plus*' interrupted their intense discussion.

The gasping, sighing voice was Jane Birkin's, a British actress married to Serge Gainsbourg. Christopher knew the song had been banned by the BBC in England because of its 'orgasmic' sound-effects.

The small parquet dance-floor cleared, leaving only one tall lone figure in a red sequined shift with matching sparkly tights, swaying on the floor, her arms raised above her head, eyes closed, body shuddering at each orgasmic sound.

Klaus nudged Christopher: 'Regine's has been known to attract the odd transvestite, eh?' he marvelled.

Christopher followed Klaus's gaze and got a jolt of surprise.

'Not this one,' he said. 'Her name's Samantha, she works for Delange and she's one hundred per cent female.'

'How do you know this?' Klaus frowned.

'I still have the bruises on my thigh! She grabbed it when I told her I wasn't gay,' Christopher said. 'She thought every man in fashion was gay.'

'What sort of woman is she?' Klaus asked, staring at her as she suddenly spun around. 'Might I be her type?'

'If you're male, you're her type,' Christopher nodded.

He stepped onto the dance-floor and touched Samantha. Her eyes blinked open. 'Christopher!' She smiled. 'I'm trying to look Rich Hippie!'

He invited her to their table, making sure she brought her drink with her. She had backcombed her hair into a mane that added to her height. Eight chains clanked around her neck as she walked.

'Klaus, meet Samantha.'

She held out her recently manicured hand. 'Klaus! Cute name. What is it, German?'

'Yes, I plead guilty to German.' Klaus bowed and clicked his heels. 'And you, Samantha, are the most exotic woman I have ever seen.'

'I like that word, exotic,' Samantha beamed.

'Also erotic,' Klaus ventured.

Samantha giggled. 'OK, *I'll* plead guilty to erotic. But I'm usually called *jolie-laide*.'

'*Jolie*, yes. Never *laide*.' Klaus corrected. 'You dance erotically, too!'

'It's that tune,' Samantha sighed. 'It *really* turns me on.'

Christopher watched with interest. It would never have occurred to him to match this couple, but he had to admit there was a spark between them. Perhaps they could be Fashion's newest odd couple?

The next day, Christopher woke up alone in the flat.

Klaus always steered his private life to his photographic studio where there was a generously sized sofa.

'That Klaus,' Samantha confided gratefully, when Christopher popped his head into her office later that morning. 'He is a *great* lover. Solid rhythm, like a German marching song. He wants to see me again. Oh Christopher, Paris is going to be better than my wildest dreams – I never thought I'd find fashion *and* passion!'

And then, in that odd way Paris life had, Samantha met another man when Audrey took her to Ghislaine de Rives' chic Sunday-night '*salon*'. Eduard de Kousmine was taller than her, and a lot wider. She noticed the intense way he stared at her, his subtle way of showing she attracted him – touching himself under cover of his blazer. She raised her eyebrows and popped her eyes, pursing her lips. Men loved it when you reacted, she thought. They take it as interest. She walked over to him. How it helped to be drunk!

'You're not at *all* my type . . .' she began.

'Eduard de Kousmine, a director of Chanel,' he said with a bow.

'. . . but there *is* something very sexy about you,' she recovered quickly. He leaned towards her.

'I keep a little apartment near here where I sometimes invite very beautiful women,' he growled. 'Perhaps you would like to see it?'

Samantha raised her eyebrows high. 'Why not?'

Samantha's imaginary perfect lover would not have been this heavy-set man with his walrus moustache and glowering black eyes. But the fun part of playing Beauty and the Beast, she

70

thought, was that *she* got to play Beauty! And if the Beast just happened to be a director of Chanel, she could file this under the heading of 'work'.

After a short taxi-ride, Samantha was ushered up some red-carpeted stairs to a tiny, luxurious apartment off the Champs-Elysées. He fell on her the moment the front door was closed, growling, unbuttoning and clutching, his eyes rolling back in his head when she began the famous Samantha routine she had perfected at Beverly Hills High. Few men could resist a bad blow-job, she nodded sagely to herself. But no man on earth could resist a really good one. It was a useful fact of life she had learned early and it saved undressing, getting wet or risking pregnancy, so it made everyone happy, *if* you were really good at it and she knew she was.

She had no inhibitions. Success depended on the man being made to believe he was irresistible. Most men were pathetically eager to believe that. Then, she had learned early on the technique of treating this part of his anatomy as if she were a master musician playing a flute. This she did, pleased that her musical talent evoked cries of astonishment from her new friend. She had learned from an incredibly gifted girl at school who had liked sex even more than Samantha had. It was a question of pressure (of lips, of tongue), speed (alternating high speed with low speed then back to high, sometimes even stopping) and lots of air-blowing (first hot air, then cool). They didn't call it a blow-job for nothing, she thought. It helped a lot if the man was not too big, far less work. So it was a simple matter to make de Kousmine groan with astonished pleasure.

The better you were, the longer you tried to make it last, but the better you were, the shorter it lasted. That was the paradox, she thought. Thank God! She got him there in a matter of minutes. As she saw only the whites of his eyes, she turned up the speed, increased the hot air, the pressure, the tongue. The satisfied wheezes of her new large lover took a while to quieten down and Samantha sat back, her work done. She had rarely had such a large degree of audience appreciation.

'I have never—' he gasped. 'Where did you learn this?' he asked suspiciously, mopping his face with a large white handkerchief.

'Beverly Hills,' Samantha said matter-of-factly, dabbing her lips with a Kleenex. 'Blow-job capital of the world. I was voted "Most Likely to Succeed" in my school yearbook. Luckily, they didn't say at what.'

'Yes, you *are* likely to succeed, Samantha,' de Kousmine grunted. 'No one this talented could not succeed.'

She shot him a sharp look. 'I want to succeed in *fashion!*' she stated very firmly.

'I must see you again!' he said.

Samantha attempted an enigmatic look. Leave them wanting more, her father had always advised.

'So you grew up in Beverly Hills?' he asked.

'Until I was eighteen,' she nodded. 'Then we moved to New York. My father's in the fashion business, too. He distributes Delange perfumes in America. Amongst other things.'

He nodded, looking intently at her.

When they left the apartment soon after, the taxi was waiting. This luxurious touch impressed her. New Yorkers *never* left the meter ticking. Samantha was dropped off at her flat. She let herself in and faced her surprised expression in the mirror.

'They're either crazy about me or they don't notice me at all,' she said aloud to her reflection. She ran a long warm perfumed bath.

On the phone to Jean-Jacques the following morning, she said, 'I must be an acquired taste. Two men in the same *month*? Feast or famine.' She giggled. 'I'll choose feast, because who knows when famine is on the way?'

'Very prudent, Samantha,' he agreed. 'But I've seen him around, he isn't very sexy. I bet he's never worn a leather garment in his life? What could possibly attract you to this man, this walrus?'

'Jean-Jacques,' she whispered shyly into the phone, 'you won't tell anybody? I think I'm Cocosexual . . .'

'And what is that?'

'Well you know what heterosexual is?' she cooed. 'And you know what homosexual is?'

He grunted.

'Cocosexual is a much rarer condition: anything with entwined Cs on it turns me on. A camelia quickens my pulse-rate. A quilted purse gets me all hot and bothered. Imagine what a Chanel *director* does to me?'

'Isn't he a Co-Director?'

'He's a Coco Director!'

'Samantha.' Jean-Jacques gave a long sigh and she could hear he was shaking his head. 'You are quite crazy. That is why I love you.'

'Crazy?' she questioned. 'No. It's that in Paris somehow nothing feels as if it's real. I'm allowed to do anything I want.' She nodded at the phone. 'De Kousmine comes under the heading of work. Klaus will come under the heading of love. De Kousmine just might lead, in a roundabout way, to Chanel?'

'You are using him!' Jean-Jacques clucked disapprovingly. 'Slutty little Cocosexual.'

Delange's perfume sales continued to improve. It was entirely thanks to their new advertising campaign, and other houses were not slow to notice that. During their subsequent meetings, de Kousmine began to appreciate that Samantha was much more than a sex object, she had a real sense of the fashion business.

'I get it from my dad,' she said, when he complimented her.

He hosted early-evening sessions in his love-nest. She made sure she asked for taxi fare. There and back.

'He talks dirty after sex,' she confided to Jean-Jacques, 'business dirt.'

'What's new?' de Kousmine would grunt after sex, lighting a cigar.

She expected him to offer her a job at Chanel. The tension between them came because he hadn't.

'Why did you put musclemen in your ads?' he asked.

'Uh-uh. I work for Delange, not Chanel,' Samantha stated.

'I know, but why *musclemen*?'

'Oh, *please*,' Samantha squawked. 'Don't tell me Chanel is too chic for sex? You won't even license bed-linen. Think of the millions of women who would *adore* to make love on Chanel sheets.'

'We must keep the name exclusive . . .' he grunted quietly.

'If Dior can license bed-sheets, why can't Chanel?' she asked. 'Not that I care. It gives us a bigger market. We are selling Delange bed-linen at J.C. Penney. It's the biggest retail chain in America!'

'We are French, not American,' Eduard sighed.

'Oh? French men don't care about money?'

'The directors feel they protect Chanel's value by *not* licensing bed-sheets,' he explained patiently. 'Maybe sunglasses are fashion, but bed-sheets . . .' He shrugged. 'Bed-sheets are not fashion.'

'Then why are *we* lying on bed-sheets discussing bed-sheets?' Samantha asked. 'Why don't we just *use* them?' She raised her eyebrows, taking hold of each end of his walrus moustache.

'A fresh generation may allow some new ideas,' he said, leaning to rest his cigar in the ashtray.

'Hmm . . .' She sighed, wanting to learn much more. This was like being an industrial spy!

Eduard began to growl, his prelude to making love seriously. She forgot fashion or even sheets. He was a very intense man. She relaxed in his firm grip. The grip of a man told you everything. She liked the way he went a little crazy at the end, his eyes rolling up in his head. She must tell Jean-Jacques all about it.

They went out for an early dinner, both ravenous. At La Coupole, Eduard ordered '*Cervelle aux Buerre Noir*'.

'Black butter?' she translated. 'Why black?' she asked.

'They burn it.'

'Sounds yummy, I'll have the same,' Samantha enthused.

The waiter made to leave when suddenly Samantha grabbed him: 'Wait! It's not something icky like frogs, is it?'

'*Cervelle* is not frogs, Mademoiselle. It is one of our most popular dishes.'

Ten minutes later, Samantha's scream was heard throughout La Coupole. She shot out of her chair, ran to the door of the Ladies' Room, and looked back in terror at her table.

'There's a *brain* on my plate!' she cried, clutching the waiter and hiding behind him.

'*Mais oui*, Mademoiselle.' The waiter nodded. 'This is what you ordered, *non*?'

'I thought it meant *veal*,' Samantha wailed.

They changed the dish and she returned very warily to the table.

'Ugh!' She shuddered at de Kousmine. 'You never know what you'll find in Paris.'

For her first morning in Monsieur Guy's workroom, Monique rose early to wash and style her hair, carefully applying some make-up: Monsieur Guy might appreciate her taking some trouble with her appearance.

It was hardly worth wearing anything 'good' if she was to hide it beneath the usual overall, but he would see her for a few moments before she put on the overall, so she wore one of her 'best' dresses, a fine grey wool shift which suited her and in which she felt pretty.

'This must be Monique!' he cried.

He jumped up to shake her hand, smiling, his grip strong and warm. He was not tall, he was starting to lose his hair, but the intensity of his stare was mesmerising. He glanced approvingly at her dress. As he talked, his eyes burned through her. When he emphasised a point, he jabbed her arm with his forefinger. He was a man who unthinkingly charmed every woman he met. Was this what all the films and songs called 'love at first sight', she wondered.

'I've heard good things about you, Monique.' He indicated a

place at a work-table. 'From Mademoiselle herself.' He made an impressed expression. 'She does not throw praise around, believe me. You'll be happy here,' he predicted. 'I respect good work. I respect my girls. I don't ask much. Just perfection.'

'*Bien sûr*, Monsieur.' She averted her eyes from his intense gaze only to alight on something equally disturbing: curls of dark hair at his open-necked white shirt. Again she averted her gaze. He spread a delicious pale blue bouclé wool flat on the table top, preparing it for cutting.

She studied his hands. They reminded her of a piece of driftwood moulded by the waves, found on the river bank near Angers. Brown, hairless, the nails cut down neatly, they showed great strength and power. These were a tailor's hands. A craftsman's hands. She watched them smooth the fabric for some moments, as if he were a blind man trying to find the flaws in it.

'Mademoiselle Chanel chooses every fabric,' he told her. 'But one never knows exactly how a fabric will "make up". Some wools fray at the edge of a jacket, if the design does not involve over-sewing. This may not be up to the task,' he decided, folding it carefully. 'I shall break the news to Mademoiselle.' He gave her a twinkling glance. 'She will not be happy.'

Monique made a sympathetic face.

'A great designer understands what a fabric is capable of . . .' Monsieur Guy sliced into a different wool with a huge pair of shears. 'Cutting a fabric is like calming a wild horse,' he went on, half to himself. 'You have to know how to discipline it, how it will react to your cuts, your stitches. Some fabrics have wills of their own and won't be tamed. We often battle against the fabric. It is far better to work *with* the fabric.'

'*Oui*, Monsieur,' she whispered under her breath.

Each time he touched her to emphasise a point, she received a tiny electric shock. Bewildered, she sat at the work-table he indicated.

'If you are half as good as they say, we shall get on very well, Monique,' he smiled.

She nodded, trying not to read into his words more than he intended. He had the gift or curse of making everything he said seem very personal. She had the impression that he was seducing her. Maybe he didn't even realise?

The other girls arrived, greeting her cheerfully. They seemed more serious and had more pride in their work than Madame Michelle's girls. Without those mournful sniffs in the background, the atmosphere would be far better here: Monique felt happier already. She was working for a master craftsman. One from who she could learn. A man who understood fabrics. A man who had such an intense gaze that when he aimed it at her she felt something stir within her. By the end of the day she felt quite different. About work, about life, about herself.

Six

Christopher called Sophie a few times during the weeks after their lunch but she either did not answer or sounded very busy.

'I often go to La Coupole in the evenings,' she told him. 'We may run into each other there . . .'

It sounded so half-hearted that he did not follow it up.

'I was a one-afternoon stand and I did not come up to her standards,' he told Klaus with a big sigh.

Klaus shrugged. 'So what?'

Christopher frowned. 'I felt that we'd fallen in love.'

'Just because you had good sex?' Klaus asked.

'It wasn't that good,' Christopher said. 'Not for her. It's *her*!' He frowned. 'She tries to be so tough and yet she's so . . . vulnerable. I want to protect her.'

'She doesn't sound so vulnerable to me,' Klaus tried.

'Don't you ever fall in love, Klaus?' Christopher asked.

'I am more involved in exploring my own sensuality,' Klaus said.

'Does that mean you just wanna screw?' Christopher laughed.

Klaus laughed, too. 'Don't put it down . . . it sounds like you could use some practice?'

Klaus went back to studying the stack of contact prints he always had piled up on his desk. He used a magnifyer and a wax crayon to mark the ones he liked.

*

Monique had chosen the couture as her career, not been forced into it through lack of education. Monsieur Guy understood that. He knew she loved beautiful fabrics, fashion. They were like two professional dancers, paid to dance, who found they danced very well together.

She tried not to read more than he intended into Monsieur Guy's glances and touches. They meant nothing, she assured herself, he touched everyone in that way. She ran more errands to the front of the house and began helping at clients' fittings. She loved accompanying Guy to the mirrored *cabines* where she took pride in having pins or scissors at the ready before he asked for them, as if reading his mind. They worked well together.

If Monsieur Guy mentioned something his wife or his daughters had done over the weekend, it brought a jolt of jealousy. She had glimpsed his wife when she'd visited the atelier – fairly pretty, small, slim, not particularly remarkable. She didn't really deserve a man like Monsieur Guy, Monique found herself thinking. But who was she to decide this? It would go against all her principles to allow herself to fall in love with a married man.

A parade of older clients trotted through the salon that week to be fitted by Christopher. Why did they all choose clothes designed for slim women, then wheedle the house into adding sleeves, lengthening skirts or substituting trousers for skirts? he wondered. Christopher supervised these 'alterations' very disapprovingly. Klaus heard him out each evening.

'They don't want fashion,' Christopher would complain. 'They try to destroy it.'

Klaus stared into his wineglass. 'Young women also are caring less about expensive fashion. They prefer to drive fast cars and wear old jeans. This will finish the couture. I do not envy you, Christopher. At least I get to photograph clothes on pretty girls.'

'These old ladies will put me off fashion for ever,' Christopher decided.

'No.' Klaus shook his head. 'We are addicted to fashion, Christopher. We could not live without it.'

Over the next few months, Camille Delange became more frail and arrived later and later at her 'studio'. Soon she only made an appearance at around noon for about an hour each day. Her retirement was rumoured. It was much too much to hope for, but Christopher could not help fantasising about being asked to replace her. His arrival at the house was too recent to allow for that. And sure enough, a new designer was appointed: Jules Callier, Belgian, about fifty, designer for the last ten years at Sacherelle, another old-fashioned house, would be Christopher's new boss.

The diminutive Jules took himself seriously. His entourage of adoring women assistants cocooned him in his safe padded cell, where he found various ways to annoy Christopher, from spraying cloying perfume around his desk 'for inspiration', to wearing thin kid gloves throughout the day, to nibbling constantly on exotic fruit from Fauchon.

'The Paris house he most admires is Balmain!' Christopher told Samantha disgustedly.

'Oh God, *Jolie Madame*?' she said, making a face at the name of Balmain's collection.

Because orders were slow, it was decided that Jules would design a mid-season 'Boutique Collection' for Spring '68. The thirty models of ready-to-wear would go directly into department stores, a new way of selling fashion which some houses were finding profitable.

Jules was a little flustered by this hurried design and soon got into a feud with Delange's other male diva, the milliner Jacques. In an inspired moment, he ripped Jacques' fur cossacks from the models' heads, sliced off the tops and told the models to carry them as muffs.

When he saw the sliced hats, Jacques stormed into the studio to complain.

'I do *not* create *muffs*! I create *hats*!'

But Jules won that round. Muffs were declared more chic, and even sold to a few clients who said they kept their hands warm as they strolled the boulevards.

In between queuing at Fauchon for exotic fruit for his new boss, Christopher sketched out designs to add to the stack on Jules' desk. These piled up until the day Jules sifted through them with a fake bored expression. It must be fake, Christopher guessed, for he selected quite a few to make up into *toiles*. In fact, he seemed to be relying on Christopher's unending stream of new ideas.

He took some fittings of the older clients, for which he insisted on wearing his thin kid gloves.

'He cannot touch female skin!' an assistant whispered to Christopher, almost admiringly. 'He is – how you say? – *allergic* to it!'

Christopher smiled. Surely a fashion designer allergic to female skin was at a distinct disadvantage?

Monsieur Guy's superb tailoring was not wasted on Chanel's simple cardigan jackets. He specialised in the jackets and coats that buttoned and fitted closer to the body. Clients in the know requested him to make up their orders. The girls told Monique that many years ago Mademoiselle herself had cut and fitted suits for favoured clients but now no longer did this. Now, Monsieur Guy cut Mademoiselle's own suits. He accepted this accolade as his due.

Whenever Monsieur Guy left the workroom for a fitting, the room would explode into gossip. There were rumours that Dior or Givenchy had tried to hire him away from Chanel, at an increased salary. Madame Avril, the *Premiere Main*, would calm them down: 'Girls, let's get on with our work.'

The house of Chanel, a little kingdom to itself, had known its staff to depart for other houses, leaving behind good friends or cousins or sisters. If a girl had a sister or a best friend at a rival house, it was like having a spy in a rival country.

Any couture employee with a husband or wife working for the

competition, hushed it up. But gossip regularly seeped through and got everyone excited. In the event that Monsieur Guy was hired away from the house, it was known that he would insist on certain girls accompanying him. He was very clear about who his favourites were: they were the girls who did the best work. Monique longed to be one of them.

Breathless mannequins would run into the workroom trailing clouds of perfume to beg Monsieur Guy to make suits for them. If the workroom was not too busy, models could order suits, paying the cost of the materials. Models flirted outrageously with Guy, and Monique watched them, feeling fiercely jealous.

She continued to take suits to the glamorous side of the house where the collection was modelled each afternoon and clients were fitted for new outfits. In this world, every woman was beautifully made-up and coiffed, the air rarefied and sweet-smelling. Sometimes, she glimpsed the *directrice*, Madame Antoine, a woman so elegant and 'snob' that Monique lowered her eyes as she passed.

Christopher came into work one Friday morning to find everyone in tears. Camille Delange had suffered a massive heart attack under the dryer in her favourite hair-salon.

At the elegant funeral, Christopher got a good look at all the historically important fashion-people still alive in Paris. It was like opening an encyclopedia of fashion, seeing these elderly couturières hobble in to the Madeleine church: Madame Alix Gres, the legendary designer of draped silk-jersey evening dresses: Guy Laroche: Maggy Rouff: Nina Ricci herself, leaning heavily on the arm of her elegant son Robert.

Jules, deciding that he was now indispensable to the house, immediately demanded a much higher salary and was quickly thrown out on his perfumed behind. Chantal Delange, the only niece who really loved fashion, persuaded the family it was time to revitalise their ancient institution. She called Christopher to her office. She was a small, blonde, pretty woman in her mid thirties. He knew she was married and had a small child.

A little nervous, he sat before her as she scrutinised him in her Parisian way. Suddenly she announced, 'I am aware that Jules chose many of your designs to be made up for the last collection. They sold quite well, not to our regular clients but to their daughters. Perhaps we should make more of an effort to appeal to a younger cliental?' She shrugged. 'Well, I may be crazy, but I am thinking of asking *you* to design the next Delange couture collection. In July we will need a full Autumn/Winter collection.'

'I can do it!' Christopher jumped to his feet. 'Wow!' he exclaimed. 'You won't be sorry.'

'Then tell me I am not crazy,' she said.

He leaned forward to assure her. 'I am young and I want to design for the young. I will drag Delange into the seventies.'

'Not all of our clients are young,' she warned. 'You must also design for them.'

'They want to *look* young!' he said.

'Ok, don't think of age. Just make wearable clothes,' she said.

'The whole point will be to attract new clients, surely?' he promised confidently.

She looked so dubious that he knew he would have to censor some of his wilder ideas and concentrate on pleasing her. But his fashion instincts, suddenly unreined, sent his imagination soaring.

'It's *only* the most fabulous thing that has happened in fashion history,' Samantha enthused with her usual understatement. 'What an opportunity. You, Christopher Hutchins, will be the next Christian Dior.'

'It hasn't quite sunk in yet,' Christopher said.

'Hey, I could be your wife – Jewish Dior!' she gagged. 'But seriously, think of the publicity? "Englishman conquers Paris".' She broke off, staring at him, alarmed. 'You *are* going to conquer it, right, Christopher? There *are* millions of brilliant designs in your fashion subconscious?'

He hugged her. 'I shall pull apart and rebuild Delange. I aim to blow their minds.'

'Yes, but don't forget "wearable",' Samanatha reminded him. 'Let's lunch at La Quetsch. I can't believe Chantal Delange is daring to do this! You have to thank her for this, you know, Christopher. It might be good public relations to give her, you know, some "thank-you sex"!'

Christopher spluttered. 'She doesn't need sex from me, she's married.'

'Yeah, but have you seen her husband?' Samantha grabbed his arm and marched him to La Quetsch, an elegant combination of food store and café-restaurant, conveniently located at the end of their street. 'I have a little problem of my own to discuss with you, Christopher.'

She ordered a dish not on the menu, changing the ingredients even as she listed them. When the waiter escaped, she hunched forward.

'I told Daddy I'm dating a German,' she groaned. 'I write to him each week, reporting on how I'm getting on. So yesterday I get this letter.' She fumbled in her bag for it. 'It's in terrible English – Daddy didn't get much of a formal education. His informal education was pretty good; he made a million by the time he was thirty. This letter is the end of my childhood. I guess at twenty-five that's long overdue, huh?'

She untied the Chanel scarf from her bag handle and arranged it over her head.

'Is this some kind of Jewish ritual?' Christopher asked, watching.

'No, but I like to feel dressed for the occasion,' Samantha explained. 'I'll read it the way Daddy would have said it. She cleared her throat. "Mine darling little Sammi," ' she began, using a strange foreign accent.

Christopher stared at her, amazed. 'Are you . . . channelling your father through your body?' he asked.

She shot him a look and ignored him.

' "Always, I am heppy when I read the wonderful 'speriences you having in Paris," ' she continued. ' "Your 'speriences make you educated young lady so Daddy is proud of you. So heppy was

I when I read you found a man who luffs you and treats you like Princess."'

['Klaus,' she broke off to nod to Christopher.]

'"But I nearly had heart attack when I read he is of German nationality. How you can do this to me, Sammi? Maybe his father or grandfather was Nazi. Did you ask that before you let him luff you? Maybe you forgot that Nazis killed your grandparents? You may be kissing the son of a murderer! Will you please now make your daddy heppier by getting rid of this Nazi? Surely, there are many nice French men in Paris for dating? A beautiful girl like you does not need to be lonely."'

She looked up tearfully. 'Daddy's the only man who thinks I'm beautiful.'

She put down the letter and removed the scarf, her eyes on Christopher.

'Is Klaus a Nazi?' she whispered.

'If I remember my history lessons, the Nazi party ceased to exist in nineteen forty-five,' Christopher said.

'Phew! That lets Klaus off the hook.' Samantha fanned her face. 'We didn't know any Germans in Beverly Hills or New York. Daddy never warned me against meeting them. It's so typical of my weird family to come up with an objection like this. My frame of reference is different: to Daddy 'German' means 'Nazi', to me it means 'great lover with irresistible marching rhythm'. I'm lucky to have a talented fashion photographer like Klaus crazy about me. I can't give him up.'

'I should hope not, he's very fond of you. What will you tell your dad?'

Samantha frowned for a moment. 'I think I'll send a postcard of the Eiffel Tower and tell him, very tactfully of course, to *go fuck himself*. I know how to say that in Hungarian.' She stared at Christopher, breaking into a brilliant smile. 'Meanwhile, I can start working on transforming Klaus. You know, make him more French and less German. It's all a question of image. I'll redesign him.'

She brightened, swallowing the rest of her Coke.

'Thanks for listening, Christopher. Now we must plan how

85

to make Delange the hottest house on the planet. *Bigger* than Chanel.'

'Girls, this is Sophie,' the atelier head announced. 'She is joining us to do her *stage*.'

Sophie entered the workroom hesitantly, the eyes of the other girls riveted on her. Monique looked very closely at this pretty new girl, a mixture of conflicting feelings rising in her. One was jealousy, for she saw this new girl as a threat.

In one glance the workroom girls took in that Sophie dressed better and spoke better than they did. She was, obviously, a spoilt rich girl who wanted a '*stage*' in their workroom to advance her to where she really wanted to be.

New entrants shared a bench, the newest squeezing into a grudged space in the very middle. To get in, Sophie raised an elegant leg, giving all the girls a good look at her expensive shoes.

Didn't she realise those shoes, more than anything, would make the other girls jealous? Monique thought. She watched Sophie out of the corner of her eye, perched alongside the Algerian girl called Maité, trying not to turn up her nose when she was handed skirt-linings to sew. She smelled of good perfume.

Her pale, pale skin, her green eyes, her wonderful red hair, her air of being from another world: Monique could hardly take her eyes from her. She tried to keep her attention on her work.

Sophie took a deep breath and began to sew the lining. She had swallowed a lot of pride to ask her mother to arrange this *stage*, but she felt that getting her fashion career started was the least her mother could do. Working at Chanel was better than attending the *Chambre Syndicale* school, even if it paid nothing. It was an entrée into the couture. The problem with skirt-linings was that it left too much time for thinking and her thoughts twisted and turned as she sewed throughout the morning.

At the lunch break, the girls rushed off to throw their little metal pails of food, *berlingots*, in a huge pot of boiling water. Sophie slipped out of her overall and pulled on a denim jacket. Down the service stairway, Monique followed her as she made towards the Place de la Madeleine. Men turned to stare at her. If Monsieur Guy fell madly in love with her, could Monique blame him? If she were a man, who would she choose: herself or Sophie? There was no contest.

Until that day, Monique had always been a disciplined person, had known exactly what she was doing, but that lunchtime, something told her not to let this girl out of her sight. She would follow her!

Sophie did nothing more suspicious than sit at an outdoor café and order a cheese *baguette* with a *café crème*. She ate her lunch when it arrived, glancing at her watch. Obviously, she was not used to forty-five-minute lunches and did not want to be late.

Monique sat a few tables away, sipping at a tiny *café*. It had become vital to know as much as she could about this 'interloper', which was how she had branded Sophie from the first sighting.

Nursing her coffee, she took bites of an apple hidden in her handbag. When Sophie paid the bill she followed her back to the house, hanging back twenty paces. How stupid to panic because a pretty girl had joined the atelier! She felt deeply ashamed of her jealousy.

The afternoon passed quickly, with many orders to fill. Sophie was told to unpick a skirt-lining because it was not quite right and Monique felt a small stab of satisfaction. It would have been unbearable if this pretty girl had proved very good at her work.

That evening, when dismissed by Monsieur Guy, Monique again found herself twenty paces behind the red frizzy hair, this time following Sophie home. Seeing where she lived might provide some clue as to why this girl had joined their atelier.

She struggled to keep up as Sophie side-stepped stragglers or moved off the kerb to overtake them. They skirted Concorde, turning into the Champs-Elysées, an avenue Monique had never liked with its oversized cafés and car showrooms. To her relief, Sophie marched straight past the first metro station, Clemenceau, and continued to walk briskly to the very top of the avenue.

At Etoile, she turned left, crossed two avenues and walked down Kleber. Offices turned to apartments, food and flower shops suddenly bloomed and the neighbourhood became solidly bourgeois. Sophie stopped, pressed a buzzer to click open a heavy wooden door and disappeared inside.

Monique crossed the avenue, staring up at the building. After a couple of minutes, the top corner flat windows opened and Sophie stepped out onto the tiny balcony. Monique made out the excited jumps of a small dog. Sophie petted it and urged it back inside, disappearing again. Monique waited. After a while, the front door clicked open and Sophie stepped out with the dog on a lead. She walked him around the block. Watching her, Monique felt certain that she lived there alone.

Monique got home late, the sisters fussing about keeping her dinner warm. She lied about work delaying her. She was completely bewildered at her behaviour and vowed never to follow Sophie again. If she revisited her apartment, it would be by invitation, though why Sophie should invite her, she couldn't say.

'You will come to the protest, Christopher?' Klaus stated one Saturday afternoon in May.

'What protest?'

'We're marching down the Boulevard St Michel and then along the Seine, protesting President Johnson sending more troops to Vietnam,' Klaus said patiently. 'We must go! To show how we feel.'

Christopher sighed. 'I was planning to sketch some new designs . . .'

'Listen, man,' Klaus placed his hand on Christopher's shoulder, 'I know you love fashion but this is more important. If we don't show America how we feel, how will we stop the wars in the world?'

'Is it *our* job to stop wars?'

'Of course it is. You know what they say: "Make Love Not War." You cannot bury yourself in fashion. There's a big, dangerous world out there! It's our duty to change it.'

Samantha joined them at their flat. She was dressed down in sweater and jeans but she eyed her black-booted feet dubiously.

'I'm not sure I'm wearing the right shoes for this,' she warned Klaus, as they left.

They took a bus across the Pont Neuf, then walked up the Boulevard St Germain towards St Michel. Van-loads of menacing, caped police lined the route, immobile and silent as black bats in their vans.

'What are they doing here?' Samantha indicated them.

'Expecting trouble,' Klaus said.

'Klaus,' Samantha warned, 'if some protestor scuffs my new boots, you will *really* see some protest!'

As they neared the crossroads of St Michel and St Germain they saw crowds of students with banners and signs and American flags waiting to join the march.

Christopher felt a burst of excitement but it was mixed with resentment. He had come to Paris for fashion not protest yet all these eager young faces together with the hippies in their embroidered Afghan coats, psychedelic make-up, holding flowers, made a fantastic spectacle. Fashion and protest had met and become one. If fashion could work its way up from the streets, clothes must also rebel, he realised. If clothes could be ripped apart and sewn back together in a new modern way, so could society. These young people could blow a raspberry in the face of staid Paris elegance and build a new order. And he could be part of all this! Suddenly he longed to design clothes for young, young women, not the old Delange clients. He also realised that these young people – the future of fashion – could not afford his clothes. Jeans were their uniform. How could he get these girls out of jeans into his dresses? When a pretty girl beckoned him to join the parade, he nudged Klaus, accepted a 'Make Love Not War' banner, and held it high.

'*This* is hippy?' Samantha stared at the hippies' clothes, shaking her head disapprovingly. 'I call it "Mix 'n' Match with medallions". I think I'll wait in this café.' She stopped at an empty table on an outdoor terrace.

'Samantha . . .' Klaus began warningly.

'No really, this is not my scene.' Samantha sat down, pushing them towards the street. 'You boys come back when you've protested enough. I'm gonna people-watch.'

Klaus stared sadly at her. 'You are making a terrible mistake, Samantha,' he told her. 'Today we can change the world!'

'I'd rather change these boots.' she shrugged. 'They're not that comfortable!'

Klaus gave up, taking his place next to Christopher.

'I cannot seem to awaken her political conscience,' he grunted.

As they waited for the march to get underway, a pretty American girl next to him smiled and offered him a flower. He took it, thanking her.

'You were right,' Christopher said. 'It's essential to protest!'

'And,' Klaus raised his eyebrows, 'a great way to meet girls?'

They began to move down the Boulevard St Michel, and Christopher began to feel part of this young, fresh, fearless movement. It was a heady sensation. He would fight war too! He couldn't wait to translate his new feelings into fashion terms. They walked the length of the Boulevard St Michel, but were stopped at Place St Michel by a barricade of police. It had been planned to turn left and walk alongside the Seine towards Les Invalides and cross over to the Right Bank. The crowd waited a few minutes, then grew noisy, demanding to be let through. The police looked as if they were not going to budge. There were cries and chants. Why was the Right Bank being protected from their protest? Was this a democracy or what? A rowdy element of the crowd was getting out of control. Christopher was just about to ask the American girl for her telephone number when he was hit on the head by a cobblestone hurtling through the air towards the police. A trickle of blood streamed down his forehead.

'Oh my God, are you OK, Chris?' Klaus grabbed him and half supporting him, dragged him all the way back to the café where Samantha sat.

She leaped to her feet when she saw them. 'Oh my God! I knew there'd be trouble!'

'I'll be fine . . . just need to sit down for a moment,' Christopher gasped.

A news photographer flashed a camera as he collapsed on the cane chair. A girl rushed to kneel by him and hold her handkerchief to his forehead.

'Christopher, you are all right?'

He opened his eyes and saw Sophie dressed in casual clothes, a scarf tied around her forehead, hippie-style.

'Sophie, what on earth are you doing here?'

'I was behind you in the march. I saw you get hurt.'

She pressed the folded handkerchief firmly to his head, clearing his tousled hair out of the way.

'I'll recover,' he laughed. 'Why are you here?'

'My friends at the Sorbonne arranged it. I wanted to march with them. Why are *you* here?'

'I came with Klaus,' Christopher said. 'I kind of got swept up in the protest. Klaus, Samantha, meet Sophie!'

Samantha leaned close to scrutinise her. 'Are you his girlfriend?' she asked her. 'Are you an actress?'

'I am not an actress,' Sophie laughed. 'And I do not accept the term "girlfriend". I am a free spirit.'

'Teh!' Samantha marvelled. 'Do you work in fashion?'

'The lowest of the low at Chanel,' Sophie nodded. 'I do a *stage* in a workroom. One day I wish to be a couturier.'

Samantha brightened. 'Really? You'll need a great publicist . . . !'

'I don't even know if I can last out my *stage*,' Sophie sighed. 'The monotony may drive me mad.'

She gently touched Christopher's hairline, removing the handkerchief to inspect the small cut.

'I am wondering if you might need a stitch or two?' she said.

He smiled. 'I didn't realise you cared so much about me?'

'Well I am worried. It was a huge stone.'

'Thanks for being worried.' He raised himself to kiss her cheek. 'It just glanced my head. If it had landed full force I'd be dead.'

He pressed his lips to hers, longing for her to suggest a taxi to her flat.

'These two think they're gonna save the world!' Samantha burst out to Sophie. 'They were *crazy* to walk in that dumb march. They coulda been killed!'

'It was peaceful until the *flics* stopped us and those idiots dug up cobblestones,' Klaus said.

'Make him promise not to march again!' Samantha told Sophie.

Sophie eyed Samantha cooly. 'Next time we will march together. I, too, am against war. I know some of the guys who organised this. They have many more marches planned. They wish to protest the entire system.'

Christopher put his arm around her. 'That's my girl. I want to promote Peace and Love from now on, too. There's a flower child inside me raring to get out!'

Samantha could not stop staring at Sophie.

'Did you ever think of being a model, Sophie?' she asked finally. 'You have the perfect face for today. You'd photograph fabulously well, don't you think, Klaus?'

Klaus nodded, studying Sophie.

Sophie shrugged. 'I've never thought about it. But why didn't *you* march, Samantha? Don't you want world peace?'

'Yeah, it would be great, but I just found these boots and they exactly match this outfit. I didn't want to risk ruining them. I mean, that cobblestone could have fallen on my foot!'

Sophie stared at her for a moment. It was very obvious what she thought of Samantha's priorities. She exchanged a glance with Christopher, snuggling closer to him.

While they ordered more drinks, Sophie slipped across the road to a *pharmacie* and bought some plasters, applying one very carefully to Christopher's wound.

The afternoon should have brought them closer together, but the moment they reached Klaus's flat, Sophie made some excuses and left.

'What's with *her*?' Samantha exploded.

'Oh, she gives Christopher a hard time,' Klaus told her. 'I've been hearing about this Sophie for weeks.' He turned to Christopher. 'You should go out with other girls. It's your turn to play hard to get. You might find someone you like better.'

Christopher sighed. 'From the moment I saw Sophie I knew she was the one. Every man has one girl made for him.'

'Oh God, that is so *fairy tale*!' Samantha gasped approvingly. 'It's just how I feel when I see a Chanel suit!'

'And you saw how worried she was about me,' Christopher went on. 'There's just something in her that stops her from—'

'She plays hard to get,' Klaus muttered. 'She thinks because she's so pretty—'

'I'm willing to wait,' Christopher declared.

'Don't wait *too* long,' Samantha advised. 'Plenty of girls would *die* for a guy like you!'

'Yeah, and he falls for the one girl who doesn't!' Klaus laughed.

'Must we discuss my private life?' Christopher cut him off, his eyes sparkling. 'Don't you want to hear how today will influence my first collection?'

'For the better?' Samantha asked, wide-eyed.

'Clothes will be more democratic, less constructed . . .'

Samantha nodded. 'They say Saint Laurent's designing a Rich Hippie collection.'

'Mine will be Poor Hippie!'

'What will Chantal Delange say?'

'*Fuck* Chantal Delange!'

'She should be so lucky!'

Seven

'We do not want this kind of publicity!' Chantal Delange brandished Monday's *Figaro*: Christopher's face on the front page, cherubic, topped with tousled blond hair, a streak of blood running down his forehead, looked strangely content as Sophie dabbed at it.

The caption read: *Chic Protest: Christopher Hutchins, new English designer at Delange fashion house, has Anti-War injury tended by Sophie Antoine, daughter of Laurent Antoine.*

'It was supposed to be peaceful,' Christopher told her.

She glanced at the small plaster still stuck to his forehead.

'Christopher, we pay you to design, not to protest!'

'Surely what I do on weekends is entirely my affair, Chantal?' he asked. 'Isn't France a democracy? Don't I have a right to express what I think?'

'We have American clients,' she reminded him. 'They won't like our designer criticising America!'

'But I don't criticise America,' he frowned. 'I criticise war!'

He strode to his office triumphantly. The protest had inspired him. There was more to life than fashion, he thought. Clothes must reflect real life. He pulled out a handful of designs inspired by Saturday's events. He now felt impelled to create a new kind of clothing for the new kind of world he had discovered last Saturday.

*

A crisp cream wool suit, trimmed in navy silk braid with gold buttons – the very essence of Chanel – made Monique sigh each time it returned from fittings. This, if she were a rich woman, was the suit *she* would choose. The wool was nubbly and springy, the entire jacket quilted, the stitching following the body's lines, which were not ruled straight but seemed so when worn. The lining – a bright silk flower print in violet and pink – was finished off inside with a flat gold chain acting as a border and weighting the hem. It was light as air. One afternoon, when Guy was out of the room, she slipped it on. It fitted wonderfully and hung just right. She buttoned it and the other girls gasped at the magic a Chanel jacket could bestow on one of their own kind. By slipping on a jacket, Monique transformed herself into a woman of quality. She felt feminine and beautiful. If she coveted any suit it was this one. As she modelled it, she heard Maité gasp. Monsieur Guy stood in the doorway, watching her, smiling indulgently.

'You really love that suit, don't you, Monique?' Monsieur Guy asked early the next morning when they were both alone in the workroom. 'If you can afford two metres of very expensive tweed, would you like me to make one up for you?'

'Oh, Monsieur Guy.' She beamed, then frowned. 'But when would I wear it?'

'Why not decide that once you have it?' He grinned. It was his way of showing her that he really valued her, she felt.

The two metres of gorgeous British wool cost fifty francs per meter. An extravagance, but one she could not resist. She could only imagine wearing the suit at Christmas, when she visited her family. The idea of wearing her own Chanel suit would be something to look forward to.

They did the fittings after working hours. As Guy helped her into the jacket, his hand brushed her breast. He did not seem to notice but she did. She must not give him the slightest sign of how she felt about him.

A girl in the workroom said she had seen Monsieur Guy kiss a mannequin during a fitting. Another girl went one better and said she had seen Monsieur Guy and a model making love on the cutting-table. Monique refused to believe any of this.

When the suit was made, she took it back to her room at Châtelet and modelled it for the sisters and other girls. They touched it, exclaiming at the workmanship and fabric. She let them all try on the jacket. In her room, she displayed it on a hanger as she sipped a glass of wine, wondering when she might wear it. The fittings had been the happiest moments of her life. How could something so simple as a man's hand on her waist or a man's eyes intently studying her silhouette trigger off such urges and thoughts? For years she had cut into thick, soft fabrics, guided a needle through them, made careful stitches in a straight line. Thousands, perhaps millions, of stitches. Hard work could drive out all other thoughts. She had denied her sensuality, she knew. But now, with this beautiful suit hanging in her room, reminding her of all those after-work moments with Guy, she faced it. He had touched her sometimes, by accident, and her body had come alive.

Christopher's first fittings for his first collection began in June, using the house-models. He was pinning a dress on one when Samantha burst into the room, her face wet with tears.

'Bobby Kennedy!' she gasped.

He looked up from fitting a dress 'What about him?'

'He's been assassinated! We'd have had another President Kennedy in the White House!'

Christopher shook his head, a little dazed. 'And Martin Luther King was killed just a few weeks ago!'

Samantha nodded. 'What is going on in my country? Why would anyone have wanted to kill another Kennedy? Why did they kill the first one?'

Christopher shook his head.

'I'm so upset. It's feels as if I knew him. I *love* the Kennedys,' she told him, blowing her nose and taking a deep breath.

'I didn't realise . . .' he faltered.

'Yes,' Samantha assured him. 'I got interested in politics when I found out Jackie Kennedy was wearing Chanel the day the President was shot? She's a Chanel-junkie too. She must be so freaked-out.'

'What about Ethel?'

'Oh, she has about a hundred children to take care of. Jackie is my idol,' she sighed, dabbing her eyes. 'I completely identify with her.'

Six weeks later, three Delange *vendeuses*, birdlike little old ladies in black, sat on a row of salon gilt chairs scowling at Christopher, awaiting the run-through of his Autumn/Winter '68 collection. Their own fashion antennae told them that Christopher was attempting something new, something daring.

'Look at their faces. They hate anything new,' he whispered to Samantha. 'They hold back fashion. They only want "bread and butter" – safe, saleable, secure.'

'They want their commission. Give them a little *pain et beurre*?' Samantha whispered back.

'There is no *pain et beurre*,' he laughed. 'Not even any crusts!'

Christopher blithely dismissed all Chantal Delange's fears that he was too young. He believed a designer must have the courage of his convictions so he had designed exactly what he wanted to design. These last two days of preparing a collection had been an emotional roller-coaster ride. Models fainted. Seamstresses burst into tears at criticism. Too much was riding on Christopher's personal vision of what women would want to wear next season. Everyone at Delange gathered in the main salon at ten thirty on Saturday morning for this final rehearsal.

The good models who modelled only at the first week's showings, sat with their feet up on the *cabine* dressing-table, awaiting the clothes to arrive warm from the workrooms. They were fully made-up with the theatrical, ballerina-like make-up they knew Christopher liked.

Standing in the centre of the *salon*, Christopher took a deep breath, frowning with concentration. Young girl assistants stood by with trays of gloves, rings, brooches, necklaces, earrings, flowers, feathers, scarves and handbags. Jacques stood hopefully by his mountain of hats.

Everyone seemed to think that he would adorn his clean-cut clothes with as many accessories as he could pile on, Christopher thought, amused. But he did not wish his pure lines to be ruined by hats, necklaces, scarves, handbags or any earrings other than the plainest pearl studs.

The models marched out, one by one, in his stark, unadorned dresses and suits. Christopher allocated plain pearl studs, ignoring the trays of gloves, jewellery and accessories.

The *vendeuses* stared disapprovingly at the stark clothes, their mouths turned down. He noticed and felt annoyed.

'*Mesdames?*' he stopped the models and approached the *vendeuses*. 'I'm sure you have a lot do this weekend. Maybe you're wasting your time here?'

They stared at him, shocked, muttering amongst themselves.

Chantal Delange ran up and took him to one side.

'The *vendeuses* always view the run-through of a collection,' she began.

'I don't mind them viewing it,' Christopher said. 'Not *judging* it. I don't need bad vibes. It's hard enough being judged by the press.'

'For God's sake, don't be a diva,' Chantal said. 'We got rid of Jules to avoid this kind of drama. What is wrong with jewellery and hats and gloves? We make money from those things. If we show them in the collection, we sell more.'

Christopher looked at her. 'They dilute the impact,' he said.

Chantal stared at him, turned on her heel and stalked off.

Samantha took him aside. 'Don't take it out on the *vendeuses*,' she warned. 'They only sell the clothes. You need them on your side, Christopher. Please apologise to them.'

She held his eyes pleadingly. He took a deep breath, walked back to the women and bowed, taking the hand of each one and kissing it.

'*Mesdames*, forgive me. I'm under a lot of stress. Please stay, I welcome your comments.'

They exchanged glances and melted under his apology.

He rolled his eyes at Samantha. 'OK, let's go . . .'

The models marched out in his unadorned, simple shapes. For a moment he forgot everything but the joy of seeing his designs in three dimensions, perfectly made and fitted. He directed them exactly how to stride down the salon, stop, turn, and march back.

'Don't smile too much,' he instructed. They glared. He had chosen sporty, active, fresh girls from the top model agency. None older than twenty-five. He changed the order of a few outfits and sent for two workroom heads to adjust a seam on a dress, a jacket, a hem. For this, his first collection, he had designed a series of outfits which he showed in groups of four. Stark, simple, unadorned shifts and suits. Tweeds, double-faced wool, plastic! Bright colours. Some pastels. A lot of white. A little gold and silver for the evening, and some black dresses with criss-crossing straps and shoulder detail.

By seven that evening, it was over.

Only one model had fainted and only one seamstress had wept. The assistants sadly returned to the store room with their trays of gloves, scarves, handbags and jewellery. He had used none of them.

The collection on which everything depended was ready to be shown.

Eight

A woman who orders a suit from a famous fashion house made to her own measurements expects to feel pampered and unique. Yet it was well-known (but never discussed) that two rich pampered 'unique' Parisian women risked coming face to face wearing the same suit. It was up to the *vendeuse* to use all her tact to steer a client away from a ordering a certain model if it had been ordered by a friend or rival.

No one warned Monique that there were two Madame Werthers, both Chanel clients.

The lavender wool suit Monique helped to fit on a Madame Werther that day seemed to be the same lavender suit she had fitted two weeks before, except that the lady had lost a little weight and seemed a little different. But Monique put that down to over-concentration on the suit and not looking too closely at the client's face on that first day.

During the fitting, Monique remarked, 'Madame has lost some weight since last time . . . we must take in the waistband.'

The client stared at Monique. '*Last* time? But this is my first fitting.'

'No, Madame,' Monique corrected, ignoring Monsieur Guy's foot touching hers, 'we fitted you two weeks ago. I remember thinking how pretty this tweed is . . .'

The client froze.

'Guy, is this young lady confusing me with someone else?' she asked in icy tones. 'Is it possible that the *other* Madame Werther ordered the same suit? If so, you can cancel this one.'

She removed the skirt and held it out to Guy as if it were a dead rat.

Guy accompanied Monique back to the workroom, his frown deepening.

'I forgot to tell you that we never talk about other clients' buys to the client we are fitting . . .'

'But, Monsieur, I didn't know there *was* another client. The same name, the same suit . . . how could I possibly know?'

He waggled his head. 'I should have told you: I am sorry. Don't worry, Monique, I shall take all the blame.'

He held her eyes and she felt her heart melting under his sincere gaze. He was going to take the blame for her stupid mistake. He was protecting her and she liked feeling protected.

That evening, Monique knocked softly on the open door of Madame Antoine's office. More a small sitting-room than an office, it held a sofa facing a couple of tartan-covered armchairs, an arrangement of fresh flowers and a Rigaud candle scenting the room with its haunting *Chypre* perfume. Madame Antoine sat at an antique writing-desk piled with copies of *Vogue* and *Women's Wear Daily*. The daily papers were spread on a coffee table.

'Monique.' Madame Antoine looked up, sadly. Her beautiful sapphire eyes and feather-cut white hair contrasted with bright red lipstick. Although slightly stocky, she had great chic and wore navy as if there was no other colour. She projected great integrity.

'We lost an important order.' The blue eyes levelled a guilt-making look at Monique. 'Two metres of very expensive tweed ruined, a good client unhappy. What did you say to her?'

Monique reddened with injustice. 'I complimented her on her loss of weight.'

'Thinking she was the first Madame Werther?' Madame Antoine nodded. 'But she is the second Madame Werther.'

'It never crossed my mind that Parisian men might have two wives, Madame,' Monique said.

Madame Antoine stared at her for a moment then burst into a peal of silvery laughter.

'Monsieur Guy says he takes all the blame,' she said finally. 'He cannot remember every little intrigue that happens in Paris society. I am not reproaching you, Monique. During fittings it's best not to volunteer any information or opinion unless asked.'

Monique nodded her head. 'Yes, Madame.'

'Guy likes you accompanying him for fittings. If there's ever a problem with a client, I'm always here in my office, my door is always open.'

'Yes, Madame.'

'*Au revoir*, Monique.'

'Thank you, Madame.'

Why am I thanking her for reprimanding me? Monique wondered. But Madame Antoine had that effect.

She had taken only a few steps towards the back stairs when she was called back.

'Oh, Monique?' The way Madame Antoine spoke her name added allure to it.

'*Oui*, Madame?'

She appeared breathless at the door of her office after running the few steps.

'I was just thinking . . . you would make such a nice friend – a good influence perhaps – for my youngest daughter. She's a bit of a rebel, you see.'

'Oh yes, Madame? And what does she do?'

The sapphire gaze faltered as Madame Antoine frowned. 'Why, Sophie's doing a *stage* in your workroom. Surely you know her?'

Monique blushed. 'Sophie is your daughter?' she stammered.

'Adopted daughter.' Madame Antoine nodded. 'Keep an eye on her, would you? I'd be so grateful.'

'We've hardly spoken but I've noticed her, of course. Does she live with you?'

Madame Antoine's eyes flickered. 'No, she recently moved out. She wants to be independent but I still worry about her. I arranged her *stage* in your workroom. She was at the Sorbonne but wanted a career in the couture.' She glanced down at her perfect hands. 'Maybe we were wrong to insist on a formal education, I don't know.'

'She's so pretty,' Monique said. 'And she works very hard.'

'She *is* pretty, isn't she?' Madame Antoine stared at Monique, as if unsure whether to confide in her. Suddenly she burst out: 'I've always felt a little guilty about her.'

'Guilty?'

Monique's eyes were so curious, so guileless that Madame Antoine went on, 'It was very important to me that, being adopted, she felt as loved as my natural daughters.'

The phone rang and Madame Antoine reached for it, picked it up and covered the mouthpiece. 'We'll talk some other time. I can see you're tired. *Bonsoir.*'

Monique walked home thoughtfully. Could she be a friend to this haughty girl? They had nothing in common but fashion. Would that be enough?

Next day, she brought her sketchbook to the workroom, something she never did in case the other girls learned of her dreams of becoming a designer and mocked them. Monique knew that she and Sophie always left the house at lunchtime. That day, she went ahead of the other girl and contrived to drop her sketchbook, spilling designs over the staircase. Sophie stopped short behind her, stooping to pick up the sketches.

'How kind of you,' Monique said, pretending to be flustered.

Sophie glanced at the drawings, then at Monique.

'Are these yours?' she asked. 'You did them?'

'Yes,' Monique said.

She held out her hand but Sophie continued to leaf through the pages.

'You *design*?' she asked in an amazed voice. 'These are very good.'

'Oh . . .' Monique brushed aside the praise, although she had put her very best sketches in the sketchbook.

Sophie handed them back, saying, 'I design, too. Do you always go out for lunch?' she asked Monique as they continued down the staircase together.

Monique withdrew an apple from her bag. 'I eat this and take a little walk.'

'Well then, I invite you to coffee,' Sophie said. She led the way to her café in the Place de la Madeleine.

'I have seen you eating here,' Monique confessed shyly.

'Why didn't you say hello?' Sophie asked.

'I didn't wish to interrupt your . . . reverie.'

Sophie laughed. 'I'm usually in a reverie, sometimes it is good to have it interrupted. Where are you from?'

'From Angers.'

'Do you like Paris?'

'The haute couture is here.'

'Of course. Do you love Mademoiselle? I mean, her style?'

'It's very elegant. She never designs anything vulgar.'

Sophie looked penetratingly at Monique. 'Balenciaga says "a touch of vulgarity doesn't hurt". I'm sure he didn't mean a woman should seem vulgar . . . it is more a case of daring.'

Monique frowned. 'I cannot criticise my idols. Chanel is one, so is Balenciaga.'

Sophie broke her baguette in two and passed half to Monique. 'Please share; I'm not hungry.'

Her gesture touched Monique and she accepted the baguette.

'Where do you live?' Sophie asked.

'I rent an attic room in Châtelet from two sisters, they are milliners.'

'How quaint,' Sophie laughed. She looked closely at Monique. 'What's your name?'

'Monique.'

'I'm Sophie.'

They shook hands.

'You don't like the workroom, do you?' Monique asked.

Sophie grimaced. 'If I'm to be a designer, I must know how to make a garment.' She pointed to the suit she was wearing.

'It's lovely,' Monique said. 'I made this dress.'

'It's perfect.' Sophie looked at it with wonder. 'We could set up our own *maison de couture* right now.'

Monique stared at her. 'Wouldn't that take a lot of money?'

'I could find someone to back a fashion venture if he thought it would be profitable.'

'You make it sound so easy.' Monique laughed. 'I've never even dreamed of my own couture house.'

'Don't set yourself limits,' Sophie urged. 'Your designs are very good.'

She lit a cigarette and puffed furiously on it.

That night, Monique hardly slept, excited by the new vistas opened by Sophie. She had never talked with someone so assured, so unconcerned about what anyone thought. Next to Sophie, she felt very dull.

'I'll stand here, to welcome the English and American fashion press,' Samantha decided, positioning herself by the Delange entrance as journalists and editors began to arrive in the salon. It was the second day of the collections and Delange had been given the three o'clock spot. Christopher's stomach made a complete somersault. He stared at the women entering. These people were about to judge him. One or two fashion editors were elegant, but most were dowdy and some were downright grotesque. One woman wore a lobster on her head as an *hommage* to Elsa Schiaparelli. He was surprised that these self-appointed fashion oracles did not always dress or even groom well, as if unwilling to compete with the lovely models they would be watching. It was only the second day but they had already seen too much fashion, up to seven or eight collections daily. Now, dazed by fashion, overfed on rich French food, saturated with good French wine, how would they tell good fashion from bad?

Christopher watched as Samantha welcomed all the *Vogue*s. He spotted British *Vogue*'s editor first, a pleasant, middle-class woman with no evident fashion flair. French *Vogue* was predictably slim, tall, elegant, intelligent-looking, perfectly groomed and dressed.

'And American *Vogue*?' Christopher whispered to Samantha.

'Not here yet!'

Some were snooty, some downright unpleasant. A smattering of men with an air of great self-importance. Everyone scrambled for gilt chairs, snarling and even weeping if they were not seated in the coveted front row.

'And these people are going to judge me?' he asked Samantha.

Samantha, breathless from air-kissing, nodded. 'Not judge, Christopher, *applaud*.' He was pleased that she wore one of his short white shifts, made very quickly for her that week, as she had decided that not even she could wear Chanel a rival designer, for that afternoon.

Three o'clock struck from the nearby church at La Madeleine.

'Let's start,' Christopher urged.

Samantha's eyes bulged. 'Without Her Fashion Highness?'

'Who?'

'Diana Vreeland, American *Vogue*.'

Just then, a flurry at the entrance produced an extraordinary woman, who strode in, three assistants twittering around her. She had a lacquered hard black hairdo and red rouged cheeks. She walked straight to the centre seat in the front row, as if by divine right it was hers. It was.

'Mrs Vreeland,' Samantha whispered reverentially, kneeling before her, proffering a press release which a minion took.

Then Samantha gave the signal and the collection began.

Christopher had banished Delange's satins, tulles and crêpes along with all her beiges, taupes and browns. He'd replaced them with bold primary colours or soft pastels in wools, knits, tweeds and gaberdines. He wanted to change the way clothes were worn. No hats, no gloves: the colours standing out, the candy pastels glimmering. There was lots of white, in crisp matte wool, plastic, lace and, for evening, black transparent chiffon, revealing more of the female body than had been seen outside of 'Le Crazy Horse', the famous Paris striptease club.

But now, hiding behind the curtain that separated the manne-quins' *cabine* from the catwalk, Christopher suddenly saw his entire collection as a giant mistake. For the first dress – a stark white plastic shift, utterly simple, utterly new – he had fantasised stunned silence followed by wild applause.

He was right only about the stunned silence, which stretched to a minute. Nobody seemed about to applaud. A *Harper's Bazaar* lady studied her nails and fished in her bag for a file. Someone near her fell asleep for a moment, waking with a jerk. Only the lady with the silk lobster on her head, a respected Italian editor named Claudia Fontana, looked impressed.

And so with the next dress, and the next. Samantha moved closer.

'Too radical?' she muttered.

Christopher watched in dismay. He had intended to revol-utionise fashion through cut and look, through hard new shiny fabrics, through banning luxurious ball-gowns. Everything was informal, a little sporty. He had stripped the glamour from fashion and designed dresses for young girls to run for buses in. Now, watching his collection through the jounalists' eyes, it occured to Christopher that young girls who ran for buses did not buy haute couture.

I've misjudged the mood, he panicked. Women may not be ready for such a drastic change.

The fashion journalists frowned, groping for words to describe these bold, sculptural shapes.

The final dress of a couture collection was traditionally a bridal gown; Christopher could not ignore this tradition, but his stark bride wore short white plastic and no gauzy veil. The other models joined her for a last parade. A polite smattering of applause and Samantha pushed Christopher forward for the quickest bow in fashion history. A magnum of champagne was popped and the models filled plastic glasses to toast Christopher.

Samantha stood before the exit, her body a little hunched, head lowered, as if ready for a fight.

The fashion editors who had fought and clawed their way in now fought and clawed to get out in time for the next showing halfway across Paris. Some headed towards Samantha, clutching lists of clothes they wanted to photograph.

'They'll look great on magazine pages . . .' she heard an editor say doubtfully, meaning, 'But perhaps not on women?'

'We're controversial . . .' Samantha nodded to Christopher. 'That's good. The main thing is to be talked about.'

Lips pursed, Chantal Delange approached Christopher for the traditional post-collection kiss. 'Women either love your clothes or hate them,' she hissed, propelling him into her office. 'Most of this crowd *hated* them.'

'Thanks, Chantal,' Christopher said lightly. 'I think I shocked them, but then fashion *is* shocking!'

'Fashion should *not* be too shocking,' she corrected him. 'I gave you too free a hand. I had my doubts. I wondered who would wear these clothes. Certainly not our usual clients. I should have insisted on a few saleble items. The *vendeuses* need "bread and butter".'

'Delange was *only* "bread and butter"!' Christopher burst out. 'Your fashion pulse was dead. Now, I must meet one or two editors. Excuse me.'

He escaped her office and found some ladies seeking him.

'You have outdated the other designers.' The lobster lady grabbed his hand and pumped it. 'Claudia Fontana, Italian *Vogue*. You are a fashion visionary. *This* is what women will be wearing . . . in *five years' time*, of course!'

'A futuristic vision,' her companion agreed. 'But remember, young man, being *too* far ahead of one's time is as dangerous as being behind.'

'That's what I'm learning,' Christopher laughed.

Samantha piloted him away from the fashion oracles. '*Vogue*, *Elle* and the *Bazaar* have chosen models,' she told him. 'It's only a disaster if they *don't* photograph anything. And *Elle* has promised a *cover!*'

The mannequins clustered around Christopher, pouring more champagne, kissing and screaming: 'Success, success!'

Diana Vreeland approached and placed a hand on Christopher's shoulder.

'Congratulations, young man. You've got something!'

'Thank you,' he said with a bow.

'Richard Avedon will photograph that wonderful white shift, number one,' she announced. 'I see it on Catherine Deneuve!' She gave him a meaningful look, before sweeping out. He stared at Samantha for a moment, then ran out after her.

'Mrs Vreeland!'

She turned around, surprised.

'Could I watch the shoot?' Christopher asked. 'I admire Avedon so much.'

She beamed. 'Dick loves a party atmosphere. Why not bring the dress yourself, tonight? He's at a studio off Avenue Montaigne.'

He scribbled down the address, his heart beating fast.

That night, he took the dress, cocooned in tissue in a Delange box, by taxi to Avedon's studio. It was half past seven. The glossy green ivy of Rue Jean Goujon appeared almost unbearably glamorous. Loud music came from a small square building set back from the street, obviously Avedon's studio. Bright flashes showed through white papered windows.

Christopher paused outside, the box under his arm, taking a deep breath of the Paris night air. This was the moment he had waited for. He entered the studio.

'I've bought the Delange dress,' he told a friendly American girl, looking past her to spot Richard Avedon sitting at a table on a stage, flicking through contact prints.

'Hi!' Avedon jumped down from the stage to shake Christopher's hand. 'I hear you showed a fantastic collection today. Mrs Vreeland was very impressed. Is this the dress?'

'I'm such a fan of yours, Mr Avedon . . .' Christopher began.

'Call me Dick. Catherine's in the dressing-room . . . wanna see her in your dress?'

The dress was passed inside. After ten minutes, Mademoiselle Deneuve peeked out of the dressing-room.

'C'mon out, Catherine,' Avedon called. 'Don't be shy.'

She walked out onto the seamless white paper. Christopher stared at his white dress on this woman.

'Catherine, this is the designer. He's English!' Avedon said.

'Oh?' The actress smiled at Christopher. '*C'est trés original!*'

The music was now cool jazz. Flash bulbs under silvered umbrellas flashed all over the studio. Christopher drank it all in. So this was how the celebrated photographer achieved his famous effects.

Avedon got his model to stride briskly across the white paper many times, snapping her in mid-stride. Christopher stared. The actress was small and seemed quite subdued. He would hardly have noticed her on the street. Like Sophie, her small, flawless features blew up to perfect proportions under a camera's eye.

The silver-lined umbrellas flashed and Christopher ascended to fashion heaven. The best fashion photographer in the world was photographing France's most celebrated actress in his dress. The photographs would be seen by hundreds of thousands of readers. Could he ever ask for more?

Camille Delange became the most talked-about house, with headlines asking: *Would YOU wear this?*

The fashion press loved the idea of a young Englishman renewing the image of a staid old Paris couture house. They ran stories like: *An Englishman Conquers Paris!*

Had he conquered it? The Delange family were doubtful because few private orders had been placed.

'It'll boost perfume sales,' Samantha assured Chantal Delange. 'Isn't this why you kept the house running all these years? This new image will revitalise you.'

'But will it be profitable?'

Samantha sighed. 'I'll find a priest to denounce the transparent dresses as "sinful",' she told her. 'That will get Christopher talked about.'

'We need orders from private clients,' Chantal spat.

Samantha tried to calm her. 'There'll be orders. It always takes a while for people to adjust their eyes to a new look.'

'I've got to see you!' Christopher told Sophie over the phone. He was at home alone one evening two weeks after the collection-showing and had finally found Sophie in, or at least answering her phone.

'You sound a little desperate,' she said. 'You know La Coupole?'

'Of course.'

'See you there in thirty minutes?' She hung up before he could agree or disagree.

He splashed some water on his hair and face, adding a squirt of *Eau Sauvage*. He threw on a jacket and ran out.

Although he was at the crowded terrace of the café within twenty-five minutes, thanks to a dangerously fast taxi, he had to wait another twenty minutes before Sophie strolled in languidly, in no hurry, dressed up in one of her more clinging outfits – a lavender-coloured silky dress with a white crocheted shawl. She hadn't quite decided whether to be Spoilt Rich Parisienne or Cool Hippie. Her shoes were strappy high heels and she was perfectly made-up, hair piled on top of her head with the usual fetching tendril drooping down. He jumped to his feet and kissed her.

'Kir Royale,' she told the waiter.

'I'll have one too,' Christopher said. 'What is it?' he asked as the waiter left.

'*Crème de cassis* and champagne.' She turned to face him. 'What's the matter, Christopher?'

'My collection. No private orders. I don't know what to do.'

'I saw photographs of it. It looked *très avancé* to me.'

'That's the trouble.' He peered at her with worried blue eyes. 'Young girls like you love it. So do some avant-garde fashion editors, but the old dears who keep Delange going aren't ordering. How do I attract new young clients?'

'My mother has a few elegant youngish friends . . .' Sophie began.

'Surely she steers them towards Chanel?'

'Yes, but not everyone adores Chanel.' Sophie gave him a stern look. 'The young ones find it a little conservative, even banal. I'll ask her to direct them to your collection. If just *one* of them orders something, all her copycat friends will follow.'

'You would do that for me?' he asked, staring into her eyes.

'Yes,' she took a cigarette out of her bag and lit it, 'I would.'

He hunched forward. 'Why?'

'Because I like you.'

'Only "like"?' he asked, still staring at her.

'Don't be so intense, Christopher,' she laughed. 'This is *fashion*, not life or death!'

'For me, fashion *is* life or death!' he said. Then he found himself blurting out,' I can't stop thinking about you, Sophie. Why aren't we seeing each other every night? Why aren't I making love to you? You said you'd teach me!'

She burst out laughing. 'Christopher, this is Paris: we flirt, we lie, we play games!'

He shook his head. 'I don't play games, Sophie,' he told her. 'I say what I think. And I want you to know that I think I love you.'

At that moment, the waiter served their drinks. Sophie was suddenly at a loss for words. Christopher's guileless, sincere declaration threw her. Out of all the men she had played with, no one had ever said anything so simple, so direct. She sipped her cocktail, fumbled for her cigarette and took a long drag on it.

'You don't say something like that so soon,' she said.

'Why not, if I feel it?'

She gazed at him for a long moment with her smoky eyes, placing her hand on his knee. Her green eyes so full of questions, doubts, tricks and guile, stared into his honest blue eyes. Her questioning gaze was accepted by his unflickering regard.

'You are so sure of what you want,' she whispered wonderingly. Suddenly, she felt sure, too. She swallowed her drink in a gulp and stood, pulling at his arm.

'Come,' she said breathlessly. 'Let's go to my flat!'

Outside, she gave the taxi-driver the address, adding, 'We're in a hurry!'

It was a dangerous thing to say to a Paris taxi-driver on a hot summer night. They careened and screeched their way across what felt like oiled streets to Avenue Kleber, his hands sneaking inside her dress to cup her breasts and gently rub his thumb across her nipples. Her hand between his legs moved rhythmically and hard against him. A groan escaped him. Their mouths were glued together. The driver was thrilled to have his own X-rated film play out on the back seat, his amused eyes alternating between glancing at the road and watching them in the rear-view mirror.

They tumbled out of the taxi, into the old-fashioned grilled lift, unable to let go of each other all the way up. She pulled down his zip and held him in her hand. His lips never left her lips, even as she fumbled the key into her door. Once inside her flat, they ripped the clothes off each other and fell onto the broderie-anglaise bed. He was here again, in her bedroom, with this exquisite body and these lips which seemed never to get enough of his lips. Thank God he'd taken a shower that evening, he thought, burying his face between her legs. As she cried and whimpered he began to lick her very gently at first then made his tongue surprisingly hard and aroused her to such pleasure and need that she pulled him onto, into, her. Arching her back, she let him enter her, whispering, 'Slowly, slowly . . .'

Again, she swung her legs up to cross behind his back, forcing him deeper into her, the feeling so overwhelming that he bit hard on his lip, giving himself distracting pain to control it. As she blew and licked in his ear, he kissed her face, trying not to move his body too much as she was doing all the moving for them. She thrust and pushed against him, giving soft little cries as if her moment was getting dangerously near . . . and suddenly, she screamed and Christopher shouted as they experienced that rare pleasure of climaxing at exactly the same moment, the shared intensity and disbelieving gasps making them sound like two people being exquisitely tortured.

'I love you, I love you, . . .' Christopher whispered urgently in her ear as the echoes of pleasure quietened within him.

Something that feels this good can almost make you fall in love, Sophie thought. *Almost, yes!* But she had to hold something back. She was not quite ready to give herself wholly to him, not body and soul. OK, her body, yes, she had often given that, but not her self. Love! She knew he expected the same word to be repeated back to him. Instead, she stroked the back of his head very firmly, grasping handfuls of his thick blond hair. She loved the cleanness of his body and inhaled his fresh smell of lusty young man, reminiscent of new-mown grass.

He was equally drunk on wine and the smell of her skin, always perfumed and heady, making him want to lick her. The urgent passion over, he still wished to kiss her very tenderly and softly on her mouth, lips closed. These were the sweetest, subtle kisses, *après-sex*! Soft kisses which, since sex was over, could only signify love, Christopher thought, couldn't they? Even if she dared not say it, he knew she must feel it. Nobody could fail to recognise this magic that covered them with rays and sparks.

Chanel's collection had been shown in a completely different atmosphere to the debut of the young Englishman. Clients or buyers neither expected nor wanted any big changes. They came to pay hommage to 'The Chanel Style'. They came to pay hommage to Mademoiselle, to worship at the Chanel altar, yes, almost like a religion. Chanel-addicts, trembling and reverential, needed their twice-a-year fix. They concentrated hard on the most minute details of the *defilé*. They confidently assumed the clothes would be almost invisibly brought up to date, a centimetre pared off the length of a slightly fuller skirt, an imperceptibly wider silk braid edging a jacket and five gilt buttons at the cuffs, perhaps, instead of four, to signpost that season's models.

The newspapers said, *More of the Same at Chanel* . . . Or, *Elegance as Usual at Chanel.* Yet the miracle of Chanel's clothes was that they were never *demodé*, that dreaded fashion word meaning 'outmoded, out of style, old-fashioned'.

These were the clothes that Paris society, actresses and rich women craved to wear and orders flooded in. Guy's workroom worked full out.

*

Two months after the collection had been shown and the first rush of orders completed, Monique watched Sophie stride off at the mid-day break as if she had important things to attend to. Why should she have expected anything else? Monique asked herself. Something told her to bide her time, not to come on too strong. Sophie was unpredictable and self-involved; Madame Antoine had hinted at problems. Perhaps she simply needed time to make new friends, she thought. And, sure enough, one weekend Sophie finally invited her to lunch.

Wearing her good grey wool dress and a new Burberry mac, Monique walked all the way, on a crisp autumn morning, to Sophie's very proper part of Paris, just off the Etoile, where all the buildings were mid-nineteenth century and very solid.

Sophie had laid lunch prettily at a round table in front of two doors open to the tiny balcony. And there her little dog lay, jumping up for tit-bits Sophie threw for him.

'I never knew my real parents. I want to find out who they were . . .'

Monique nodded. 'That must be hard. I adored my father. He died when I was twelve. I still miss him.'

'And your mother?'

Monique looked questioningly at Sophie. 'Can a mother feel jealous of a daughter being very close to her father?' she asked.

Sophie laughed. 'Some daughters and mothers hate each other.'

'It's not hate,' Monique said thoughtfully. 'But she never made me feel pretty. She talked about me as "Poor Monique".'

'That's unforgivable,' Sophie spat. 'Mothers *should* make their daughters feel beautiful.' She poured some wine. 'My real mother must have died in some accident . . . I can't accept the idea that I was given away.'

'Madame Antoine never told you about her?'

'She says she doesn't know.' Sophie sipped her drink thoughtfully. Monique watched her.

'In these circumstances, Sophie, I think you are remarkably brave,' she said.

'No one has ever called me brave,' Sophie said. She put down her glass, leaned towards Monique and kissed her.

After lunch, Sophie modelled some new clothes she had designed and made. She believed in simplicity, nothing frilly or fussy, and she used good fabrics. Monique's sharp eyes saw the defects, but she did not mention them.

'You have some nice ideas,' she said. 'How set are you on being a couturier?'

'What else would I do?' Sophie asked. 'Maybe I am not driven and terribly ambitious, but I do want to work in fashion. I always have.'

Monique left around five o'clock and walked down the Champs-Elysées in a dream. After this glimpse of another world she felt excited by the sudden potential of Paris and all it had to offer. Paris would become her town. She doubted she'd ever return to Angers.

Back at her room she found a letter waiting for her from her sister.

Why did you leave me here? this one began. Monique felt more and more guilty as she read on. *When can I join you? Maman is being difficult,* it continued. *Please visit soon. It is all so much easier and more fun when you are here.*

Of course she felt guilty. She had been so intent on coming to Paris that she had not considered Caterine. Now she realised that she had left her in a difficult position.

Before meeting Sophie, she had imagined that life was easy for a pretty girl. She had thought Caterine, with her slim figure and pretty face, would have no big problems, not realising that their mother would be selfish and clinging. She should be looking for a flat and inviting Caterine to join her.

Nine

Weeks had passed since Delange's first collection showing. It continued to be shown three times weekly at three o'clock. As the bride emerged, the *vendeuses* always hunched forward expectantly, order-books at the ready, only to watch clients walk right past with waves and smiles.

Eventually Christopher was summoned to Chantal Delange's office. As he entered, a pile of fashion magazines featuring his clothes on the covers sailed past him and crashed into the wall.

'Press, *oui!* Clients, *non!*' Chantal screamed.

Christopher stared at her. 'If those had hit me—' he began, then turned and walked out.

'She doesn't seem to understand that as long as your designs get photographed, they serve their purpose,' Samantha said over lunch at La Quetsch. 'They get us *space*. Every cover we get sells more perfume. It doesn't matter if the clothes don't sell.'

'It matters to *me*,' Christopher said. 'I *want* to see women buying and wearing what I design. What do I care how much perfume Delange sells?'

Samantha looked at him with an expression of disbelief.

'Perfume pays your salary,' she told him finally. 'It pays everyone's salary!'

*

Monique grew so efficient that she could get a suit ready for its first fitting in a day. She was tactful with clients, listening to them and studying their reflection intently in the *cabine* mirror. She made it seem like a matter of life or death that the clothes fitted perfectly and flattered their figures. The *vendeuses* loved her. The clients requested her. She had a waiting-list. She was well on the way to heading her own workroom in a quarter of the time it usually took.

Madame Antoine sent for her again. This time, she ordered two tiny espressos from the café downstairs. Watching Monique stir some sugar into hers, she said, 'Thank you for befriending Sophie.'

Monique nodded. 'But does Sophie need a friend like me?' she asked, puzzled.

The blue eyes stared deeply into hers. 'Monique, you have a rare quality in the fashion world. Perhaps you don't realise *how* rare? You're real. It might help Sophie towards . . . well, a more balanced life.'

'She mentioned starting a couture house,' Monique said with a smile.

'Sophie is always in a hurry,' Madame Antoine said. 'You'll find your own levels at this house first. From what I'm hearing, *you*, Monique, will advance faster than anyone in this house ever has.'

Next day, Sophie invited her to lunch at Le Drugstore at the top of the Champs-Elysées, ordering two huge hamburgers.

'My mother sent for you last night: why?' Sophie asked.

'She hinted I might be made Head of Atelier. Don't tell any of the girls.'

'Good. You'll earn more money. You deserve it, Monique.' Sophie smiled. 'You work so hard.'

'You'll be next,' Monique assured her.

'I'll never sew that well,' Sophie said slowly. 'I don't have the dexterity of your fingers.'

'Of course you will.'

There was a short silence, and then Sophie said, 'Monique, have you ever had a lover? You seem so innocent.'

Monique blushed scarlet, lost for words.

'You're not still a virgin?' Sophie asked.

Monique continued to blush.

'So you are?' Sophie frowned.

Monique turned to stare at her.

'Don't try to make me feel ashamed about a perfectly normal situation,' she answered.

'Oh, it's nothing to be ashamed of,' Sophie agreed quickly. 'How old are you, Monique?'

'Twenty-six.'

'Don't you want to fall in love?'

Monique stared at her friend, feeling inadequate and provincial. Finally, she said, 'I *am* in love, Sophie.' She felt more grown-up, less of a country bumpkin, saying this to Sophie.

Sophie's eyes opened wide, all curiosity. 'But that's marvellous. Who?'

'I must keep it secret. I will never be able to marry him. Do you wish to be married?'

'I would like to fall in love, Monique,' Sophie admitted, lighting a cigarette. 'I almost get there, then I am afraid.'

'What is there to be afraid of?'

'I don't know. It's a question of putting your trust in a man, isn't it?' She gazed at Monique for a long moment before leaning to kiss her on both cheeks. 'We will "*tutoyer*" each other now, Monique, agreed? Let's be sisters. I miss my sisters sometimes. I could use someone to confide in. I'll be the same for you.'

'I miss my sister, too.' Monique touched Sophie's arm. 'I am happy to be your friend,' she said.

Sophie sat cross-legged on her living-room floor on a November Saturday night, 'Dog' beside her, picking at cheese and fruit, sipping wine. Her life seemed out of kilter. The Chanel magic had not rubbed off on her. The rigid social order of the couture prevented that. Once she donned that white overall each morning, she was just another seamstress, invisible, unable to mix with other people in the house. The routine of her apprenticeship was dulling her.

But she had always felt challenged by rules and sometimes escaped the workroom, slipping off her overall (she was smartly dressed beneath it) to wander the office floors or visit the *salons*, pretending to be on some errand. If you walked quickly, people believed you were going somewhere. But the Chanel magic had not rubbed off. Instead, the taint of the workrooms had. That odour of reheated lunches and seamstresses' sweat seemed to cling to her, no matter how much perfume she applied.

The following week, she came across three mannequins in the street when she left work, girls she had often chatted with at social events. When she tried to join them for a drink they brushed her off. A Chanel model had told them she toiled in a workroom. That really hurt. The models didn't accept her and the workroom girls certainly didn't.

The next day, she bought an expensive box of Fauchon chocolates to offer around the workroom in the afternoon but Maité, the Algerian girl, refused to take one. She looked at Sophie with impudent amazement.

'You think you can buy me with a chocolate?' she taunted her.

Sophie was so angry she popped out of the workroom as if to go to the lavatory, took off her overall and strolled around the offices, bumping into Monsieur de Kousmine.

'Sophie.' He kissed each cheek, holding her at arm's length, studying her. 'How is the *stage* going?'

'Boring.'

'Couldn't we have found you something a little more fun?'

'I really must learn the couture,' she told him seriously.

He tried a benevolent smile but it came out as a lascivious leer. He had visited her parents' house ever since she could remember and she had flirted with him during her precocious adolescence. They had once gone as far as a frenzied grope on the second-floor landing.

'Your mother tells me you have your own apartment, now?' he asked. 'I'd love to see it . . .'

'One day I may give a little housewarming,' she said.

He laughed, bending to kiss her. 'The more you elude me, the more you excite me,' he whispered. 'I've known you since you were a little girl, Sophie . . .'

'Yes, and you always seemed about to rape me!'

'Well . . .' he shrugged. 'That's how I look with beautiful females. You know where to find me. My office is right here. I have a busy afternoon. It seems Mademoiselle has just found something new to sue us about.'

When she returned to the workroom. Monsieur Guy was standing with a jacket in his hands. He looked furious.

'Where have you been?' he asked her. 'Did *you* do this lining for Madame Guibourg's jacket?'

Sophie hurriedly buttoned her overall. 'I . . . I . . .' She felt all eyes on her and could not answer.

Maité delightedly called out, 'Sophie did it! Sophie sews all the linings! That's all she can do!'

Guy showed her the suit. 'How did you manage to sew the armhole closed? Madame Guibourg could not get her arm through. This is Chanel, Sophie, we have a reputation for sewing the most beautiful clothes in the world!'

'I am so sorry, Monsieur . . .' Sophie apologised.

Guy ripped out the lining, shaking his head. He returned to the *salon* and Maité burst into a cackle of malicious laughter.

'Of all the stupid mistakes, sewing up an armhole tops the lot!' she crowed. 'You shouldn't even *be* in this workroom, Sophie. You're taking the place of a girl who really needs the money!'

'Leave her alone, Maité!' Monique called out.

Sophie suddenly burst into tears.

Maité laughed. 'And now she's crying,' she announced.

Sophie ran out of the workroom.

She sat on the top step of the worn staircase, sobbing into her hanky. It had been a ridiculous mistake to imagine she could fit into a workroom and sew for months on end. There was nowhere in this world where she could feel comfortable. She simply didn't fit anywhere.

'Now, now, what is all this?' asked a voice. A stooped figure in black bent over her. Sophie scrambled to her feet, attempting to pull herself together.

'Don't I know you?' Mademoiselle Chanel peered at her.

'I am Sophie Antoine, Mademoiselle . . .' she said. She blew her nose. 'I am doing a *stage* in Monsieur Guy's atelier.'

'Did Monsieur Guy make you cry like this?'

'I made a stupid mistake. And the other girls . . .'

'They don't feel you belong there?' the old lady guessed. 'Well you probably don't. Come up to my *salon*, I want to take a good look at you. I have known you since you were a little girl.'

Before they went downstairs together, Mademoiselle popped her head around Guy's door. Sophie's eyes closed, resignedly.

'I'm just borrowing this little girl Sophie for a few minutes,' Mademoiselle told the atelier head. There was a shared intake of breaths. Mademoiselle was rarely seen in an atelier. Sophie shook her head to herself. Now the girls would really hate her.

They went down the back stairs together, re-entering the house through the front doors and climbing the mirrored staircase. Sophie had once sat on this staircase with her mother to watch a collection. It had been even more chic to sit there than in the front row. It proved you were a member of Mademoiselle's inner circle. She had heard that Mademoiselle knew the name of everyone in the house of Chanel, but surely the high turnover of seamstresses made that impossible?

She vaguely remembered a small, vital woman visiting her parents' house and talking for hours after lunch.

Up in her salon, Mademoiselle reclined on a caramel-coloured suede sofa. She glowed in her setting, surrounded by the most exquisite coromandel screens. Some of them depicted camelias, Sophie noticed. There were lifesized blackamoor figures and shelves of leather-bound books. The diffused afternoon light added a cool glamour. Sophie hesitated at the doorway.

'You're pretty!' The words rapped out almost as an accusation. 'Take off that overall.'

Sophie removed the garment. She wore a skinny ribbed sweater and a short skirt.

'Turn around,' Mademoiselle instructed.

Sophie pirouetted, feeling like a prize dog.

'You have a perfectly proportioned body. Sit down over there. At my age, it is better to have the light behind me.'

Mademoiselle was a black silhouette against a bright window – Sophie could not make out her eyes, but she felt their intensity. When a lamp was suddenly snapped on, the bitter expression, the thin lips, the ravages time had brought to a once-pretty face were cruelly illuminated. The tiny chic figure lit a cigarette and let it dangle from her mouth, its smoke curling to the ceiling. She had a presence, Sophie thought. After all, she herself had invented the image she now presented. The energy coiled inside revealed itself each time she darted forward to flick her ash into an ashtray.

'What *are* you doing in a workroom?' she asked.

'I wish to become a *couturière* like you, Mademoiselle,' Sophie began. 'Isn't a workroom the best place to start?'

'Do you have talent? Do you have ideas?'

'I worship your style, Mademoiselle. I use it as the basis for improvising and variations—'

'What about *your* style?'

'In time, I hope I shall find it, Mademoiselle,' Sophie said.

Mademoiselle stubbed out her cigarette. 'It takes hard work to get to where you wish to get. Can you work hard?'

'I think so, Mademoiselle.'

The old woman leaned forward. 'Show me your hands.'

Sophie held out her hands. Mademoiselle peered doubtfully at them.

'They don't look as if they have bled recently,' she said.

'I try not to bleed on your fine fabrics, Mademoiselle.'

Mademoiselle leaned back for a moment, considering Sophie.

'Do you eat properly? I like healthy girls. Only homosexuals like skeletons. But I like fresh blood entering my house. You have a way of wearing clothes. Here, try this on.'

She leaned forward to shrug out of her jacket, handing it to Sophie.

Sophie put on the still-warm, black wool jacket.

'Walk up and down, then turn slowly . . .'

Sophie felt the eyes scrutinising her.

'The pockets are there to be used,' she was told. 'Dig your hands into them.'

Mademoiselle watched, nodding, as Sophie strode the length of the salon then made a dramatic turn. She lit a fresh cigarette, took back the jacket and allowed Sophie to help her on with it.

'Have you ever considered modelling?' she asked.

Sophie raised her eyebrows. 'Aren't I too small?'

Chanel cocked her head. 'We have many clients your size. The pay is good. Most models manage to get a new Chanel suit each season. Think about it. It could not happen before next year, but I see you modelling my clothes more than sewing them. Especially if you sew up the armholes!' She gave her a pointed look. 'Send up your mother if you see her in the salon.'

'Apprentices use the back staircase, Mademoiselle.'

'If anyone stops you, tell them I gave you permission.'

Sophie gave a little bow, as if leaving royalty, resisting the impulse to walk backwards from the room. Then she went to find Madame Antoine. Perhaps she should learn to call her what everyone else called her, not *Maman*. Her door was open as usual. Sophie peered in.

Madame Antoine was writing a note with a fountain-pen at her desk. A flickering *Rigaud* candle sent its haunting *Chypre* aroma floating around the room. Sophie hesitated, torn between running away and making contact with the woman who, for all her life, she had considered her mother. She knocked softly on the open door. Madame Antoine looked up.

'Sophie!' She removed her reading-glasses.

'I was just with Mademoiselle. She would like to see you.'

'On the top floor?'

Sophie nodded. She was about to leave when she suddenly said, 'Why is Mademoiselle interested in me? Because of you?'

Madame Antoine stared, clear-eyed, at her. 'Of course, I told her you wanted a *stage* in a workroom. She authorised it.'

'Why would she invite me to her *salon*?'

Madame Antoine continued to regard her. 'Well, I suppose because she knew you as a little girl.'

Again, Sophie made to leave, then suddenly she heard herself blurt out: '*Maman* . . .'

A crack in the blue stare appeared as hurt entered Madame Antoine's eyes.

'I don't feel good about what I did,' Sophie whispered. 'That necklace. I want you to know I regret it. And I am lonely.'

Madame Antoine gave a little laugh. 'Whose fault is that?' she asked. 'You sold the necklace to get away from us. How do you think *we* felt? Didn't you realise it would hurt your father when you sold something he gave to you with love, something which had been his mother's?'

'It seemed like the only way to get what I wanted,' Sophie said softly.

There was a silence.

'And what *do* you want, Sophie?' Madame Antoine asked. 'Do you even know? I don't think you do.'

'I *did* know!' Sophie blurted out urgently. 'I wanted to leave the Sorbonne. I wanted to live independently. I wanted to work hard to be a *couturière*. I did not expect to be told I was adopted. That has changed everything. It's made me feel . . . different.'

'I'm sorry Papa told you so brusquely,' Madame Antoine said. 'He shouldn't have.'

They stared at each other. 'He's tried to track down the necklace to buy it back but the bidder cannot be found. Why don't you come to lunch on Sunday? Apologise to your father. Begin to repair the damage.'

Sophie swallowed. 'I don't know if I am ready to come, yet. Let me think about it.'

Madame Antoine inclined her head. 'When you want to come, you are welcome,' she said softly. 'And you have friends, there is no need to be lonely, Sophie. Your sisters miss you. Remember, you chose to leave. We did not throw you out of the house – we never would.'

Sophie left the office. As she passed the mannequins' *cabine*, she pulled back the curtain to peer in. It was empty, the lights left blazing around the long mirror over the dressing-table like a theatre's dressing-room. As a little girl, visiting Chanel twice each year with her mother was as magical and predictable as a fairy tale, always ending the same way with a bride walking out in a wedding-dress, alone.

'Where is her husband, *Maman*?' she had once cried out, making the women around them laugh. Her mother explained that the model was not a real bride, just pretending to be one. Sophie had nodded gravely at the explanation. What fun to *pretend* to be a bride, she had thought, and not have the bother of a husband to cope with.

As her mother chatted with friends after the showing, Sophie would peek into the mannequins' *cabine* to watch six beautiful models sitting in complete silence facing their reflections, as if awed at their own beauty. The lights blazed down yet they always seemed cool. Now and then a hand raised a sharpened eyebrow pencil to correct a tiny imaginary fault. Dressed in their Chanel suits, they'd wave goodbye to the staff at the front desk. Sophie's eyes would widen in wonder at the thought of these mythical creatures wandering out into the city and mixing with ordinary people on the street. She had never imagined she might be one of these women.

She walked home slowly that night, thinking. If she expected to find out about her parents, she must keep a relationship with her adoptive parents, *Maman* and *Papa*. She must not cut herself off from them as she had intended, and now she realised she did not really want to. By rights, her parents should be angry with her. But the lunch invitation and Mademoiselle's suggestion of a modelling job seemed to add up to something. What?

Halfway up the Champs-Elysées, she stopped dead in her tracks as a new thought hit her. Maybe Mademoiselle Chanel knew who her real parents were?

Ten

Sometimes the house of Chanel joined other couture houses to present some models from their collections at charity gala presentations. These showings, held mid-season, could attract new clients to the house. A prize perk for a Chanel seamstress was to travel with the models to these events, to do fittings or last-minute repairs. Monsieur Guy asked Monique to accompany him to a forthcoming gala at Deauville Casino to dress the models and help with any alterations. One thing about this invitation made an impression on her dazed brain: she would be staying in the same luxurious hotel as Monsieur Guy.

'So, finally, you will seduce Monsieur Guy?' Sophie suggested over a drink after work at a little bar on the Rue des Capucines. She was wearing one of her most clinging knitted dresses in a burnt orange and she smoothed her red hair back with a languid gesture.

Monique choked on a sip of wine. 'How did you know it was him?' she gasped.

'The way you look at him. The way you behave around him.' Sophie shrugged. 'And now, this opportunity of sleeping under the same roof! You won't waste it?'

'I hadn't thought about it,' Monique said.

But she had, and just hearing the phrase 'sleeping under the same roof' quickened her pulse.

Sophie raised her eyebrows, then spoke of other subjects. They enjoyed their lunch, but as Sophie walked her to the metro at L'Opera, Monique suddenly stopped.

'So you think I should profit from being under the same roof as Monsieur Guy?' she asked.

'Well, *I* would!'

'What would you do?'

Sophie gave a little shrug. 'I'd put on my sexiest nightgown and go to his room.' She made it sound like the simplest thing in the world.

Monique squinted her eyes, trying to imagine doing this. 'Do men like sexy nightgowns so much?'

'Of course they do! Black ones. As transparent as possible.'

'So you would go to his room?' Monique frowned. 'And if he didn't want you?'

'Monique!' Sophie laughed. 'Very few men won't welcome a woman into their bedroom.'

Monique took the metro home in a daze. How wonderful to possess such confidence. If I was that pretty, I would also be confident, she thought. Perhaps a new nightdress would lend her confidence? She could buy the nightdress, then think again when she saw how she looked in it.

The next lunchtime, Monique bought a new nightgown, spending more on it than she usually spent on a pretty new dress. She modelled it that night before her bedroom mirror, trying to see her body through the sheer black the way Guy might see it. She saw only the plumpness, her pink skin flushed from a warm shower. Perhaps she was 'pleasingly plump'? But attractive? Desirable? It was so hard to say. The sheer black nightgown was so foreign to her, she had been embarrassed even to buy it. She tried to picture herself in this robe, floating down a Deauville hotel corridor late at night to Guy's room.

On the Friday before the gala they accompanied six models to the Deauville Casino's hotel. In the train carriage, she studied Guy as he read *Le Figaro*. Was he even conscious of her? She knew she wasn't conventionally pretty, but when people work together so well, they communicate on the same wavelength. It is another way of being intimate. If that was so, something would push them, sweep them, into . . . well, she hardly knew what.

'If Guy doesn't betray his wife with you, he'll only betray her with someone else,' Sophie had warned her. 'Then, why not you?'

This had a certain Sophie logic, she had to agree. By the time they reached Deauville, she saw this trip almost as a honeymoon. The nightdress was in her suitcase. If she allowed herself to imagine Guy's brown, strong hands on her body, she felt near to fainting. She could not think clearly enough to form a real plan. She would do as Sophie suggested and go to his room. That was the plan.

The top-level, high-priced models did not deign to do jobs like Deauville. Of the various tiers of models used at Chanel, the very top included society ladies who were paid with Chanel clothing, since they turned up their noses at cash. If a society woman found favour with Mademoiselle, she would model the first few collection showings almost as a favour, but a favour well rewarded with a new suit. The year-round house-models reported to work five mornings a week for fittings and modelled the collection every other afternoon throughout the season. The bottom tier of girls had the right measurements but did not have pretty faces: they were used only for fittings. They earned the lowest salaries and Monique always felt a little sorry for them. The fashion world was so cruel, paying you according to your looks.

For the gala they took three house models and two freelancers, all pretty, all in their twenties and thirties. Mademoiselle Chanel was very particular about the models who showed her clothes, auditioning them all. She liked a certain type, a little sporty, elegant in a throwaway style. The French word was *racé* or thoroughbred. To girls whose rich boyfriends sometimes took them to Morocco for the weekend, a working trip to Deauville was not a very exciting prospect. They were a little spoiled and definitely blasé. Gossip and chatter was the background to their fussing and primping.

They checked into the smart hotel and Monique directed trunks of clothing to the ballroom where a catwalk was being set up between the tables.

Guy's room was on the same floor as hers, she learned. Even if it hadn't been, she had made up her mind to visit it. She would profit from this night 'under the same roof'. The weight of her virginity had always felt like some guilty secret. She would change that, and Guy was the man she wished to change it with. Not the first night, she wasn't quite ready: the next, when she had got her bearings. That way, if it all went wrong, they would be returning to Paris the following day. Although the outcome was supposed to be pleasurable, she had only the greatest misgivings. But now there was no turning back: she was going to carry out her plan whether it was a good one or not.

The next morning, a raised catwalk ran down the centre of the ballroom. They rehearsed the *defilé* there. It would be presented after dinner. Tables were being laid with cloths and floral decorations, waiters bustling around adjusting cutlery and crystal.

A technician tested the loudspeakers for the music that always accompanied these showings, tapping a microphone for the commentator. It was an opportunity for some fifteen models to get together, with their hair stylists and *maquillistes*, to cause sheer havoc.

The day was spent helping Guy inspect each outfit, pinning, then hand-sewing any alterations.

'Take a little rest, Monique,' Guy urged at the end of the afternoon. They had been working since early that morning and he could see she was tired. 'If there's an emergency I know where to find you.'

He patted her arm in a friendly manner. What would he say if he knew she had a new nightgown, one to wear as she walked the few steps to his room? Perhaps he did know and was not letting on. She was amazed at her determination to go through with something she knew, deep down, was wrong. She did want a nap, yes, but she was worried that she might sleep until the next morning. A model agreed to call her room after an hour, so that she could press the clothes before lining them up on their hangers for the *defilé*.

They ate an early dinner at a nearby bistro, as the dressed-up charity audience filed in for dinner at the casino. Then the models had their hair done and were made up and it was nine thirty, the chosen hour.

Monique tried to ignore the fact that her heart was starting to beat faster.

That weekend, Samantha and Christopher attended a World Orphans Organisation reception. Delange had paid seventy-five francs each for them to watch a 'fashion auction' and hear about the world's orphans.

'So we must drink at least a hundred and fifty francs' worth of champagne to make this worthwhile,' Samantha cautioned. She was wearing Christopher's white plastic shift, cut extra short, with navy tights that elongated her legs to fashion-drawing proportions. 'At the charity auction of "priceless vintage Delange clothing",' she winked, 'also known as "old stock found in a closet", I'll bid up to a hundred bucks on a gold lamé gown that Camille Delange cut on the bias a million years ago. I think I'd look fabulous in it.'

They arrived at six o'clock and Samantha's eyes zeroed-in immediately on huge platters of seafood waiting on a long buffet-table. As she passed, her bangled hand sneaked towards a plump shrimp when an officious waiter suddenly slapped it down.

She slapped his hand back. '*Ne me touche pas!*' she cried.

'*Le buffet* does not open until *after* the charity appeal, Madame,' the little squirt smirked.

'*Mademoiselle,*' she corrected with a glare.

She returned to Christopher, looking back longingly at the buffet.

The room was crammed with familiar faces, and Samantha checked them all out, testing her fashion knowledge by matching designers' names to dresses, one of her favourite pasttimes.

Ghislaine de Rives wandered by in a white leather mini-skirt, glancing sharply at Christopher. Monsieur de Kousmine passed with his very un-chic wife ('married *before* he joined Chanel, of course,' Samantha whispered) in what looked like a burlap potato sack. He ignored her, of course, after a quick flash of his black eyes. The speeches and appeals began. An official quoted orphan statistics.

'God, this is dull,' Samantha groaned to Christopher. He silenced her with a frown. This was the good cause for which they had come and everyone's attention was on the speaker.

Samantha rolled her eyes. 'How long is this gonna *take*?'

She looked behind her at the shrimp. She had forgotten to buy pastries the day before, and she was starving. These little sea-monsters were pretty plump . . . her mouth watered at the prospect.

'When I was a kid. Daddy used to take me to those "All You Can Eat" buffets in the Valley,' she whispered to Christopher. 'I always won. I could probably consume more shrimp than anyone here.'

'Take it easy, Samantha . . .' Christopher tried to calm her. 'We're not here for the food.'

'You're damn right,' she agreed. 'We're here for the booze.'

The speeches showed no signs of ending.

'This stuff about orphans is so *depressing*,' she sighed when one speaker ended, only to introduce a new one. She glanced back at the seafood platter. It was unattended: who would notice if she sneaked one, just to stave off painful pangs of hunger?

'Those shrimp aren't a treat,' she groaned to Christopher, 'they're a medical necessity. I may faint.'

'In 1965, there were two million orphans in the world,' the speaker was saying. 'Taking into consideration a fast-growing Chinese population, we calculate that . . .'

Samantha edged around the table. Checking that everyone's attention was on the speaker, she popped two fat shrimp into her mouth.

'. . . in ten years there will be ten million unloved, unwanted orphans!' the speaker ended.

'Oh! My! *God*!'

Everyone turned to look sympathetically at the woman so affected by these statistics. But it was the shrimp not the orphans that had caused Samantha's outcry. 'These must be the most delicious shrimp I've *ever* tasted,' she swooned.

There was complete silence. Everyone, including the speaker, glared at her. Delicately, she blotted her lips with a napkin until their attention turned back to the speaker.

Christopher rolled his eyes at her.

'Oh, so what?' she hissed.

The buffet was finally declared open. Samantha ate more shrimp, washing them down with as many champagne cocktails as she could swipe off passing trays. She seemed to be taking all these cocktails in her stride, but at the eighth, they suddenly hit her. Holding a small bowl of *oeuf mayonnaise*, she walked past a distinguished older man who was eyeing her.

Samantha stopped dead in her tracks.

'Hello, you want some sex?' She thought she'd try Jean-Jacques' method on the man.

He looked a little surprised but smiled and murmured, 'I am married, but my wife and I have an understanding . . .'

'You do?' she asked, her eyes going out of focus. She swayed, feeling very dizzy. Suddenly she parked herself in his lap.

She rested there only a moment before a very determined hand caught her and she was strong-armed off the lap and deposited on the floor.

'Ouch!' She rubbed her bottom, picked some egg out of her hair and glowered at the woman standing over her.

'First you eat our shrimp,' the woman said, 'then you sit on our husbands! Don't you Americans *know* how to behave?'

'You're lucky I didn't sit on the shrimp and eat your husband,' Samantha cried. 'The shrimp tasted better. And how should I know he was your husband, anyway?'

As she focused on this woman, she felt a deep hidden pang of horror as Ghislaine de Rives suddenly swam into view.

'Why is this woman on your lap, Bertrand?' Ghislaine demanded.

'So sorry, my darling.' He struggled to his feet, bowing. 'She lost her balance.' He mimed drinking a few cocktails.

Samantha threw the remains of her champagne in his face, hurled a shrimp at the elegant Ghislaine and stalked out, dignity defiantly intact.

The hour-long *defilé* seemed to pass in a frenzied minute. Never had so many legs been thrust into skirts, arms into sleeves, hats onto heads and feet into two-toned shoes in so short a time. The models, cool and professional, managed not to rip linings or tear any sleeves. Between dresses, they were almost naked. Monique glanced at Guy to see whether he registered the nudity. Of course, he didn't. He studied only the suit or dress and the way it hung on the girl. That is what she loved about him: his professionalism.

After the gala, Monique folded and packed all the clothes, then found Guy and the girls relaxing outside in a nearby café. It was a cool night and the wine was on their expense account so they drank a lot. It seemed that Guy rather enjoyed being the only man amongst a group of beautiful women. Monique noticed Nadine, one of the prettiest models, refilling his glass constantly. She ordered coffee. But even tiny strong espressos failed to dampen the general merriment.

At one o'clock, Guy stood to kiss them all goodnight, including Monique. He kissed her cheek, lost his balance and clung to her for a moment. He had drunk a few *vins rosé* too many and seemed to overlook that she was his employee and should not be kissed. The warmth of him, the smell of Chanel's *Monsieur* cologne so spicy on his neck, made her giddy. She was close to what she suddenly realised she had always longed for. She tore herself away from his embrace with a little laugh. This, she was convinced, was a sign to go ahead with her plan.

She went up to her room, showered, changed into her new nightdress, arranged her hair, retouched her make-up and refused to think any more: it was time to just live, to act. A last glance in the mirror and she left her room to walk, in a dream, down the quiet corridor to his room.

She knocked gently on his door. No answer. She tried it and found it to be open.

'*Guy?*' she whispered, stepping into the dark room.

Groping her way into the room, she stumbled. She heard a noise. A bedside lamp snapped on and she found herself staring at Guy and the model who had plied him with wine all that evening, Nadine. They stared at each other for a frozen second before Monique turned and ran. She ran along the corridor back to her room. Closing the door, she threw herself face down on her bed.

She sobbed for some minutes before there was a knock on her door. She cried 'Come in,' wondering if that stupid model had come to apologise. Footsteps padded to her bed, then stopped. She looked up and saw Guy in a white bathrobe, his face twisted.

'Monique, I am so sorry,' he said.

She could not speak. Instead, her arms instinctively went out to him. After his split-second hesitation, she felt herself melting into a man's body for the first time in her life. The weight of his body on hers was wonderful.

'I never considered you this way . . .' he whispered in her ear. 'I thought of you almost as a daughter . . .'

He could not have chosen a more electrifying word: its effect on her was instant. Her mouth sought his, and she clutched him tightly to her. He kissed her, his mouth still tasting of coffee. She was on the verge of swooning. She parted her legs, drew up her nightdress. He held her and she began to know the pleasures of love for the very first time. She felt him against her but as if he sensed this was her first time, Guy was gentle and solicitous, urging her to such a height of longing that no sooner did he begin to make love to her than she felt immediately that gathering wave she had read about so many times. It had been described in different ways, disguised, in songs, in books or in films. She thought she'd be ready for it, but it took her unawares, sweeping across her so intensely that she cried out, then screamed. Guy's hand gently covered her mouth. Gasping, sobbing, with tears coursing down her face, his body's jerks were so exciting to her that they set off further explosions of pleasure within her. She did not want to let him go. Her body wanted him to stay inside her. The body seems to know what to do, she thought, holding him. It *receives* the man, she thought, and then it does not want to let him go. Guy soothed away her tears and cries, now little whimpers, his soft lips kissing over her face, her eyes, her neck. Her entire body was alive, glowing, as if super-sensitive. She began to weep.

This weeping was the most unexpected part. All the grief for her father, all her yearning for love, all the loneliness borne until this moment, exploded within her. This was what life was really about, this fitting together, this slotting of two bodies one into the other, two puzzle pieces locking together, solving the mystery of love. She clutched tighter, wanting them to be inseparable. Guy held her, as if he completely understood her weeping.

'What good can possibly come of this?' she sobbed.

Guy chuckled. 'It's a little late to ask that,' he muttered.

She lay quietly in his arms, her senses slowly calming, her brain a flurry of activity. What could she compare this to? She could not drift off to sleep. She hardly dared to move as he slept, holding her, the way she had always dreamed of being held in a man's arms. All through the night, secure, firm, loved. The dawn came up and still her brain raced. When two people felt like this together . . . it couldn't mean nothing, could it? It had to mean *something*?

Eleven

'Samantha, I heard an eye-witness account of your behaviour at the charity reception,' a triumphant Chantal Delange announced with undisguised satisfaction on Monday morning. 'Did you forget that you were representing Delange? A public relations person must behave with great tact and discretion. We cannot have employees behaving the way you did. And at an orphans' charity event, too! We French are very liberal but . . .' she shrugged.

'You? Liberal?' Samantha laughed. 'You're the most closed-minded society I have ever seen. *Californians* are liberal! Americans are liberal!'

'Then maybe you should return there?' Chantal suggested. 'Because this time you have gone too far. We will have to let you go.'

Samantha stared at her, open-mouthed. 'You mean, like . . . *fire* me?' she asked.

Chantal nodded.

'You *can't* fire me!' Samantha cried. 'I've increased your perfume sales by seventy per cent! My father will stop distributing your perfume.'

Chantal smiled grimly. 'I don't think even your father would approve of your behaviour. *Especially* your father! You're a *guest* in our country, Samantha! You must conduct yourself accordingly.'

Samantha stared at her. 'You can't fire me for eating two

137

shrimp!' she said. 'Or are you jealous because I get more sex than you? Who the fuck do you think you are? I can get a job at Chanel any time I want it!'

'Our loss will be Chanel's gain,' Chantal sighed.

An hour later, Samantha shook out the contents of her desk drawers, mostly chocolate and make-up, into two large Chanel shopping bags. After this painful task, Christopher supported his ex-publicist out into the street. She stopped for a moment to stare longingly at a phone-booth before shaking her head.

'Nope!' she decided. 'I'm too proud to ask Daddy to get me out of this one.'

Christopher hailed a taxi. Samantha climbed in and wound down the window to stare pleadingly at him.

'Oh, Christopher,' she began to cry, 'is this the end of gay Paree? Just because of a couple of fucking shrimp?'

'Maybe it's just the beginning? The sudden notoriety might help your career?' Christopher suggested.

'That song, "*Je ne regrette rien*"?' she asked. 'I'm writing my version – '*Je regrette tout!*' But I'm not going back to New York until I achieve something here.'

The cab drove off, Samantha's hand fluttering out the window.

Monique woke alone. She stared at the rumpled bed then got up to study her reflection in the bathroom mirror. There was a difference in her face, or, to be more accurate, in her eyes. She felt languorous and relaxed, as though intense massage had removed all the kinks and aches in her muscles. Above all, she felt like a woman.

She hesitated before entering the dining-room for breakfast. Surely Guy would pretend that nothing had happened and she would do the same. Her only fear was that the model, Nadine, had told all the other models about last night, but she found herself not caring.

She hugged to herself the smell of Guy on her body, the

knowledge that she was no longer a virgin. She would never be a giggling old spinster like the Catroux sisters. That in itself was a weight off her shoulders.

One can change overnight, she thought. Life changes in one second.

Walking into the dining-room, she felt more attractive. Guy had desired her! Guy had kissed her, embraced her, held her to him with such force, as though he could barely control his feelings. Perhaps he even loved her?

The day after her firing, the doorbell rang at nine in the morning. Samantha stumbled to her front door in flannel nightwear. Her eyes were bloodshot, she looked as if she had been crying. Christopher stood outside with a sympathetic expression.

'How sweet of you to come,' she cried. 'Come in, I'll make coffee . . .' She fussed with coffee and cups as he sat in her small kitchen, watching her.

She poured coffee and served pastries from the fridge as if it were normal to eat éclairs for breakfast. Suddenly she stopped, hunched over the sink, shaking with sobs. He ran to her and put an arm around her.

'Now, don't take this so hard,' he said. 'It's no good crying over spilt champagne. Delange was always just a starting-off point, wasn't it? For both of us?'

'Yup.' She dabbed her eyes, straightened up and served the coffee. She was silent as she sat down and devoured two éclairs, gazing at him mournfully between bites.

'You're not going to mope, are you?' he asked.

'Well, I'm not ready to dress up and go out as if nothing has happened. Not when *le tout Paris* is laughing at me!'

'*Le tout Paris* has completely forgotten,' he assured her. 'Except perhaps Ghislaine de Rives. Expect a dry-cleaning bill for removal of shrimp stains. Won't de Kousmine help you find a job?'

'He'd *better!*' Samantha said threateningly. 'I never said I was a saint but I'm a terrific publicist. Parisians are just so good at making you feel crass!'

'You must control your impulsive behaviour,' he began. 'The French—'

'Don't!' she cut him off. 'The French kill their wives and it's a "crime of passion". I nibble a shrimp and I'm a social reject.' She sipped her coffee sulkily. 'You're my only friend here, Christopher.' She touched his arm. 'Maybe this is the moment to ask myself the really difficult questions? Like,' she glanced at him expectantly, 'do I change my dry-cleaner? They lost a button off a Chanel jacket. Should I go home to New York? Everything is tumble-drying in my head! Oh, Christopher, do I have a future in the French couture?'

'Of course you do.'

'There's something else,' she stared into her coffee. 'I'm always comparing other women's Before and After makeover pictures and,' she glanced up at him, 'sometimes I prefer the Before picture. Is that kinky? Maybe I looked better before Jean-Jacques exaggerated my *worst* features?'

'You looked good before, and you look good now,' Christopher soothed her. 'I have to go to work . . .' He stood up.

'I'll pray for a sign,' she patted his hand, 'from Dior, from Yves Saint Laurent, from Givenchy . . . from all the houses I've sent Special Delivery requests for employment to. Delange's perfume sales-figures prove I did a fabulous job. You'll back me up, won't you? You'll be my reference?'

'Of course I will.'

She kissed him.

'I've approached everyone *but* Chanel,' she raised her eyebrows. 'I'm just a tad shy about the de Kousmine connection.'

'I am extremely disappointed in you, Monique,' Mademoiselle said.

Monique stood her ground before Mademoiselle Chanel in her top-floor salon as Mademoiselle's eyes burned deeply into her, reminding her of a childhood priest who had always tried to scare her into confession when there was nothing to confess. This time there was plenty to confess but she was damned if she'd confess it.

'Have you never heard of self-discipline?' Chanel asked.

'I don't know what you mean, Mademoiselle,' Monique said.

'I hear everything that happens in my house,' Mademoiselle said.

'Well, Mademoiselle, whatever gossip you may have heard, it did not happen in your house.'

'No . . .' Mademoiselle allowed. 'It happened in Deauville where you were *representing* my house. Guy is a first-class tailor but he never could resist a pretty girl batting her eyes at him: he's been making free suits for models for years.'

'That is surely just gossip, Mademoiselle.'

'Monique, I'm taking you out of Guy's workroom.'

'You can't do that!' Monique cried out.

'Yes, I can,' the old lady replied implacably. 'Next season, I am giving you your own atelier. Because of your fine work. You'll bypass all the usual steps and go straight to the top.'

Monique stared at her.

'Because of my work?' she asked. 'Or are you *judging* me, Mademoiselle?' she said. 'I think I should be judged on what I do for the house and the clients, and I do my very best.'

Mademoiselle stared at her. 'Your work is superb. But I thought you and I share a devotion to work that no man can disturb?'

'Monsieur Guy does not disturb my work, Mademoiselle,' Monique said. 'One of the things he and I have in common is that we both—'

Chanel cut her off. 'Guy is married.'

'And did Mademoiselle never fall in love with a married man?' Monique regretted her words the moment they fell out.

Chanel's face changed. 'How dare you ask such a question? Perhaps you have slightly lost your composure? Don't you realise what having your own atelier means? It will—'

'Keep me away from Guy?' Monique finished for her.

Chanel stared at her.

'I must have order in my house, Monique,' she said calmly. 'Guy works all day in his atelier. At night, it's home to his wife and family. Isn't that how things should be?'

Monique said nothing.

'It takes most seamstresses ten years to be given their own atelier. You will be on an equal footing with Guy. Your salary will be tripled, you will select your own team of seamstresses, you will be your own boss, responsible for the quality of your output. I expect a huge demand for your suits.'

Monique tried to think. She knew this news should be making her feel triumphant. She would be utterly unique in the house, having gained this position so quickly.

'Thank you for this promotion, Mademoiselle,' she said carefully. 'I will continue to do my very best for you.' She hoped this would end the interview.

Chanel looked at her penetratingly. 'You will not let me down,' she stated.

When everyone had left the workroom that night, Monique found herself alone with Guy. As she arranged her work, she told him her news.

'Mademoiselle is giving me my own workroom,' she said.

'I know,' he said quietly. Even from across the room, his eyes struck directly into her soul. 'You deserve it. When Mademoiselle asked me, I had to agree.'

Monique frowned. 'She knew about us, Guy. Does she think she owns you?'

'She's a little nosy about her employees' lives,' Guy allowed with a shrug. 'But she is a canny old girl and knows something of life.'

Monique sighed. 'She's a difficult woman and you know it. There were some charming nieces here the other day. They only wished to say hello to their aunt but she would not see them. I think she is jealous of anyone who finds happiness.'

He stared at her. 'You think she's jealous of our half-hour of passion?'

'Is that all we had, Guy? A half-hour?' she asked him. 'Were you looking at your watch? For me, it wasn't just passion. Can't you see? I am in love with you, Guy! I think I was from the first day.'

Guy shot her an alarmed look. 'Monique, I am very sorry, I

don't know what to say . . .' he said slowly. 'There's no future with me . . . I am not about to make my wife, my two daughters, and, finally, you and me, unhappy.'

'So . . .' she frowned, trying to collect her thoughts. 'This promotion, this salary raise, this putting me on the same level as you in the house . . . it will all be meaningless?'

'Why meaningless? It is wonderful! I am happy for you!'

She stared at him, disappointment pulling her mouth down.

She took a deep breath and leaned to kiss his forehead.

'Will you sometimes visit my workroom, Guy?' she asked.

She hesitated for a moment, too proud to hug him. Holding her jacket, she left the room, tears welling up. She was a few steps down the back staircase when she heard him behind her. He caught her arm, spun her around. And suddenly his mouth was on hers and again she felt that sensation of her entire body being on fire. She fell back against the wall, steadying herself against the force of his embrace, opening her lips to his kiss. She could feel he was aroused as he pressed into her.

She pushed him away. 'It was only half an hour of passion, remember? Why didn't you beg to keep me in your workroom?'

'Because you deserve your own workroom, Monique,' he said. 'From the day I saw your work I knew you would get it very quickly.'

She smoothed down her jacket.

'Good night, Guy.' She left him standing on the staircase.

'Monique, wait,' he called after her. 'If we saw each other once a week . . . maybe meeting at a hotel near here? If that was all I could offer right now . . . would you please say yes, Monique?'

She stared at him for a long moment, turned and left.

She walked along the Grands Boulevards, following the crowds. She was getting her own workroom and she was assured of Guy loving her for one hour a week. Should she be happy? If so, why wasn't she? For the first time in her life she needed a drink, something strong that would burn. She stopped at the first bar she came to, ordered Scotch, and swallowed it down quickly, the way she had seen men standing at the counter do. The warmth quickly spread through her, comforting and giving strength. It took the edge off things, *blurred* the edges so that she did not have to see life quite so clearly.

A virginal girl from Angers had become an alcoholic adulteress, she marvelled as she continued on her way home, walking down to the Seine to follow its path. She had not imagined this happening when she came to Paris. No, what she was doing now, walking the streets of Paris alone, was what she had imagined for herself. And now she would have her own workroom! Was this fate telling her that work would always prove more rewarding than her personal life?

For now her personal life would be hurried meetings in a hotel that probably rented out rooms by the hour. What sort of people went there, met there, made love there?

Very quietly, she answered herself: people like herself and Guy.

Three days later, she sat across a café table from Sophie.

'Did you think he'd leave his wife?' Sophie asked gently.

Monique looked up. 'I thought we had begun a love affair. I expected a little more than one hour a week.'

Sophie raised her eyes to heaven as she spooned sugar into her coffee.

'You don't have any idea of how men and women *are*, Monique. For him, it was just another conquest.'

'No. Guy is not like that.' Monique held Sophie's eyes.

'Maybe loving a married man is too complicated,' Sophie said. 'I could use a little advice myself. I'm also in love. But I keep this man at a distance.'

'Why?' Monique asked.

Sophie's eyes clouded. 'Something in me resists trusting any man,' she began slowly. 'I protect myself from getting hurt. So you see? I refuse to give myself pain.'

Monique nodded. 'You and I are very different, Sophie. It's true that I have a softer view of life than most Parisians. But I

144

cannot do without love in order to spare myself a little pain. And who knows what might happen?'

Sophie shrugged as she lit a cigarette.

'Nothing will happen, Monique,' she advised. 'Guy is married.'

Twelve

Delange clients were not ordering zipless, buttonless, plastic sheaths or transparent blouses.

'They have no wish to reveal their withered breasts, Chris,' Klaus told him drily one night.

An older client did order the white plastic shift but on condition that it was made up in grey wool, with long sleeves and a much longer skirt.

'I'm not letting some old dear completely ruin my design philosophy,' Christopher told Samantha at their weekly La Quetsch lunch.

She stared at him. 'I thought you wanted to sell your clothes?'

'Yes, *my* clothes,' he nodded, 'not the clients' own designs.'

Then one afternoon, a *vendeuse* ran triumphantly into Christopher's office and stopped, wheezing slightly, at his desk.

'Madame Ghislaine de Rives is coming to see the collection!' she announced. 'A little late in the season! But if she orders something, we're saved!'

He raised his eyebrows. 'Saved by the Rives?' he asked.

Ghislaine de Rives, one of the most elegant women in Paris, was easily look-up-able in some back issues of *Vogue*. A devoted follower of fashion, Christopher learned, and also editor of a chic magazine of the arts. Married to a successful businessman, she hosted a weekly *salon* in their apartment at Les Invalides. She viewed the collection that afternoon and promptly ordered six outfits.

146

'She'll expect you to take her fittings,' Madame Genevieve, the haughty *directrice*, couldn't wait to tell him. She stared at him with that distasteful expression that always made him feel he had forgotten to apply deodorant.

'You won't be complaining about *this* client's figure,' she went on. 'She's perfect! Visit her *cabine*. Study her reflection in the mirror *very* intently,' she advised. 'Try to please her. If *she* is happy with your clothes, a flock of her socialite friends will follow. They're like sheep, those women.'

At their next lunch, seated at their favourite window table in *La Quetsch* Christopher sought Samantha's advice.

'She assumes I'm only too eager to prostitute myself for the sake of one client,' he told her.

'You are, of course?' Samantha nodded.

'Well, yes. I just don't like her assuming it.'

'Ghislaine de Rives! I was fired because of her. She probably saw you that night and got the hots for you,' Samantha guessed.

'Or she may like my clothes?' Christopher pretended to be offended. 'You did look pretty fabulous in that white shift. Before they threw you out.'

'Well, it's fantastic publicity. She'll save Delange. We should celebrate.'

'For you, every meal is a celebration. But I'm not so great at fittings . . .' he mused. 'It's hard getting pins through the plastic I used in this collection. I kind of left the technical stuff to the seamstresses. I'll have to fake it, squinting in the dressing-room mirror, pretending to see the faults.'

'Yeah, fake it,' Samantha agreed happily. 'If you keep touching her ass she won't notice the odd pin sticking into her. The French love a little *oooh la la!*' She glanced around the restaurant. 'Did you know Pierre La Chasse is making his collection on fourteen-year-old *boys?*' she asked. 'Kinky? He says they have the right "boyish shape". Well, that's no surprise, they *are* boys.'

Christopher frowned. 'How do I handle Ghislaine de Rives?'

'You just answered the question: *handle* her. Handle her a *lot*.

Pretend her back seam is crooked, it'll give you an excuse to keep touching her ass.'

Christopher stared at her. 'Honestly, Samantha, your view of couture is so different to mine. It's not *all* about sex!'

She glanced up from the menu. 'Wanna bet?'

The waiter came for their orders.

'How is the *Croque Madame* different to the *Croque Monsieur*?' Samantha asked.

The waiter said, 'There is a poached egg.'

'How about we substitute a fried tomato?' Samantha tried.

'Then it will no longer be a *Croque Madame*, Mademoiselle.'

'That's OK. And does the salad contain lettuce?'

'Of course! That is why it is a salad!'

'Can you replace it with endive?'

The waiter rolled his eyes and scuttled away.

'Christopher,' Samantha resumed, 'this de Rives Chanel-junkie is probably trying to kick her Chanel habit, cold turkey. She's always dressed there. I bet she seduces you into the Paris tradition of young man becoming willing pupil of older woman, learning how to really please a woman. It's like riding a bicycle – priceless knowledge you *never* forget.'

Christopher made an impressed face.

Samantha nodded. 'Bored married couples do this to rekindle their interest. She'll be seen around with her new boyfriend. It lasts until the guy falls in love with someone his own age. Like Sophie.'

'Yes, you're forgetting I'm in love with her.'

'Well, Ghislaine's interest in you may rekindle *her* interest. Jealousy can be an aphrodisiac,' she said, nodding knowingly.

Madame de Rives came to be measured by a *Premiere Main* for the white plastic shift. A week later, the shift cut out and tacked together, Christopher splashed on some *Eau Sauvage* before taking the dress to a *cabine*, knocking on the door.

'*Entrez*,' came a young-sounding voice.

Ghislaine de Rives stood lithe and tall in white silk bikini and

148

bra. The mirrored *cabine* reflected back several images of her elegant body as she took his hand.

'It's you.' She stared amusedly into his eyes. 'Well! Already, I am your big fan.'

Her freshness and vitality wiped out the fact that Ghislaine de Rives was old enough to be Christopher's mother. Her alive dark eyes were full of mischief and gave everything she said a hint of innuendo. Her slightly long face had a sharp look, nose a little long and mouth a little thin. She compensated for this with silky shoulder-length hair, which she tossed girlishly. Perfect grooming and a crisp *chic* made her younger than her photographs. She held up her arms for him to slip the shift over her head: he had banished buttons or zips as *demodé*.

She gave a delighted gurgle as the dress settled on her, regarding herself in the mirror. 'Young! New! Advanced!' She struck a few poses, becoming one of his fashion drawings turned into animated cartoon. 'Oh, I got so bored with Chanel! I cannot wear what every other woman is wearing. Being daring is part of fashion, no? And now . . . Chanel? *Pouff!* Nobody could call her daring. I *love* how this looks on me. And so short! I must not blush as I sit down.'

Ghislaine de Rives was what the French called '*bien dans sa peau*'. This expression meant 'feeling good in one's skin' without apologising for anything. Another description (the French were so good at coining them) was: '*un certain age*'. It meant a woman no longer in the first flush of youth. She seemed ready for an adventure, flashing her eyes at him as if he were a delicious morsel she was about to gobble up.

Non-stop flattery, little compliments, knowing looks . . . how could it make him feel anything but utterly irresistible? Little touches of her fingertips gave the impression that she could barely keep her hands off him. She gazed at Christopher adoringly as if he were the handsomest man she'd seen.

He stood just behind her, facing her reflection in the mirror. Firmly, he placed both hands on her body to smooth some slight wrinkling in the fitting white plastic. He moved from the top of her ribcage to her waist. Instead of facing her reflection, she threw her head back, closed her eyes and nestled against him, her hand 'accidentally' coming to rest in his crotch. She moved just the back of her wrist against him, blinked opened her eyes and said, 'Do you think just a centimetre longer?'

'Would you feel more comfortable?' he asked, reaching for some pins.

He knelt on the floor by her feet to unpin the hem, rolling the plastic down to make it a tiny bit longer. Normally a young girl assistant would have done this, but he had decided to fit her unaccompanied, to make her feel more special. When the laborious task was done, he stood behind her again.

They stared into the mirror. He got the impression that she was testing him.

'You're from London?'

'Yes, Madame.'

'Oh, please call me Ghislaine.'

The hand was back in his crotch and so was the suggestive look in her eyes.

'We go to England every other weekend to stay with friends in the country,' she said. 'My husband loves to shoot. It makes him feel big and strong to kill innocent little animals. We return on Sunday afternoon in time for our weekly 'salon'. You must come to one. How do you like Paris?'

'I love it, Madame. I mean, Ghislaine.'

'Good.'

She turned suddenly to face him, looking down. Again, he cursed his tight-fitting trousers for revealing his arousal. She raised her eyebrows, looking at him with a wicked glint in her eyes.

'Well! This is very unusual for the haute couture,' she said. 'This never happens at Chanel!'

'I . . .' Christopher fidgeted, not knowing what to say. He moved away.

'I mean the white plastic material, of course!' she laughed.

Christopher helped her off with the shift.

'We'll try to have it ready in a few days,' he said.

He took her hand to say goodbye but she pulled him to her for a kiss on each cheek. They exchanged a glance which said that this fitting was just the first of many fittings. Not just of clothes.

Drunk on her aroma, the kind of unique scent that made you want more and which clung to him for hours afterward, he left the *cabine* flushed with pleasure, the dress over one arm covering him. Madame Genevieve hovered outside. She smiled approvingly at him for the first time ever.

Ghislaine de Rives wore his clothes from that moment on. It was as if their couture coupling was destined: chic, advanced clothes on perfect model-muse, enhanced by a mutual attraction that disturbed and confused him.

'Our fashion antennae got kind of intertwined,' Christopher later told Samantha.

'Oh my God, that is just so *romantic*,' she sighed. 'Make sure the new publicity person quotes that in your press release.'

'Samantha, there isn't a new publicity person. You are irreplaceable.'

Sophie was blowing cold again, not accepting Christopher's invitations to dinner or drinks. He called her to tell her the news about Ghislaine.

'Congratulations,' she said. 'But watch out for her,' she laughed. 'She eats up little boys like you for breakfast.'

'How is your fashion career going?' he asked.

'I'd like to show you some new designs,' she suggested.

'Complete with private fitting-cubicle?' he asked.

She laughed. 'Last time, I was acting out a fantasy.'

'Let's act it out again,' he suggested.

There was a pause.

'Christopher, I don't always know what I need,' Sophie replied finally. 'Maybe I need something different each day? This time, I'm simply asking for some advice. Will you give me some?'

'Of course,' Christopher said.

He visited her the next weekend, a visit very different to the others. Sophie gave him a friendly hello kiss, then kept her distance, he noticed disappointedly.

'This is all I do now . . .' She led him into her bedroom, indicating clothes laid out on her bed. 'I work hard. I design. I sew.'

She showed him into the living-room and disappeared. Five minutes later, she returned in a cream linen shift. It was very simple, short, fitted to her body.

'Nicely cut,' he nodded. 'Cool and wearable.'

The next dress was in thin black silk with some interesting draping on one shoulder. She modelled five other outfits for him. She had a certain taste and he liked it. It was quite different to his. She was more classic, but with quirky details.

'This is known in the ready-to-wear trade as "classic with a twist",' he told her.

'Funny, I never think of myself as classic . . .'

She prepared one of her elegant little lunches and they ate it at the table in the window. He could not quite make out her mood.

'I don't understand,' he said finally. 'Last time, I told you how much I love you. When we were together here, it was . . . well, I know you felt it too. I didn't imagine it. You snuggled next to me as if we were lovers. And now you're acting as if we're meeting for the first time?'

'Christopher,' she lit a cigarette, staring directly at him, 'Ghislaine de Rives is telling everyone how seductive you are in the fitting *cabine*. Maybe we should just be friends while *you* live out *your* little fitting-room fantasy?'

He held her eyes. 'But we're more than friends, Sophie. I love you. Ghislaine is only a client. I hope to have many of them.'

'She won't stay a client for long.' She shrugged. 'That woman lives for conquests.'

'You told me you did, too. And you beat her to it. You've *made* a conquest. Of *me*!'

She took a puff on her cigarette, staring at him. 'If I admit to a man and to myself that I am in love with him, I must be one hundred per cent sure of him . . .' She blew out smoke.

'Well, don't let Ghislaine de Rives come between us: she's only a very important client.'

She stubbed out her cigarette with a slight shrug.

'You're not a very good liar, Christopher,' she said. 'That's actually a point in your favour. Ghislaine *will* seduce you. Her interest flatters you and she will boost your career.'

He remained silent, watching her.

'Do I have talent?' she asked, looking up at him. 'Is it worth my while to carry on?'

'Of course you have talent. And you seem very determined . . .'

'I don't know how determined I am. Mademoiselle has offered me the chance to be a model. It would be better than that Chanel atelier.'

'Is it very boring?' he asked.

'You cannot imagine,' she groaned. 'But I'll see it out.'

Her goodbye kiss was warmer than her greeting and he held her to him, pressing his lips to hers for a few moments, trying to make it last. He felt his body react, but she made it clear this visit was not going to end up in her bed. He left, disappointed, his body aching. And, yes, he did feel a little guilty because he knew Ghislaine de Rives would seduce him and a part of him was curious to see just how.

'Ghislaine and her husband Bertrand have this . . . understanding,' Samantha told Christopher approvingly. 'He chats up young girls, she feels up young men.'

They were sitting outside the Flore. Sunday noon was the perfect moment to be there; there was just the right mix of chic and shabby intellectuals. Now a sprinkling of fashion-junkies added a little colour as they ordered *le brunch*. Samantha was in full Chanel regalia: a gorgeous pink tweed suit, two-toned sling-backs and a grosgrain bow incongruously perched at the side of her hair.

'She felt *me* up,' Christopher confessed, 'in the *cabine*.'

'She did? What happened?'

'What d'you think? I reacted. I'm a man.'

'Really? In the *cabine*?'

'Yup.' He reached out to finger the navy silk braiding and gilt buttons of her jacket.

'How much did *that* cost?' he asked her.

'Kinda expensive.' Samantha rolled her eyes and began counting on her fingers. 'Twenty blow-jobs.'

'Is that what Chanel charges these days?' he laughed.

She made a face. 'It's how de Kousmine charges,' she said. 'He had it made for me. It fits pretty good, considering there were no fittings . . .' she shrugged. 'A girl can't have too many Chanels, right? I wanna hear about the *cabine* fondling . . .'

'If you tell nobody about it. Especially Sophie. She's jealous!'

'I won't tell anybody if you don't tell Klaus what this suit cost.'

They shook hands solemnly.

'Our fitting stopped just short of actual sex,' Christopher said.

'My God, she wastes no time, that woman. I don't think I like her.'

'Do you behave so differently from her?'

'I'm American!' she reminded him 'What I do doesn't count.'

'She's actually very nice. I'm invited for drinks tonight.'

'You'll have fun, what will you wear?'

'My "British Boy" outfit!'

'Don't tell me, let me guess. Frilly white shirt, tight pants, velvet jacket and boots?'

Bertrand and Ghislaine de Rives' evenings became the most enjoyable *salon* in Paris. Their recipe was no secret: take a huge Quai D'Orsay apartment with romantic views over the Seine. Add several handfuls of Paris society. Stir in a dozen chic models, some with faces familiar from magazines. Sprinkle in a few grizzled intellectuals in tobacco-drenched, elbow-patched clothing. Season with a pinch of avant-garde artists in paint-spattered dungarees. Garnish with pretty maids in lacy white aprons serving delicious hot nibbles. Wash down with Scotch or champagne that is never allowed to run dry. Simmer for an hour or two, then garnish with the surprise late arrival of a world-famous actress or opera singer. Marlene Dietrich or Maria Callas would do nicely.

It was not, of course, called a *salon*. It was *le drinks*. At his first Christopher stuck out as the only male under forty, a situation Ghislaine had surely engineered to flatter a young British boy dressed in black velvet blazer, white frilly dress shirt, flared trousers and black shiny British boots with pull-on loops at the back.

The walls were covered with lapis lazuli brocade as if specially ordered to match his eyes. Apart from two huge navy velvet modern sofas framing a marble fireplace, everything was Louis Quatorze style, including the heels of the women's Roger Vivier shoes. The Aubusson rug was so thick that Christopher's black leather boots sank a centimetre into it. The ancient chandelier with its glinting crystal drops looked as if it had been borrowed from Versailles. The museum-quality marqueted furniture were surely family heirlooms. The only thing modern were large, vivid abstract paintings filling the walls. They were by a new artist Ghislaine had recently discovered and he stood beneath his paintings, paint-spattered and bearded, accepting compliments and orders from guests who always wanted what Ghislaine had.

Glancing around, Christopher recognised the tiny privileged world he had read about and aspired to: he reinvented himself on the spot. Everyone was 'on', sparkling, competing to be the best in one of the four Paris categories: 'Sexy', 'Amusing', 'Successful' or 'Intellectual'.

These people would not wish to hear of his modest suburban London life unless he presented it as some fantastic story, hilarious and quaint. He would forget his background and enter their game, pretending that tonight he had sprung fully-formed into this room, this world. A world where mundane tasks were done by servants and where illness, poverty or misery did not exist. In this world, one did not complain or whine or worry . . . not out loud, anyway. One pretended that life was about success, love, champagne, fun and money.

'Christopher! I'm so glad you could come!' Ghislaine greeted him, wearing his white plastic shift. 'Come, meet my husband!'

She was as sparkling as her chandelier, long legs in perfect light grey tights, swinging glossy hair held back by a gold ribbon, make-up slightly theatrical and perfectly applied.

She presented him to a portly, bald, bespectacled man in a dark suit who grasped his hand firmly and cried, 'Thank you for the liberation of my wife from that ghastly Chanel!'

'I thought everybody loved Chanel?' Christopher said.

'This is the problem!' Monsieur de Rives laughed. 'My wife is not *everybody*! She likes to be different!'

'Yes I do!' she nodded enthusiastically, stopping a waiter with a tray of champagne and handing Christopher a glass. 'Life is too short to all dress the same, all feel the same. I *feel* different in this, Christopher. That's why I love it!'

She certainly stood out from all the other guests who were wearing little black floaty dresses. Christopher felt a thrill of pride to think this was his dress. She towered over most of them, eyes sparkling, glossy hair swinging. Was fashion nothing more than perfect grooming? he wondered. It helped, too, that she wore the shift just as he'd shown it, without jewellery or adornment, just plain pearl stud earrings.

A few more champagne cocktails later, Christopher's French became more fluent and he was becoming quite witty. Then he spotted Sophie across the room.

Her fluttery cocktail dress in black silk chiffon was intricate and expensive and she wore it with great style, hair piled atop her head in a just-got-out-of-bed look. Her eyes were carefully made-up, revealing a deeper, more intense gaze due to shadow in the crease of her eye-lid, and long silky lashes. More than just a pretty girl that night, she was a breathtakingly beautiful woman.

She was laughing and flirting with a big bulky man with a walrus moustache.

'Who's that man?' he asked Ghislaine.

'Monsieur de Kousmine,' she replied, 'a big noise at Chanel.'

He recognised the name and nodded. Samantha's friend. How many females did this man juggle?

He stared at Sophie, his newfound sophistication melting like an ice-cream in the sun. In that moment, he suddenly became plain old Christopher Hutchins again. Love did this, he decided. Love removed all pretence and forced you to be the person you really are.

He reached for another glass of champagne, still staring at Sophie, and just then she looked across the room and saw him. Their eyes connected with a shock at the very moment Ghislaine passed by to collect Christopher and present him to a woman in a skimpy black shift.

'The man who dresses me!' She put as much sexy innuendo as she could cram into the phrase. Christopher saw that Sophie had heard.

'It took an Englishman to wean me off Chanel!' Ghislaine added.

As he stared across the crowded salon, he could sense that Sophie was jealous that he was being monopolised by Ghislaine. Now they were quits, he thought, for he was jealous of that bear of a man, Monsieur de Kousmine.

'My best friend, Marianne Brenner,' Ghislaine introduced him to her friend. 'She's absolutely in love with your clothes. You're lucky, her husband's the King of—'

Christopher waited with bated breath.

'—Soap!' Ghislaine finished.

He took the woman's hand and kissed it, both women expressing delight at an Englishman making such a French gesture. If they knew how utterly hopeless he felt at that moment, Christopher thought, as the sincere feeling of his love for Sophie cut through the elegant evening like a sharp knife through Brie. He felt suddenly sober. This was all show and pretence. Seventy-five per cent of these people did not belong here. They had bluffed their way in. That includes me, he thought.

And yet wasn't this how an ambitious young couturier must conduct himself in Paris if he was to get anywhere? He needed Ghislaine and her friends, and Sophie probably needed someone like de Kousmine. How banal, how French, and what utter bullshit, he thought. He finished off his champagne in a gulp.

'How would you propose to dress *me*?' Marianne Brenner asked him.

'First, I would *undress* you,' Christopher cried.

In a burst of bravado, he grasped at where her non-existent breasts should have been and she screamed with delight.

Later that evening, he noticed Sophie standing alone, slightly dazed, as if she had drunk too much or taken some drug.

He approached her. 'Are you stalking me?'

She nodded. 'Yes. I follow you all over Paris. From protest marches to the de Rives' *salon*. You are quite famous now, you made the *Figaro* front page.'

'Ha!' he laughed. 'But there have not been many orders for my clothes.'

'You have the most famous client in Paris!' She jerked her head towards Ghislaine.

'And *your* companion?' he asked.

'He's an old friend of my family . . .'

'He doesn't look at you like an old friend.'

'Oh, I just tease him. He enjoys that. He's what you call in English a little "kinky". He will never have me!'

Christopher felt a wave of relief. He leaned towards her, taking in the beautiful swell of her bosom, the soft skin of her shoulders and her delicious scent.

'You look absolutely gorgeous.'

She smiled. 'I'm surprised you noticed me with all these women fighting over you?'

'You're sometimes so sweet . . .' Christopher began. 'When I got hurt in that protest march, when we made love. Why do you change and suddenly seem so unavailable?'

She stared at him. 'Me, unavailable? What serious conversation for such a light-hearted *salon*. Perhaps I *am* unavailable. Not just for you, for anyone.'

'If I like someone, I want to see them,' he said. 'And you like me, I know you do! We feel magical together, Sophie . . . we make a good couple.'

She laughed, grabbing a glass of champagne from a passing waiter and quickly sipping from it.

'You flirt with these society women, then come over and tell me I like you?'

He nodded. 'You *do* like me.'

She finished the champagne in a gulp.

'Go back to your society ladies,' she said, fishing in her bag for a cigarette.

He stared intently at her. 'I will if you really want me to. But I don't think you do. I'm serious, Sophie.'

'Yes? Well, maybe I am not ready for anyone so serious,' she said.

She walked away. She had once said that 'Men and Women' was a game and had its own rules. Tonight provided a good illustration of the rules: they were both with older, more powerful people. People who might help them. Yet seeing Ghislaine de Rive's hands on Christopher was somehow worse than seeing a young girl with an older man. And watching Christopher act like an affectionate puppy licking its mistress made her sick.

She found de Kousmine, told him she was tired and wandered out into the night.

Monique waited for Guy at a small hotel a few streets away from Chanel. It was a rather grey area on the other side of the Grands Boulevards where many two- and three-star hotels were available to lovers. They went up to the room separately. The hotel was discreet and posed no problems. She admitted Guy to the room. They did not talk. He did not undress. He simply held her in his arms. When she stole a glance at his face, his eyes were tightly shut.

Eventually she peeled his jacket off him and removed his shoes. His touch, his caresses, blended with hers as if she was echoing him or gazing into a mirror. Whatever he did, she did. His body felt so familiar, surely because she had dreamed of it so often? He said very little. She enjoyed remaining in his arms after they had made love. Perhaps this was the best part? She tried to talk to him, but he seemed so exhausted after work that she was scared to annoy or tire him.

He kissed her goodnight and he left the room first.

She walked home thoughtfully. If she had heard of a woman doing this, she would have called the situation sordid. But tonight hadn't felt sordid. It had felt like visiting a fount of love, as if love was pure spring water and she had been thirsty. She had taken a long sip of this water and felt much better afterwards. Could love be as simple as that? Could she settle for this weekly meeting, passionate and sensual and not at all satisfying her desire to share life with a man? Guy was someone she could think about, dream about, consider the possibility she hated herself for considering – that he might one day leave his wife.

Thirteen

A last-minute rush in Guy's workroom came when eight clients suddenly decided they needed new Chanel suits for delivery before Christmas Eve. It had resulted in panic, and in the frenzy a girl was badly burned on the arm by a scalding iron.

Helping to pack a finished suit into a luxurious, tissue-lined Chanel box, Monique thought about the human pain that went into a simple suit. Not just sweat, tears and often blood, but in this case a bad scalding which would leave a life-long scar. Each suit was swaddled like a baby in white, with plenty of folded pristine white silk tissue placed inside the jacket and to puff out sleeves. More tissue, pleated like a Fortuny gown, filled gaps in the box so that the suit would not roll about and get creased. The lid was placed on the black box and it was tied with white ribbon which repeated 'CHANEL' every fifteen centimetres. Placed in a stiff card bag with cord handles, the suit was driven to each of the eight clients' homes on the afternoon before Christmas.

Monique imagined the client holding up her new jacket to the complimentary cries of friends or family. No one would register that the cost was equal to six months of a seamstress's wages.

Not every Paris couture house had such demanding personal clients. Most houses were already preparing their new spring collections and Christmas was regarded as little more than a nuisance for interrupting this.

*

On the train taking her home to Angers, Monique leaned back to the comforting rhythm, looking forward to being with her sister and mother. She would wear her unworn Chanel suit, carefully packed in her suitcase, on Christmas Day.

Her mother was waiting at the station. They greeted each other, kissed cheeks and walked out of the station as Monique glanced around her. Angers was a provincial little town, she realised with a jolt. It was colder than Paris, and she shivered, wrapping the scarf closer to her throat.

'Dr Martin is joining us for Christmas lunch,' was the first thing her mother said as they walked the few streets to home.

Monique groaned. 'It's not just us?'

'He's a little lonely and he's always made it clear he was interested in you,' her mother began eagerly. 'Such a nice man: this could be your chance.'

'Yes, a nice man,' Monique sighed, 'but not my style and he's too old for me.'

They reached home. Nothing had changed in the house. The old-fashioned, bulky sofas and armchairs and a few reproduction or 'family' pieces of mahogany or heavy dark wood seemed to cling to the walls. The paintings were so dark and dull she did not even register them. The curtains and carpets could use replacing, she noted. It was her childhood home with all the memories and resentments of anyone's childhood home. She knew that she could never live there again.

Caterine clattered down the stairs, throwing herself into her sister's arms and whispering, 'Oh, I've missed you. What is it like to work for Chanel?'

She was prettier than ever. And for her, Monique made a great effort to describe her work, making it sound exciting, cutting out her feelings for Monsieur Guy. She had left a Christmas gift for him on his work-table – a beautiful cashmere scarf from Galleries Lafayette, something he could wear next to his body. Lovely stripes of blue and grey: it would suit him.

In her bedroom, she realised why she had not returned to the house for any time until now. She had not wanted to see her face in her old dressing-table mirror until she was no longer a virgin.

'Make a big effort with your appearance,' her mother reminded her at breakfast the next morning. 'Be attentive to the doctor, sit next to him, talk.'

Monique controlled her irritation.

Her mother was roasting a goose and made a great fuss about the potatoes, which had to be roasted alongside the goose, in its fat, at just the right temperature and for just the right time. There would be a green salad and an hors d'oeuvre of *celeri rémoulade* with *oeuf en gelée*, another speciality of her mother. Monique went out for the baguette, which had to be bought that day, retracing her steps to the *boulangerie* which she had taken so many times in her childhood. It was a cold, clear Christmas Day and the streets were deserted. There were different people selling the bread. Coming back, her nose turned quite red.

At noon, she changed into her Chanel suit. She admired it in the mirror: it never failed to make her feel wonderful.

When she went downstairs, her mother regarded the outfit doubtfully.

'My first real Chanel suit.' Monique said. 'Made for me, *Maman*. Isn't it beautiful?'

'Isn't it a little formal for today?' her mother asked.

'I thought it would be nice to wear it here,' Monique said. 'Where else can I wear it?'

Her mother shrugged. 'Do you go to the kind of places where women wear Chanel?'

Monique shook her head. 'No, but if I cannot wear Chanel on Christmas Day in my own home, where can I wear it?' she exploded.

'The doctor will think you always expect to dress in Chanel,' her mother sighed.

Monique felt sorry for the poor man when he arrived at one o'clock. He was polite, pleasant, with little hair, wire-rimmed spectacles and kind blue eyes. He must have been in his mid-sixties. Glancing at his freckled white hands, she couldn't help imagining them examining rashes on an inflamed skin. Not very romantic compared to Monsieur Guy's strong hands moulding beautiful fabric over a woman's body. She suddenly wished she were back in the workroom, watching those strong capable hands slice into some rich fabric then coax it into submission.

At the end of lunch, her mother ushered out Caterine.

'You two will have things you want to talk about . . .' she said, leaving Monique in the dining room with the doctor.

Monique blushed and the poor man made an effort to ask her about Paris. 'Are you enjoying it?' he asked.

'Oh yes, very much.'

He turned his chair to face her.

'Well, Monique, I know we did not see much of each other but I liked knowing you were here. It sounds silly, I suppose.'

'You are very kind, Monsieur.' She tried to sound formal, not at all encouraging. When he left soon after, professing to have enjoyed himself, Monique heaved a sigh of relief.

She removed the suit, realising she would never wear it again. The expression on her mother's face had made her feel ridiculous in it. She'd had no right to think she could wear a lady's outfit, a couture suit. She returned to the kitchen to help her mother and Caterine.

'That's better,' her mother said, eyeing her grey wool dress. 'You seemed so stiff in that suit.'

'She looked lovely,' Caterine said quickly.

Monique said nothing.

'Didn't Chanel say "a suit cannot wear you"?' her mother asked. '*You* must wear *it*.'

'Yes, she did. Thank you, mother,' Monique said.

'You'll soon be twenty-seven,' her mother reminded her as they worked. 'Don't you *want* to be married? To have children?'

She gave her younger daughter a look which made her leave the kitchen. Monique replaced pots and pans, trying to quell a rising anger.

'Because if you really aren't planning marriage,' her mother continued, 'I'm sure your father would have wanted you to keep me company as I get older.'

Monique turned to face her.

'Perhaps he would have wanted me to fulfil myself by staying in Paris?' she surprised herself by saying.

'I was counting on your coming back,' her mother said.

Monique said nothing, finished clearing up and went upstairs with a new issue of *Vogue*. She wanted to sink into fashion, beautiful fabrics and shapes, to escape the mood of her mother, but she leafed through a few pages without really seeing them. She got up to peer in the dressing-table mirror.

'I have changed,' she assured her reflection.

A knock came on her door. It was Caterine.

'Will you really stay in Paris?'

Monique hugged Caterine, feeling horribly guilty. 'You'll join me one day.'

'When? When *Maman* dies?' Caterine asked. 'She's pinned her hopes on my making some *wonderful* marriage here as soon as I'm old enough. It will sweep her into local society. It's pitiful.'

Monique soothed her sister's soft hair. 'You are still so young and so pretty. Life has truly wonderful things in store for you.'

'You'll be on my side when I try to leave?'

'I'll send the fare. You will find work in Paris. What do you think you'd like to do?'

'I'll think of that when I escape *Maman*. And Monique, you looked beautiful in that suit.'

'Take it.' She reached for the suit on its hanger and handed it to Caterine. 'It will look better on you. Wear it at your next important event.'

'I couldn't, Monique!'

But Caterine could not resist slipping on the jacket and looking in the mirror. The beautiful fresh cream wool looked wonderful against her slightly olive skin.

Monique hardly slept that night. Staying on another day would undo all the good that Paris had done her. She left the next morning. She actually missed the workroom. And Guy.

'New year, new job,' Samantha decided, after seeing in 1969 at Regine's with Klaus. 'I'll ask de Kousmine,' she murmured into the telephone to Jean-Jacques on New Year's Day, still a little hungover at noon. Klaus was asleep. 'I'll be subtle. Any suggestion I make to de Kousmine will be almost subliminal.'

'Oh? Subtle?' Jean-Jacques echoed drily. 'This is something new.'

'I didn't see *you* at Regine's?'

'I was in the Flore at midnight,' Jean-Jacques confessed. 'They turn out all the lights then for one or two minutes. When they went up I found I was groping a black lesbian!' His strangled laugh made it very clear what he thought of that.

'Didn't you say, "Want some sex?"' she asked.

'Samantha! Everyone wants sex on New Year's Eve.'

Klaus seemed ready to loll about her apartment for a few days, but she had to get rid of him before de Kousmine arrived at six o'clock on the second day of the year, the first day he could escape his family.

She opened the door to him and heard herself scream: 'Get me a job in your house, godammit! It's the easiest thing in the world for you to do. Tell them I'm a great publicist.'

So much for subliminal, she thought.

'Happy New Year, Samantha,' he said, sitting down heavily in her only armchair and handing her a little Chanel shopping bag. 'I am not sure that your style goes with Mademoiselle Chanel's style.'

She ripped open the bag and withdrew a jewelled bangle. 'Oh, this is cute. Thanks. What *is* my style?' she demanded.

'American,' he stated. 'And Chanel is very French. You use naked men in your advertisements. Chanel could never do that.'

'So, I'll put tuxedos on them,' she shrugged. 'I'll adapt to Chanel's style. Just get me in or, so help me God, I'll have my mid-life crisis a couple of decades early.' She tugged on his moustache. 'I will not leave Paris defeated. I have to find employment. Chanel would do nicely. You could easily slip me in there.'

'No, Samantha darling . . .' He stroked her hair. 'You expect to be *Chef de Publicité*? Only Mademoiselle herself can slip you into that.'

'So introduce me to her and I'll do the rest.'

De Kousmine frowned. 'I cannot picture you and Mademoiselle Chanel discussing fashion. Anyway, she already has a *chef de publicité*,' he pronounced.

'What does *she* do all day? Sit on her ass? I *work* for my living. I nag people. I work magic. I get *coverage!*'

She stopped, staring at him in frustration. In some ways, he reminded her of her father, but she could always nag her father until he agreed with her. Now she saw that he was not going to help, she would have to advance herself.

'Work your wonderful Samantha magic on me,' de Kousmine suggested, lying back.

He left soon after. Samantha sank onto a couch and dialled Jean-Jacques' number.

'I'll have to go over his head,' she explained into the phone.

'How?' he asked, always eager for gossip.

'I'll dine at the Ritz. What do I have to lose? At least I'll eat well. And I may meet Mademoiselle Chanel, the woman I came to Paris to meet.'

Jean-Jacques made an encouraging growl.

'Jean-Jacques, *mon cheri* . . .' she cooed. '*You* know people who know Chanel? Which night does she eats alone?'

'From what I hear, most nights.'

'I'll dine there on a night I know Mademoiselle is alone!'

'But Samantha, tell me why, with so many other houses to work for, must it be Chanel?'

'Because I'm a Chanel freak!' she sighed. 'A Chanel-junkie! In my dreams, I run a chapter of Chanel Anonymous to cure women of their addiction! I've got to work for her. I have *always* had this dream. It's time I lived it.'

The seduction was underway. After yet another successful Sunday *salon*, naked under lavender-scented Porthault linen in Ghislaine's huge bed, Christopher rose to the next level in his conquest of Paris.

It was midnight. The guests had left, Bertrand de Rives was out of town, and staff had silently tidied the large room.

In an exquisite silk kimono, Ghislaine wafted out of the bathroom and came over to the bed.

'I've been wanting this since I met you that day in the Delange *cabine*!' she told him.

There was something thrilling about a woman showing such interest in him. She desired him and that had always excited him. She touched his lips lightly and he stretched as she traced her finger all the way down his chest.

She slowly drew down the sheet. 'The clue to your becoming the most successful couturier in Paris . . .' she uncovered his excitement, her raised eyebrows crowning a 'not bad' expression, 'is here, in one word!'

'Cock?' he asked.

She shook her head. '*Heterosexual.* You are, aren't you?'

'What do you think?' he countered.

'All the signs are there,' she laughed.

This was a far cry from his seduction scene with Sophie. Here, *he* felt like the love object and thus more in control. 'Making love' took on a whole new aspect: neither gooey nor romantic, this was more as if Ghislaine had decided to cook a certain dish which, no matter how long it took, must be perfect.

She took him in hand: he flexed his muscle.

'This is what I like, Christopher . . .' she began.

She gave a quick rundown of her preferences: he couldn't help thinking of Samantha asking for endives instead of lettuce, or a *Croque Monsieur* without cheese, except that Ghislaine's 'substitutes' applied to the sexual act. A hard touch there, a soft touch here, a kiss, a bite. Where to touch, how long to touch, how hard to touch. Once glued together, she directed his movements . . . The act of love with Ghislaine was certainly a learning experience. She left nothing to chance. Hers was the most pampered body, lean and taut, and so obviously massaged and annointed with expensive creams each day.

He nodded as she ordered up her sex, wanting to say, 'A good choice, Madame.'

Ghislaine's quick course in 'How to please a woman . . .' would prove the foundation-course for his sex-life.

The first lesson reached its climax when Ghislaine deemed it the right moment.

'Don't stop! Don't stop! Don't stop!' she cried and then, as elegantly as if sipping a fine wine, she arched her back, shut her eyes tight and sighed. Relaxed and satisfied on her fresh linen, she traced his profile with her finger.

'A *young* Englishman . . .' she purred. 'Don't worry, *cher ami*, I am not about to fall in love with you.'

'Why not?'

She pulled a funny face. 'It is too banal.'

'What if I made you?' he threatened.

'How would you do that, my darling?' she asked, lighting a cigarette.

'Send you flowers, love letters, stuff like that . . .'

'A little too sweet for me, Christopher.' She exhaled smoke. 'But I could enjoy teaching you how to drive the women of Paris quite wild. Make you the most sought-after man in town . . .'

'Why would you do that?' he asked.

'It would amuse me . . .' she shrugged. 'A little revenge for my experiences with couturiers. Some actually dislike women. How dare they dress people they dislike!'

She relaxed back on her huge square pillow, glancing at him.

'It's a luxury to have a designer who actually *enjoys* touching a woman's body.'

He placed his hands on either side of her ribcage and she wriggled with enjoyment.

'I'm already planning new, outrageous dresses for you,' he said.

She gurgled. 'Fittings will be so delicious!'

'How many times will you compare me to a plate of food?' he asked.

'Oh, *why* did you say that?' She jumped from the bed and ran towards the kitchen, pulling on the kimono and throwing him a white bathrobe. 'I'm always ravenous after a good fitting.'

The *après-sex* snack – an omelette, crusty baguette, ripe Brie and endives sprinkled with walnuts and blue cheese – was soon ready.

'That's the same expression I saw on your face twenty minutes ago . . .' he laughed as she chewed with her eyes closed in a heavenly expression.

'Yes . . .' she allowed, sipping wine. 'Good food *is* a little like good sex.'

'You feel a bit sick after it?' he guessed.

'Oh God, you English!' she cried. 'No, I don't mean that at all. I mean that it should be beautifully prepared, then slowly savoured.'

He nodded, feeling terribly gauche and somewhat out of his depth.

'And your husband doesn't get jealous?' he asked.

Ghislaine shrugged. 'I want him to like you. He can make my dream of having my own couture house come true. With you as designer, of course! And I would insist on being your muse.'

Christopher leaned back in his chair. 'What's for afters?' he asked cheerfully.

'*Afters*?' Ghislaine frowned.

'The sweet. The pastry?'

'Oh.' She laughed. 'Well, sometimes we French end on cheese or something savoury. You prefer sweet?'

'If you have something. A chocolate biscuit will do . . .'

'There must be something more interesting than a chocolate biscuit.'

She disappeared into the pantry for a few moments. He imagined she was preparing something delicious. When she came out she was doubled up.

'Are you all right?' he eyed her, alarmed.

'Oh yes, follow me . . . we'll have something sweet in my bedroom . . .'

He followed her, frowning.

On her bed she lay back, threw off her robe and presented herself to him with a giggle.

'What's this?' he cried, staring at her.

'*Afters!*' she announced, bursting into laughter. 'Don't worry, it's only cocoa powder and icing sugar!' The penny dropped and he licked it off to her little cries and giggles. It was almost too sweet for him, but more exciting than a chocolate biscuit.

'Have you ever done this before?' she asked.

'I've dreamed of doing it,' he gasped.

'If you ever find you are not quite up to the task,' she told him, arching her back, 'highly unlikely, I'm sure,' she took him in her hand, 'you can always give a woman pleasure with a different organ . . .'

'The tongue?'

'Yes. Look at me. Stick out just the tip. Now make it very hard by curving it. Now try to insert just the tip.'

He followed her instructions and she cried out 'Yes!', her eyes shut tightly. 'Keep doing it. Whatever you do don't stop. Oh . . . oh!!! Oh! Oh!'

She clutched him so tightly to her, he could hardly breathe. There was no doubt she thought him a quick pupil.

He walked home from Ghislaine's deep in thought, nursing a sore tongue and sore lips. He had heard of singing for your supper, but licking for your supper took it to a new level.

Klaus was studying contact-prints through a magnifier as he came in. He looked up.

'What happened to you?' he asked.

'Sex on very posh sheets,' Christopher told him. 'Very enjoyable.'

'What's wrong with your voice?' Klaus held the magnifier to Christopher's mouth. 'Your lips are swollen!'

'She made me lick her!'

Klaus put down the magnifier. 'A woman like that will eat you up then spit you out,' he said.

'Well, as long as she doesn't spit me out before backing my own house. She said her husband might do that.'

'You should be happy?' Klaus poured them each a glass of wine.

'Would she really launch my own house, Klaus? *Could* she? Or am I doomed to conducting sexy fittings in mirrored *cabines*?'

Klaus sipped his wine. 'And you are the boy who said there was no such thing as sleeping your way to the top?'

'The second collection makes or breaks you,' Ghislaine warned him the following Sunday. 'After an acclaimed first collection, you must show an even better second collection to consolidate your reputation.'

Christopher nodded. They were on rumpled sheets at the end of a love-making session. Ghislaine had served up a four-course sexual banquet beginning with *amuse-bouches* of tender kisses, hors d'oeuvres of touches and embraces, then a hot *entrée* (the act of love), followed by *tarte aux citron* – an acid critique of his career.

'The first collection displays exciting new talent. The second shows you can do *wearable* clothes, which this time *must* include some breathtaking ball-gowns.'

'Oh God, ball-gowns,' Christopher groaned. 'The women I design for don't attend balls.'

'Oh, but we do!' she said. 'We are forced to for our husbands' sakes.' She lit a cigarette and puffed furiously on it. '*Learn* about French women if you wish to dress them. Learn what they do!'

He watched her, sighing. 'I am trying, Ghislaine . . .' he began.

'Expensive, embroidered ball-gowns are part of a woman's wardrobe and a profitable part of a house's wares,' she said.

'*Embroidered?*' Christopher groaned.

'Yes, but don't say it like that. Embroidery does not have to be flowers or birds! It can be something wildly modern like political slogans or graffiti. Imagine a fabulous gown with "Down With Everything" beautifully appliquéd across the skirt? So rebellious, so protest, so flower power!'

Christopher nodded. Ghislaine could always put a new slant on something and make it modern, exciting.

Spring collections were presented in January with enormous fanfare to the press and to buyers. Manufacturers, store directors, buyers, journalists, photographers, stylists and models flooded into the city and booked the best suites at the best hotels, the Scribe, George V and the Ritz. Tables at restaurants like Tour de l'Argent and Maxim's were reserved months in advance. Powerful buyers from stores like Saks, Ohrbach's and B. Altman brought useful dollars into the French economy.

Buyers paid five thousand dollars to see a collection. This ensured that they bought one *toile* and one paper pattern to copy hopefully by the thousand, in stores across America. Sometimes they even used the original French fabric for 'line-for-line' copies: near-couture for a fraction of the Paris price.

You could say that collection time in Paris was a festival of glamour and fashion. But if you worked in the couture you felt that Paris became an insane asylum.

The ladies of the fashion press were mostly treated as nuisances by the fashion houses who enjoyed refusing entry to the less important publications. When they did, there was lots of mascara running pathetically down cheeks. Nothing was more humiliating than being denied entry into a house to view a collection.

Vogue and *Harper's Bazaar* editors were fawned over, their names beautifully handwritten on labels tied to the backs of front-row gilt chairs. The humbler journalists from lesser magazines were pushed to the back of the smaller rooms and craned to catch glimpses of the models flashing by.

At this time, La Coupole, in Montparnasse, became the fashion world's meeting-place.

'If you don't make an appearance here at least twice an evening, you are not officially in Paris,' Samantha told Christopher and Klaus as they dined in the buzzing restaurant on the Sunday evening before Collection Week.

The famous had one thing in common, they often arrived

after midnight. Anouk Aimeé was spotted at a terrace table, brushing her hair furiously as her handsome young companion read a newspaper. World-famous models ran in for a lettuce leaf and bottle of water before hurrying out for their next booking. Photographers like Richard Avedon or David Bailey came to sample local atmosphere then rush back to their white-papered studios.

The narrow aisles between La Coupole's tables turned into runways for models as they table-hopped, ran to the cloakroom or telephone-kiosk if paged by La Coupole's uniformed 'bell-boy'.

'To make sure your name is heard, you get your mother to page you every hour throughout the evening,' Samantha said, watching the models running around.

Telescoped into a week, the collections were fuelled by black coffee and wine. By the time a few hundred American buyers and press collapsed onto first-class flights back to New York, the buyers had planned their own fall collections of Paris copies, and *Vogue* or *Harper's Bazaar* had plotted their thick 'collection issues' for September and March.

Christopher began fitting *toiles* for the new collection. These garments – made from muslin to save ruining expensive fabric – were ripped apart, changed and sometimes discarded. Three workrooms, each with twelve girls, worked to translate Christopher's designs from sketches to three-dimensional clothes.

With her typical charm, Chantal Delange reminded him that his future depended on this collection.

'Deliver the goods, Christopher, or this will be your last Delange collection.'

Chantal had become the guiding force in the Delange house, mostly because of the others' indifference. She was the one who had offered Christopher his job in the first place, and now the other members of the family left things to her, happy to receive their share of the perfume profits. Samantha's idea that the clothes were only there to sell the perfume had filtered down to them and they now left the design direction to Chantal.

'Her idea of fashion is very different to mine,' Christopher sighed to Klaus.

'Use that famous Christopher charm!' he advised.

He laughed. 'Chantal Delange is the one woman resistant to charm. I never got through to her and I never will. I look into her eyes and see only dollar-signs. If you don't look back with equal amounts of dollar-signs, she loses interest.'

Fourteen

For her new workroom, Monique tried to pick serious crafts-women, often from outside Paris, girls who loved their work and excelled at it. She felt she could judge a girl immediately.

Her workroom at the top of a neighbouring building had her own personality stamped on it. Not in the decor: she had no say in that beyond getting the room whitewashed and the floor polished. But the routine, the way the work was handed out, and, above all, the way girls were treated with appreciation and respect, made work a lot more enjoyable, she knew. And the work *better*. As for the clients, she now knew very well how to please them.

A woman investing thousands of francs in an outfit expected perfection: it was the *Chef d'Atelier*'s job to ensure that she got it. When neurotic clients changed their minds about a garment at the first fitting, it was up to the fitter to make calming murmurs or cries of admiration. She must save the suit by flattering the client and telling her how slim, how tall, how beautiful she looked.

Guy had appreciated this aspect of her. As they had climbed the back stairs to the workroom, he used to chuckle, 'You handled her well, Monique. You gave no sign at all that you thought she was a stupid old lady!'

She would laugh and say, 'Oh, she is not stupid, Guy. But sometimes these women have more money and time than they know what to do with.'

Christopher wanted his second collection to be different in every respect to anything shown in Paris. No rock music, no bridal gown, no gloves, no hats. But he was always aware of Chantal Delange watching disapprovingly from the sidelines. She was only in her late thirties, he guessed, married with two small daughters, and yet she seemed to be from a completely different generation.

The more disapproving her expression, the more he wanted to shock her. Getting rid of gloves and hats wasn't enough . . . he would ban interlining, canvas, stiffeners, whale-bones, anything that interrupted the sensual flow of fabric across a body.

The cutters and tailors thought him quite mad.

'If you get rid of interlining . . .' an older tailor cried, 'how does the collar stand up?'

'That's just the point. I want it to just flop!'

'*Flop?*' the tailor repeated, rolling his eyes.

'Yes,' Christopher nodded. 'Less constructed, less constricted clothes; less lining, less interlining, no stiff canvas, no stiffness at all.'

'The French are experts at tongue-clicking,' he complained to Klaus. 'They try to make me feel too extravagant, too daring, too cocky, too English, too different, too close to being fired. But the more threatened I feel, the more determined I become.'

Klaus nodded. 'I too wish to simplify things. I try to rid photography of bulky lighting, complicated backgrounds, stiff posed models . . . I want to make natural, unposed, relaxed pictures.'

Delange's new collection was shown with as much fanfare as their new publicity director could whip up. It wasn't a lot. The management had been obliged to find a replacement for Samantha. A tiny, freckled, red-haired girl named Arianne Brunner, she exuded arrogance but did not form any bond with Christopher. He missed Samantha's moral support.

Fifteen minutes before the showing, the fashion journalists trooped in. Christopher watched them fighting for their seats.

They sat there, looking fiercely critical before the collection had even begun. They were ready to sentence the victim. And of what was he being accused? Trying to make women look more modern?

Christopher had been up working so many late nights, changing and ripping apart his dresses and suits. The result of all that creativity was to be judged by a *salon* of glassy-eyed women, tired and dizzy from scrutinising too many dresses. These women would decide whether Christopher Hutchins was a designer to be taken seriously.

Ghislaine de Rives wore her favourite Hutchins dress as she took her front-row seat. It was rare for a private client to be seated front-row on press day, but the Delange *direction* knew they owed their success to her and this was their way of repaying her. She leaned across two assistants to kiss Diana Vreeland, missing the heavily rouged cheek by a good six inches. This was not an air-kiss, more an outer-space kiss. They assured each other this collection would be 'marvellous'.

Christopher wished Samantha were there. He wished Sophie was modelling his clothes. He wished – but there was no time for more wishing, the showing began and Christopher sensed a good reception. His loose, draped, subtly clinging clothes were sexy and classy, the fashionistas glanced at each other's reactions to see if they agreed. And different! There were tiny bursts of applause for certain dresses. A group of trouser-suits made in reversible wools, more feminine and softer than the usual ones, got some scribbled notes and applause.

Diana Vreeland reached out to touch the fabric of one – considered an incredible compliment. She noted down a few numbers. The more clothes photographed for American *Vogue*, the better. Money in the bank, for if American *Vogue* chose a dress, a manufacturer would be sure to buy the pattern to manufacture it. An editorial page in *Vogue* guaranteed it would sell.

He watched the house's *vendeuses*. These women, much as he disliked them, knew whether clothes were saleable. He had always felt their critical faces were a curse. They hated anything new or too jarring. No one watched their faces more closely than Chantal Delange. She didn't care if Mrs Vreeland thought a particular dress was amusing to photograph. It was the *vendeuses* who signalled the house's future: they alone knew which models would *sell*. If they noted down the number it meant they had a client in mind for it. And to his horror, Christopher realised that no *vendeuse* was scribbling. He should have bribed a few to scribble, even if it were just doodles, to keep Chantal happy. Lesson number five hundred and twenty-two: don't forget to bribe the *vendeuses*.

The 'bride' wore a pin-striped suit with a white gauzy veil – Christopher's wry comment on career-women getting married as if between business meetings.

There was luke-warm applause. Christopher resisted taking a bow, despite Arianne's prod. The mannequins popped the cork of a champagne magnum: everyone else made for the exit. Chantal Delange aimed a deadly look. Would anyone buy these clothes? *Wear* them? Were they too original? Too different to everything in Paris that season? Ghislaine also gave him looks to kill, furious that he had not taken a bow.

Nevertheless, she despatched all her friends to view the collection in the following days and they duly placed their orders. Christopher had been reprieved, for one more season at least.

When spring finally arrived it was with a sense of déjà vu, as they had already designed for it and lived through it in January.

'Madame Antoine has invited me for lunch on Sunday . . .' Sophie told Ines one April Saturday morning. They were in her apartment, Sophie pinning a new dress on her old friend.

'And you refused?' Ines asked.

Sophie nodded, her mouth full of pins. She removed them. 'But perhaps I *should* make friends with them, Ines? I need them, in some ways, if only to find out who my real parents were . . .'

'They won't tell you!'

Sophie replaced the pins in a box and sat on the bed.

'If I apologised,' she whispered, 'would you think me weak?'

Ines considered her. 'If they invite you for Sunday lunch, they'll be ready to forgive you, no?'

Sophie sat back on her heels and lit a cigarette. She wore faded jeans and a huge baggy man's sweater, with several holes. She blew out a very discontented breath of smoke.

'Sophie, will you ever be happy?' Ines sighed.

Sophie shrugged, taking a puff.

'Happiness is only a concept, Ines. At least I learned that in my Sorbonne philosophy class. Real life is more complex. There is something I've never asked you,' she began. 'How do you know when you are in love with someone?'

'Oh God, how banal! With whom? Not that beast de Kousmine?'

'No, it's Christopher. The last time I saw him was months ago at Ghislaine de Rives' salon. He is her toy. I felt jealous when I saw them together. Why would I feel jealous?'

'Because you care about him, why else?'

'I suppose so. Anyway, I shall not do anything about it. My problem with my family is more important . . . Should I call them? Should I go to their lunch?'

Ines frowned, thinking hard. Suddenly, her eyes opened wide.

'Solve both problems!' she said. 'Call the Antoines and ask if you can bring Christopher with you? Is he presentable?'

'Very.'

'Introduce him. They'll be impressed. He'll be impressed. Everyone will be happy. Except you, of course.'

Sophie stared at her friend for a long moment.

'Not a bad idea,' she allowed. 'And I'll borrow a Chanel suit from the workroom to wear for lunch. That'll surprise them!'

Over the next few days, Sophie made sure she was the first in the workroom, going through the rail of muslin-shrouded suits awaiting fittings before anyone arrived. Sometimes a client was travelling for weeks and the suit just hung there. A cream shantung suit seemed to be her size. She tried on the jacket, keeping an eye on the door. It fitted perfectly: she folded it carefully into a large shopping-bag she had brought with her that day. No one would notice.

Christopher's love-lessons with Ghislaine continued.

'I am a diligent pupil,' he told Klaus.

'In the art of love?'

Christopher made a face. 'I'll never quite see sex as a series of courses in a gourmet meal. But Ghislaine truly loves fashion and she is the only client who understands my clothes.'

Klaus shrugged. 'Parisians are a pragmatic race, but a little cold, no? Your friend Samantha is much warmer. But she can be strange, too. She changes the ingredients in every dish she orders, even at La Coupole! This is such an American thing to do, Chris.'

Half a dozen society ladies had followed Ghislaine to Delange and Christopher's reputation had begun to take off. They all demanded personal fittings from the designer. He wasn't sure how much Ghislaine had told them but there was always a definite atmosphere of expectation in the fitting *cabine*, and it was not just for the clothes. No one was as flirtatious as Ghislaine. One rather repressed lady threw her head back and kept her eyes tightly shut as Christopher fitted her, mouth pursed. Others daringly hugged him or kissed him as he fitted them, but he was learning to walk the fine line of being friendly without being overtly sexual. He found ways of wriggling out of difficult situations.

As in any capital city, circles of friends sometimes overlapped each other: as they pulled in their friends, it amounted to a growing number of clients.

'You now have a following,' Ghislaine announced triumphantly one Sunday evening. 'Do anything more than air-kiss any of these women and I will kill you!'

She went off into peals of laughter after her threats, but he always felt a slight undercurrent.

'Christopher, things are a little difficult with my family . . .' Sophie began. She always managed to surprise him. Just when he had given up any hope of hearing from her, she suddenly called. It was late at night.

'I'm all ears, Sophie,' he said.

'You know I left home to live alone? It insulted them. But now I'm attempting a kind of *rapprochement*,' she went on. 'They've invited me for Sunday family lunch. You will be my escort this Sunday, maybe?'

'I'd love to.'

It was more than he had dared hope for. He was so happy to be with her, he would have accompanied her to meet General de Gaulle.

They had dinner at La Coupole on Saturday night. They shared a bottle of wine and in her white knitted clinging top and faded jeans, she attracted a lot of looks. Her defenses were down that evening, and she allowed him to touch her knees under the table, and now and then to nuzzle her neck.

They were the perfect lovers and after a shared dessert of ice-cream drizzled with blackcurrant liqueur, they wandered out to the taxi-rank and he gave the driver her address.

'Come with me,' she whispered huskily.

She liked to catch him off-guard.

When they reached her flat, she disappeared to make them two coffees. She came back with the coffee on a tray, naked.

He threw a magazine aside. 'Wow!' he said.

She was just breathtakingly sexy, he thought. Her pert little bottom was a sexy turn-on, and when she'd carefully placed the tray on a table, she sat in his lap, her naked body seeming even sexier against his jeans and shirt.

They kissed so gently and so lovingly, and she gave a little moan as he curved his hand under her and gently stroked her. What a difference it made when sex had this extra element of love!

An entire night of love as delicious as their first time except that now he knew a little more about the art of love. He could wait for her pleasure to begin before he indulged his own. He could prolong her pleasure to last longer than a few moments. And he was getting rather good at preparing a dessert of cocoa powder and sugar, amazing Sophie with his skills.

'I wonder how you became such a good lover?' she asked in mock innocence.

Next morning, after much time preparing in her bedroom as Christopher lolled on the sofa playing with Dog, she emerged wearing the Chanel suit. The contrast of her red hair against the cream shantung tailored jacket was striking. It changed not only his image of Sophie, but his view of fashion. For the Chanel suit looked just right. It always did, it always would, blotting out all other fashions, as if no other way of dressing existed. Sophie refused to consider matching hat or accessories but added her own black tote-bag and higher heeled shoes.

'Where did you get it?' he asked.

'I borrowed it. I'm seriously thinking of becoming a model. Months ago Mademoiselle suggested it.'

He studied her as she guyed walking a catwalk, striking poses and turning.

'Wouldn't you get awfully bored standing there having garments pinned on you?' he asked.

Sophie pouted. 'The pay's better than a *stagière*'s. And I wouldn't remain a model for ever. When I finally become a designer, the experience might even help? I'd watch and note everything the tailors do. I won't just stare into space like the other models.'

'Why did Mademoiselle Chanel suggest this to you?'

She struck another pose, shrugged and lit a cigarette, taking a long sultry drag, regarding him through narrowed eyes.

'She likes the way I wear her clothes. She made me try on her jacket.'

'And why did you leave home?' Christopher asked her.

She stopped posing, shooting him a serious look.

'I sold a very valuable necklace my father had given me,' she told him. 'He was so angry he told me I was adopted. It was a shock to learn so brusquely. It changed everything, of course.' She ran over and knelt at his feet, staring into his eyes pleadingly. 'If this lunch achieves a reconciliation, it might help me find out who my parents really were.'

He watched her as she spoke, thinking how beautiful she became when she spoke passionately about something.

'You're so complicated.' He shook his head. 'Why can't you just live your life, without being so tormented about everything?'

She got to her feet with a little laugh. 'That's easy to say when you know who your parents are,' she said. 'This is like living through an earthquake. The ground beneath you moves and shakes. You don't know where you are or who you are! From what you told me of your life, you had the cosiest, most secure upbringing.'

He nodded, watching her.

'It will make things so much easier for me if you are there, Christopher,' she said. 'I couldn't do this without you. Now, let me look at you,' she commanded.

He stood to show off his well-pressed grey flannel trousers and navy blazer found in St Michel. There were two slits at the back and it was double-breasted, buttoned tightly to his lean frame.

She scrutinised him, then nodded, satisfied.

'She likes people to be punctual,' Sophie said. 'Let's go! Right now, before I change my mind.'

Fifteen

'Sophie! Christopher! How pleased I am to meet you.' Madame Antoine opened the door to them herself, wearing a grey fitted dress, a white cardigan draped over her shoulders, her concession to Sunday.

'I hear you're dressing Ghislaine de Rives?' she said, shaking Christopher's hand. 'She is a very dear friend of mine . . .'

Society ladies had the charm of making you feel so welcome, he thought. He shook the white hand tipped with scarlet fingernails, deciding not to kiss it. She hugged Sophie, holding her at arm's length to study her suit.

'Suspiciously like the real thing,' she said with a frown. 'Borrowed?'

'Stolen!' Sophie said.

Madame Antoine's silvery peal of laughter sounded unamused.

Laurent Antoine arrived in the hall, greeting them with his easy bonhomie. He kissed Sophie on both cheeks and gave Christopher a firm handshake.

Christopher took a deep, relieved breath: they were going to pretend that everything was quite normal. But he noticed that Sophie was not normal. As she stepped over the threshold of the house, it was as if an evil fairy had waved a magic wand, turning her into the sort of person he would not be attracted to. Gushing, laughing too loudly, making pointed remarks, she was doing a parody of a society lady. He wanted to shake her and tell her to be herself.

Perfectly iced champagne was served in the *salon*. As she handed Sophie a glass, Madame Antoine asked, 'How do you find Mademoiselle these days?'

Sophie took a swallow of wine. 'Lonely,' she said. 'And rather sad. Is it possible that the richest, most successful woman in Paris feels sorry for herself?'

'Well, she *is* lonely.' Madame Antoine nodded. 'She's lost most of her good friends. Most women of her age have . . .' She turned to Christopher. 'I invite her here, of course. She was invited today. But she's wretched on Sundays because she cannot work. Ripping clothes apart, that's what keeps her going. She doesn't go out much. It is so much easier for her to go downstairs to the Ritz restaurant and order what she wants . . .' she shrugged. 'For her, the Ritz is an exclusive retirement residence. Except she has definitely not retired.'

Turning back to Sophie, she asked: 'Does she see you often?'

Sophie began to answer when her sisters, Isabelle and Francine, arrived and fell on her with hugs and kisses. They very charmingly said 'How do you do?' to Christopher. They were the usual well-brought-up Parisian girls in their Westaway cashmere sweaters and kilts with big safety pins worn on the hip.

They stared at Sophie's suit in awe. 'That is so grown up,' Francine exclaimed. 'Is it yours?

'I borrowed it,' Sophie said.

And this time, Madame Antoine gave a strangled sound of mirth, adding, 'Mind you give it back.'

Other guests arrived, all middle-aged and rather formal. Madame Antoine bent towards Christopher. 'There was no time to invite amusing young people for you . . . please excuse us. You'll have to make do with my daughters.'

During lunch, Madame Antoine suddenly announced, 'I lunched with Audrey Hepburn!'

There were approving, interested murmurs.

'We're on the same international charity committee,' she

explained. 'She is absolutely impeccable. Head-to-toe Givenchy, of course.'

'And you'd prefer head-to-toe Chanel?' Monsieur Antoine teased her. 'Did you get anywhere?'

Madame Antoine shook her head. 'I tried, of course. But she feels Chanel is almost a uniform for many women . . .' She treated each of them to an expression of great surprise, as though such a statement was sacrilege. 'In Givenchy, she feels a little different. I couldn't change her mind. I offered to lend her a suit. It was very charmingly refused.'

Christopher frowned.

'Perhaps Audrey Hepburn is right,' he blurted out. All faces turned to him. He cleared his throat. 'When I saw Sophie in her Chanel suit this morning, I got the feeling that it was the "only" way to dress,' he told the table. 'Is that what is meant by a "uniform"?'

Madame Antoine gave him a penetrating gaze. 'If so, it's a very beautiful uniform.'

'You are so excited by celebrities, my darling,' Laurent Antoine teased.

'Mademoiselle has turned down many, when she thought they had the wrong "image".'

After lunch and a lot more gossip, Sophie tapped her spoon against her glass for silence. All heads turned towards her.

'I would like to introduce you to the newest Chanel model,' she announced to the table.

She got to her feet and struck a pose. Everyone applauded. Madame Antoine exchanged a sharp look with Christopher.

'I thought you intended to be a *couturière*?' she asked Sophie.

'I can learn a lot by being a model,' Sophie said.

'Learn what? How to stand still?' Madame Antoine asked with a disapproving gurgle.

After lunch, Madame Antoine took Christopher aside with the excuse of showing him her English roses. In the small garden behind the house, she kept a calm, pleasant expression on her face in case anyone was watching.

'This is utter madness!' she exploded. 'A model? Whose idea was this?'

'Mademoiselle's, I think,' he replied. 'Don't worry, Sophie will tire of modelling. Being fitted for hours is not very interesting work.'

She regarded him gravely.

'I was apprehensive about meeting you, I must confess.' She smiled. 'But now that I have, I can't help feeling that Sophie has fallen into the right hands. *Has* she . . . er, fallen into your hands?'

He nodded. 'I adore her. I want her to be happy . . .'

She raised her eyebrows. 'Will *modelling* make her happy? Chanel models do have a certain cachet. The favourites are wined and dined at the Ritz. They can become celebrities but . . . keep an eye on her, Christopher. It would be fatal for Sophie to become a celebrity. She needs a lot of calm attention and care.'

'I thought you threw her out?' he replied cheekily.

He saw immediately he had overstepped the mark.

'You were misinformed,' she said, her gaze turning icy. 'She left home of her own accord. She had done something which made us very angry. Perhaps it wasn't the best way to learn she is adopted. But I still care very much about her and she is still our daughter.'

'I will do my best for her, Madame,' he promised. 'I love her, too. I have this absurd idea that she is the only girl for me.'

'Really?' she asked. 'And where does Ghislaine de Rives stand in all this?'

He held her clear blue gaze without flinching.

'She loves my clothes, Madame Antoine.'

She shot him a sharp look. 'Just your clothes? Parisians love gossip, you realise? I have no interest in your private life but I don't want Sophie to get hurt. She has been hurt enough in her young life and I don't want her hurt any more.'

They were slowly walking back to the drawing room when he asked, 'How was she hurt, Madame?'

She shot him a look. 'I can only say that something in her past makes her more vulnerable than most girls her age. She needs a little extra care, that's all.'

He stared into her sincere, moral, azure gaze, so searching that it made him feel a little ashamed.

By the time coffee was served in the *salon*, Sophie longed to leave. A meaningful glance from Madame Antoine reminded her of some unfinished business.

Laurent Antoine stood, holding his *demi-tasse*. 'Please excuse us,' he said to his guests. He motioned to Sophie, who stood and followed him to his library.

He closed the door and set the coffee carefully on his desk, glancing at her.

'You look very beautiful today, Sophie,' he said. 'I'm glad you came. And your English friend seems like a very decent young man.'

Sophie stared at him. She took a deep breath then said, '*Papa*, I'm sorry about the necklace. I apologise. I may call you *Papa*? It would feel so strange to say "Monsieur Antoine".'

'Of *course* you must call me *Papa*,' he replied. 'I am your legal father. We adopted you.'

He remained looking quizzically at her but he did not hug her as she'd half-expected.

'Am I forgiven?' she asked.

'Well . . . forgiveness must be earned, Sophie,' he said. 'I'm disappointed that you left the Sorbonne. I had to pull a few strings to get you in there, you know.'

'Because I was not Sorbonne material,' she reminded him. 'It is wonderful that Francine and Isabelle wish to be lawyers but I have other genes in me. And you should tell me what those genes are, *Papa*. I have a right to know who my parents were.'

He gazed at her, soberly. 'We don't know.'

'*Papa*, you're such a bad liar. Why won't you tell me?'

He looked slightly helpless. He did not answer. Instead he stood and said, 'Continue to visit us, Sophie. In time, hopefully, we will get back to our old ways.'

When she rejoined Christopher, she dug him in the ribs and muttered, 'Get me out of here.'

They made their excuses and said goodbye. The moment they were out of the house, Sophie tore off her jacket, unpinned her hair, and ran towards the nearby park. There she laughed, skipped, lit a cigarette and puffed on it. Christopher watched her with mixed feelings.

'You didn't tell me you'd decided to be a model,' he said, sitting on a bench.

'I decided as the first course was served. I suddenly realised I am so bored in that workroom, I need a change.' She gave a few more skips, taking hungry puffs on her cigarette. 'I'm so happy that lunch is over. That house suffocates me. It always did.'

'But your family seem really charming,' he told her.

'You *enjoyed* the lunch?' She widened her eyes.

He looked at her seriously. 'It's the first time I've seen women actually *wearing* couture clothing. I saw how clothes adjust to the occasion, how the details above the waist – the neckline, the bodice, the lapels, become more important because that's what you see above a dining table.'

She shook her head, making a tutting noise.

'After lunch, in the *salon*, I saw how women pluck at their skirts to cover their knees,' he went on. 'Unless she has wonderful legs, a woman can feel quite uncomfortable in a short skirt. Trousers could be the solution?'

Sophie sighed. 'You saw that lunch in fashion terms,' she said sadly. She sat next to him and lit a fresh cigarette, blowing out an exasperated breath. 'I see it as a glimpse into a narrow privileged strata of society,' she said. 'You don't see why I had to escape?'

'I see I want to catch you in my arms and protect you,' he told her. 'Although I'm not sure from what.'

Her mood changed. She hugged him, her guard down for a moment.

'Yes, protect me, please, Christopher. From life,' she pleaded. 'And thank you for coming with me today.' She took his arm. 'I couldn't have done it without you.'

When all her defences were down, as then, she was the most adorable person he had known.

'When you meet a girl's parents . . .' Christopher mused to Samantha on the following Monday. 'It puts things on a more serious level. I should really break with Ghislaine.'

'But you need her goodwill, Christopher.'

'You think she wouldn't be half so eager to help me if I stopped sleeping with her?'

'Christopher, *c'est Paris*,' Samantha said patiently. 'Don't kid yourself.'

'I'll keep our date tonight,' he decided.

'Balenciaga is closing his house,' Mademoiselle said in a dead voice. 'He says the couture is over. He is only seventy-three. Surely he had ten good years left in him?'

Madame Antoine watched the blue smoke from Mademoiselle's cigarette curl towards the ceiling. The two women sat on the honey-coloured suede sofa in the private *salon* upstairs. They were old friends who could almost read each other's minds.

'*Is* it over?' Madame Antoine asked softly.

'If Balenciaga closes, there is only me,' Chanel shot her a sideways glance. 'I feel terrible.'

'But Yves Saint Laurent is doing very well. *He* is couture, surely?' Madame Antoine pointed out.

'He sketches!' Mademoiselle retorted.

'I've heard he has a good eye, he scrutinises the fittings . . .'

'It's not the same.' Chanel shrugged. 'When you cut and drape on the model, the result is more three-dimensional, more chic. Balenciaga knew that, and now there is only me.'

Madame Antoine glanced at her friend and employer's sad face.

'It's true that you have never sketched a dress or suit in your life. The things you create with a length of fabric, scissors and a pin-cushion are indeed miracles.'

Mademoiselle leaned forward suddenly, peering at Madame Antoine's grey tweed skirt. 'There is a pucker in that seam . . . give me your skirt, I'll fix it.'

'Mademoiselle, I don't really feel like undressing.'

'Just slip out of it.' Mademoiselle snapped her fingers. 'There's no one here.'

She reached for her work box as Madame Antoine sighed, stood and undid the skirt, stepped out of it, and handed it to her. Mademoiselle fell on it like a hungry vulture.

'You can never just sit and relax!' her friend complained.

'I won't have my *directrice* looking like a scarecrow!' Mademoiselle snapped.

After a little snip with the sharp scissors, she nimbly pulled apart the seam. Threading a needle, she sewed the seam by hand.

'Now I can say Mademoiselle Chanel made my skirt herself!' Madame Antoine laughed.

'Didier Brunewald saw Sophie at the last collection,' Chanel announced between stitches. 'He asked for an introduction.'

Madame Antoine's eyes narrowed.

'Should playboys be viewing our collection to meet girls?' she asked with a smile. 'People will say you're running a bordello!'

'Didier is the nephew of a very good client,' Mademoiselle said. 'He finds Sophie charming. She could do far worse.' She snapped the thread, stretched and smoothed the seam and handed the skirt back to Madame Antoine.

'This is like a man going shopping, spotting a pretty girl and . . . ordering her,' Madame Antoine said, slipping into the skirt and zipping it up. 'Anyway, Sophie has an English boyfriend.'

'Oh yes? From a good family?'

'Well, he's not a Duke.' Madame Antoine smiled. 'He is a couturier. The only British one in Paris.'

'How original! Who does he work for?'

'Designs for Delange. Remember Camille Delange? He came to lunch recently. He seems polite and nice. They've known each other some months; it appears to be serious. But Sophie enjoys leading her admirers a merry dance. To make it more complicated, he is a protogé of Ghislaine de Rives, the notorious cradle-snatcher.'

Mademoiselle stared at her, lighting a fresh cigarette.

'You see? Didier Brunewald is a much better bet,' she said. 'His aunt has millions, which will all go to Didier one day. You do want Sophie to marry well?'

Madame Antoine laughed. 'Marriage is a long way off for Sophie. I'm concerned that modelling may turn her head?'

'Modelling won't turn her head but men in general might,' the old lady grunted. 'She has such allure.'

'Isn't she going to wonder why you are so very interested in her?' Madame Antoine cautioned. 'You don't want that, do you?'

Mademoiselle Chanel gave her a long stare. 'No,' she allowed, 'I don't want that.'

Sixteen

'What do you wear to meet Chanel?' Samantha asked everyone she knew. Her problem began the moment she learned that Sunday evening was the night Mademoiselle usually dined alone at the Ritz's L'Espadon restaurant.

Samantha finally answered her own question.

'What *can* you wear to meet Chanel but Chanel?'

As much Chanel as she could pile on, she thought. Then make one of her fabulous entrances, nonchalantly passing Chanel's table as if she had no idea that she dined there each night. Chanel would look up, see her, and be so impressed that – if she was as lonely as everyone said – she was bound to invite Samantha to join her. They would become firm friends.

'I'll make a reservation for one,' she told Christopher. 'And I shall do my best to be at the next table to her. I know exactly which table that is.'

'Samantha, I'm not sure the Ritz accepts reservations for women dining alone.'

'Are you saying they'll think I'm a prostitute?' she cried.

'Maybe, yes.'

'That is so—' she broke off with a splutter. 'OK, I'll reserve a table for two and pretend I've been stood up.'

Christopher looked at her admiringly. She always seemed to find a way around obstacles.

*

194

It look Samantha most of Sunday to prepare for the encounter. She popped a Valium and forked pastries. The more nervous she was, the more pastry she needed. She ran downstairs for more éclairs.

Jean-Jacques came to make her up, doing it better than she ever could. He stayed to watch her dress. At around six o'clock, she popped another Valium. By the time she began to dress she hadn't a fear in the world. She asked Jean-Jacques to arrange her hair around her Chanel straw boater, grosgrain ribbons streaming behind it, Gigi-style. Grumbling, he did so.

Her favourite pink tweed Chanel was six years old: surely Chanel would appreciate the fact that it still looked fabulous? She layered ropes and ropes of genuine Chanel jewellery, given each birthday (under her strict guidance) by her father. Several bangles jangled on each wrist. Three Maltese crosses swung casually amongst the pearls. She carried a Chanel quilted handbag and pinned two white Chanel camellias to her shoulder. For extra confidence, she wore Chanel sunglasses, Jackie Onassis style. Her eyes were slightly glazed by the time she was ready.

'Oh, Samanatha, you look *fabulous*!' Jean-Jacques assured her as she stumbled into the taxi. 'All that Chanel! Only another Cocosexual would know you were Cocosexual . . . I hope you are not turning yourself on *too* much?'

'Just for tonight, *cher* Jean-Jacques,' Samantha replied, 'keep the bitchy remarks to yourself. I need to stay *very* calm and *very* chic.'

The taxi delivered Samantha to the Ritz just after eight. The Maître d' did not seem too surprised that an elegant woman dressed in Chanel wished to dine alone, especially when a neatly folded twenty-franc note slid from her palm to his.

He probably thinks I'm much too well-dressed to be a prostitute, she thought.

The Espadon Grill was dimly lit, only half-full: truly chic Parisians dined later. As the Maître d' scanned his Reservations book, Samantha spotted Mademoiselle in a black suit at the table

Christopher had described. She felt a little dizzy. She had entered her dream, she was in the same room as her idol. From now on, she could function on automatic Chanel pilot.

'I'll sit there,' she said firmly, indicating the table nearest her idol. Henri hesitated but Samantha had a second twenty-franc bill at the ready for just such a hesitation.

She followed the head waiter, staring at Mademoiselle picking at her *hors d'oeuvres varieé.*

She's kind of shrivelled, Samantha thought disappointedly, but she was well into her eighties. She was too skinny, but her style and presence left no doubt that this was indeed Gabrielle Sidonie Chanel, the woman Samantha had idolised ever since learning to sign a credit-card bill.

Unfortunately, she was too busy checking out Mademoiselle Chanel to watch where she was going, her dark glasses too dark for the dim dining-room. The head waiter pulled out a chair but, twisted to watch Mademoiselle, Samantha did not see it. There was an almighty crash, the room whirled and she felt a painful bump on her Chanel-ed behind.

When she opened her eyes she was sprawled on the floor, one lens of her dark glasses still in its frame, the other in her mouth. She removed it, focusing on the waiter and the old lady bending over her. In gruff French, the lady asked, '*Vous êtes bien, Mademoiselle?*'

Samantha groaned. This was not the way she'd planned to meet Mademoiselle Chanel.

'I . . . I think so,' she muttered, grabbing a chair back as the head waiter hauled her to her feet.

She collapsed into the nearest chair, rubbing her *derrière* as discreetly as she could. She'd wear navy lingerie all next week to match it. There was an awkward silence as waiters hovered and the old lady sat down opposite her. She cleared her throat as Samantha stared dazedly at her.

'I don't recall inviting you to share my table,' Mademoiselle suddenly barked.

Samantha tried to sit up straight. 'Oh, I'm at your table? Do you mind if I rest here for five minutes, Madame?' she asked. 'Just to recover my equilibrium.'

'*Bien sûr*. Do you feel all right?'

'I could use some water,' she croaked.

A waiter poured some. She gulped it down, then weakly held out a hand. 'Samantha Lipstaadt,' she introduced herself. '*Enchanté!*'

Staring at all the Chanel bangles, Mademoiselle gave her hand. 'Mademoiselle Chanel,' she muttered.

Samantha struggled to her feet, staggering slightly as she held tightly onto the famous hand.

'Oh my God! *The* Chanel?' she gasped. 'The "Chanel No. 5" Chanel? If you only knew what an honour—'

'Sit down before you fall again,' Mademoiselle snapped.

She stared at Samantha for a moment. 'What are you wearing?' she asked.

'Don't you recognise it, Mademoiselle? *You* designed it. It's *Chanel*. Real Chanel, not copies!'

'Are you one of my clients?'

Samantha frowned. 'In a way, I guess I am. I mean, I bought this in New York.'

'You are American?'

'Yes, Mademoiselle. And I am your greatest fan. I absolutely love everything you design.'

'That is all very well, but it was not designed to be worn all at once.'

Samantha frowned. 'I love it all! I can never choose!'

'Are you able to walk now?' Mademoiselle asked her.

'Oh, *please* don't send me away just yet,' Samantha begged. 'I have so much to ask you. I admire you more than any human being on this planet!'

'Very well, but I would like to show you a way to look much better. Go to the cloakroom. Deposit at least sixty per cent of your clothing and accessories. *Then* return and sit with me.'

'*Oh.*' Samantha looked very surprised. 'OK!'

She left some things in the cloakroom, making sure she got

a numbered ticket for the thousand dollars' worth of handbag, bracelets, necklaces and camellias.

When she returned to the table ten minutes later, Chanel examined her.

'Isn't that better?' she asked.

'I feel lighter,' Samantha admitted, secretly feeling half-naked.

Chanel nodded. 'As they say: less is more.'

'And I always thought *more* was more,' Samantha said, sitting down. 'Oh, Mademoiselle, you have already taught me so much.'

A waiter appeared to take her order. 'Mademoiselle, you have decided?'

She glanced at Chanel's plate.

'I'll have what she's having,' she said, perhaps a tad impulsively.

'Mademoiselle Chanel ordered snails and chicory salad,' the waiter announced, almost as a warning.

'Oh, OK.' Samantha swallowed hard. 'But can you remove the snails and substitute – I don't know – *cheese*, maybe?'

The waiter scurried away and Mademoiselle stared at her, her face a mixture of horror and fascination.

'I know, I'm doing everything wrong. I guess you've never met anyone like me before?' Samantha asked hopefully.

She began to ply her idol with questions, ones she had stored up for years: how she'd begun, how she designed, what she really thought of fashion. And Chanel responded in a fast-spoken French that Samantha only *just* understood, as if the taps of her memories had turned full on.

After thirty minutes of listening, Samantha thought: My God, I could be this woman's personal shrink! What a lot of emotional baggage: it spilled out in a flurry of talk. How she hated being alone, how other designers made women look ridiculous, how resentful she felt towards the *parfumeurs* who had taken over 'her' house.

Samantha took it all with a generous pinch of salt. Mademoiselle didn't mention the millions of dollars they were paying her for the right to do this.

Samantha finally managed to put in a few words, suggesting ways of selling accessories, finding loopholes in her contract which, if it did not allow Chanel bed-linen, might allow a larger range of handbags and purses, lingerie and luxury items.

'You need me, Mademoiselle!' she assured her. 'I would fight for you!'

Chanel stared at her, enthralled. Samantha had used the magic word: *fight*.

'Maybe you could?' Mademoiselle allowed. 'You certainly have energy.'

They made an unlikely couple, but Samantha quickly realised that Mademoiselle responded to admiration and interest more than anyone she had ever met. And nobody, *nobody*, can provide more sincere admiration and genuine interest than me, Samanatha thought happily. She could now achieve her life's ambition. She would help the designer she admired most in the entire world. She would wear nothing but Chanel clothing, and smell of nothing but No. 5.

Dîner avec Coco ended just the way she had dreamed it would, with Samantha accompanying Mademoiselle up to her suite and practically tucking her up in her bed, having talked her way into a job at Chanel. She wasn't sure what the job was, but it was a job!

'*And* she paid for dinner,' Samantha delivered the punchline to the previous night's exploits to de Kousmine.

De Kousmine stared at her.

'No,' he growled, '*we* paid for dinner. So glad you enjoyed it. We pay all Mademoiselle's living-expenses at the Ritz, including restaurant bills. That is why she is so generous.'

'Oh?' Samantha raised her eyebrows. They were in her apartment. It did not look as if sex was on the menu. In fact, de Kousmine's limp reaction to her fabulous news was a distinct turn-off.

'You're not very happy for me,' she wailed. 'I'll be working for the same firm you work for, and I didn't even need your help! I got this job on my own merits!'

'You think you scored a victory,' he grunted. 'But all you did was take advantage of a lonely old lady.'

'I'd never do that,' Samantha gasped. 'I worship her. I would do anything for her.'

'Don't worry. She will ask you to do plenty . . . mostly to annoy *us*. It's time you learned something, Samantha. Mademoiselle Chanel is a pain in the neck to us. We have a full-time lawyer on the payroll just to deal with her *emmerdeuses!*'

Samantha frowned, not sure what that last word meant: it had '*merde*' in it, so she could guess.

'How can you speak about her that way, Eduard?' she protested. 'If it wasn't for her—'

'If it wasn't for her, I'd have a much easier life,' he cut in.

She let him grumble on. And she let him leave her apartment without even asking for sex. He was jealous, she decided.

'This will be the end of my Paris problems,' she sighed to Jean-Jacques on the telephone later that night.

'You think so, *cherie*?' he asked. 'I think it will be the start!'

Seventeen

The phone jangled into Christopher's dream. He squinted at the clock as he grabbed the receiver. It was three thirty.

'Mmmmmmm?' he groaned.

'I've had the most horrible nightmare,' Sophie's voice sobbed. 'The first I've had in this apartment. I feel so alone. Christopher, could you possibly come over?'

'You mean *now*?'

'You would do that for me?'

He was in a taxi within ten minutes, still half asleep. The streets were dark, glittering, almost deserted, with just a few taxis whizzing up and down the Champs-Elysées.

She opened the door to him in a white nightgown, her face scrubbed of make-up.

'I dreamed I was a little girl!' She fell into his arms. 'I woke up realising that I don't remember my childhood – about five years are just a blank. Why did I never realise that before?' She broke off, clinging to him.

Her body pressed against his through the thin nightgown. He was ashamed to be aroused by a girl in distress, at her most vulnerable. They kissed and it was so obvious that she needed him to comfort her and reassure her that his male pride and strength was stirred in a way it had never been stirred before. With all her sexual knowledge, Ghislaine could not make him feel like this. Here, *he* was the man, the protector, his body pressing urgently against a woman who did not view him as the appetiser of a delicious meal – a human *hors d'oeuvre* – but as a man.

He led her back to her rumpled bed and she got into it.

'I cannot remember anything before the house at *Ecole Militaire* . . .' she said, wonderingly. 'It's as if someone stole my childhood from me, Christopher.'

'Can't your parents fill in the missing parts?' he suggested.

'They are *not* my parents,' she cried. 'That is the point.'

'Why must you know?'

She sat up in the bed. 'How can I know who I am if I don't know a basic fact like that?'

'*I* know who you are; Sophie, isn't that enough?' he asked earnestly.

'No,' she shook her head. 'It isn't. And I have an instinct that Mademoiselle is somehow involved. The way she looks at me. As if she owns me. I can't explain it, but I'll keep trying to find out. I've promised myself I will.'

'Should I go now?' he asked.

'No.' She pulled back the covers. 'Stay the rest of the night. Hold me in your arms.'

He did not need much persuasion. Naked against her, he enjoyed the luxury of holding her, unhurried, the rest of the night before them. The thin barrier of her nightgown made their closeness even more sexy . . . perhaps only a fellow couturier would realise how much sexier than nudity this fragile layer of fabric was?

Kissing her, holding her breasts, then allowing his hand to massage between her legs, her cries urging him on. He sensed she needed the pleasure to wipe out her nightmare. Was sex as tranquilliser better than sex as appetiser? He decided it was.

He gently pressed his lips to hers and she bit on his full lower lip. He pulled up her nightdress, the last cloth barrier between them, and now he sensed her soft skin against his. She cried out, a raw, hoarse pleasured cry, the moment he entered her. But now he knew how to move quickly, rhythmically, without fear of it all ending in a few moments. He could move until she sobbed and cried with pleasure, he could move until she finally begged him *not* to stop. She screamed and only then, as Ghislaine had so carefully trained him to do, did he allow his own intense pleasure to rocket and explode in the sky, showering him with stars. His pleasure so loud and so heartfelt, began yet another wave of pleasure in her. Sexual bliss could be contagious, desire could reflect like the mirrors on Chanel's staircase. Multiple reflections, multiple orgasms! As Sophie echoed his moans, his arms tightened around her and her cries became disbelieving ones of surprise, surprise that she could experience so much intense feeling so often.

He knew how to arouse and satisfy a woman and he couldn't help thinking that Ghislaine would be proud of him. Sophie might take him more seriously. Why intense sexual pleasure should help make love seem even more loving, he did not know.

Sophie, too, as her body calmed, had thoughts and impressions she had never felt before. He had said *he* knew who she was. If so, he was the first man who had bothered to discover that. His new assured manner made her trust him a little more. And she realised so well that she had never fully trusted a man. She had flirted with men, tested her attractions, pleasured herself with men, done just about everything but trust one. Trusting a man would be the sexiest, most luxurious thing she had ever allowed herself, increasing her pleasure to an almost unbearable intensity. She hugged this new discovery to herself.

For a few moments they found themselves in a world above and apart from the usual one. Christopher was thinking that he never had this feeling with Ghislaine, so surely it could only be credited to love?

Sophie discovered a feeling she had not experienced with anyone, so surely it could be credited only to trust? Had she found, by accident, a man she could trust? They drifted back to the real world holding each other so closely that they almost became the same person.

This is what love is, each thought, holding the other so tightly.

The thought thrilled Christopher but scared Sophie.

Sophie sat before the brightly lit, long mirror of the *cabine*. Now *she* was one of the beautiful mannequins staring silently at their reflections, as if in awe of their own beauty. After the drudgery of sewing, the luxury of being a model whose job was simply to look pretty seemed like sheer heaven. She didn't miss the workroom at all. She loved coming in to work at ten o'clock. She took to a model's routine as if born to it. She liked the way Chanel's afternoon *defilé* was put together like a forty-five-minute dramatic play. Each afternoon, it felt entirely natural to perfect her make-up and hair, then don, in quick succession, six suits, four dresses, two cocktail dresses, two long evening gowns and glide up and down the *salon*, showing them off. She was like an actress assuming several roles, it became her aim to get the Japanese tourists present to focus all their attention on her, murmuring excitedly each time she appeared. If there was a man in the audience, so much the better, she would stare through him and try to excite him.

Mademoiselle Chanel had visited the salon to watch her first *defilés* with a critical but approving eye. An approving glance from Mademoiselle was worth fifty Japanese gazes. The presence Sophie projected was extraordinary. It made people sit up and take notice. Each model developed her own special walk. One walked languidly, one trotted in little steps, another took the runway at face value and ran down it.

One girl showed suits very grandly, as if they were evening dresses, and evening dresses very casually, as if they were suits. Sophie invented her own style. In a suit, she would stride into the *salon* unhurried, almost languid. She speeded up the walk until it was quite brisk, then suddenly stopped to turn. The soft folds of the skirt came to rest against her legs as she froze for one second in a pose. It was strangely hypnotic. Then she went into stylised slow-motion and moved forward exaggeratedly slowly, leaning back, her arm out, returning to normally paced gait.

Each outfit suggested a different character until she reached the full-length evening dresses and became a femme fatale. Here,

Sophie turned up the sexual power, fixed her eyes on a male in the audience and emoted. She was the model people watched, she was the girl people waited to see emerge again in a different outfit.

Two girls in the *cabine* assisted the models, held their shoes for them to step into, caught the jacket they flung off as they passed through the curtain screening them from the *salon*. They were helped into coats, handed hats, bags, gloves and pushed out back into the *salon*. To perfect a languid gliding walk in the midst of all this panic was a talent, indeed.

Sophie absorbed tips about hair and make-up from the other models and had soon perfected the art of *maquillage*, making her eyes smoky and deep using layers of shadow, her lips even fuller with lipstick and darker outlining pencil. In contrast to all the sleek dark cuts, her hair was tousled, sexy and red. She was admired just for being Sophie. Her ambition to design began to slip away: this was so easy!

A few girls were bitchy, but on the whole the Chanel *cabine* was a friendly group, united in their mixed feelings of love for their boss.

A press photographer recognised the special magic that only a camera could pick up. He soon spotted Sophie on Chanel's runway. He predicted how fashion photographers would jump on that careless, nonchalant shrug and make her a star. The camera moved in close on that perfect nose, that gleam in her eye, that air of being unattainable, that mood. The lens seized on and enhanced what the human eye did not see. With the luck that landed her in the right place at the right time, Sophie was offered magazine work and was signed up by a top modelling agency.

Samantha shook the flacon of *eau de toilette* close to her ear, hearing it bubble. Toilet water – the cheapest item you could buy with a couture label attached: twenty dollars. She sprinkled a few drops on her pillow so the scent of haute couture permeated her dreams.

'A tiny piece of the dream', her new mantra, that wonderful

word the hippies used. She lay her head on the fragrant pillow, careful not to smudge her face-cream.

The dream was the glamour of the haute couture. A luxurious name like Chanel was beyond most women's means, but attached to a twenty-dollar bottle of *eau de toilette* it was suddenly within a woman's means. Dreams and means . . . she followed her train of thought.

When she was sixteen, Beverly Hills High had arranged a trip to Italy for twenty students. She had run into Rome's most expensive boutique and come out with a key-chain. Why? Because Daddy had put her on a strict budget and that was all she could afford. But the key-chain had been beautifully wrapped in pleated grey tissue and placed in a stiff grey shopping-bag with silk cord handles that she had used as a purse for the next year. She had left that boutique with a little piece of the dream.

A five-thousand-dollar Chanel dress was bought by perhaps five women. A twenty-dollar bottle of toilet water might sell to five million women. She fell asleep on the brink of discovering something vitally important.

The next morning, she awoke thinking, why just toilet water? Why not bath-oils, bubble-bath, soaps, make-up, creams, an entire Chanel *drugstore*?

An entire new class of woman could be using Dior or Chanel products. It might only be a tiny piece of the dream, but it was *real* Dior, *real* Chanel! Or so Samantha's thinking went. She was a little disappointed with her new job, so far. She had done little but listen to Mademoiselle spouting advice, memories and opinions on fashion. She longed to share her 'little piece of a dream' discovery with her and, more importantly, with the Chanel directors.

'Every woman needs certain rocks in her life,' Ghislaine told Christopher, one evening in the George V bar. '*Couturier*, *visagiste*, hairdresser, gynaecologist, masseur, florist, travel agent, dentist, dry-cleaner.' She ticked them off. 'As your clients come to believe that you know their lives, their bodies, they begin to think that only *you* know how to make them beautiful, slim and young.'

'Where does "love" come in that list, Ghislaine?' Christopher asked. 'Between travel agent and dry-cleaner?'

'Please don't be sulky,' she pouted.

She lit a cigarette in her practised older-woman French way and blew out a stream of smoke. He watched her lithe body, so at ease as she sat on a high stool at the bar, showing off her long legs in his short white knitted shift.

'Isn't life about our need for people who provide us with something?' She raised her eyebrows. 'Good sex, good care, good food, good flowers?'

Christopher frowned. 'I'm from a country where one doesn't order up sex as if ordering flowers or plane tickets.'

'Why not?' Ghislaine laughed. 'I'd like to order up sex right now. D'you think they have a free room here?'

'I'm not really in the mood, Ghislaine.'

'My little English boy is offended because I desire him? What a pity, because I think he is sooo sexy. Would it make things better if I kissed you here?' She touched him. 'And here?' She moved her hand up further. 'Does that get you into the mood?'

He twisted away from the gaze of other people. He could not resist her admiration. And the hotel was happy to rent them a room, pretending to believe Ghislaine's story that their luggage would arrive later.

In the lift going up, Ghislaine whispered, 'Here is the scenario. We are strangers. I am a *poule de luxe* you picked up in the lobby. You will keep all your clothes on—'

'*Poule de luxe?*' He frowned, trying to translate. 'A luxurious chicken?'

'A very classy expensive prosit-tute,' she corrected. 'One you'd never find on the street or in the Bois de Boulogne!'

Amongst her many gifts, Ghislaine was an actress. In the hotel room, she acted the part of a *poule de luxe* very convincingly. She stripped down to her underwear and he remained dressed. He watched her, excited.

'I want to please monsieur,' she said in a sexy voice. 'What is monsieur in the mood for tonight?'

There was never a dull moment with Ghislaine. She was soon on her knees before him, pretending to be a hungry woman finding a *ficelle*, the narrow bread loaf Samantha liked. In her way, Ghislaine was as skilled as Samantha and she practised French twists on an old classic. Spirals of pressure and spirals of pleasure soon made Christopher breathless.

She angled an open wardrobe door mirror behind them, so that the glass reflected her hand between her legs as she took him to *poule de luxe* heaven.

Five minutes later, she picked up the telephone, winking at him, 'Room service, please.'

She waited, cross-legged on the bed in her underwear.

'Room Service? I'd like a bottle of Veuve Cliquot '61 with two glasses, a cup of cocoa powder and a cup of icing-sugar, please.'

Later, puffing an *après-sex* cigarette, Ghislaine went back to outlining her plans for him.

'As Paris's first heterosexual couturiér, you could—'

'Ghislaine, *please* stop saying that, he cut her off. 'Ungaro and Courrèges are heterosexual. There won't be a sign reading "heterosexual" on my forehead! And I cannot make love to every client.'

Ghislaine made a face. 'Just fit them the way you fit me, touching – here and here . . .' She indicated places on her body. 'By accident, of course. They will come to you for that.'

'I want them to come for my *clothes*,' he said, jumping out of bed. 'This is starting to get ridiculous, Ghislaine.' He began to dress. 'Do I need talent to reach the top in Paris, or just a hard cock?'

She laughed. 'You have a very big talent, darling! We poor fashion victims so rarely feel *anything* hard against us during fittings. Usually only some nasty shears!'

He dressed hastily, staring down at her.

'I didn't come to Paris to be a gigolo, Ghislaine,' he told her.

'But we must make the most of your talents!'

He closed the door as she lit a cigarette. He walked all the way home, fuming.

Eighteen

By early Summer, Christopher was on his third collection for Delange. From the many warnings Chantal had issued, he was in no doubt that his collection for Spring '69 was important. *Women's Wear Daily* was already calling it his 'make or break' showing.

Ghislaine wanted wearable, easy clothes. So did Sophie and Samantha. But the more advice and warnings he received, the more Christopher felt a mounting rebellion to make his own statement about how women should dress for 1970. He could not ignore politics and he could not ignore 'the street'.

On the eve of beginning his work, he felt torn in two, wanting to keep his position at Delange and wanting to express his own design philosophy. He won.

He began with the conviction that no one but himself should see, or make suggestions about, his new collection. If he could, he'd have blindfolded the models.

'You've become a diva!' Samantha warned.

He forged ahead with fittings, refusing previews to Sophie or Samantha or Ghislaine. Above all, to Chantal Delange.

He wanted no comments and no discouragement. Street fashion must march into the haute couture salon, his inspiration coming from the students' protests and the Boulevard Saint Michel. His influences – hippies with their psychedelic designs, Flower Power floral floating dresses, mock military gear and camouflage outfits – mixed together for a 'guerilla warfare' look or an art gallery 'Happening'. Made up in much better fabrics than the average hippie or protestor could afford.

A *Women's Wear Daily* reporter waylaid a model as she left the house and gleefully wrote, 'Christopher Hutchins' make-or-break collection for Delange is like the musical *Hair* without the music.'

Over a pre-collection drink with Ghislaine at La Coupole, crammed with American and British press and buyers, he enjoyed her showing off an orange plastic tent-dress he had made that season, waving across the café to all the faces she knew.

'A designer needs a muse,' she told Christopher, '*and* an editor. Even brilliant writers have editors. As your muse, I would also be your fashion editor.' Ghislaine sipped at her Kir Royale and puffed on her cigarette. 'I wanted to be your muse, Christopher.'

'I didn't feel in need of one,' he said.

She shook her head at him. 'Christopher, this time I really don't know what has got into you. I don't know what to expect, now.'

'I don't either. I just know I have to make my own statement. My view of fashion, uncontaminated and un-influenced by anyone else.'

The collection was unveiled on an afternoon in July in Delange's packed *salon*, in the middle of collection week. The bored fashion press stared straight ahead, not even bothering to turn their heads to watch the models' progress. Flower power, camouflage, military, hippie . . . it seemed to make no impression at all on anyone. Ghislaine, centre front-row, looked on, dismayed. When it ended with two brides, one black and one white, walking hand in hand down the *salon* to suggest racial harmony, the press got to its feet and filed out, silent, eyes lowered. Ghislaine remained seated, staring sadly at him.

Christopher was twenty-six and the average age of the fashion-audience was around fifty. The generation gap and the fashion gap joined to form one big gap, a fashion calamity.

Chantal Delange called Christopher into her office. 'I've had enough of this . . .' she groaned. 'I am so sick of youth. I want maturity on my runway, and elegance.'

'I'm sorry you didn't like it,' he said gruffly.

'Christopher, do you have any idea how many hundreds of thousands of francs that collection cost us? Do you even know what seamstresses earn per hour? Or how many hundreds of hours' work each dress needs?'

He shook his head.

'I thought not.' Chantal sighed, shaking her head. 'Well, I cannot go through this again. It is simply not feasible. This pose of not letting anyone see the collection was the last straw.'

She fired him that very night.

'The best possible career move.' Samantha nodded approvingly later that night in Christopher's apartment.

'That's what they said when James Dean died,' Christopher groaned, refilling her glass with flat champagne. Klaus had opened a bottle of champagne which had barely popped. They had realised that it was flat. Was it symbolic?

'And look how successful his movies were!' Samantha cried.

'Hmm, I seem to recall saying something like that to you to cheer you up when Delange terminated *your* contract.'

'And look at me now.' Samantha struck a pose, arms out, resplendent in a purple Chanel suit. '*I'm* at Chanel. So *fuck* Delange! They never really appreciated you. *Or* me!'

She sat on Klaus's lap.

Christopher sipped the flat champagne, watching them.

'Does Chanel appreciate you?' he asked Samantha.

'No, but they will!' Samantha vowed. 'I'm working on it right now.'

'Chantal Delange needed a little faith in me,' Christopher sighed, holding out his glass for Samantha to refill. 'The press are photographing my clothes right now. It takes time to get used to them, but with Ghislaine and her friends wearing them . . .'

'Did Ghislaine like them?' Samantha asked.

'No,' Christopher admitted.

'And Sophie?'

'I cannot face her or Ghislaine. They are both furious because I didn't give them previews.'

'So the guy with two girlfriends is all alone!' Samantha said. 'Well, well, well! You wanted to do it all by yourself. And now you're *by* yourself.'

'You'll meet other fashion folk,' Klaus promised. 'You still have a name, a reputation. We'll go to clubs, try to meet some helpful people.'

Sophie rang later that evening. 'I just heard,' she said. 'Oh Christopher, I am so sorry. Do you feel terrible?'

'Now that you've called, I feel better.'

'You are asking around at other houses?'

'I don't know if I have the energy to drag another old-fashioned house into the seventies. Even Delange didn't seem to want it.'

'Listen to me, Christopher. It took great courage to do what you did. At least you tried something new. Mademoiselle's collection was the same old story.'

'She's eighty-something!' Christopher declared. 'No one expects groundbreaking clothes from her.'

'You *must* find the energy to approach other people,' Sophie said.

'Maybe this is the time to open my own business . . .'

'Who would back it? Ghislaine de Rives?'

'I don't know.'

'Christopher, I must see you soon . . . Call me, OK? What are you doing right now?'

'I'm sharing a bottle of flat champagne with Klaus and Samantha but I have no idea what we're celebrating.'

After he'd hung up he told Samantha and Klaus, 'She said it took a lot of courage to do what I did! Ha!'

'Yeah, we'll propose you for the Red Lobster Award for Courageous Chic!' Samantha toasted him.

Ghislaine offered a consolation dinner at Les Petits Pavés on the Left Bank the next night.

'Look at this!' She indicated her dress, one of his black clingy numbers from the last collection with a cut-out diamond at the breast revealing her white skin. A thin band of pearls kept her hair back and real jewels glittered on her long white fingers. He had to admit she looked beautiful.

'You *can* do it! What happened?'

He stared at her. 'I don't know.'

'Every designer is allowed *one* dud collection,' Ghislaine began.

'I don't consider my collection a dud,' Christopher said quietly. 'I'm proud of it.'

She covered his hand with hers.

'Fashion works only if women want to wear it, that's a basic rule. You need a woman to look at and comment on your clothes as you design them. I wanted to be your muse. I might have influenced some of these clothes, made them wearable? I don't want to be a hippie or a flower-child. Kids wear camouflage clothing on the Boulevard St Michel, but did you ask yourself why an elegant woman would spend five thousand francs on a camouflage dress? Did you even have a client in mind?'

He stared at her. 'I wanted to make my own fashion statement with nobody looking over my shoulder.'

'Well, now you've made it!' She pulled an expectant face. 'Now what?'

'I'm thinking of returning to London,' he blurted out.

She lowered her glass. 'Don't start dinner with a threat. It will ruin my digestion.'

'Are you hungry?'

'Yes, but not for food.' She held his eyes. 'We haven't been together in a while.'

He sighed. 'Maybe there's no future for me in Paris.'

She cocked her head, considering him gravely.

'What if there's a new future? What if this is the moment to start again from the beginning? Learn how to cut, sew and make a suit from scratch, the way Chanel and Balenciaga can? Learn your craft!'

'Where?'

'In a Chanel workroom.'

He looked at her, incredulous. 'A couturier who has designed three collections suddenly disappearing into a workroom?' he asked.

'Now that *would* be revolutionary, wouldn't it?' Ghislaine leaned forward. 'You see, great couturiers know how to form a collar,' she went on, 'how hundreds of stitches on canvas interlining will beautifully curve a lapel, how a skirt is softly gathered with *two* invisible drawstrings, how a bodice is draped, how a sleeve set in. When you know these things, you start understanding what a woman wants to wear, what flatters a woman.'

'I have no sewing talent,' he burst out. 'Why torture myself when qualified seamstresses can do it for me?'

'What happened to the rebellious boy open to revolutionary new tactics?' she asked. 'Learning your craft is a beautiful, modern thing to do. It shows people how very serious you are. It can only further your career.'

'And what would I live on? Delange's pay-off was not very generous.'

She lowered her voice. 'I'd subsidise you in return for a share in your eventual success. Chanel can't live for ever and now that Balenciaga has retired . . . Paris needs new designers.'

He thought for a moment. 'I don't have the patience, Ghislaine,' he decided. 'If I returned to London I could get a job in some up-market ready-to-wear house.'

'One of those dreary ones that dresses your Queen Mother?' she laughed. 'Somehow I cannot picture you there, Christopher.'

'*OUT!*' cried the front page of *Women's Wear Daily*, which Samantha showed him at lunch the next day. A close-up of Christopher's face was splashed over some pictures from his collection.

'All publicity is good publicity,' Samantha said.

Christopher raised his eyebrows. Whoever would believe that a gossip-filled lunch with Samantha would be the high spot of his day? It entertained him and he came away from it thoughtful, it was so odd to be idle. Out of work. During the next few days he had time to think about what Ghislaine had said. He knew she was right about the sewing. Every biography of every great couturier since Vionnet had stressed how nimble he or she had been with scissors and needle. But could he possibly learn?

There was a great deal of pride to swallow but finally one call to Ghislaine and her impeccable contacts got him into a Chanel workroom as an apprentice. He was placed in a relatively new workroom and told to report to its head, Mademoiselle Monique. The most overworked workroom in Chanel, it desperately needed apprentices.

A beautiful statue named Sophie sat before the Chanel *cabine* mirror staring into her own eyes. Why was she meeting Didier Brunwald? Two reasons. She had not liked to say 'no' to Mademoiselle. And his eager phone-call had turned her on, pushing her back in time to when she was a sexy young girl teasing her parents' friends. A man assuming that he was irresistible was in itself an irresistible challenge. This would provide some light relief from thinking about Christopher. She was a little surprised at how much he was on her mind. The idea that Ghislaine might back him in a new business was alarming. How deeply would Ghislaine sink her well-manicured claws into him? Just as she was beginning to trust him, she saw that he was not really free. It was easy to be cynical about Paris love-affairs as long as they did not involve Christopher. She should be seeking a partner, perhaps even a husband? Of course, Didier Brunwald was neither, but he might prove useful to practise on.

She took a taxi to the Scribe, making sure to be fifteen minutes late. Didier jumped to his feet as she ran into the American Bar. He was wearing dark glasses. He pulled out a chair and she sank into it. She wore a striped knitted shift, her model make-up expertly applied, the blended grey and brown eye-shadow giving her eyes a deep, smoky expression, false lashes veiling her gaze. As they leaned towards each other, they made a perfect page from

Vogue, one of those spreads by Bob Richardson, a fashion photographer who liked quoting scenes from old movies.

Didier was exactly as she'd expected: a 'playboy-gigolo' as supplied by a casting agency. Or a male model of the breed that usually got into fashion shots with half his body cut off – a human fashion accessory. Smoothed-back, Alain Delon hair, expensive tan, impeccable grooming, a rather thin, cruel mouth with sardonic expression completed 'The Look'.

'Why am I here?' she murmured.

'You were unable to resist?' He pushed his dark glasses up into his hair, revealing periwinkle blue eyes. 'Since I saw you modelling at Chanel, I cannot get you out of my mind—' he broke off, signalling the waiter for two champagne cocktails. 'And see? You came?'

He expected her to be very impressed by his blue eyes, she realised.

'Mademoiselle Chanel likes to play matchmaker,' she told him. 'Her heart was set on our meeting.'

'So you met me to please an old lady?' he laughed. 'Not very flattering.' His blue eyes were bright, yet strangely empty. 'But you were staring directly at me when you modelled the evening wear.'

Sophie shrugged. 'Yes, I usually choose a man to stare at when I model, but I don't really see him! Why were you at Chanel anyway?' she asked. 'Don't tell me you're interested in fashion.'

He shrugged. 'It is a lovely spectacle. I had to meet you to see if you match the little fantasy I spun about you . . . that beneath your icy exterior is a little sex-bomb.'

'Oh.' She blew out her lips. 'I put on an icy act in the *salon*. Chanel clothes are not for striptease. They are not obviously sexy.'

'*You* manage to look sexy in them, Sophie.' He glanced at her skimpy little shift, touching it. 'Is this Chanel?'

'It's Sonia Rykiel.'

'Well, I have learned something,' he laughed.

He tossed a peanut in his mouth. Sophie realised they had nothing in common. This date was a mistake.

He did not let much more time elapse – just a second cocktail – before announcing, 'I am staying here tonight. Would you like to see my room?'

Sophie pouted. 'I have seen a hotel room before, thanks.'

He laughed. 'Playing hard to get?'

She shook her head. 'No, not playing, I really *am* hard to get! I don't go to a guy's bedroom twenty minutes after meeting him.'

He shrugged. 'Why waste time if we want the same thing?'

She crossed her legs. 'I thought we wanted a drink.'

'So have another drink. You are very much my type, you know.'

'I'm seeing an English guy. A couturier.'

'English? Couturier?' He spluttered into his glass. '*That* can't be a very satisfying combination!'

She gave him her sexiest pout. 'Do I look unsatisfied?'

'You have a delicious air of "divine discontent". You should be served up like a glorious cocktail, naked in an oversized Martini glass, with a glacé cherry on top of you . . .'

She giggled.

'Why did you come if you are so satisfied with your English fag? Does he even speak French?'

'He's no fag, believe me. He speaks French and makes love in French.'

'*Makes love in French*?' He smiled. 'Maybe you could show me what that is? Wait . . . you said a couturier? Not the *petit ami* of Ghislaine de Rives? The one who resembles one of the Rolling Stones?'

'That's him. Christopher Hutchins.'

'You *share* him with Ghislaine?' he asked incredulously. 'A girl like you should not need to share. So why did you meet me?'

'The models gossip about you. I was curious.'

'Come up to my room, I'll show you the real me.'

'I can see now.' She stood up. 'Thanks for the drink.'

'The night is still young. Why would you leave?' he cried.

Sophie stopped for a moment, thinking. 'Would you like to know, Didier?' she asked him.

'Of course. But sit down and tell me.'

'I am going because you have not asked me what goes on up here.' She tapped her head, 'I have a brain, you know.'

He frowned. 'I thought you were a model?'

She laughed. 'Only temporarily. I intend to be a designer one day.' She held out her hand. 'It was nice meeting you.'

He took her hand in his, kissed it gently, looking up at her with his blue eyes.

'Cock-teasing little bitch,' he hissed.

She swivelled on her right high heel and stalked out of the Scribe. She had wanted to see what a man like that was like and he was exactly as she had thought. Perhaps a little more unpleasant.

Christopher stepped self-consciously into the Chanel workroom of Mademoiselle Monique one hot Monday August morning.

This is utterly ridiculous, he thought. Revolutionary, perhaps, but ridiculous just the same. He introduced himself to Mademoiselle Monique, shaking her hand. She indicated a stool. The girls stared at him as if he were an extraterrestrial. He smiled at them, pulled on a white overall and sat on the hard stool to tack a silk lining for a jacket. I will never get through a year, he decided.

It was a very busy workroom and he saw immediately that their standards were high. No one spoke except to hand him another lining. When he completed his work it was put on a table where it was examined by the *Premiere Main*, passed or handed back for him to resew. It was utter routine and after one day he feared he would go insane.

On the Left Bank, students had begun 'sit-ins' at the Sorbonne, occupying classrooms to protest against an outdated educational system. The protests escalated into riots and van after van of *gendarmes* in black uniforms appeared on the scene. Old cobblestoned streets were ripped up by the bare hands of angry protestors who aimed the newly liberated stones at the enemy, the '*flics*'.

Injuries were suffered, blood flowed, arrests were made as France slowly metamorphosed into a new 'liberated' society.

The couture houses boarded their boutique windows at weekends but on the whole *les protestations* were treated as if they were happening in another country. Another country called *le Rive Gauche*.

During those first days of the workroom, Christopher tried to adapt, tried to pretend that he wasn't there or sewed automatically, his mind elsewhere. But some little incident would happen to show he didn't belong.

There would be a scream of '*Christopher!*' and a model-girl he had known at Delange would recognise him and run over to kiss him. The familiar name of a client told him he was sewing a coat-lining for a society friend of Ghislaine with whom he had dined a few nights before.

'It's like serving a term in prison,' he told Samantha when they met at La Quetsch for lunch. 'My sole crime being fashion. I am guilty of an obsession with fashion.'

'I think it's terrific what you're doing, Christopher,' she said brightly. She frowned, trying to find a comparison. 'It's like dieting or body-waxing. An unpleasant chore you have to do.'

She was in head-to-toe lavender Chanel and he had to admire her look.

'You should see what *I* put up with,' she said. 'I thought I'd be Chanel's new publicist. But they're so secretive at Chanel, they release, like, one press release per year! So I'm nothing but an old lady's companion. What I do has nothing to do with *couture*. I must stick it out. I'll try to parlay it to something better.'

Back in the workroom, head lowered over his work, he found some comfort in Mademoiselle Monique's smile each time he caught her round dark eyes. He pricked himself with the needle, he undid badly matched pieces, he was a disaster, he felt.

Next day, when the lunch-break bell sounded, Monique was one of the only ones to leave the house. The other girls ran to their canteen to heat up their metal *berlingots*.

'You are English?' Monique enquired shyly, as they walked down the back stairs together.

'How did you know?'

She gave a little smile. 'You are in the magazines. Before she became a model, Sophie Antoine was in Monsieur Guy's workroom with me, I become her friend. She told me about you.'

She spoke English to him – the first friendly gesture he had received in a long time. He invited her to lunch.

'I cannot understand why you do this *stage*,' she said over lunch. 'You are already quite famous.'

'I was fired from Delange.' He smiled. 'A friend advised that unless I knew how to make a suit, coat and dress, I won't amount to anything in the couture.'

'But you studied before, no?'

'Yes, at a very good London school called Saint Martins. But we did not learn "couture". Most people went into Prêt-à-porter.'

She nodded. 'It's true that all the great couturiers knew how to make clothes. Mademoiselle cannot even sketch. She cuts and drapes directly on the model.'

They ordered giant *café crèmes* and baguettes filled with ham.

'Why do workrooms take *stagières*?' he asked Monique before biting into his.

'You are cheap labour,' she laughed. 'We have big workloads. The more *stagières* to help, the better.'

He nodded, glumly.

'You have met Mademoiselle Chanel?' she asked.

'No, have you?'

'I introduced myself to her on the street the day before I began work. Since then she has received me in her *salon* upstairs.'

'Received? You make her sound like the Queen,' he laughed. 'Or the Pope.'

'Yes, more like the Pope,' she agreed. 'A very strict Pope!'

'What is she really like?'

'Lonely. Unique and obviously quite special,' Monique said. 'But she can be very difficult. Not for me, because she likes my work and so far has not ripped anything apart. But she is terrible at collection-time.'

From then, Monique kept an eye on Christopher in the work-room, correcting his mistakes quickly so he would not have too much to undo. A *stagière* usually did the donkey-work and was not really taught anything, but Monique went out of her way to teach him. Whatever happened between them, he would always be grateful to her for that.

He tried to settle down to a year's hard labour. But there was too much thinking time. And just as he was questioning his relationship with an older woman, he met a much older one.

Ghislaine visited Christopher's flat for the first time, looked around and shuddered.

'How to be a couturier,' she announced, handing him some sheets of paper.

The list included lunching fashion editors, being friendly to the *vendeuses*, the clients, the *direction* . . . juggling all the women a designer needed to ensure that his career works.

He looked up from the list. 'Any time for designing?'

'We take that for granted,' Ghislaine laughed. 'But you must lunch with as many of these people as you can. And dine with the rest. And perhaps a drinks party for the others every fortnight in your lovely new drawing-room. *Voilà!*'

'I don't have a lovely new drawing-room.'

'So I see!' She threw a disgusted glance around the untidy room. They still used a cardboard box that had once packaged a TV set as their coffee table. The beanbags were lying slumped on the floor.

'It could use a little smartening up,' she said. 'Who is your decorator?'

'The dustbin men. Sometimes they throw out some really useful boxes.'

'Oh Christopher, really.' She stood, suddenly exasperated, opened the window, picked up the 'coffee table' and threw it out. There was a squawk from the concierge downstairs. 'You cannot live like this. You may borrow my drawing-room, if you wish?'

She poked around a little more and sighed, 'Beanbags!'

When she left, he gritted his teeth and buried his head in his hands.

Ghislaine called a halt to her Sunday *salons* for a while. A week later, Christopher sat alone at a table for two in the Ritz, staring forlornly into his wineglass. 'The Ritz is quiet on a Sunday evening,' Ghislaine had assured him.

Earning nothing, yet dining at the Ritz, he thought. Just one of the many contradictory facets of his life. In love with a beautiful girl and carrying on an affair with an older woman was another. He was the youngest person in the restaurant. Everyone else appeared ancient. Another five minutes passed. It looked as if Ghislaine had stood him up. He sipped his wine, wondering whether to leave.

A waiter approached him.

'A message from Madame de Rives, Monsieur,' he bent to whisper. 'She is absolutely *desolé*, she is unable to come.'

'Oh. Thank you,' Christopher muttered.

'Two solitary people dining alone at separate tables?' said a hoarse voice near him. 'What a waste of a perfectly good table-cloth!'

He looked up into a grinning tortoise's face, the grin more a grimace than an expression of joy. As he recognised her, the blood froze in his veins.

Mademoiselle Chanel indicated the empty chair opposite her.

'Excuse me, I couldn't help overhearing your message. If you are anything like me, you will detest dining alone? Food tastes much better *à deux*.'

Christopher took a deep breath and went along with the charade.

'*Enchanté*.' He got to his feet and gave a small bow. '*Je m'appelle* Christopher, *Madame*.'

'*Mademoiselle*,' she said, motioning to a waiter. Christopher sat down opposite her and she watched the waiter transfer his cutlery, wineglass and napkin, arranging them before him.

'Doesn't speaking to strange men sometimes get you into trouble, Mademoiselle?' he tried.

She gave a dry laugh, poking the waiter.

'Did you hear that, Henri? My days of getting into trouble are long over, young man,' she told him. 'The waiters are my chaperones. Henri here even escorts me to my room sometimes. I live here, you know.'

'Yes, I know.'

'You know who I am?' The friendly glance became black suspicious eyes.

'I do indeed and I consider it an honour to—'

She cut him off. 'Use words like "honour" and you can return to your table! Words like "honour" make me feel two hundred years old.'

'I promise never to use such a terrible word again, Mademoiselle.'

She gave a penetrating look to see if he was being serious, then relaxed. 'I have missed dry English humour,' she sighed. 'Where are you from?'

'London, Mademoiselle.'

She shook her head regretfully. 'Haven't set foot in that city for years. Who is the woman who has abandoned you, here, alone? It *is* a woman?'

'Forgive me, Mademoiselle, I am too discreet to say her name. I will only tell you that she is twenty years older than me.'

She burst into a laugh. 'Ha! And now you are with someone fifty years older. If you ever see this mystery woman again she will appear a mere slip of a girl.'

Their conversation took off from there. She was charming and fascinating when she had a male listener's attention and Christopher listened and reacted to her stories. She had a non-stop stream of anecdotes, history and remembered conversations . . . it was difficult to sort out the truth from the ravings of an extremely intelligent old lady who had survived several different lives. Also, she sometimes spoke an old-fashioned French complete with slang expressions from the nineteen-twenties that he did not always understand.

It took until the cheese course for him to confess that he

worked in her house, and she was a little shocked to hear that he was a mere *stagièr* in Mademoiselle Monique's workroom.

'But what are you doing in a workroom?' she exploded. 'The house of Chanel is not a school.'

'But Mademoiselle, you surely know that *stagières* are used in busy workrooms. Didn't Ghislaine de Rives ask you whether an Englishman could do a *stage*?' he asked.

Chanel shook her head. 'She probably asked Madame Antoine, my *directrice*. They are old friends. Nobody tells me anything.' She shot him a sharp look. 'Ghislaine de Rives? Is she the mystery woman who stood you up tonight? What a coincidence, she was once the Face of Chanel.'

He said nothing, merely raised his eyebrows.

'Wait a minute, I think I know who you are. Are you Sophie's friend, the English couturier?'

'Guilty, Mademoiselle.'

'Well, you are very charming. I see why she likes you. But make up your mind what you want and don't play with her.'

'I want Sophie, Mademoiselle. She is playing with me.'

'*You* are the one who had an assignation with this de Rives woman tonight,' Mademoiselle said sharply. 'Were you planning to talk about the weather?'

'She is paying for my *stage*, Mademoiselle,' he admitted embarrassedly.

She shot him a very dubious look.

'Sometimes I'm glad I am too old for these intrigues . . . I had enough of those in my time. But in this case, you should do the right thing with Sophie and be true to her.'

There was a moment of awkward silence. She soon began to talk again. He reminded himself that she was in her eighties and the wine very good. If he sat this out, her eyelids would surely droop and end the evening.

He did not have to wait long. At ten thirty, she asked him to accompany her to the lift. He signalled for the bill hoping he had enough money to pay it and was told it had been taken care of. He offered his arm to walk her to the lift. She made herself stand erect as if it was shameful to admit to tiredness.

The lift arrived, the doors opened and Mademoiselle turned to say, 'I have always enjoyed an Englishman's conversation. My English is getting rusty, so it's good practice for me. We will meet for dinner every Sunday night. It's the least you can do if you are learning to be a couturier in *my* house.'

Nineteen

'So you're Coco's new friend . . . well, well . . .' Sophie looked at him with renewed interest as she followed him up the Rue Cambon on Monday morning.

'This must be the gossipiest city on the world!' Christopher marvelled.

'A friend spotted you last night at the Ritz being very attentive and charming.' Sophie shrugged. 'I suppose I cannot be jealous of Mademoiselle. Did you put her to bed?'

'I think the maid did that,' he said. 'Actually, she picked me up. Invited me to join her. She had no idea I work in her house.'

'Why were you alone?' she asked. 'And how can you afford to dine at the Ritz on your non-existent salary?'

'A *Woman's Wear* journalist invited me,' he lied, not wanting Sophie to know his date had been with Ghislaine. 'She thought a couturier learning his craft would make an interesting story. I was getting dinner in return for "Confessions of the Haute Couture". She stood me up and Mademoiselle took pity on me sitting alone.'

'What did you think of her?'

He laughed. 'I wish I'd known her when she was a young woman.'

'Yes, can you imagine?'

They arrived at the staff door and stopped as he fumbled for his card to stamp in the time-machine.

'Why are you here so early?' he asked.

'Monsieur Guy is making a suit for me.'

'How did you get him to agree to that?' he asked jealously.

'I didn't sleep with him, if that's what you mean. It is perfectly legal. Not that you have any right to be jealous.'

'I miss you, Sophie,' he told her. 'I wish we could see each other.'

Sophie stared at him penetratingly. 'Well, you must let me know when you are free . . .' she said meaningfully.

'I get it.' He nodded. 'I'm a *stagière*, you're a model. Once again, fashion has made us very unequal.'

She shook her head. 'You know I am not a snob. But I won't share you, Christopher, especially with that woman. Someone has to protect me, so *I* do it.'

She left him at the staff entrance, making her own entrance through the Chanel boutique doors.

That evening, Klaus wanted to hear about Mademoiselle Chanel.

'That old girl could really help you,' he said. 'She must be a millionaire several times over. I read that Chanel No. 5 is the biggest selling perfume in the world.'

Christopher stared at him. 'Everyone tries to profit from that old lady. But I shall be different. I shall dine with her and share a nice meal each Sunday night, if that is what she wants. I'll listen. And I won't try to take advantage of her at all . . . how's that?'

'You're a fool,' Klaus muttered.

The three women who met at Les Trois Asperges, an intimate Left Bank restaurant with candlelight on tables crammed incestuously close, made an unlikely trio. It was a late summer evening, warm and slightly humid, and they turned quite a few heads as they entered, dressed to the nines in their Chanel wardrobes. Sophie, an almost-famous Chanel model, wore one of Mademoiselle's famous little black dresses, a soufflé of gently gathered silk chiffon which fell in soft folds around her slim body, a transparent black stole over her shoulders. Samantha, a tall, striking Chanel employee in charge of 'special events' wore her trademark Chanel suit, this time a dark burgundy bouclé wool jacket over a flower-printed silk blouse. And Monique, the head of her own Chanel workroom, wore her own dark grey linen dress, which she felt was smart but inconspicuous. Even so, she had sewn a 'Chanel' label into it. She had no intention of competing with her glamorous friends.

On one thing they were united: their boss, Mademoiselle Chanel, was a fascinating, demanding, possessive employer, and too much of their time was consumed in trying to please her.

They leafed through the menu, steered Samantha away from items she deemed 'icky', ordered, then sat back, looking at each other.

'You look absolutely gorgeous,' Samantha whispered, staring at Sophie.

'You mean this old Chanel, found at the back of a boutique closet?' Sophie brushed aside the compliment. 'It's only genuine nineteen-fifties Chanel. Can you imagine?'

Monique reached out to touch the delicate, black silk chiffon.

'Someone must catalogue these vintage Chanels,' she said. 'Then donate them to the *Musée des Arts Decoratifs*.'

Samantha nodded. 'I shall raise the matter.'

Sophie sipped some wine. 'Meanwhile, I have adopted this dress and given it a very good home. On my back!'

Monique regarded her. 'Christopher is an English gentleman. It breaks my heart to see him struggling in my workroom. Why is he doing this?'

Sophie rolled her eyes. 'Someone gave him this obsession that he must learn to sew. You saw where that got me? I don't think he'll last as long as I did. I'm sorry, Monique, but it was so boring!'

Monique laughed, 'It's boring if you hate sewing. And I can see that he hates it! Like you did! You and he must make such an attractive couple, Sophie. You would make beautiful babies.'

'Except that we are not a couple, Monique,' Sophie corrected. 'Just part of a ménage à trois. Ghislaine de Rives is still very much in the picture. It is her idea that he does this ridiculous *stage*. She pretends that she is only interested in his clothes, but . . .' She gave a 'pouff' and lit her cigarette.

'You don't believe her?' Monique looked shocked.

'Monique, don't be naive. I am *sharing* him. Even if it is only for his career. Ghislaine's husband might back him in his own house. I have to be realistic.'

'That is a little too realistic,' Monique said.

'Why?' Samantha laughed. '*I* juggle two lovers. And I wouldn't mind a third.'

'Samantha,' Monique gasped. 'Sophie! You make me feel like some little old spinster, afraid of men. If I was not so in love, this is how I would feel.'

'But what good is this love doing you, Monique?' Sophie asked.

Monique put down the menu and looked at her.

'It gives me a little hope when I get up in the morning.' She glanced at each of them in turn with her big round eyes. 'It puts something else in my head apart from buttonholes. I have a man in my life. In my heart. No one is more dedicated to work than I am, but a woman needs other things . . .'

'Like praying a bus runs over Guy's wife?' Samantha said innocently.

'Samantha!' Monique's eyes popped. 'I would never think that. I am not that wicked. I think about *him*, that's all.'

Samantha and Sophie exchanged looks, their hors d'oeuvres arrived and they changed the subject.

Monique chose a good wine. It amused the other two that she knew about good years and vintages. She remembered the hot summers of Angers.

Monique had been fitting Sophie for the new collection. She knew Sophie's body better than anybody, except perhaps Christopher. She was still fascinated by her. In a way, Sophie replaced Caterine as a younger sister, someone to be protected.

As Special Events Director, Samantha had an excuse to be all over the house.

'But what exactly *is* a "Special Event" at Chanel?' Sophie asked her now. 'In fact, what is your job, Samantha?'

'That's what I keep asking,' Samantha groaned. 'I think it's mostly putting Mademoiselle to bed at night, after being a sounding-board for her,' she laughed. 'I arrange charity fashion-shows, meet a lot of lawyers and nag for new ideas to be introduced. My intention was to make Chanel the biggest house on the planet, but they won't let me.'

'Who is "they"?' Monique asked.

'The *direction*,' Samantha said. 'They are ultra-conservative!'

'Do you ever wonder who will continue the Chanel style when she dies?' Monique mused. 'Who she might leave her house to?'

'Nobody,' Sophie shrugged. 'When I was a little girl I heard my mother say that Mademoiselle earned a million dollars a year from perfume royalties alone. That sum stuck in my head. Can you imagine, a million dollars? Every year? And she doesn't spend one penny of it.'

'Yeah, what good does that money do her?' Samantha said. 'It just accumulates in Swiss banks.'

'Being a model . . .' Monique stared at Sophie admiringly. 'Is it wonderful?'

'Oh, it's just like being a prostitute.' Sophie shrugged.

'How can you say such a thing?' Monique covered her mouth with her hand, her eyes wide.

'Oh please, Monique,' Sophie said. 'Sometimes the salon is full of playboys looking for girlfriends. Why would handsome single men attend Chanel showings, if not to drool over the models? Are they so interested in fashion? Yesterday, a guy had his hand in his pocket – I swear he was playing with himself.'

'Couture porno?' Samantha cried.

'But if they want to watch girls, they should go to the Crazy Horse Saloon,' Monique said, 'Not to Chanel.'

'Mademoiselle likes beautiful young girls,' Sophie laughed. 'So do men. I am not in the least tempted by these guys. I know their reputations from my parents' *salon*. I know exactly what they have to offer.'

'Big cocks?' Samantha asked hopefully.

Sophie shot her a look. 'Sometimes not so big,' she said.

They collapsed in laughter and Monique turned bright red. Although the most prudish, she loved the way they let their hair down when together. It made a delicious contrast to the old spinsters she lived with. Finishing her wine in a gulp, she fixed them with her dark eyes.

'I survive on an hour a week with Guy. We meet at a hotel—' she broke off, staring at them helplessly. 'How guilty and grubby I feel afterward.'

'Use a better hotel,' Samantha advised.

'It is not the hotel. It is the fact that Guy is married. I feel so ashamed.'

'I'm sure you get over it, dear,' Samantha snorted. 'Good regular sex is as important as great pastries and great dry-cleaning.'

'He makes me feel that I'm a woman,' Monique agreed. 'I cannot look at other men. Something marks out Guy as the only man I can ever love or even notice. Why?'

'Yes . . . why?' Samantha mused, inspecting an olive before popping it in her mouth. 'You should ask yourself that.'

'I do, every night. And I still do not know the answer. He has something that . . . somehow . . . gets inside me.'

'Monique,' Samantha giggled, 'did you really mean to say that?'

Monique blushed and glared at her. Sometimes Americans were so crude, she thought. Or was it just Samantha?

Sophie did not feel well during the following week. She always took good health for granted and was terrified of doctors, but eventually she felt that she should consult one.

She made an appointment with the fashionable society doctor her mother used: his office on the Faubourg St Honoré was almost next to Hermes' boutique. This in itself seemed reassuring. She needed permission from a Chanel bigwig to take time off from posing for her ten o'clock appointment.

At eleven, the beautiful young girl with a mane of red hair, stepped out of a doorway, took a few halting steps along the Faubourg St Honoré and collapsed on the pavement.

Passers-by glanced down at the impeccably groomed girl lying, as if peacefully sleeping, spread out on the pavement in a lavender coloured Chanel suit: was she posing for some surrealist fashion shot by Guy Bourdin, a *Vogue* photographer who did rather morbid shots of beautifully dressed girls seemingly unconscious?

When they realised that there was no photographer around, they ran to her aid. Men knelt by her and old ladies gingerly touched her . . . everyone asked if she was all right.

She was gently helped to her feet and guided into a nearby café where the kindly proprietor pulled out a chair, poured a glass of water and offered a stiff Scotch: Sophie shook her head. She slowly sipped some water, trying to digest the news the doctor had delivered.

Twenty

That afternoon, Sophie sat before the *cabine* mirror, trying to organise her thoughts as she drew on eye-liner.

'Hangover, *cherie*?' her neighbour, a gorgeous girl named Rebecca, asked. 'You seem a little fragile.'

'I'm fine, thanks,' Sophie replied.

She modelled the collection as usual, then relaxed in the *cabine* with her feet up until late afternoon.

Mademoiselle liked to receive Sophie for gossip and Scotch in the top-floor *salon* at around six o'clock. That evening, as Sophie entered, she received the full blast of a penetrating X-ray stare aimed at her.

'You're pregnant,' Mademoiselle said.

Sophie was so surprised that she blurted out, 'How do you know?'

'A gift I have.' Mademoiselle smiled grimly. 'I'm like a water-diviner. You intend to get rid of it? Girls go to London, don't they?'

'I want it.'

She would have answered the opposite to just about anything Mademoiselle Chanel suggested, just to provoke her. But, as she spoke, she realised that she had been given away as a baby and she was not going to repeat the pattern. She *did* want this baby.

Chanel's mouth twisted downward. 'Who is the father?' she snapped. 'I assume you know?'

'Yes, I know,' Sophie nodded gravely. 'It is Christopher Hutchins your new friend.'

'Have you told him?'

'Not yet.'

'Well, wait and think about it. You have a wonderful career ahead of you,' she said. 'Why ruin it?'

Sophie shook her head, wonderingly. 'Mademoiselle,' she began quietly, 'this is my own child growing inside me. How can you suggest I murder it?'

'It is not yet a child. End it,' Chanel grunted.

'I won't do that.' Sophie shook her head.

Mademoiselle arched forward like a snake.

'Then give *me* the child!' she hissed. '*I'll* take care of it. I'll give it a wonderful life.'

Sophie sat down, suddenly. Was this the solution? If Mademoiselle adopted the child, could she watch it grow up, well cared for? And how long did Mademoiselle have to live? If she died, would the child then be hers again?

'Because I was thrown into an orphanage—' Sophie began.

'You were *not* thrown into an orphanage. How *dare* you say that?' Chanel erupted.

Her outburst was fierce and Sophie saw that she immediately regretted it.

'You know who my parents were?' Sophie cried.

Chanel's eyes darted around the room. 'No,' she said. 'No, but I do know that you were not given away. And certainly *not* to an orphanage.'

Sophie studied her, shaking her head. 'You know all about me, don't you?' she asked wonderingly.

Chanel ignored the question.

'Give me the child,' she said. 'She'll inherit my empire.'

Sophie turned to Mademoiselle with a searching look.

'And this empire,' she asked softly, indicating the elegant *salon*, 'did it make *you* happy, Mademoiselle?'

She watched the light in Mademoiselle's eyes flicker and die.

'I think you know who my parents were, Mademoiselle,' Sophie said. 'What I don't understand is why you won't tell me.'

'What did she say?' Ines asked later that evening.

'Nothing,' Sophie told her. 'She is a stubborn lady.'

They sat on Sophie's sofa, bare feet tucked beneath them, sipping a little wine.

'She must be mad,' Sophie said. 'Can you imagine such an old woman adopting a baby? She's eighty-six, Ines! She lives in a hotel room. Can she believe my baby would make her happy? Perhaps she's senile? Would *she* care for it? She needs care herself.'

Ines stared at her. 'So you are having it?'

'I must speak to Christopher first.'

'He will want the child. He will also want *you*.'

'We'll see,' Sophie said.

There was a lonely moment when Ines left. Then she realised that a child was actually growing inside her, so how could she ever feel lonely again? The idea of a daughter had already taken hold, but imagine if it were a little boy? Well, fathers liked sons, didn't they? She knew she would have to tell Christopher about it. Later that night, she called to tell him her news.

'We will marry,' Christopher said, without any hesitation.

'Oh, really?' Sophie handed him a glass of wine. He was in her flat the following evening. 'And how will three people live on a *stagière*'s salary? I don't even understand how *you* live on it?'

He held her eyes. 'I'm living off my pay-off from Delange. If we married, I'd leave the workroom and find a job. Any job.'

'Christopher,' she sighed, fixing him with her grey-green stare, 'I know Ghislaine pays for your *stage*. I also know you are sleeping with her. Everyone knows. I have no intention of marrying you.'

His gaze wavered slightly.

'If you don't sleep with me, I have to sleep with someone,' he tried.

'I do not sleep with you because you sleep with *her*!'

236

'OK!' He faced her. 'Yes, Ghislaine pays for my *stage*. As an investment. She intends to back me in my own house.'

'Well? Don't you see? If you married me, you would lose her support.'

His hand sought hers and held it.

'That's why I said I must find some job . . .' he brought her hand to his lips and kissed it.

'The other solution,' she removed her hand to search for a cigarette, 'is an abortion in London.'

A pained expression crossed his face. He began to say something, then stopped.

'Men think everything is so easy,' Sophie said, inhaling. 'Have a baby. Get married. Not always in that order. But Christopher, one must consider the consequences of one's actions.'

'Oh?' he laughed. 'Do *you* consider the consequences of your actions?'

'I don't know what to think. An abortion might save both our careers but I don't know that I am capable of such a thing.'

'It would be such a beautiful child, Sophie. It would have the best of both of us.'

'What if it had the worst?'

'No, he'd be a beautiful, tough little boy.'

'But I see an adorable, strong little girl.'

He leaned to kiss her gently on her lips.

'This baby is a blessing, Sophie.'

She looked at him for a long time, saying nothing.

'I need a little time,' she said, finally. 'One should not rush into parenthood.'

'Nor an abortion,' he said.

After a gentle kiss goodbye, Christopher walked down the Champs-Elysées, and around the Place de la Concorde, reversing the route he'd taken on his first visit to Sophie. What a mess his life was turning into. And it didn't have to be a mess. He and Sophie could be happily married with a beautiful child, one of several, on the way. It just needed . . . plans, money, security. All the things he did not have right then.

Why did life happen in the wrong order?

'If she hadn't told me,' he said to Klaus when he got home later that night, 'she could have gone to London for a long weekend, come back without being pregnant and I would be none the wiser.'

'But she *did* tell you, Christopher,' Klaus pointed out. 'She wanted you to know. Maybe she wanted you to persuade her to have the baby.'

'I asked her to marry me,' Christopher said.

Tired and hungry, he made a sandwich and ate it ravenously.

He took a sleeping pill in order to sleep, waking up thinking he must speak to Ghislaine. She had once told him she regretted not having children. He could talk this over with her.

Ghislaine was waiting for him at Olivier, the bar of the moment, in a narrow street off the Boulevard St Germain des Prés. She wore the smartest little navy dress. One of his, of course. Just seeing her sitting on a bar-stool, cigarette in hand, a glass on the counter, gave him ten new ideas for dresses. He shook them from his head.

He kissed her and sighed. 'I suppose it's best to get right to the point?'

'Oh yes, my darling, I love getting to the point,' Ghislaine giggled.

'I'm sorry this isn't a joke, Ghislaine. My girlfriend is pregnant,' he told her.

'What a brutal way to tell me!' Ghislaine drained her cocktail and signalled for another, stubbing out her cigarette. 'Are you sure it's yours?'

'Yes.'

'Well, you'd better find out what a long weekend in London costs?'

'I want this child.'

She set down the cigarette she had been about to light, staring at him, then gave a quick shrug and lit it, taking a long draw. She seemed about to scream at him, then changed her mind and said quietly, 'Christopher. Just get on with your *stage* and leave this to me.'

'What does that mean?' He held her gaze. 'It is my child. I want it.'

She pushed back her chair and stood up. 'I know Sophie and I will speak to her.'

'But what business is it of yours?' he burst out.

She gave him a grim look, slithering off the bar-stool. 'If you don't think it my business, why are you here? What is there to discuss?' she asked.

She stalked out of the bar, leaving him to throw down some money. He ran after her, just catching her taxi as it drove off, Ghislaine's profile at the window, staring straight ahead.

'Does Christopher know you are here?' Sophie asked.

'This is strictly between us,' Ghislaine replied.

She leaned across Angelina's marble table-top. She had dressed for the occasion in a guipure lace dress and tiny jacket – the perfect outfit in which to take care of your boyfriend's girlfriend. Her make-up was barely noticeable, but it was more artfully applied than Sophie's. Her gleaming dark hair was tied back with a wide black grosgrain ribbon.

Angelina, a Rue de Rivoli tea-shop for ladies who took *le thé Anglais*, was across the street from the Jardin des Tuileries. It had dainty wrought-iron tables with excruciatingly uncomfortable matching chairs. Late afternoons, it was packed with women gorging on cakes and gossip. When the French chose tea, they made more fuss than the English. Tea-pots were swaddled like babies in white linen napkins, then carried lovingly to tables and carefully set down.

Sophie wore an oatmeal tweed Chanel jacket over tight worn jeans and a white shirt. From the waist up she was a Chanel mannequin. From the waist down, a rebellious young student. Her hair was tied in a purple chiffon scarf drooping down on either side of her head. Another fashion photograph, she thought, wryly: two ladies, backs arching as they faced each other across a tea table, shot in black and white by William Klein. She could almost see the caption: *Jacket by Chanel, scarf by Pucci, shoes by Roger Vivier, model's own Levi's* . . .

'I invited you here to discuss your little . . . problem,' Ghislaine began.

'Why would I discuss it with you?' Sophie asked. 'Haven't you caused enough trouble?'

'Well, it's my problem, too. You see, I have enormous faith in Christopher's talent. I have invested in it. And this could prove a real stumbling-block.'

'Stumbling-block?' Sophie lit a cigarette and Ghislaine leaned in to get hers lit, too. 'Not a very nice thing to call a beautiful baby.'

The waitress placed a plate of tiny *sandwichs au concombre* between them. They ignored them, watching each other warily.

Sophie regarded Ghislaine so blankly that Ghislaine finally laughed and said, '*Voyons*, Sophie. You agreed to meet. Obviously you thought there was something to discuss.'

'I often meet people without knowing why,' Sophie murmured.

'Yes, I heard you met Didier Brunwald recently. What did Christopher think of that?'

Sophie shrugged. 'Christopher is in no position to judge any-thing I do. Anyway, Ghislaine, I know very well what you are about to propose.'

'You do? Then why not tell me what I intend to say?'

'You're going to advise me to abort this "stumbling-block".'

Ghislaine sat back in her chair. 'Sophie, I have known you since you were a little girl.'

'Perhaps, but not very well,' Sophie added.

'I respect your mother enormously.'

'Everyone respects my mother,' Sophie said, tersely.

'Yes,' Ghislaine giggled. 'We really should propose her as the new Patron Saint of the Haute Couture! To replace that dreary old St Caterine!'

The waitress slipped a platter of petits fours onto the table.

240

Thin slices of lemon impaled by toothpicks lay in a saucer alongside a milk jug.

'I always wanted to be as admirable and moral as your mother, but . . .' Ghislaine shrugged. 'I found out it was more fun being immoral.' She laughed. 'Shouldn't *she* be sitting here instead of me?'

'She doesn't know,' Sophie said. 'And you won't tell her.'

'First the necklace, now a baby,' Ghislaine said. 'How many more secrets of yours must I keep? You'll always be found out in the end, Sophie.'

They sipped their tea.

'Christopher is a gentleman,' Sophie said suddenly. 'The moment I told him, he proposed marriage.'

'Christopher is not the most practical of men,' Ghislaine said, pouring their tea. 'He is an artist, so I must speak for him in this matter. And do we even know it is his child?'

'I am not like you,' Sophie stated cooly. 'I do not sleep with many different men.'

Ghislaine gave her a quick glance, pouring more tea, unsure whether to feel insulted or complimented. She withdrew an envelope from her quilted Chanel bag.

'There's enough in here for a safe, clean, recommended "weekend" in London,' she said, holding Sophie's eyes meaningfully. 'And the phone number of a reliable doctor. It's a weekend I have sometimes taken. And it wasn't that bad,' she assured her. 'I even lost a little weight and bought some nice boots.'

She pushed the envelope across the table. After a moment of hesitation, Sophie took it.

Ghislaine nodded, as if this was the correct procedure.

'I suggest you book your trip as soon as you can,' she said. 'Next Friday, even. And when it is all over, why don't you treat yourself to a super pair of Anello and Davide thigh-high leather boots?'

'Is that what you think a human life is worth?' Sophie said tonelessly.

'*Voyons*, Sophie, it is not a question of money or worth, it is a question of planning one's life.'

'Did you plan yours?'

Ghislaine smiled icily. 'Nobody has the perfect life, Sophie. I have had more experience than you. This London weekend *will* solve most of the problems.'

Many curious glances were cast their way. Discovering Ghislaine de Rives in their midst reassured many of these tea-drinking Parisiennes that they had chosen the chic place. But none of the women watching these two sipping tea so charmingly in their contrasting yet of-the-moment outfits would have dreamed they were discussing anything so serious.

'And then?' Ines prompted that evening in Sophie's flat.

'I took the envelope and left,' Sophie told her.

'You weren't too proud to take the money?'

'She thinks she can buy off anything. If she wishes to hand out money . . .' Sophie shrugged, rummaging in her bag for the envelope. 'I didn't even look inside.'

She passed the envelope to Ines who tore it open greedily, fanning out crisp fifty-franc notes.

'Three thousand francs!' she marvelled. 'What will you do with it?'

Sophie shrugged. 'I may not use it for what she suggested. I haven't decided. All I know is . . . the more I picture this baby, the more I want it.'

Sophie went up to see Mademoiselle the following evening, double-checking her reflection to make sure she looked perfect. The pale blue Chanel suit set off her red hair beautifully. She would never wear jeans with a Chanel jacket in front of Mademoiselle; she knew it would seem insulting to the old lady.

'I am thinking of going to London . . .' Sophie began hesitantly.

'For how long?' the sharp question came.

'For a while, perhaps; I don't know.'

Mademoiselle reared back. 'You're not leaving Chanel?' she

asked, 'I *like* the way you wear my clothes. Did you know we sell more of the outfits you model? You are one of those rare models who *sells* the clothes. And you are getting magazine work! It would be most inconvenient if—'

'I must go to London, Mademoiselle.'

'For that?' She gestured at Sophie's stomach.

'Perhaps. I haven't decided. I could return if you wanted me to . . . ?'

'Sit here, next to me.' Chanel patted the sofa.

Sophie sat stiffly on the edge of the suede cushion.

The old lady reached out to take her face gently between her hands.

Sophie flinched. Mademoiselle turned her face this way and that, peering at it. 'You *must* return, Sophie, you are to be my Face,' she whispered urgently.

Sophie watched, puzzled. 'Your "Face", Mademoiselle?' She frowned.

'Yes,' the old lady said, touching her chin, watching Sophie's cheek-bones catch the light. 'This face will sell a lot of perfume.' She let go, watching Sophie expectantly.

'I don't understand.'

'Each year, we choose a girl whose "look" represents Chanel,' Mademoiselle explained. 'She becomes The Face of Chanel. Her face advertises the perfume all over the world. This year, when you began to be featured in the magazines, I showed them a cover from *Elle* proposing *you* as our new Face. Usually they don't listen to me but this time everyone agreed. *You* will be the new Face of Chanel. Every girl we have used has become a top model. Everybody wants the Chanel Face.'

As Mademoiselle watched her, Sophie tried to think quickly. She gave a delighted smile, knowing she should be feeling triumphant. But she no longer had ambition. It had been replaced with the ambition to become a mother.

'I will be paid for this?' she asked.

'The usual fees for posing for photographs,' Chanel nodded. 'And you will sign an agreement to be exclusively *our* Face.'

'Exclusive?' Sophie blurted out. 'Surely that deserves more than the usual modelling fees, Mademoiselle?' she broke off, shrugging.

Mademoiselle stared at her. 'I thought you would be thrilled.'

'I *am* thrilled, Mademoiselle,' Sophie bent towards the old lady to kiss both her cheeks. 'It *is* an honour to be chosen. But I want what I am worth. I have a child to think about, remember.'

Chanel pushed her away, flustered.

'You were born with that face,' she said gruffly. 'It's a certain look you have. It could be your fortune. The model agency will negotiate your fees. You cannot leave before they take the photographs. This is an important event for you.'

Sophie left Mademoiselle, going straight to Samantha's office.

Samantha listened, frowning. 'I'll ask the advertising people to arrange the photographs as soon as possible,' she promised.

Sophie kissed her.

The shoot was set for early the following week.

Sophie had days to wonder why Mademoiselle was insisting on her. The Chanel Face – personified by models like Suzy Parker or actresses like Catherine Deneuve – had always been a face whose class, beauty and elegance put across the Chanel image. It usually involved at least a one-year contract.

The next morning, Sophie called the head of her modelling agency and told her to ask ten times the usual fee of a Chanel Face.

'But we have never asked so much,' the woman gasped.

'If Mademoiselle Chanel herself wants me, you can ask anything,' Sophie told her. 'Times are changing. Publicity has become more valuable.'

She got it.

A few days later, Sophie underwent two hours of make-up, an hour of hair-styling and several hours of excited studio assistants jumping around as she emoted for the camera of an English photographer and *Elle* favourite. They began with a fresh clean look. Then Sophie's hair was tied back, frizzed up, covered with a wig of straight silky Dynel hair or adorned with twisted silk scarves. She tried a long evening dress and then a white tennis sweater and slacks. With jewellery and without. For close-ups, she was urged to express every emotion from tragic sadness to wide-eyed happiness. They wanted a lot of shots to choose from and she estimated, as she staggered from the studio to a waiting taxi, that they had taken thousands.

There was no guarantee that any of the photographs would be used, but she was told very definitely that if they were used, she would become the most sought-after model in France.

The next day Sophie went to see the agency who booked her magazine modelling sessions. She asked about the possibility of modelling work in London and they promised they would speak to their London branch.

She wrote a note to Christopher and left it with Ines, who had agreed to stay in her apartment and take care of Dog.

Outside the apartment, as the taxi to the airport awaited, Ines hugged her friend hard and suddenly began to cry.

'Let me come with you, Sophie?' she wept. 'You should have someone taking care of you, in case . . . well, you *are* going to get rid of it?'

'I'll decide in London.' Sophie got into the taxi. 'I shall come back either very slim and pale or holding the new heir to Chanel and Co.'

'It takes longer than a weekend to have a baby—' Ines began, but Sophie slammed the door shut and gave a wave.

'Take care of Dog!' she cried.

And with that she disappeared.

Twenty-one

This London was very different to the city Sophie had visited several times with her parents. They had stayed at grand hotels, visited the National Gallery and the Tate, met some rather stuffy people, seen a staid city. Now, although rainy and grey, London seemed a lot more fun. She liked the Bloomsbury bed and breakfast near the British Museum recommended by her agency, and after spreading a few Chanel scarves around her room, she felt quite at home.

The chill autumn weather did not dampen her spirits but she was slightly unnerved by the changes she had begun to notice in her body. On her second morning in London, she suffered morning sickness for the first time. It was a reminder that her life and body were about to change and it made her realise that she had never for one moment seriously considered an abortion. So why was she here? Perhaps to make a new life for herself?

She visited the London branch of her agency: they were wonderfully optimistic about getting her bookings. Her book, which she had brought with her, showed her most glamorous shots from *Elle* and *Vogue*. The agents were impressed by her different looks. They made a big fuss of her, dubbing her 'the anti-Twiggy' because she was rounded and feminine and not at all boyish. Many bookers mentioned her breasts, a novelty in the fashion world. They booked her on 'go-sees' to magazine editors, photographers and advertisers.

On the third day, she had dates with a few photographers and had to call to delay them an hour as she recovered from her nausea. Luckily her pale face only seemed to interest them more. Her cheek-bones benefited from a slight weight-loss, becoming more defined. She would have to tell the agency about her pregnancy – maybe later they could book her for face and hair shots. One advantage of being pregnant was that her skin glowed and her hair seemed stronger and glossier.

That morning, she discovered the trendy Chelsea streets off the King's Road where many photographers had their studios. They seemed enthusiastic as they pored over her portfolio, muttering 'Super!' or 'Far out!' at her better shots. It was the moment when the French found the British 'fresh' and the British found the French slightly exotic.

After some 'go-sees', Sophie found herself wandering the King's Road. It had a different atmosphere to the rest of London. It was full of fashion boutiques like Mary Quant's Bazaar, showing new-looking clothes, a little whackier than Paris styles. Passers-by seemed younger, better made-up and better dressed than the rest of London. On this street, she realised that London could be a lot of fun. King's Road seemed to go on for ever. Since she had no other appointments that day, she decided to walk the entire length of it.

Ghislaine had put Christopher on a gruelling regime.

'All day in the workroom learning my craft,' he complained to Klaus. 'Thinking up designs and sketching them out at home. Then sparkling with witty conversation at dinner, and performing well in bed.'

'Sounds good to me, Chris,' Klaus said.

Christopher shot him a dark look. 'I race to keep up with her and her crowd. I miss people my own age. It's a strain always pretending to be more sophisticated than you really are. And I am out of my mind about Sophie, she seems to have disappeared.'

A telephone-call from Ines told him she had a note from Sophie:

I have gone to London. Please don't try to find me. I will decide what to do and let you know . . .

'What did she decide?' he asked Ines.

She shook her head. 'She had not yet decided anything.'

'What mood was she in?'

'Unsure,' Ines said. 'Even as she got into the taxi.'

'Well, I can't let her find some back-street abortionist on her own,' Christopher cried. 'I must find her, mustn't I?'

He had almost forgotten London. That big city with a vibrant life of its own had carried on perfectly well without him and he without it. He had dutifully called his mother each week. She was delighted when he announced his visit for the next weekend. His first since he'd left.

'I kept your room just as you left it,' his mother said.

'It's not a shrine, is it, Mum?' he laughed.

How weird it would be to sleep in the room he had left as a callow young man with no experience of the world. He was returning to it a different person. Wiser, he hoped, and a little nearer to his dream.

'Ghislaine, Sophie has just vanished into thin air.'

'*Vanished?*' Ghislaine tried for a sympathetic expression.

They were sitting in Les Deux Magots celebrating the end of another day in the Chanel workroom.

'She's in London,' Christopher sighed. 'I don't know what exactly she is doing there. She is going to be Chanel's new Face.'

'Congratulations. I was the Face in 1959, you know . . .'

She began to describe her days as Chanel's Face. He thought, very hard, of Sophie's enigmatic note. Surely an abortion could be her only reason for going to London, although Ines said she had spoken of modelling work.

'Are you listening to a word I say?' Ghislaine suddenly cut in on his thoughts.

'What? Sorry. It blows your mind when your girlfriend disappears.'

'She'll be back in a few days,' she soothed. 'You know what young girls are like today.'

He looked at her. 'London can only be to get rid of my child or to give birth to it?'

Her eyebrows shot up. 'Well, that's easy. If she returns in a few days, you'll know. If she does not return for eight months, you'll also know.'

'Ghislaine,' he began, 'I don't think I can—'

'Sshhhh,' she placed a finger on his lips. 'Don't say anything you might regret.'

He stopped, staring at her.

'Wait until you hear what she plans to do,' she said.

Meanwhile, I cannot sleep with you, he wanted to say, swallowing the words. If only he could have swallowed his food that easily when they dined later at a nearby bistro.

'I'm going to London,' he told her near the end of the meal. 'I must try to find her.'

'Walking out of your *stage*?' she asked. 'After all the trouble I had arranging it?'

'This is more important.' Christopher got to his feet. 'I've had enough of the *stage*. I am not a seamstress, Ghislaine.'

Ghislaine threw down her fork with a clatter.

'I have *completely* lost my appetite!' she cried accusingly.

'I'm *so* sorry,' he said as ironically as he could. 'I've tried really hard. I just don't think I am cut out to sew. Excuse the pun.'

'Instead, you'll run all over London looking for a girl?'

'It's not *a girl*, it's *Sophie*. I'll see her agency; I am sure they'll have an address for her. I must find her. And I will!'

'I'm getting rather tired of de Kousmine and his grunts,' Samantha confided to Jean-Jacques on one of her nightly phone-calls.

'I knew you would!' he sighed with satisfaction.

'I found my own job at Chanel, without his help; why do I need him?' she asked.

'Free Chanel suits and jewellery?' he suggested.

'I don't need de Kousmine,' she said. 'But if I limit myself only to Klaus—' she broke off for a long pause. 'The man in my life must be very successful,' Samantha continued. 'Klaus cannot go on being a hippie. I need to redesign him and start directing his photography. His shots are in focus but they need oomph. So does he!'

'Well, if anyone can give someone oomph, it's you, *cherie*. I can't wait to see the new Klaus!'

'While you're in London, I'm redesigning Klaus,' Samantha announced at Christopher's goodbye lunch at La Quetsch.

'With his agreement?' Christopher questioned.

'I don't need his agreement, I need him to be more successful. It's nice to have a little doll of my own to dress up,' she added defensively.

Christopher nodded. 'I began designing with paper dolls. But they were six inches. Klaus is six feet four.'

'That'll be even more fun. He'll love it!'

They ordered club sandwiches and cokes.

'Why do this to poor Klaus?'

'Because I'm bored. Did you ever think you'd hear me say that? Bored with Chanel? It's not the challenge I expected. If being bored means lining up everything to be perpendicular on your desk, then I'm bored. I'm supposed to plan Special Events. Since when did showing lawyers into Mademoiselle's *salon* count as a Special Event?'

'You could turn it into something better.'

'Meanwhile, I'm giving Klaus "Oooomph"! For his photography and for his image.' She took a gulp of coke. 'He needs a new wardrobe, a new haircut, a new beard, and a terrific new folio to show around.'

Christopher nodded. 'I have to confess, I always thought Klaus's work lacked something.'

'Exactly! Ooomph. In my book that's *fabulous* lighting, for a start.' Samantha took a deep breath. 'It's a technical thing. I may not understand it, but I *know* it when I see it and I think I could direct Klaus into it.'

Christopher nodded.

'I'd also help pose the model,' Samantha said. 'Klaus has watched *Blow-Up* too many times. It's too late to straddle a model and cry; "Come on, baby! Give it to me, baby! Groovy! Yeah, yeah, yeah!" She took a sip of coke. 'We're approaching the seventies! He's gotta be cooler, moodier. And he needs a *great* model. If only we could get Sophie. What d'you think?'

'I'm sure she'd pose for him if I can get her back to Paris.'

'Of course she'll be back,' Samantha said airily. 'Sophie couldn't exist anywhere but Paris.'

Christopher gazed around London in amazement. Hearing English spoken everywhere, seeing girls in mini-skirts under maxi-coats, staying in his old room at the modest family house, which now seemed like a squeaky-clean doll's house, eating English food – so tasteless after French: it all added up to a time-machine sensation.

Even his father seemed less gruff, asking a lot of questions about his Paris life and revealing that he had compiled a scrap-book of *Daily Express* cuttings about Christopher. When they asked what his life was like, what could he tell them? He could only think of the things he could not possibly tell them: *I'm in love with the Face of Chanel and she's either having or aborting my baby. I'm sleeping with a married society lady almost as old as you, Mum! I just walked out of a non-paying job.*

He spent his first evening at home with his parents, taking care not to contradict their rosy view of his Paris life, enjoying his favourite meat-pie which his mother had lovingly prepared. The quaintness of the flowered carpet and genteel curtains and the huge old television set made him smile.

'She never makes me meat-pie,' his father pointed out.

'It's hardly worth doing just for two,' his mother said, gazing fondly at Christopher as he ate.

Next morning, he flew out of the house at half past nine to find Sophie's agency in New Bond Street. He was there by ten, just as it opened. It was, buzzing with activity and the rather snooty girls were not very helpful at first. They seemed to think that working in a model agency made them superior in some way to normal people. They wore blunt clipped haircuts and smart clothes, but their brusque, arrogant attitudes gave them away. He marvelled again at how self-deluding the fashion business was; model-bookers thought they were models!

One or two real models popped in while he was there.

He did not get very far when he requested, then begged for, Sophie's address.

'How do we know you're her boyfriend?' they asked. 'Some of our girls get stalked by men who've seen them on posters.'

'I am not a stalker. This is rather urgent!' Christopher cried.

He was advised to await the agency director, who rolled in at eleven.

A no-nonsense type, she offered to pass on a message.

'I guarantee Sophie will get it,' she promised. 'Leave your number with me.'

He scribbled a quick message telling Sophie he was in London. He wrote his parents' phone number in large black numbers and handed it to the woman, ignoring her doubtful look.

After all the *soignée* Parisian women, everyone in London seemed slightly shabby, their clothing cheaply made, the seams about to unravel, the hems uneven. His critical eye took in everything, including his mother. To overcome these shameful thoughts, he made an effort to be nice to her, gifting her with a huge flacon of Chanel No. 5 and inviting his parents to dinner at a Chelsea restaurant he could not afford.

He heard his mother telling someone on the phone: 'He's working for Chanel now. Yes, that's right, *the* Coco Chanel.'

He did not have the heart to ruin their conviction that he was successful. They would be incredulous that he worked for nothing, learning to sew. Already, he had decided he must leave the atelier; it was a waste of time.

For their dinner out, his mother dressed in what she called her best 'frock', a word he had not heard in a while. She touched a careful drop of Chanel No. 5 behind her ears with the bottle's stopper. When they entered the Italian restaurant in Chelsea, she did not seem to feel out of place amongst all the young people in jeans or mini-skirts. But she was happy and her eyes sparkled. Christopher loved her for that.

He heard nothing from Sophie and called the agency director to confirm she had indeed been given his message. Then there was no choice but to return, unsuccesful, to Paris. He felt wretched. He imagined Sophie bleeding to death in some backstreet abortionist's grubby room. Recent 'working-class' English films had portrayed these rooms very graphically. He had no one in London to ask about such things or he would have made a tour of back-street addresses. It looked as if he would not find Sophie and he returned to Paris empty-handed.

Samantha, Jean-Jacques and Klaus sat at an outdoor table at the Flore.

'I've done a *fabulous* job, if I do say so myself,' Samantha cried, holding up a glass of champagne. 'I *love* redesigning!'

Book-ended by tiny Jean-Jacques and tall Klaus, Samantha had trawled Paris for the right men's hair-stylist, the right boot-seller and the right 'eyebrow shaper'. Even Klaus was surprised at the end result.

Cropped short, his hair enhanced by a henna rinse, his eyebrows 'reshaped', his little Vandyke beard shaved clean away, Klaus really wasn't so bad at all, Samantha thought. In black turtleneck, black jeans, black boots, black leather jacket, he was quite dashing. Would the new Klaus have a new marching rhythm? Samantha studied him, then relaxed.

'Now we're a *jolie-laide* couple,' she said happily.

*

Back in Paris, Christopher fell on the phone each time it rang, but it was always Samantha, asking, 'Heard anything yet?'

For a few days he avoided Ghislaine. Unable to contact other houses for work, he fell into a slump. Worrying about Sophie had resulted in one long dull ache. He drank too much, he slept too much and he even considered dating a pretty model he ran into.

Suddenly, Ghislaine made one of her early-morning 'have to see you' phone-calls.

'Did you find her?' Ghislaine did not beat about the bush.

'No.'

'Are you returning to your *stage*?' she asked.

'No.'

'Well, what *are* you doing?'

'Nothing.'

She gave a huge sigh. 'I am willing to admit I may be wrong, Christopher,' she announced. 'I have a new idea. Meet me at Les Deux Magots. Noon.'

He walked the leafy October streets of Saint Germain des Prés, enjoying the nip in the air and shuffling his feet through the leaves piling up in the gutters. This would be the first time since coming to Paris that Christmas approached without a Spring Collection to design. He found Ghislaine sitting at an outside table amongst the usual bunch of intellectuals. She air-kissed her entourage, and, still talking, moved to another table.

She was wearing one of his designs, a clean-cut, simple suit in white wool, to which she had added ropes of chains, hair ribbon and pins.

'Christopher, I have been wrong,' she announced excitedly when he had sat down and ordered coffee. 'A new idea was staring me in the face but I could not see it!'

'What?'

She rested her chin on her hands, her eyes alive with excitement.

'I always thought haute couture was the only way to dress,' she began. 'Until now! This new spirit of democracy in Paris – the student protests and street fashion – well, my more serious friends think it's obscene to spend what I spend on clothes. They've made me feel horribly guilty and suddenly expensive, handmade clothes seem so Marie-Antoinette! I deserve to be guillotined, don't I?' She gave a peal of laughter. 'But I cannot suddenly wear cheap clothing. So what can replace the couture? Because many women are thinking like me, and their daughters even more so.'

He frowned. 'Paper clothes? Disposable clothing?'

She leaned forward eagerly.

'Christopher, people got so excited about ready-to-wear clothing that they didn't realise the huge gap they were creating. Clothing doesn't have to be either obscenely expensive or shoddily cheap! A whole in-between market is being ignored. *Good* ready-to-wear!'

'What is "good ready-to-wear"?'

'Better made clothes with better quality fabrics. It won't be one hundred francs, but it doesn't have to be ten thousand francs, either!'

He nodded. 'I never really believed any outfit was worth ten thousand francs. It would be great to produce reasonably priced fashion.'

'But it must sell from a new kind of enterprise,' Ghislaine suggested. 'Situated a little "dangerously", like St Michel or right here in St Germain des Prés?' She popped her eyes at him excitedly. 'A new kind of place selling directly to clients, perhaps with one fitting to adjust the clothes to their bodies?'

'A shop?'

'Nothing so commonplace!'

'Sorry, a boutique?'

'Something so new it doesn't yet have a name,' Ghislaine mused, lighting a cigarette. 'We must come up with a fabulous new one.'

'Almost-Couture?' he suggested.

'*Prêt-à-Choquer?*'

'Ready to Bare?'

'Ready to Strip? Well, we'll think of something.'

He nodded. ' Place St Sulpice has always struck me as—'

'Leave the real estate details to me,' Ghislaine cut him off. 'All you have to do is start sketching wonderful clothes, Christopher. We'll need a terrific publicist . . .'

'Samantha?' he suggested.

Ghislaine pouted. 'If I can forgive her for that ghastly evening.'

'Oh come on,' he groaned. 'She's suffered enough. And what is "almost" couture, Ghislaine?'

'Off-the-peg but well made by a good firm. Generous hems to allow for alterations. Clients could buy a dress, fit it and have it altered while they had a coffee next door. It's the future, Christopher!'

'What sort of prices were you thinking of?' he asked.

She screwed up her face. 'Couture starts at seven or eight thousand francs . . . our off-the-peg should hover around five hundred francs, don't you think? Better than off-the-peg, but far cheaper than the couture. We'd get what the Americans call "impulse buys"?'

They fell silent, staring at each other.

'You keep saying "we",' Christopher said, finally.

She held his eyes. 'Yes, I say "we". Are you or are you not a designer, Christopher?'

He returned her intense stare.

'Yes, I am a designer, Ghislaine.'

Klaus's new look gave him confidence to zoom around Paris in a 'blitz' on fashion magazines. Samantha set up lunches at the Ritz with art editors and drinks with fashion editors at the Crillon. Her generous gifts of Chanel handbags to editors propelled Klaus into a *Vogue* commission.

Ghislaine's friends encouraged her new career choice of fashion entrepreneuse . . . everyone agreed it was what she would be best at. She quit the arts magazine the same morning Christopher called Monique to say he would not be returning to her work-room. The Sunday *salons* resumed. And so did his Sunday-evening sessions on the Porthault sheets. He changed his weekly dinner with Mademoiselle to Saturday.

Ghislaine's mood had changed, too. Their affair was starting to mean more to her than the light-hearted little romp she had always liked to portray. And one evening his passion failed him and she stared disappointedly at his less-than-ready body.

'You're going to leave me, aren't you?' she asked lightly.

Christopher found himself unable to say yes or no.

Ghislaine skated over the awkward moment in her usual graceful way, making a joke, rushing to the kitchen to serve a delicious snack and open a bottle of champagne. The important thing, he could see, was to keep it light.

Samantha had taught him an American saying: 'Never let them see you sweat!' The French equivalent must be: 'Never let them see you hurt!'

Ghislaine looked at boutiques in Odeon, St Sulpice and along the Boulevard St Germain. Christopher worked on a prototype collection of clothes, cheaper than he had ever produced.

'If your fashions are wildly successful, you'll be really committing yourself to Ghislaine,' Samantha warned.

He shrugged. 'I'll cross that bridge when it comes.'

It was one of the weirdest Christmases of his life, thinking of Sophie pregnant in London, no real job in Paris, sketching design after design for a new ready-to-wear collection.

In the new decade of 1970, Ghislaine rented a large room in Saint Germain des Prés to serve as her office and his studio. Monique recommended seamstresses, Ghislaine happily served as his sole fitting model, and, soon after New Year, Hutchins Rives Rive Gauche 'almost-couture' filled the air with the comforting hum of sewing-machines.

Twenty-two

'Your girlfriend is back,' Mademoiselle Chanel announced.

Christopher's heart gave a thump. He was dining with Chanel in the Ritz on a Saturday. It was too cold for her to go outside the hotel. Ten days after her new spring collection had been shown, she seemed exhausted and dissatisfied. Although it had received the usual headlines of 'Chanel reigns supreme', he had heard that she had been very difficult during the making of her collection, cantankerous and more critical than ever.

'Sophie has returned for more photographs,' the old lady said implacably. 'I'll see her tomorrow.'

He nodded, taking a big swallow of wine.

'You know about her . . . condition?' She peered at him sharply.

'Of course, Mademoiselle, it is my child.'

'What are you going to do about it?'

'I want to marry her. Can I offer more than that?'

She looked at him, nodding her head. 'She is lucky. No man ever offered me that,' she said quietly. 'Do you know why she has not accepted?'

'I think she has some idea that she must have this baby on her own.'

'Well, you see how times have changed?' She glanced quickly at him. 'In my day, a girl from a good family having a baby out of wedlock would be quite unthinkable.'

He nodded, and moved on to other, less dangerous, topics.

She had asked several writers to help her write an auto-biography. Each writer had backed out when they had realised she was drawing a veil of mystery over her origins instead of revealing them. Something in her early past struck her as so shameful and sad that she would not reveal it. Instead of sticking to one new story, she invented a dozen different beginnings.

One respected editor had recently left French *Vogue* and became impatient with Chanel's varying versions of her life. She announced an unauthorised version to appear after Chanel's death.

Nobody seemed to agree on where Gabrielle Chanel had sprung from, but it was rumoured to be a very modest orphanage run by nuns.

There was always plenty to talk about during their dinners.

'The food of my youth,' Mademoiselle said as their table was cleared that evening. 'One could not stop eating. Not from hunger, but for the *taste*. It came from the earth – no chemicals, no refrigeration. Even the cheap table wine was delicious where I grew up. Unadulterated. God knows what goes into it today.'

He tried to keep his attention on her but he could barely eat his dinner and could not wait to take Mademoiselle to the lifts.

As he bade her goodnight, she suddenly asked him, 'What do you want from me?'

He started, surprised. 'Nothing but your friendship, Mademoiselle,' he said.

Her face softened as she looked at him.

'You are very kind to me, Christopher, you keep me good company. This last collection was very difficult. I don't know how many more I can do. Someone must design for the House of Chanel when I stop, should it be you?'

He burst out laughing. 'Why me?'

She leaned against the wall, watching him.

'You understand my style . . .'

He nodded. 'I understand it, but my style could not be more different, Mademoiselle. I want nothing from you but our dinners and our conversations.'

'Yes . . .' she said. 'I believe you mean that.'

'I do.' He kissed the wrinkled cheeks, saw her into the lift and walked home.

Should he find out when Sophie was expected? Could he continue to love a girl, carrying his child, who did not call him?

After posing for more photographs for the Chanel campaign, Sophie had promised to give two hours of her precious time to Klaus.

'Why don't you come over and surprise her?' Samantha suggested over a quick coffee with Christopher. 'Women love surprises. And I'll be there, making sure Klaus takes the best pictures of his life.'

'*Surprise* her?' Christopher asked tersely. 'She hasn't answered my calls or letters. Would you "surprise" Klaus if he'd walked out on you?'

'Depends how horny I was,' Samantha giggled.

'No.' He shook his head firmly. 'I wouldn't dream of visiting your session and spoiling the atmosphere.'

'You wouldn't spoil it!' Samantha wailed.

'Samantha, I'm angry, hurt and disappointed. Don't you understand what she is doing to me?'

She looked up at him, her eyes going a little out of focus, as they always did at anything serious.

'I'll talk to her,' she promised. 'See if I can find out what's going on.'

'Sophie, you look *fabulous*!' Samantha cried at her friend. 'A trip to London and you come back with a whole new *look*?'

Sophie had gained a new beauty. Her red hair, redder than usual, had been straightened and cut in a London bob with a blunt fringe, which suited her face and brought out the expression in her eyes.

'A whole new look,' Samantha repeated, studying her closely. She picked up Sophie's eye-lid and tried to look under it. 'Are those coloured contacts?'

Sophie darted away. 'They are my own eyes, Samantha. How is Christopher?'

'He's great. I thought he might stop by to see you . . .'

Sophie grimaced. 'Better that he doesn't.' She indicated a softly rounded stomach. 'I hope you picked the right clothes to disguise this?'

Samantha handed her a Chanel dress. 'Right, dear. We want you to be happy. It'll mostly be close-ups. We need you to emote. We want an *ambiance* . . .'

'Play some Yves Montand,' Sophie suggested.

'What's wrong with the Rolling Stones?' Klaus called out, adjusting his white paper roll.

'What's *right* with them?' Sophie cried. 'I'm French, I need Yves Montand. If I give you two free hours of my time, I can at least choose my own music, no?'

Samantha scurried away to the record-player, making a surprised face. 'A diva is born,' she muttered to Klaus. 'Poor Christopher. Good thing he didn't come.'

Sophie disappeared into the make-up *cabine* where Jean-Jacques, also borrowed for the occasion, got to work on her face.

'If she goes on like this,' Samantha went on, 'The new Face of Chanel will soon be the new asshole of Chanel.'

Thanks to well-iced champagne, Klaus took some wonderful pictures. His harder, brighter lighting (synchronised flash-lights under silver-lined umbrellas), added a dramatic quality. Shadows were blacker, with more contrast between blacks and whites.

Samantha struck some poses and got Sophie to copy them.

The exaggerated positions looked far less comical when Sophie did them. She told them British photographers had asked models to kneel and sit at a recent British *Vogue* shoot, believing it gave Art Directors different 'shapes' to set against the usual full-length standing poses. Everyone now copied the idea of models running or jumping across a white studio, caught by the camera in mid-flight. Movement, action, emotion were the key words.

Armfuls of drop-dead gorgeous Chanel clothes were mixed

with worn jeans and T-shirts for 'Protest' contrast; Sophie's wardrobe portrayed a girl of today or even tomorrow. It was Sophie's idea to throw a Chanel jacket over tight old jeans.

'Mademoiselle will swoon at the sacrilege,' Samantha said. 'But it looks very nineteen seventy.'

Jean-Jacques did various looks, ranging from make-up that looked like no make-up at all to little white and yellow daisies painted over Sophie's face. His best effort was the romantic look – smudgy, shadowed eyes in deep sockets, blushed cheeks and pretty rosebud lips. This was Sophie at her most beautiful and ethereal, a fashion angel.

'What are you doing, Sophie?' Samantha asked, when she finally emerged from the dressing-room in her own clothes. 'I mean, with your life?'

Klaus was on the other side of the studio, labelling film cannisters.

'What am I doing?' Sophie lit a cigarette and blew out a long, troubled breath. It was the first quiet moment between the two of them and she held Samantha's stare without flinching.

'Trying to live my own life,' she said finally. 'I have a lot to understand and plan, you know? I like London and . . . I like being alone.'

Samantha, so rarely called upon for genuine advice or feeling, suddenly felt compelled to give it. She put her arm around Sophie.

'Don't lose Christopher, Sophie,' she warned her. 'He's one in a million. You don't know how lucky you are to have found him. And he loves you, I just know that.'

Sophie nodded, exhaling smoke. She looked into Samantha's eyes pleadingly.

'Samantha, I want to ask you something . . .' she began.

'Ask away!' Samantha cried.

'Just—' Sophie began and stopped. 'I miss him. I miss him so much. I know he's a good person. I'm even prepared to tell you I love him. But,' she made a helpless gesture, 'promise me you won't tell Christopher how screwed-up I am. This is something I must work out for myself.'

Samantha nodded. 'I promise. But, Sophie, there's so much I don't understand. You're so *beautiful!* You're going to be the world's top model. Every man will be in love with you. When that campaign gets underway you'll be the most famous face in the world! Even Twiggy didn't—'

Sophie touched her hand and her face changed. It made Samantha stop and suddenly see her as the saddest person she knew.

'All that shit about being the most beautiful, famous face in the world means absolutely nothing if you don't know who you are,' Sophie said.

'Oh!' Samantha gasped.

'I have a difficult year ahead of me,' Sophie said. 'Please don't mention my pregnancy to everyone. Nearer the time, I shall try to get only face or hair shots, and I must recover from the birth in record time. I must be discreet and stay in London. It would be scandalous if everyone here knew the Chanel Face was having an illegitimate baby.'

Samantha laughed. 'If Catherine Deneuve can marry in a black dress, surely you're allowed a love-child? If it was me, I'd use the publicity to become notorious! I'd—'

'It's not you, Samantha,' Sophie said softly. 'It's me. I don't want to be notorious. I just want to be a good mother.'

Each evening, Monique dutifully visited Madame Antoine to report on the day's fittings before going home.

'Where do you live, Monique?' Madame Antoine asked one evening. 'It seems strange that I don't know.'

'I rent a room at Châtelet from two milliners who are sisters,' Monique replied. 'I am one of several lodgers with them.'

Madame Antoine frowned, looking slightly pained.

'But now you have the means to make a comfortable home for yourself in Paris, why not find your own flat, create your own atmosphere?'

'*Oui, Madame*,' Monique said.

Madame Antoine began to discuss various areas of Paris and Monique let her talk. She means well, she thought, listening to all the plans she should be making. So far, she had felt no great motive to leave the sisters to make her own home, her own life.

'I really think you should consider it,' Madame Antoine ended. 'It would make Paris seem like home. And I'd feel more secure about you staying in Paris.'

'I am staying in Paris, Madame Antoine,' Monique said simply.

'Good.' Madame Antoine stood to show that their little meeting was over. Monique took the white, bejewelled hand Madame Antoine held out, glancing down at the red-lacquered nails and the perfect soft skin of hands that never scrubbed a floor or even a dish.

'Sophie has simply disappeared, Monique,' Madame Antoine said. The blue, intense gaze bored into her. 'Do you know where she is?'

'I believe she is in London, Madame, doing photographic modelling work. And she was recently here, for a few days.'

Madame Antoine shook her head to herself. 'But why wouldn't *she* tell me that?'

Monique made a sympathetic face. Then she allowed herself to ask, 'You said you adopted her, Madame?'

'Yes.' Madame Antoine inclined her head. 'I had two daughters: Sophie became our third.'

Monique nodded.

'I speak to you in confidence, Monique,' Madame Antoine reminded her. 'You don't repeat anything I tell you?'

'I never gossip, Madame, but . . .' she hesitated.

'Yes?'

'Why not tell Sophie about her parents? She really wants to know.'

Madame Antoine gave a troubled sigh and glanced up at Monique. 'I cannot. You'll have to take my word for that.'

'She *needs* to know!' Monique burst out.

Madame Antoine turned an icy gaze on her. It was chilling and it paralysed Monique.

'Monique, I think I know what is best for my daughter,' Madame Antoine said.

Monique nodded.

She walked slowly back, opened the mirrored door into the shabby part of the house. The part that smelled of sweat and toil and that day's warmed-up lunches. *Her* part. She thought she had learned how to deal with Madame Antoine. Not to be in awe of her but to speak honestly to her. But every now and then she misjudged. Why would you not tell a child who its parents were? she wondered.

The Chanel campaign splashed Sophie's face all over Paris. Billboards in the street and posters in the metro magnified her petite features to cinema-screen size. Simply by smiling enigmatically into the camera, she created an instant 'rapport' with the spectator. Only six letters appeared on the photograph: CHANEL. The glamorous, charismatic 'Face of Chanel' attracted a lot of attention. The campaign moved to magazines and newspapers.

Models were poised to become celebrities. Twiggy had begun the trend, and she was followed by Veruschka, Lauren Hutton and Donyale Luna, the first famous black model. Now it was Sophie's turn. Samantha used the sudden interest in their Face to get more publicity for Chanel. She sent out press releases detailing Sophie's 'discovery' by Mademoiselle Chanel herself, calling it 'A fashion fairy tale' and 'Chanel Cinderella', dramatising Sophie's mysterious 'disappearance' to London where photographers now demanded her services.

'If you love someone and they ignore you, the logical thing to do is to try to forget that person,' Christopher told Samantha and Klaus one evening. 'Isn't it?'

He sounded as if he were trying to convince himself.

They had dined at La Coupole and now sat sipping coffee on the plastic-covered terrace, which was surprisingly cosy in

February. His friends exchanged glances, looking at him sympathetically.

'Do I embarrass you when I speak about Sophie?' he asked.

'Christopher!' Samantha was shocked. 'Look at me. Has anything *ever* embarrassed *me*? It's just that,' she gulped some coffee, 'we love both you guys, so . . .' she made a helpless gesture. 'I did try to talk to her, when she posed for Klaus. I couldn't figure out what her problems are exactly, Christopher, but she seems to need to work things out for herself. I think she loves you. I am ninety-nine per cent sure there is no other guy around.'

He nodded. 'I know. But the best thing I can do is to forget her.' He swallowed the rest of his coffee. 'How do I do that?'

Unable to find a taxi that night, Christopher took the metro home. He walked down one of the long, connecting tunnels at a *correspondance*. It was emblazoned on both sides with the same Chanel poster featuring a giant close-up of Sophie. Sophie's eyes followed him as he strode by, the perfume advertisement repeating her face to infinity. He stopped, looking up into her eyes for a moment. Were they mocking? Were they sorrowful? Were they asking him to wait? He made himself believe they were asking him to wait. When you are in love, you can make yourself believe anything. One thing he knew: the story with Sophie was by no means over.

Twenty-three

Skirts could not get any shorter so they grew longer, and the maxi-coat grew so long it doubled as floor-sweeper. For women to buy fashion, it had to change each season. But this last change proved one too many and stores were left with racks full of unsold maxi-coats. But Fashion survived and although she had threatened her last collection might be her very last, the oldest lady who lived at the Ritz, Gabrielle Sidonie Chanel, began to think about her next.

She still had only one reason for leaving the Ritz – the forty steps to her *maison de couture*, where she began work on her autumn collection.

She was frail, but her mind was as sharply critical as ever. At the first fittings, she was almost demonic, ripping apart *toiles*, wrenching out sleeves and reducing workroom heads to tears. They felt that she had become over-critical, even senile.

Sunday was still her least-favoured day of the week. Without work, it passed interminably slowly. Without work, she was little more than an infirm, old, lonely lady. At work, she was head of the most famous fashion house in the world. She chose work. She rested in the same reluctant way as she ate, because she had to, not because she wanted to.

Although she went through the motions of lunching with a friend and taking a drive through the Bois de Boulogne with a new chauffeur, she lived for Monday morning when she could return to work, rip a jacket apart, *criticise*, be 'Mademoiselle Chanel'.

Monique's week centred around her hour with Guy. The precious ritual scarcely varied. It was the high point of her week. For one hour, in a three-star hotel bedroom, she greedily accumulated his caresses and love, to be cherished in memory later. Outside of that hotel room, when they passed each other in the house, they kept a formal distance. She lived off the emotion she felt at their love sessions, a remembered film to rerun in her mind whenever she felt lonely. A film complete with feelings, touch, skin texture and Guy's rough chest, against which she would nuzzle her nose. A film where Guy touched her body and made it come alive. Where Guy entered her body and gave her feelings and sensations no one else could give her and no one else would ever be allowed to give her. Yes, he was precious. He was irreplaceable. She had come to depend entirely, emotionally, upon him.

Would things be different if they did not meet in that dreary hotel room? Was Madame Antoine right, was it ridiculous to continue to live with two spinster milliners, like a poor student? If she welcomed Guy into her own home, would he feel more loved? Want to see her more often?

The sisters were always turning down requests to rent rooms. Leaving them would free a room for some other young girl, newly arrived in Paris.

She began to view properties and finally, rather half-heartedly, found a welcoming apartment in Le Marais, now an up and coming *quartier*.

It was a spacious, solid apartment; too good to turn down. A coat of white paint and it would be fit to live in. In a month, she was ready to move.

There was a tearful goodbye to the sisters, then Klaus gave her a lift, in his new second-hand car, to her new apartment. She was amazed at how few possessions she had accumulated in three years. Now, she could shop in the *Marché aux Puces* for pieces to make the flat a home.

With a kitchen of her own, she rediscovered a love for cooking. She liked to experiment and she also liked to eat. Her cooking attracted her friends, Christopher and Samantha, often accompanied by Klaus, to her new home for a Saturday or Sunday lunch.

'Dear Caterine,' she wrote her sister. 'I have my own apartment now in Paris. There is a spare bedroom which I call "Caterine's room". It is yours if you ever join me in Paris.'

Now that she had her own place, she asked Guy to visit her there.

'I can still spare only an hour,' he said.

He was alone in his atelier after everyone had gone home.

Swallowing her pride and her hurt, Monique replied, 'Perhaps you will extend it to ninety minutes?'

A few different expressions crossed Guy's face. Suddenly, his face softened and he reached for her.

'Yes. We will extend it to ninety minutes. Excuse me, Monique. I am not a very nice man, am I?'

He held her in his arms for a moment and she felt a surge of love for him.

'No,' she agreed. 'Sometimes you are not very nice.'

'Who will guarantee the quality of workmanship in my house when I am no longer capable? When I die?' Mademoiselle asked Monique one late afternoon in her *salon*.

Monique looked over at her, surprised.

'Mademoiselle, we all expect you to live to well over a hundred.'

'You made this jacket, didn't you?' Chanel asked sharply, indicating the jacket she herself wore.

'Yes, Mademoiselle.'

Being chosen to make Mademoiselle's own clothes was the greatest accolade for anyone who worked at Chanel.

'Then you are probably the best person to take over from me.'

'But I am not a designer.'

'Superb workmanship is more important,' Mademoiselle said.

269

'The clothes evolve out of that. What do you think? You don't talk very much. Don't be afraid to say what you think.'

'I am not afraid, Mademoiselle. I admire you enormously.'

'Being admired,' the old lady said acidly, 'is not what I want.'

'What *do* you want, Mademoiselle?' Monique sighed.

Chanel gave a hard little laugh. 'To be listened to,' she said. 'To be kept company.'

Yes, Monique thought. Isn't that what we all want?

'Why did you choose fashion. Mademoiselle?' she asked.

'Oh, I tried many other things before fashion found me. I wanted to be a singer, but I didn't have much of a voice. I had an amusing personality and I was a bit of a clown. I managed to get through a song or two. I made some hats for the ladies of Deauville, and . . .' she made an impatient gesture, adding, 'it's ancient history. I became successful because I didn't upholster women as male designers do!'

'I hate to talk of the past. Fetch some glasses. We'll toast your future!'

She did not like to drink alone, Monique knew, reaching for the Scotch Mademoiselle had indicated. She poured her boss half an inch and the merest drop for herself.

'Shall we drink to work?' Chanel clinked her glass. 'Good work.'

'Good work,' Monique echoed, sipping. 'Is that all there will ever be?' she asked suddenly.

Chanel sat bolt upright. 'Why? What do *you* want?' she barked.

'I would prefer to have found a man who wanted to marry me, Mademoiselle.'

Chanel stared penetratingly at Monique, the drink frozen on its way to her mouth.

'So would I,' she said and tossed down the Scotch.

In March, sales representatives of the main fabric companies lined up in the corridors to show their new fabrics for the next season. Beneath the jokes and casual cheerfulness, a lot depended on how much of their fabrics Mademoiselle ordered.

She favoured traditional houses like Garigue and Leseur, who specialised in wools and tweeds. Silk jerseys were usually supplied by an old firm called Abraham, there were some English tweeds, and whatever else caught her eye from various firms. These bluff, hearty salesman were not the most sophisticated men: some were quite vulgar, Monique thought. But one little plump salesman with a moustache made a point of catching her eye and winking when she passed him. She didn't wink back.

The fabric people were followed by the specialists: traditional old firms that sold braiding or flowers or feathers or buttons. Mademoiselle selected great stocks of these and all the other trimmings that might go into a suit or coat.

Flat gold chains decorated and weighted the jacket hems so that they hung properly. The chains were glimpsed only if the jacket was opened. She continued to use the finest silk for the linings. She never stinted on interlinings and stiffeners or pads, which were hand-sewn by seamstresses for shoulders or used to fill out hollows at the collarbone or neck.

If she used fur, it was as a lining: she believed that to hide luxury, so that it was visible only to the wearer, was the richest way to use it.

No one expected Mademoiselle to abandon her classic suits and little black dresses. No surprises were awaited from an eighty-seven-year-old who had more or less invented modern fashion.

The refinements she made to her cardigan suits delighted Chanelistas. She updated them, made them that year's models. The braid decorating the jackets might be a different width, or she might outline the entire pocket instead of only the top edge, the braid looped into a frogged 'o' or dispensed with altogether. Heavy gilt buttons were added or subtracted. The suit was refined and improved like a Volkswagen, or the Coca Cola bottle, subtly updated yet remaining essentially the same.

Chanel-addicts understood these tiny signs and knew if there were two, three or four buttons at the cuffs or whether that season's silk lining was flowered, contrasted or matching. All these details both inside and outside were hidden signs denoting the jacket's vintage, which, like a fine wine, had its year sniffed out by true connoiseurs.

Monique placated weeping seamstresses when their perfect work was ripped by Mademoiselle's shears. These last-minute panics when Mademoiselle went into a destructive frenzy were about power, people said. Others called it senility. Others interpreted it as her rage at life's unfairness. Meanwhile, models and cutters were reduced to tears. That season was the most difficult collection her staff lived through. Her attacks appeared almost demented, as if she were in pursuit of the perfect garment. The more she pursued it, the greater the impossibility of finding it.

Hutchins Rives Rive Gauche, christened HRRG, was a success from the first day.

The rails of 'almost-couture' clothes made in Italy sold out each week at a fraction of couture prices. They appealed to savvy Parisiennes.

Christopher and Ghislaine won over all types of customers and soon learned which sizes and alterations were most requested.

'Shopping at HRRG must be an act of rebellion, a protest against the exclusivity of couture,' Samantha announced with her usual hyperbole. Unofficially engaged to do their public relations in her spare time, she had attacked it with relish.

Brown paper shopping-bags were stencilled with portraits of Che Guevara and Mao and slogans like 'Down With Everything!'. The handles were elegant braided cord. Samantha managed to establish HRRG as a slightly 'dangerous' place to shop, despite prices of up to a thousand francs.

It was ironic that a client of the couture would back this, but Ghislaine, exhilarated by their success, found that she enjoyed providing an alternative to the strict exclusivity and privilege of the haute couture.

They scheduled their first 'real' collection for July, the same time as the couture showings.

'We'll catch the buyers and press in town for the collections and ready for a change . . .' Samantha advised. 'But we'll have no little gilt chairs giving people little gilt asses,' she decreed. 'We'll show the collection on live models in the windows with people

272

outside peering in. It can run continuously so four or five lots of spectators can see it. Anyone can watch. It's open to the people.'

'Maybe you could persuade your girlfriend to model in our window?' Ghislaine suggested.

'We are no longer in contact,' Christopher confessed.

Ghislaine raised her eyebrows.

He had managed to form a professional working relationship with Ghislaine. They were on the same fashion wavelength and all the meetings, fittings, sketchings, plans, made the time pass quickly, and his brain too tired to brood.

It was hard to forget Sophie when pages of her photographs were appearing in English *Vogue* each month. Christopher hoped her current love-affair was only with the camera. He noticed when she began to be photographed in bulky outfits or shown only from the shoulders up, modelling jewellery, hats, hair-styles or make-up. He knew her pregnancy must be starting to show.

Christopher got time off when Ghislaine's husband Bertrand was in town, using it to date other girls. He saw young models, usually only once or twice. He had dated some pretty ones, dropping them before they became serious, but nobody had taken Sophie's place in his heart. He could not get over the conviction that she was the only woman in the world for him.

He did not approve at all of his own behaviour. It puzzled him and he plunged into more work to try to forget what he'd done the previous night. He drank too much.

He still saw fashion as a sacrosanct calling. He refused to profit from Mademoiselle's loneliness in any way, apart from dining with her at the Ritz each Saturday night. So he felt a mixture of feelings when, one Saturday evening, Chanel suggested he should work for her.

'What would I possibly do for you?' he asked.

'Make my life easier,' she said. 'Smooth things between me and my cutters, my models, my workroom heads . . . there is too much friction. I can be difficult, I know. You could control my perfectionism.'

273

'I don't see myself as a "smoother", Mademoiselle,' he said gently. 'I am a designer. I have just escaped the couture to form my own company,' he told her. 'You are the most modern of all designers. And I have found a new way to be a designer. So far, this idea of Ghislaine's is working very well.'

She nodded sadly.

'Perhaps you are right. Perhaps the couture *is* over. Balenciaga certainly thought so when he closed his house! And if I find no one to replace me, I'll be next.'

'How do you end a love affair tactfully?' he asked Klaus later that week.

Klaus shrugged: 'This is something I never had to do, Christopher. The girl always ended it – *un*tactfully.'

It was one of their rare evenings out on their own and they had ended up at Le Flore at midnight.

'Ghislaine is hinting that she might leave her husband,' Christopher said. 'It's my cue to encourage her, but I don't. Sophie will come back to me, I feel certain. Have you seen her recently?'

'Yes – in London the other day. At Vogue House,' Klaus said. 'She is more beautiful than ever.'

'Does she have a boyfriend?'

'She doesn't mention one.'

Christopher nodded, feeling a little better. He tried to keep his mind so full of work that his feelings were hidden. He was drinking too much and it did not help his memory. Many aquaintances passed a joint around late at night and it was unhip to refuse. But however much he tried to blur the edges, he knew very well that soon Sophie would give birth to his baby. How would he feel then? It was much easier to pour another glass of wine than to answer that question.

'Is that Samantha?'

'Ye-e-e-s-s. Who's this?'

Her face was covered in yoghurt – a good beauty mask, she had read recently – and she wondered if it was also good for the telephone mouthpiece into which it dripped.

'Jerry, here. Jerold Von Schlossberg. Your father gave me your number.'

He told her he was tall, handsome, American, single, a friend of her father's and staying at the Ritz, six things that really turned her on, especially single, tall, handsome and Ritz.

He invited her for a drink.

It would be fun to have someone new to dress up for. This one sounded interesting, even slightly dangerous? He might be a spy sent by her father? She must look her very best.

'Nobody is more worth dressing up for than a man I've never met!' she confided to Jean-Jacques.

At three o'clock on Friday afternoon, Mademoiselle summoned Monsieur de Kousmine to her salon. He knew from experience that this was the most dangerous time of the week, just before the weekend when she faced two days of loneliness.

The big lumbering man was the only Chanel director she somewhat trusted. At least he was not a Wertheimer, the family who had bought the rights to Chanel perfume and, finally, to her house. No matter how many lawyers told her they were honest and honourable, she had always felt cheated. But she felt cheated by life, too.

She offered him a drink before launching into her subject.

'I am eighty-seven.'

He nodded.

'Who do I leave in charge of my house? There are four young people I have become very fond of,' she began. 'Three of them work here: Sophie Antoine, Monique Far and Samantha Lipstaadt. Then there is Christopher Hutchins, the English boy. They under-stand my style, my spirit.'

He nodded.

She peered closely at him.

'Can I count on you to see that anyone named in my will would actually receive what I intend them to have?'

'Surely that is a matter for the executors of your estate, Mademoiselle?'

'They are in Switzerland. I would feel safer knowing that there was someone in this house safeguarding my wishes. You are the only person I can ask.'

Monsieur de Kousmine gave his classic shrug. 'It would be a conflict of interests, Mademoiselle. I would be powerless.'

'But the Wertheimers trust you.' She stared at him, steely. 'You have some influence, surely?'

Monsieur de Kousmine stared mournfully at her.

'As a director of Chanel, how could I operate in a neutral way? I suggest Mademoiselle appoints an outsider.'

'Could you refuse a million dollars?' she asked bluntly.

'A bribe, Mademoiselle?' He frowned.

'Don't call it that,' she said. 'I would leave you a considerable sum in the "expectation" that you honour my other bequests. I want this house to be run by a person I know and *like* – someone who has been kind to me. Is that so unreasonable?'

De Kousmine cleared his throat. 'Mademoiselle, you overlook one rather important fact,' he began tactfully. 'It is no longer your house.'

Unreasonable? De Kousmine thought, walking home. Ha! Hadn't Mademoiselle's entire career been based on being unreasonable? Hats off, eh? he thought. One gets nowhere in this world by being reasonable. 'Reasonable' meant letting people walk all over you, in his opinion. Even so, he had to smile at the old girl's attempt to control Chanel & Co. even after her death.

He had been appointed to the board for his administrative skills. The Wertheimer family listened to him on some subjects, but they outnumbered him. He did not have enough boardroom influence to ensure that anyone chosen to 'take over' could actually run the house? The old girl was asking too much.

Sophie was just a little girl, he thought, a model, whose interest in a career would always be secondary to her own life. Christopher Hutchins was ambitious and dedicated but not at all in

Mademoiselle's style. Monique Farr did perfect work but would probably be capable only of recycling Chanel's designs.

As for Samantha – the Wertheimers would never allow even a *sane* American to head their company, and he was starting to wonder if Samantha could be described as sane.

So he could not guarantee Mademoiselle's choices even for a million dollars. The Wertheimers, who were honest and bright, would over-ride any last eccentric wishes. He could not accept the 'bequest', as Mademoiselle termed it. On that, Monsieur de Kousmine felt immovable and sure. Having provided his own answer, he grew tired of walking and, at the Place de la Concorde, hailed a taxi.

Samantha watched the cosmetic floor of Galleries Lafeyette as Christian Dior launched its new make-up range of lipsticks, foundations, mascaras, pencils and anything else a woman could apply to her face or body gleamed, glossy and glamorous, from special displays. Yes, cosmetics with a couture name would sell more than clothing, and perhaps more than perfume.

Women clustered around the large golden logos spelling out 'Christian Dior'. Experts offered make-overs, *visagistes* painted *visages*, samples were handed out. What woman alive could resist a Dior lipstick? Luxurious, glamorous, yet still affordable. A tiny bit of the dream, Samantha reminded herself, just as she had predicted. She stood watching the scene, fiercely jealous.

Chanel must follow suit as soon as possible, she thought, walking back to the house. She must make them introduce a range of products.

But de Kousmine firmly barred her entry to any of the secretive directors' meetings, hissing, 'You're not yet at that level.'

Far from helping her rise in the house of Chanel, he was a barrier to any progress. She could talk with Mademoiselle but the board of directors would not listen or be interested. She was powerless. And Samantha rendered powerless was a peculiarly upsetting sight.

'How long should I hang around here?' she asked Christopher over dinner at La Quetsch, paid for by her modest Chanel expense account. 'De Kousmine is no help. Working in the same house has ruined our relationship. If I believe all Mademoiselle tells me, I find myself hating de Kousmine. If I believe his account, I hate her.'

'What's her story?'

'That she was tricked into selling the rights to her name . . .'

Christopher smiled. 'Could anyone trick Mademoiselle into anything?'

Samantha looked up from her Salade Niçoise.

'She's hinted she might leave Chanel to *me*. Can you imagine?'

'She suggested the same thing to me. She probably says it to everyone.'

Samantha sighed. 'So why am I knocking myself out? I'm not getting some fabulous salary. I should devote myself to Klaus's career.' She sipped her *vin blanc cassis*. 'Klaus is the reliable fixture in my life. He still has that wonderful marching rythym. He's getting so much work I hardly see him. He's in London, Germany, even New York, taking fashion spreads. All thanks to me, of course.'

She waved at a woman on a nearby table.

'*Vogue* editor,' she said out of the side of her mouth. 'They may sign Klaus to an exclusive contract. I've always been attracted to men who need me. Klaus needs me, de Kousmine doesn't. Ever hear of an American named Jerold Von Schlossberg?'

Christopher shook his head.

'He called last night just after my bubble-bath. That's a very dangerous time, for me, Christopher; I'm all soft and warm and . . . alone! So I agreed to meet him for a drink at the Ritz. I hope I haven't done anything dumb? I get so lonely when Klaus is away. Remember, there are two things in Paris I can't resist, Christopher: pastries and men. If this guy is half as good-looking as a chocolate éclair, I'll be unable to resist.'

Twenty-four

Samantha slithered out of a taxi at the Ritz's Place Vendôme entrance. It made a nice change from Mademoiselle's usual back entrance. This way, someone opened the taxi door for you.

She wore Chanel's latest black cocktail dress with Roger Vivier Louis Quatorze heels. As she made her way into the bar, someone jumped out of an armchair to grab her.

'You must be Samantha! You're too fabulous *not* to be! I'm Jerry!'

He pressed his lips to the back of her hand as she looked down onto black glossy hair. He was a mixture of every fantasy she had ever had. Tall and muscular, sun-tanned (or sun-lamped?), with that shiny (yet slightly cheesy) look of a Las Vegas croupier. It brought out all her repressed Las Vegas fantasies of sex on a gaming-table with casino chips spilling everywhere! And yes, there was something a little cruel about his mouth . . . she must try to direct her mind into cruel mode. That wouldn't be easy, after sweet Klaus.

He sniffed her hand, appreciatively.

'Chanel No. 5!' he identified. 'I'd know it a mile away!'

'Have I used that much?' she grinned.

'You're as beautiful as your father told me you were.'

'Oh, how gallant.'

Her heart was thumping but this was a little too good to be true.

This guy was better than her wildest fantasy. He *was* her wildest fantasy.

'There's something very James Bond about you,' she cooed. 'Are you a spy?'

'Mmmmm . . . perhaps a fashion spy.'

'How do you know my father?'

'You know how fashion people schmooze? I schmooze too.'

'What do you make? Perfume?'

'I manufacture fake Chanels.'

'So *that's* why you wanted to meet me?' She nodded knowingly. 'You want to pay back some of the money you owe Mademoiselle Chanel?'

She sat down as the fantasy dissolved: she might have known no man sent by her father could be any good.

'You're sassy,' he nodded. 'I like that. Champagne!' He clicked his fingers at a passing waiter. Samantha frowned. Should she drink champagne with the kind of American who gave Americans a bad name?

'I'm not sure I should have a drink with you . . . even if you are very handsome.' She perched on the edge of the seat, staring at him. 'You should be ashamed of yourself,' she added.

'Ninety-five per cent of the industry do knock-offs, don't they?' he said.

She shuddered. 'If Mademoiselle Chanel sees anyone using cameras, they're thown out – Japanese, German, British *or* American.'

The waiter brought champagne in an ice-bucket. She was impressed: a cheapskate would have ordered two cocktails. But a cheapskate doesn't stay at the Ritz. Was he really staying there, or just pretending? she wondered. She would have to visit his bedroom to be sure.

'I thought if I played my cards right, you'd arrange a sneak preview of the new collection for me . . .' he tried.

She shot him a dark look. 'I hope you're kidding?' she said.

She cursed the fact that he had chosen a horny night. But then any night without Klaus was horny.

The champagne was popped and poured.

'A toast to beautiful women?' Jerry held up his glass.

She shot him a look and checked out the strong thighs beneath his trousers.

'Let me get this straight,' she said slowly, before taking a sip. 'You think I would betray Mademoiselle Chanel, the most famous designer in the world, for a *fuck*?'

'Hey, make love not war,' Jerry said automatically. 'Who said anything about a fuck? I want to *marry* you. Your father thinks you need kids and a stable life.'

'You'd *marry* me for some fashion secrets?'

'As soon as my divorce is final,' he nodded, gulping his wine.

She knew she must not do this. Enjoy the champagne then skedaddle, Samantha, she told herself. But she didn't seem to hear.

'I've never seen a Ritz bedroom, are they pretty?' she asked.

Oh my God! Samantha thought an hour later. Forget love, forget romance! This was a man who considered his appendage as a slick, firm dependable tool guaranteed to give a woman pleasure. This was nothing less than good old American efficiency!

'Best sex you've ever had, right?' Jerry asked, throwing himself back on the bed.

Samantha shot him a look, the pleasure still echoing throughout her body.

'You wouldn't ask if you weren't sure that the answer wasn't a resounding "Yes!"' she told him.

'Well?'

'Hmmmmm . . . I'll look up my diaries,' she promised.

'You write about sex in your diaries?'

'I have to tell someone!'

'What will you write about me?'

She shot him a patient look.

'I said "*endless* foreplay",' she reminded him.

He glanced at his watch. 'Thirty minutes isn't endless?'

'OK, then I'd probably write: "Not bad. Had worse".'

His pained expression turned her on all over again.

He rummaged amongst his belongings, tossing her a large pad.

'Here! Sketch some of Coco's details for next spring. It'll give me a headstart on my rivals.'

'You have some nerve,' Samantha cried, searching for her undies, scattered over the suite. 'I wouldn't do such a thing for my father. Or even my husband.'

She dressed indignantly, while he ordered more champagne from Room Service. At least he knew how to treat a lady.

But he was nothing more than a *schmatta* manufacturer, a 'knock-off artist' with delusions of grandeur.

Who did this guy think he was? She found the answer to that as she repaired her make-up in the bathroom: the address label on his subscription copy of *Time* read 'Baron Von Schlossberg'. He thought he was a Baron!

She left soon after and called her father the moment she got home.

'Did you give out my number to a guy called Jerry Schlossberg?'

'If that son of a bitch has harmed one hair on your head, I'll have him killed,' the voice crackled over the Atlantic.

'Did you tell him I want to marry and settle down?'

'I told him *I'd* like you to settle down. Is that a crime? He's a handsome guy, you're in the same business. Samantha, you could do a lot worse.'

'But he's a knock-off artist!'

'Is that so bad? Knock-offs make millions.'

'He expected me to betray Mademoiselle Chanel.'

'What did he do to you, Samantha?'

She gave a big sigh. 'Daddy, Mademoiselle Chanel is part of *history*. Jackie Kennedy was wearing a Chanel suit when our last President was assassinated. I'm so proud to know Mademoiselle. Please don't expect me to betray her.'

'But he's offering to marry you.'

'Daddy, we're on such different wavelengths, it's a wonder I can even hear you! You're freaking me out. I'm hanging up now. Goodbye.'

When she'd replaced the telephone, she stared at it, shaking her head.

'But thanks for some super sex, Daddy,' she added.

Her experience with the 'Baron' made Klaus seem more dependable than ever. Feeling guilty, Samantha dressed in black lingerie to give him a big welcome home two evenings later when he returned from a German assignment.

'I don't appreciate you enough,' she gushed, hugging him. 'I've been so lonely.'

'This is worth coming home for,' Klaus beamed.

Chanel called all three of them up to her salon.

Monique wore glasses, her eyes tired from sewing.

Samantha was in a pink Chanel suit she had borrowed from the boutique, promising to pay the dry-cleaning bill.

Christopher had taken a taxi from the Left Bank.

She poured them each a glass of champagne. '*A votre santé!*' She held up her glass.

They sipped, expectant.

'I didn't sleep well,' Mademoiselle began. 'At four in the morning, I awoke with a lot of questions about what will happen here when I've gone? Who will run this house? I am eighty-seven, I cannot keep going for ever.'

'You have more energy than any of us, Mademoiselle,' Monique murmured soothingly, glancing at the others.

'I have no family,' Chanel complained. A lie, as they all knew, exchanging glances. 'Who will design for this house?'

Nobody said anything, they just sipped their champagne.

'The *direction* will keep the couture going, if only to sell the perfume,' she said, almost to herself.

More exchanged glances.

'I would like the three of you to be involved,' she announced dramatically.

They all stared at her.

'You all have something special to offer,' she said. 'No one person could do all I do. And if Sophie ever returns to Paris, I want her, too. As the Face of Chanel she has sold more perfume than any other model.'

They did not dare exchange any more glances. Christopher cleared his throat.

'You pay us the most wonderful compliment, Mademoiselle,' he began. 'More than a compliment, it's an honour.'

'But I am not awarding honours, I am trying to assure the continuity of my house.'

'We appreciate it more than we can say, Mademoiselle . . .' Monique spoke up.

There was a long, uncomfortable silence. They made some small talk, exchanged some gossip which Mademoiselle loved, and finally escorted her to the back entrance of the Ritz, so that she could change for dinner.

Only when she had been safely seen into the lift did Samantha let out a whoop.

'The most prestigious fashion house on the planet?' she cried. 'Ours? Maybe I won't quit this job after all?'

'She could live to one hundred and three,' Christopher reminded her.

Monique began to cry.

'What's wrong?' Samantha stuffed a hanky in her hand. 'Let's have a drink at the bar.'

Monique looked up at them, red-eyed. 'Alcohol does not agree with me; I should not have drunk the champagne.'

They found a table in a corner of the American Bar, and ordered Coca Colas.

Monique took a deep breath before announcing, 'I think she is senile.'

'What makes you think that?' Christopher asked quietly.

Monique dabbed her eyes. 'She signed away her house years ago. She cannot leave it to anyone.'

'Isn't it more a question of who takes over as head designer?' Christopher asked.

'She's always meeting clever lawyers, she's capable of wrangling back the rights to her own name,' Samantha pointed out.

'Could you design a Chanel collection?' Monique asked Christopher.

He shook his head. 'I would take Chanel in a completely different direction.'

'*I* could do it,' Monique suddenly said.

The other two looked at her.

'Chanel's look has not really changed for years,' she insisted. 'It's only a question of details, fit, skirt-length . . .'

'But what would *I* get to do?' Samantha wailed. 'There are so many things I could introduce this house to. I could double its income!'

'You'd launch a huge range of cosmetics and beauty products,' Christopher suggested.

'And bed-sheets!' Samantha raised her eyebrows.

'Only if Monique agrees.'

They watched Monique as she demurely sipped at her coke and dabbed her eyes.

'Bed-sheets?' She looked at them reprovingly. 'I am not sure that would be correct. We must protect the name,' she said.

They walked out into the darkening Rue Cambon, kissed goodnight and gave Samantha the first taxi.

Christopher decided to walk. He would take all conjecture about deaths and wills with a huge pinch of salt and a French shrug.

The man following Monique along the Grands Boulevards was too well-dressed and too good-looking to be a criminal, she assured herself. She glanced behind and saw that he was about to approach.

'Are you Monique?'

She flinched. It had been so long since a good-looking man had spoken to her. In fact, a good-looking man had never spoken to her.

'How do you know my name?' she replied in her soft English.

'I'm a friend of Samantha Lipstaadt. I know her father. She told me about you.' He held out his hand: 'Jerry von Schlossberg!'

Automatically, she took his hand. It was warm and enveloping. Added to the way he looked deeply into her eyes, she felt a little flutter in her heart.

'Samantha spoke of me?' she asked, surprised.

'*Spoke* of you? Oh man, she said you do the most beautiful work in Chanel. "Exquisite", she calls it. Also that you know Coco really well.'

'I work for Mademoiselle Chanel,' she nodded. 'You are a journalist?'

'Oh no, I just love beautiful things.'

'You are in the fashion business?'

'I'm a connoisseur. I appreciate art, sculpture, haute couture, women, whatever . . .'

'I see.' She stared at him uncertainly as people bustled past.

'May I invite you to a drink?' he asked. 'I'd really like to talk.'

Before she decided whether to accept, he pulled out a chair and almost pushed her into it, at a table outside Le Café de la Paix, a place she had never dreamed of going.

On the large terrace, amidst excited tourists, Monique frowned. 'I don't understand,' she said. 'What do you want?'

'Can't you enjoy a drink with a friend without wondering what he wants?' he laughed.

'Excuse me, Monsieur,' Monique blushed, 'but we are not yet friends. I would like to know your intentions.'

Jerry stared in amazement, not quite understanding if she was joking or serious. Then he burst out laughing. Impulsively, he grabbed her hand and kissed the back of it.

'My "intentions"? Well, Monique, that's a word I haven't heard in a while. Let's see, tonight my intentions are to enjoy, for as long as possible, the company of a beautiful Frenchwoman.'

He ordered champagne. Monique frowned. Was this a dream, a film, what?

Thirty minutes later, she was floating. This must be a dream! she thought.

'Just to see the interior of Chanel,' Jerry said wonderingly, as they walked down the boulevard, his hand firmly grasping her elbow. 'Just once, before I die. So I can tell my grandchildren about it.'

'Do you have grandchildren?' Monique asked.

'Not yet.'

She laughed. They had finished the bottle of champagne and she felt quite light-headed. She had never drunk half a bottle of champagne in her life, not even at weddings, but Jerry had been pretty insistent about refilling her glass.

'Tell me something, Monique.' He leaned towards her and looked very sincerely into her eyes. 'Do you believe in love at first sight?'

She giggled. They were slowly approaching the Rue Cambon, it was the next street on the left. He seemed to think she wished to give him a private tour of Chanel.

She did have the keys and she did know the doorman, and, rather than turn down this very charming American who appeared to have fallen in love at first sight with her, she wondered where the harm would be in giving him a brief tour. He seemed as besotted with Chanel as she had once been, and she found that rather endearing.

They turned into the Rue Cambon. Outside Chanel, Jerry leaned closer.

'I've never felt like this with a woman before,' he murmured.

She rang, hearing the old-fashioned, shrill bell echo inside like an alarm. Louis let them in. He looked surprised but a stern look from Monique stopped him saying anything. No one was there at that hour. It was around nine, Mademoiselle would be dining at the Ritz.

'Let me see her room,' Jerry pleaded.

She led him up the mirrored staircase, so light-headed that she stumbled. He caught her and, for a brief moment, they swayed on the steep staircase, as if about to fall. Then suddenly he kissed her.

287

His kisses were so different to Guy's. He was eating her lips as though he were ravenous. She resisted before allowing his tongue to enter her mouth in that most intimate of kisses. His tongue moved gently over hers. He tasted of champagne. He obviously did not smoke. Her fingers touched the back of his neck, caressing the short shaved hair there, which seemed so masculine and comforting and yes, sexy, to her. With a hot flush of shame, desire stirred in her: she would do anything this man wanted her to do.

She was ashamed that she could allow a stranger, a man she had met not two hours before, to do what he was doing to her, to touch where he was touching. And yet somehow that very shame made it more exciting. She felt his hardness pressing into her. A low moan escaped and she realised it was hers. Was she this hungry for a man's touch? Wasn't that weekly hour with Guy enough?

Suddenly, he pulled up her skirt and pulled down her panties and he was gently pushing his way into what she realised to her even greater shame was her ready, willing, welcoming body pressing back.

'But . . . Louis?' she gasped, trying to look behind her, down the staircase.

'I gave him twenty francs to get a beer,' Jerry gasped. 'Said we'd keep an eye on the house.'

He slid right up with a rather brutal jerk and she cried out – falling back against the mirrored wall as he began a rhythmic slow thrust, which made her feel a pleasure she now realised she had always craved. He was more brutal than Guy and she was surprised to find that she liked it. She opened her eyes for a moment to see many images of a man thrusting into a woman reflected in the silvered slices of mirror set at different angles following the staircase. The mirrors curved around them and she realised with a shock that the woman she was watching was herself, doing things she had never seen herself do before. However shameful, it was also unbearably exciting. There was something about his confident thrusts that was so sure and so strong that she knew she could count on them to last as long as she wished, as long as she needed. Her hands clasped his hard buttocks, their thrusting echoing the mirrors' images as he pushed harder into her. His tongue guyed his movements by darting in and out of her mouth.

Taking her by surprise, the first spark of pleasure began in her, spreading throughout her body until it reached her feet and hands . . . and then . . . a sudden burst of forbidden ecstasy which suffused her entire being until she felt herself completely overcome by it. She cried out, almost a scream.

'My God, you are a French volcano!' he gasped, and then he closed his eyes tightly, and jolted, like one of those American film gangsters sentenced to the electric chair. As his body jolted again and again, his mouth did not leave hers.

A few moments passed. The house had never been so quiet. They remained tightly pressed together. Each time she clutched him tightly to her, she felt a new burst of pleasure. She tried to regain some composure.

'Now suppose you show me some workrooms,' Jerry suggested.

She gave a quick tour of some workrooms, hardly taking in his noting the details of the suits on hangers or mannequins, ignoring the flashes of his Polaroid camera, just longing for the moment she could be rid of him.

Fifteen minutes later, after a brief tour of the house, she found herself on the street with him.

'Dinner?' he suggested.

'I must go home, it's very late,' she murmured, unable to meet his eyes. She felt flustered, ashamed.

'I don't do things like this . . .' she told him suddenly.

'Well, you should! You should do it more often! You're good at it!' he said.

She shuddered.

'Monique, has anyone ever told you you're a very attractive woman?' he asked.

She saw a passing taxi and quickly hailed it. Now, all she wanted was to get away from him as soon as possible.

'No,' she answered him. 'I know I am not so attractive.'

He thrust something into her hand as he opened the taxi door for her.

'Let's do this again sometime,' he suggested. 'Here, please take this for the cab.'

The taxi drove off and she opened her hand. A fifty-franc note was in it.

She had been treated like a common prostitute, she thought miserably.

A fifty-franc prostitute. But isn't that exactly how she had acted?

At home later, no amount of hot water gushing over her in the shower could remove her sense of shame.

The next morning, after opening her workroom, Monique ran down to Samantha's office, carefully closing the door behind her.

'Last night, I—' she began, then stopped, covering her face with her hands.

'Why Monique, what's the matter?' Samantha ran forward and grasped her friend, pushing her into a chair.

'I can't tell you,' Monique sobbed. 'I'm too ashamed!'

Samantha poured her some water and held the glass to her lips.

'Now, swallow, then take some deep breaths . . .' she soothed her. 'This is *me*, Samantha, remember? Nothing is too shameful to tell *me*!'

Monique sipped some water and dabbed at her cheeks. Looking up at Samantha with her big dark eyes, she began very hesitantly.

'Last night . . . I don't know how it happened but . . . an American man called Jerry got me drunk.' She shook her head. 'I behaved so badly, Samantha. I feel so ashamed.'

Samantha stared at her, frowning.

'Oh, *him*! I know that guy. He tried this on me. I didn't buy it. But . . . if you only got drunk, that's nothing to be ashamed of.'

Monique nodded. 'I drank too much.' she said.

'Of course, you realised what kind of guy he was, didn't you,

Monique? On the make? Looking for stuff to copy? A knock-off artist!'

'Knock-off?' Monique frowned, dabbing at her eyes. 'What is this?'

'Cheap copies of the couture. He tried to get *me* to show him around Chanel. Can you imagine?' Samantha laughed. 'He must have thought I was stupid or something.'

Monique blushed deep red, staring at Samantha.

'Oh Samantha, what have I done?' She began to cry fresh tears.

'Don't take it so to heart,' Samantha consoled her. 'It was just a drink.'

Monique stared at her for a long moment, then burst out: 'That is not all I have done. I brought him *here*. I allowed him into workrooms. He took photographs.'

'Of you? Undressed?'

'No, of the new models! He made little sketches.'

'All that for a drink?'

Monique looked anguished. 'It was *more* than a drink. It was an entire bottle of champagne. It went to my head and I allowed him to . . .' her voice dropped to a whisper, '. . . do whatever he wanted.'

Samantha's mouth fell open. She stared at Monique.

'What did he do?' she whispered back.

Monique's dark eyes continued to stare at Samantha.

'He . . . made love to me. On the staircase.'

'Back staircase or *mirrored* staircase?' Samantha asked quickly.

Monique made a pained face. 'Mirrored?' she tried.

'*Mirrored!*' Samantha screamed. 'Monique, how *could* you? That staircase is part of fashion history!'

Monique collapsed into sobs. Her shoulders heaved and Samantha could only feel sorry and protective towards her. She held Monique until she finally got herself under control.

'Blow your nose,' Samantha instructed. 'Nobody needs to know.'

'But I betrayed Mademoiselle.' Monique gave a huge blow into a handkerchief, dabbing her eyes. 'And . . . he *paid* me. For the taxi! Fifty francs, as if I were some common prostitute.'

'Oh Monique, don't be so hard on yourself. He's a very persuasive guy, and he got you drunk. You have nothing to blame yourself for. But fifty francs for some new Chanel designs? Boy, that jerk got himself a bargain.'

Monique began to sob again.

'Now, come on.' Samantha patted her arm. 'Look at the good side, Monique. At least you got laid, right? And he was very good at it, wasn't he?'

Monique began to cry again 'Ah *oui*, Samantha,' she agreed sadly, dabbing her eyes, 'he was very good!'

There was a short silence, then they suddenly caught each other's eye and burst out laughing.

Twenty-five

A few days after Christmas, Samantha reported to work and ripped a new fashion journal out of its wrapper.

Schlossberg Modes first out of the starting-gate for Chanel knock-offs, read the caption under a photograph of a downtown Manhattan department-store window filled with lookalike Chanels. *Even before the first showing of the new Chanel collection, which our spies tell us will show identical models . . .* the article went on. It ended with the immortal quote: '*Couture telepathy . . .*' founder Jerold Von Schlossberg tells WWD. '*I tried to put myself in the place of Coco Chanel and – it's kind of transcendental meditation – I came up with these designs.*'

He pooh-poohed the idea that spies at Chanel had passed on new details and designs to him.

Monique saw the article too, when the paper was brandished in her face by Mademoiselle.

'How did this criminal get his hands on my designs?' Mademoiselle demanded.

Monique's face grew hot. She burst into tears.

'Please don't cry, Monique, they say "identical models" but I doubt they will be,' Chanel explained. 'The workmanship will be shoddy, fabrics poor quality. No one can copy the essential qualities of a Chanel.'

She tossed away the paper and Monique felt a huge wave of relief wash over her.

The cheeky little fabric salesman was in the corridor when she walked back to her workroom. She received the usual wink and smile from him. She took a good look at him. He was short, stocky, with an old-fashioned moustache and neat, clean clothes. There was a twinkle in his eye. Today she winked back.

However shameful that experience with Jerold Von somebody, it had made her realise an important thing about herself: she needed more than an hour each week from a man. She took twelve more steps before she felt a light touch on her arm.

'Mademoiselle?'

It was the fabric salesman.

'Allow me to introduce myself. My name is Frederic Jablon, Mademoiselle . . .'

'I am Monique Far.' She took his hand. It was warm and firm. 'But I do not buy fabrics . . . Monsieur Jablon.'

'But you do drink champagne?'

She stared at him, a smile appearing on her face.

'Oh no, Monsieur,' she said, widening her eyes, 'I never drink champagne. It gets me into too much trouble.'

Their weekly ritual of being together, saying few words, had continued. Guy would hold Monique in his arms, make love to her, then hold her some more.

And the following night, after their usual peaceful hour, she watched him sitting on the edge of her bed before getting dressed. He sat with his face buried in his hands.

With a start, she realised his shoulders were shaking.

'Guy, what's wrong?' she sat down on the bed next to him, her arm around him.

He looked up at her. 'My wife has found out that I am not the most loyal of husbands . . . Monique, she's throwing me out.'

She sighed. 'She knows about me?'

He shook his head.

'It's the models. They're so pretty, and you know how outrageously they flirt? Maybe it's only to get a suit out of me, but . . . I'm a man! One of them, well, I ended up not making the suit. She met my wife and told her.'

Monique nodded, trying to digest this.

'So your wife and also me, we were not enough?' she said, shaking her head sadly. 'How many women must you have?'

Guy looked at her helplessly. 'How many men can resist a pretty girl?'

'Some men can,' she said. 'But not you, Guy. What are you going to do?'

He blew out his breath. 'Some friends, a married couple with a large apartment at La République, have rented me a room. I'll miss the children. They are at such an impressionable age and they need their papa.'

'How old are they?'

'Eleven and nine.'

'Yes, that is very impressionable,' Monique said thoughtfully. 'That is around the age I was when my father died. Where are you staying meanwhile?'

'I've been sleeping in the spare room.'

'*Come and live here with me.* She thought it but could not say it.

When he was ready to leave he bent to kiss her goodbye.

'It's no good asking you not to tell anyone,' he said. 'The way that house is, everyone will know in a few days.'

Mademoiselle tried to make Monique's Friday-night visits stretch until dinner-time and Monique usually indulged her. Only a single woman understood that gap of two whole days which yawned before another unmarried woman, a Saturday and Sunday without work, sometimes without people, without activity.

Monique filled her weekend with cooking and housework, but Mademoiselle didn't cook and her friends had long since tired of the Ritz's menu. It never occurred to her to eat anywhere else.

'Guy's leaving,' Chanel told her, that Friday night.

'Yes, Mademoiselle, he is leaving his wife—'

'Not only his wife: *me!*'

Monique's eyes opened wide. 'You mean the house?'

'Yes, and guess where he's going . . . nowhere else but Yves Saint Laurent!'

Monique swallowed. 'I cannot imagine that, Mademoiselle. He said nothing to me of this.'

'He was too embarrassed to tell you. I ripped apart a fitting of his. Perhaps I shouldn't have. You see him every week, I know. Monique, get him back.'

'How? Maybe he needs more money. Did you offer him more?'

'Certainly not. He already earns more than anyone else here.'

'But, Mademoiselle, if he has to rent a flat, he will now have double the expenses.'

Chanel raised her eyebrows.

'I suppose you think he's *yours,* now?' she asked. 'Well, he isn't. He could never resist a pretty girl. The models sleep with him in return for his cutting their suits. He has cut a lot of suits. Get him back!'

'Mademoiselle will authorise me to offer him a little more money, *quand même?*'

The old lady glared at her for a moment before scribbling a sum on the back of a stiff white Chanel card, growling: 'Offer him that!'

Monique pocketed the card. Where did a newly free man go in the evenings? She would seek him out in the bars. If he was staying at La République with married friends, she would look around that area.

Paris bars or cafés attract their own little following. Some cafés are obviously marked out for intellectuals, for old men, for young students, chic women or a mixed crowd.

She had an idea that Guy would be in a bar where men drank seriously, alone, hunched over tables.

She found him in a red-banqueted bar on the Place itself.

He heard her out, staring intently at her, nodding.

'Mademoiselle likes to think that everything is about money,' he said with a short laugh. 'Of course it's nice to earn more, but I also wanted to change my life completely, including the place I work.'

'How can you work anywhere else after having worked at Chanel?' she asked.

Guy laughed. 'There are other houses, Monique. And she is getting very difficult. She ripped the arms off a jacket of mine which was absolutely impeccable. Monsieur Saint Laurent appreciates fine craftsmanship. He's been wooing me for months. He idolises Mademoiselle. I can get away with anything if I tell him "Mademoiselle does it like that"!'

'And are Saint Laurent's mannequins very beautiful?' Monique asked him wistfully.

'Very.' He shot her a look, then smiled. 'Don't worry, Monique. I am not allowed to cut suits for them, so suddenly they do not find me very attractive.'

She longed to ask him what he felt about 'their' future. She had heard Samantha use the word 'relationship' in English so often . . . did that word apply to what they had? Did meeting for an hour each week make for a relationship?

'Mademoiselle wants you back, Guy. The house won't be the same without you. I am here as her spokesman.'

'Oh? I thought *you* might miss me.'

'Of course I will.'

'Mademoiselle won't miss me: your workroom produces clothes the equal of mine,' he muttered. 'Perhaps better.'

'Thank you. But it's not just the clothes, Guy. It's your presence . . . you have become part of the Chanel philosophy.'

'Oh, Monique, you know I don't believe in all that stuff. I am a tailor, not a philosopher. Anyway, even a philosopher can change philosophies. Monsieur Saint Laurent has a philosophy, too.'

'Mademoiselle has authorised me to offer you this,' she held out the white card with the figure Chanel had scrawled on it.

Guy glanced at it.

'Not enough!' he snapped.

'This is the moment to install him in your apartment, Monique,' Samantha exploded. 'While he's lost, lonely and vulnerable. Pounce!'

'Yes, he is lonely and vulnerable.' Monique looked sadly at her. 'And he drinks too much. But it is not my way to profit from a man under these conditions, Samantha. An offer to share life must come from the man.'

'Oh, for God's sake.' Samantha downed her cocktail in a gulp, signalling for another. They were in a café in Le Marais near to Monique's flat. 'In a relationship—' she began.

'An hour in a hotel room each week?' Monique cut in. 'That is not a relationship.'

'Married men sometimes divorce, Monique,' Samantha pointed out.

HRRG's *Futur/Couture* collection was their most successful ever. Exuberant and new, Christopher's designs had needed Ghislaine's disciplined eye to restrain them and make them wearable. Together they achieved a collection that women loved. More than loved, had to have!

And Samantha, working part time and in secret, had indulged her wildest promotional ideas. She had followed the open showings in the store-windows by renting large spaces on the outskirts of Paris and busing fashion journalists to stand in disused railway stations to watch lavish presentations.

A trainful of models wearing HRRG was one of her latest ideas.

Christopher's 'casual-evening' clothes were not embroidered and not formal. He liked slim, long dresses to be draped, romantic, gauzy, never stiff or full-skirted. His favourite evening outfit for a woman was a tailored white shirt, sometimes in finest silk or thinnest cotton, open low, over a softly gathered long skirt in a jewel-coloured velvet or silk satin, of any length from above the knee to floor-length.

He designed, the customer chose. This formula worked.

Ghislaine seemed a little subdued over one of their mid-morning coffees at the Flore. She turned to Christopher.

'Bertrand has fallen in love with a young model. He wants a divorce.'

She sipped her coffee, eyes wide open at Christopher over the cup. He groped for comforting words to murmur.

Don't worry, I'll marry you! Was that what he was expected to say?

Ghislaine put down her cup. 'I suppose this means you can make an honest woman out of me?'

'Is this a proposal?' he tried to joke.

'We share a business, we're in tune sexually: why not?' She gave a light laugh.

'I thought you knew I was in love with Sophie,' he blurted out.

' "Was", yes. But hasn't the Face of Chanel been ignoring you?'

'There's more to marriage than sharing a business and being sexually compatible, Ghislaine . . .'

'How would you know?'

'I'm guessing.'

They did not say another word about marriage, but something told him this was the time to bow out. Lightly.

That night, he called Samantha, his expert on love and sex, to report the conversation.

'So do I just assume it's over?' he asked hopefully.

'No, you don't,' Samantha cried. 'What if she invites you to one of her Sunday-night icing-sugar sessions?'

Christopher groaned. 'I'm sorry I ever told you that. Just tell me how *you* would most like to learn that an affair is over?' he asked her. 'Give me a few clues.'

Samantha thought for a few moments.

'If a man was about to dump me,' she began slowly, 'I'd like to think he'd have the class to tell me over a quiet dinner,' she decided. 'And for dessert, a serious piece of jewellery!' she added.

She closed her eyes trying to imagine the scene. 'I'd float off into the Paris streets and it wouldn't really hit me until the next day, by which time I'd be wearing some gorgeous Cartier diamonds and feeling a whole lot better.'

'What if you shared an office and a successful business?'

'That would be a little more difficult,' she admitted. 'Of course, Ghislaine won't like it. But I'd still go with the dinner and the jewellery to bring everything to a nice, romantic conclusion. Aux Petits Pavés is the perfect place for breaking up. Very kind rosy lighting. Ask for a booth.'

'I'll consider that,' Christopher said.

'Is there some partnership bug going around? Klaus wants to make an honest woman out of *me*!'

'Congratulations.'

'Yeah . . .' she sighed thoughtfully. 'Do I wanna be an honest woman?'

Monique missed her hour with Guy. He had told her he would contact her and she had heard nothing. What would he do? Was he lonely?

Finally, he invited Monique to the room he rented in La République. She went there the following evening when his friends were out.

Guy opened the door.

'Monique,' he greeted her, 'thank you for coming all the way here.' He seemed very low.

'What is it? Is it work?' she asked carefully.

He had the run of the apartment when his friends were out. It could not have been more middle-class and conventional. They sat on a red velvet sofa in the window of the large empty living-room, and she took his hand and gently stroked it. His hands were still the hands of a craftsman, she thought. She lifted one to her lips and kissed it.

He smiled at her. 'Work is work, whether for Mademoiselle Chanel or Monsieur Saint Laurent. You know what she said about him, once?'

'What?'

'I very much admire Monsieur Saint Laurent,' Guy imitated Chanel's gruff voice, 'for having the courage to copy me!'

They laughed.

'He's a little less demanding, but as I am demanding of myself, it amounts to the same. He knows less about materials than Mademoiselle, but no one could know as much as she does. I was always in awe of her knowledge. Monsieur Saint Laurent relies more on sketches. If I produce an outfit that resembles his sketch, he is happy.'

'What about you, Guy?' she asked.

He stared down at their hands. 'It's the children,' he said in a low voice. 'I feel terrible about not seeing enough of them.'

'Show me the room you sleep in,' she asked. 'So I can picture you there.'

He led her down the corridor. His room had the unloved, unlived-in look of all spare rooms. His open suitcase on the floor, spilling over with shirts, made her sad.

'Come and live with me, Guy . . .' The words simply fell from her lips.

She tensed, expecting a rueful shake of the head: instead, he looked up with a grateful look in his eyes.

'It can just be a temporary measure,' she added.

He took her hand and kissed it. She said nothing. He kissed her and began to make love to her. Slowly, he eased her out of her clothes and began to kiss all over her body. From his touch, a new touch, she could feel the last reserve deserting the deep font of love she had in her. Without any doubt, he was the man for her. She'd rather be alone than have anyone else. Enwrapped in his arms, she felt so safe . . . she knew it was because he reminded her of her father, and she didn't care. Their brief separation had already aged him a little, as had moving from Chanel to a rival house. That only added to all she felt for him. Miracles happen, she thought, holding him close, hardly able to believe this. She had accepted that one unsatisfactory hour for so long, she had never expected this. Miracles can happen, if you wait long enough and, most importantly, don't expect them.

Christopher reserved the corner booth for dinner at Aux Petits Pavés. Samantha had assured him it was the most romantic in the restaurant.

He had showered and changed into a fresh white shirt, dark jacket and tie. The gift-wrapped, diamond brooch carefully chosen from Chopard, a rather grand jewellery shop in the Place Vendôme, was in his pocket.

He leaned on the tiny bar just inside the door.

The minute he saw Ghislaine, he knew that her dress had been carefully selected for this occasion. They were so attuned to fashion that they could communicate through clothes. This slinky black matt jersey dress practically shouted, 'I expect a proposal!'

A *proposal*, Christopher thought glumly, not the old heave-ho.

But it was too late now. Ghislaine's eyes sparkled, a wide gold ribbon tied back her hair, she couldn't have looked prettier or chicer and his heart sank.

They got through dinner by discussing fashion and food. When two tiny demi-tasses of black coffee arrived with a plate of petits fours, he wiped his sweating hands on his trousers, swallowed and gave Ghislaine the tiny package.

'Oh Christopher!' she cried. 'So an Englishman *can* be a romantic, crazy fool?'

She ripped off the paper and popped open the box and her face dropped.

'A *brooch*!' she gave a strangled cry.

'I thought this would be a nice way to commemorate the end of our . . .' he swallowed hard, ' . . . beautiful affair.'

'The *end* of it,' she repeated blankly. Her eyes lost their romantic sparkle and quickly filled with a new sparkle – rage!

'I was under the impression—' she began then stopped, hunting for a cigarette in her small bag. 'So . . . this dinner, this . . . gift, is your gauche English way of saying goodbye?'

'I was advised that it was the French way . . .' he began.

'Well, you were wrongly advised, my friend,' she exploded.

'When I think how carefully I dressed for this evening! I thought it was the *start* of something, not the end.'

He stared at her, at a loss for words. Why had he listened to Samantha? What did she know? About *anything*? Why hadn't he asked Mademoiselle how one breaks up with an older woman?

'*Garçon!*' Ghislaine cried.

The waiter appeared as Ghislaine stood up. 'Telephone this man's mother,' she ordered loudly, making everyone look up. 'Tell her her son is ready to be put to bed!'

She threw the brooch across the table, grabbed her stole and left the restaurant. Christopher ran after her and caught up with her on the street, pulling her around to face him.

'Ghislaine, please don't—'

'You are waiting for the Face of Chanel?' she cried. 'I call her the "*Disgrace* of Chanel", a spoiled little girl who has been trouble since she was a child. What kind of woman has a man's baby and says nothing to him about it? And you're *waiting* for her? How many years will you wait?'

Christopher held her arms, shaking his head. 'There are good reasons for what she's doing. One day I'll find them out.'

'It'll be too late by then!'

She hailed a taxi.

'You're making a stupid mistake, Christopher,' she said as she got in.

'Hell hath no fury like a socialite scorned,' Samantha said. She had called Christopher at eight thirty the next morning for an update.

'How do I face her now?' he asked.

'You just walk into work as if nothing happened,' Samantha advised. 'She's too smart a cookie not to realise that you must remain business partners. She'll have a new guy licking icing-sugar off of her within a few weeks.'

Christopher groaned. 'I shouldn't listen to you . . .' he said.

But he decided to do what she said.

He walked into work and found Ghislaine on the sales floor teaching selling techniques to a handsome young sales assistant.

Maybe she was only trying to make him jealous, but, watching her flirting, he had never felt less jealous. Instead he felt wonderfully free for the first time.

At a table for two at La Coupole the following night, Klaus suddenly said, 'So we live together, right?' He looked expectantly at Samantha.

'The words I've always longed to hear,' Samantha said, staring blankly at him. 'But you gotta make it more romantic than that, Klaus.'

'I have seen this enormous old apartment in Le Marais,' he went on. 'Fixed up, it could be fabulous. So much space. There is one huge room, which could be my studio, I believe it was once a ballroom . . .'

'Is there a room that could be a nursery?' She batted her eyes at him.

'There are rooms for *three* nurseries,' Klaus nodded, obviously moved.

'Oh, Klaus!' Samantha cried, her eyes moist. 'I'll turn them into three walk-in closets!'

'The new redesigned Klaus still has the old marching rythym. . .' she told Monique when they met next Sunday for *le thé* at Angelina. 'He's *probably* the best man for me?' She glanced up doubtfully from stirring her tea. 'I mean, he's taller than me, he's a top fashion photographer, he proposes to buy a huge studio in Le Marais . . .' She ticked off the points on her fingers. 'We could have the largest living-room in Paris.'

'But do you love him, Samantha?' Monique nodded, her big eyes on Samantha's.

'Oh, *I* don't know,' Samantha exploded. 'I *guess* I do.'

'He will be the father of your children you *must* know this . . . for sure,' Monique insisted.

Samantha stared at her for a moment.

'Oh, how do you know if you love someone, anyway?' she asked.

Monique stared at her. 'You know. You *know*, Samantha,' she said sorrowfully. 'When I marry I will be certain that I am in love.'

'OK, so stay romantic and stay unmarried. Samantha shrugged. 'I can see just how far being romantic gets you. Marriage *is* a calm, cool decision you make, thinking of the future, the options, the probability of ever finding someone better. I don't think I'll find anyone better than Klaus.'

They stared at each other over the tea-table, almost hostile; two women with very different approaches to life and love.

It was time for a new Chanel collection. Mademoiselle asked Monique to be next to her when she began to fit models in the *Grand Salon*. Monique had heard all about Mademoiselle making a hundred changes at the last moment, how she was never satisfied with any garment. She remembered the ripped jackets coming up to the workroom from the fittings. But watching this furious woman slash seams and rip sleeves out of jackets was more dramatic than even Monique had realised.

'This will kill her!' Monique whispered to Madame Antoine as she visited the *salon* to stand beside them for a moment.

Madame Antoine's glance swept coolly over the wilting model, the weeping cutter and Mademoiselle's grim face.

'On the contrary,' she told Monique drily. 'This keeps her alive.'

Suddenly Mademoiselle had started wearing a rather ugly black brace on her right arm. It was rumoured she had suffered a small stroke. No one mentioned the brace and Mademoiselle adopted a variety of disguises for it, mostly scarves. She put on a good front, but Monique knew fatigue and anger when she saw it.

'Mademoiselle, that sleeve was perfectly set-in . . .' Monique could not help defending poor Madame Michelle as she burst into tears. 'You are seeing faults and puckers which do not exist. The collection will never be ready if you go on like this.'

Mademoiselle levered a stare at Monique. 'What do I care if the collection isn't ready?' she barked. 'I do this for me, do you understand, Monique? For *me!*'

Monique kept her company for many dinners at the Ritz, listening to her non-stop list of complaints and regrets about her life . . . and what a life! What friends! Jean Cocteau, Picasso, Stravinsky, Cecil B. DeMille and Sam Goldwyn, who had once imported her to Hollywood to dress stars like Gloria Swanson. She really had known everyone it was worth knowing in the last eighty years.

And the most heartbreaking stories of all were the love affairs with important men who had not wanted to marry her. Amongst the many lost loves, Mademoiselle spoke of a rich English man. She told Monique about wanting to give him a baby, an heir, at the age of forty-five. She had been advised to keep her legs in the air after making love, but it had not worked. Mademoiselle laughed bitterly when recounting these stories, but there was a mixture of cruel comedy and spite in her laugh. Finally, fatigue would overcome her and she would excuse herself.

Maybe Madame Antoine was right, Monique thought. Maybe designing and destroying for yet another collection did keep her alive?

Sunday was always the worst day. There was usually a woman friend to lunch with and she had taken on a chauffeur for drives in the afternoon, often through the Bois de Boulogne. She had managed to convince the *Direction* to open for a few Saturdays before the new collection, but the *Chambre Syndicale*, the union of the seamstresses, would not allow Sundays.

She rested unwillingly, gathering strength to return to her workroom the following day. She lay on the made bed, in the empty white Ritz bedroom where no painting or photograph hung on the walls; 'a room for sleeping', she had always said. She thought of her beautiful Roquebrune country house. It was fun to wander in her memory through that jewel of a house. No need to rifle through boxes of photographs, she saw only too clearly the happy faces of Picasso, Stravinsky, and Misia, her best woman friend who had died many years ago. They had loved the special buffet lunches she had created for their delight. The fun they'd had! She could smell the fresh salad and rich wine she'd provided so plentifully, as she summoned guests to the table.

'Come everyone! *A table! Mangeons!*' She heard her strong happy voice ringing out.

A sharp pain cut into her reverie. Suddenly, she felt very ill. She screamed, calling for Jeanne, her maid, fidding with a syringe and trying to break a glass phial of a drug which had saved her life before. But she could not manage the injection. She fell back on her white bed.

Angrily, she cried out, 'They want to kill me!' In a quieter voice, she added, 'So this is what death is like?' From her tone, it was obvious she didn't think much of it: why should she?

Jeanne reported those as her last words. On her hated Sunday afternoon, in a small Ritz bedroom, life lost its meaning and Gabrielle 'Coco' Chanel died of a bitter boredom. Fashion died alongside her.

Twenty-six

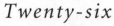

The phone jangled in the large Marais apartment where Samantha perched on a ladder, helping Klaus decorate.

'I'll get it,' Samantha called to Klaus. He was on another ladder painting a moulding.

It was 17th January 1971 and every Paris couturier was preparing his new collection.

'She is dead,' de Kousmine's voice said. 'Be in my office at nine sharp tomorrow morning.' He hung up.

Samantha replaced the phone then tottered, as if about to faint. Klaus rushed to her side, cradling her head, holding a glass of water to her mouth as she sipped.

'I feel as if I have lost my mother all over again,' Samantha moaned.

'She did not sound very maternal, from all accounts,' Klaus said.

The news was all over Paris within hours. There was no hint of the state funeral most people expected. It was rumoured that the body would be whisked away to Switzerland, for tax reasons.

'Surely she deserves a state funeral?' Monique called Guy to ask. 'I thought she would be alongside Colette and Piaf as one of France's most-admired women?'

'There are things about Mademoiselle that we will never know . . .' Guy told her.

Something was odd . . . some rush, some hurry, some lack of dignity.

The following morning, Samantha arrived in tears in a black Chanel suit. She went straight to de Kousmine's office. He was speaking on the phone, dark eyes flashing as he looked up at her, gently shaking his head. This did not put her off. She waited until his conversation ended and he had replaced the phone.

'We have a lot of work to do,' he told her bluntly. 'We have to keep this house going.'

Samantha stared at him.

'What's the good of being your mistress if you don't tell me anything?' she cried.

'As fate would have it, our Press Officer is on holiday. So during working hours, *you* are Press Officer of the house of Chanel. Please make up a press release.'

Samantha shot him a black look and positioned her pad.

'The directors of Chanel are grieved to announce that legendary designer Gabrielle "Coco" Chanel passed away on Sunday afternoon,' de Kousmine dictated. 'Death was from a heart attack. Mademoiselle wished to be buried in her beloved Switzerland, in Lausanne where she lived for twelve years and is still registered as a resident. A private funeral will be held there later in the week.' He stopped.

'What happens now?' Samantha asked.

He smiled. 'You're American, you know "Ding Dong, The Witch is Dead" from *The Wizard of Oz*? Maybe we should play it over, loudspeakers outside the house?'

Samantha gave him a horrified look. 'How can you say that? She was a wonderful woman, an icon, an idol, an example to us all.'

De Kousmine heaved a great sigh. 'Evidently, the French Government does not agree with you. Despite the Antoines' impeccable connections, there will be no state funeral.'

'Who'll design the next collection?' Samantha blurted out, tears welling.

'That will be decided in due course after we've presented this one,' de Kousmine said.

'Tell me, Eduard,' she begged, 'is it one of us? Mademoiselle always hinted it would be.'

'There will be a meeting of the directors. We have a lot of decisions to make.'

Samantha sighed and went to her office to start calling people.

'A mythically rich fashion designer on a one-way flight to Fashion Heaven,' was how Samantha began, as she called journalist after journalist. '*Without* heirs?' She broke off to gulp some coffee. 'Of course, everyone is speculating! A torrent of rumours and gossip flood in and out of Rue Cambon, and you know something? I have no answers, I've been told nothing. Mademoiselle's death, Mademoiselle's funeral, Mademoiselle's legacy will be like her life: full of mystery and intrigue.'

Faithful to their usual secrecy, the owners of Chanel & Co issued only one more press statement later that week, announcing the private funeral in Lausanne, Mademoiselle's official residence. It was rumoured that four billion dollars had been salted away in Switzerland.

'I want to be at the burial,' Christopher told Madame Antoine. She had approval of the guest-list: the funeral in Lausanne was shaping up to be the most exclusive event of the couture season. 'By Invitation only' had already been decided; hysterical Chanel-junkies would be ruthlessly edited out.

She glanced up at him from her writing desk. 'There will be a small service tomorrow afternoon at the Madeleine church,' she told him. 'But of course, the Lausanne funeral is the main event. I'll add your name to the list.'

'Thank you.' He bent to kiss her cheek then turned to go.

'Christopher', does this request have anything to do with Sophie?' she asked.

He hesitated for a moment. She'll be there,' he told her. 'I am certain.'

'She's not on my list.'

'If anyone is desolated by Chanel's death, it will be Sophie,' he said. 'She sometimes fantasised that there was some kind of link between her and Mademoiselle.'

Madame Antoine laughed her strangled laugh. 'I wonder why?'

'I want to be there,' Christopher said urgently, 'in case she needs me.'

Madame Antoine looked at him, raising her eyebrows.

'Or in case you need her?'

Twenty-seven

A small chic crowd of Parisians advanced into the Lausanne graveyard, crunching frosty gravel beneath their feet. Their breath showed steamy in the cold air. Cypress trees, dark green and tipped with ice, loomed up and seemed to hem them in.

There were many familiar Paris faces: models, actresses and society ladies, alongside employees of Chanel who had been with her for decades. Some wore Chanel coats or suits, with fur linings, muffs or scarves to keep out the cold.

There were also several representatives of the Wertheimer family, dignified and solemn.

The press photographers were not allowed into the grounds, and contented themselves with photographing the glamorous arrivals at the entrance.

Mourners followed the path until they reached a tall marble rectangle decorated with five lion's heads, Mademoiselle's star sign of Leo. The sounds of sobbing came from only one person – Monique.

The people who stood around the tomb included a group of current and former models. They were unmistakable; tall, elegant, with carefully styled hair, wearing black coats or black suits. Their white make-up, false eyelashes and red mouths made it seem as if Chanel had cloned a perfect female race. Most pinned white camellias to the black grosgrain ribbons in their hair, as a kind of hommage. They seemed genuinely sad, and Christopher, watching, realised that Chanel had acted as a mentor to many of them.

Their grave exchanged glances showed that this was the end of an era.

'The very last social event we share with Mademoiselle,' he murmured to Monique, holding her arm.

He saw Sophie, and a jolt shot through him like an electric shock.

She was quietly greeting the other models, gravely brushing cheeks and exchanging knowing looks with them. She was by far the smallest of them, so was half-hidden. She was pale and moved like a sleepwalker. She wore a cream-coloured silk coat and her uncovered, red hair had grown longer, making her stand out in the sober crowd. She held something which he thought was a large bouquet of flowers as she buried her face in it. Then she turned and he realized she was carrying a baby.

To a father longing to hold his child for the first time, the service, in a sing-song Swiss French, seemed to take for ever.

After it, some mourners paid tributes, saying how important to France, to women, to fashion, to the world, Chanel had been. Christopher waited out the eulogies, his heart beating madly.

Suddenly, as if she sensed his intense stare, Sophie turned. He saw her full face and also the face of his *daughter*. He could barely resist pushing the chic mourners out of his way to grab her and hold her close to him.

Two men slid the coffin into its final home and gently covered the entrance with a marble slab. The crowd turned, women dabbed at their eyes. He saw Madame Antoine, her eyes reddened by tears. Clinging to her husband's arm, she did not see him. There were faces from the film world, actresses who had worn Chanel in their films and private lives.

The people at the front found their way blocked by the ones behind trying to approach the tomb. The crowd froze. He heard the click of cameras and the whirr of filming. Voices were raised, someone was pushed, a few moments of Parisian couture chaos invaded the cold Swiss churchyard.

The situation resolved itself, the two-toned Chanel shoes took a firmer stand on the slippery ground and people continued to stream out.

Christopher stood by the gates, waiting for Sophie, trying to spot her in the crowd. Suddenly they were face to face. She had been crying, and was thinner, her lipstick a red slash in a pale face. Still so beautiful, he thought. The child stared at him curiously. It was like looking into the mirror at his own blue eyes in a child's face. She had Sophie's red hair.

Sophie's eyes opened wide and she smiled.

'Christopher. Say hello to your daughter, Gabrielle. Gaby, this is your father.'

Time spun back two years in two seconds. Sophie wore the same haunting perfume she had worn when he'd first met her. Love is an extraordinary thing, he thought, a kind of power she had over him . . . maybe not even a sexual power, just a power. She thrust the child into his arms.

'This is your papa,' she said again.

The little girl twisted around to look up at him, her eyes intent and serious, as if she realised the importance of this moment. Christopher tried to say 'I'm your daddy' in English, but he was so choked up that the words would not come. Instead, he touched his lips to her head, smelling the sweet hair of his daughter.

'Why? Why? Why?' Christopher cried.

It was the only word he could express. He sat across from Sophie in a café, the little girl on his lap. The weight of the sturdy little body and the way she gripped his forefingers so firmly as he gently jiggled her, slowly calmed him. So did the words 'my daughter' as he thought them.

They had been obliged to get through fifteen minutes of Monique and Samantha and Laurent and Madame Antoine, admiring and fussing over the child.

Madame Antoine had held her close, obviously moved.

'What a beautiful thing, this new life giving us hope after a death,' she said. 'Especially if it's my first grandchild.'

She nodded when Sophie told her the name was Gabrielle. 'After Mademoiselle?' she asked.

Sophie nodded.

Christopher and Sophie finally excused themselves and found a nearby café. They sat across the table from each other as Sophie considered him soberly.

'I will try to explain, Christopher,' she began. 'I know it is almost unforgivable, but this baby was something I had to do alone. I needed her first months to myself, to make me strong. Do you see?'

'No, I don't see,' he said bitterly. 'After what happened to you, why would you wish to deprive your child of her father?'

'I did not intend to deprive her,' Sophie said softly, looking at the child. 'The idea was to recapture my own childhood. Time passed so quickly, and there was something . . . addictive about having her all to myself, not sharing her with anyone, not even you.'

Christopher blew out an impatient breath. 'I just don't understand that.'

Sophie leaned forward, her hand on his arm. 'Some day I will make you understand what is so deep and wonderful that it can only happen between a mother and her daughter. It has enriched me. It has restored me. Can't you see how different I am?'

He touched his daughter's head and she turned to peer up at him.

'But she is *my* daughter, too,' he said. 'You have stolen her first six months from me.'

'I had to watch this baby become a little person . . . I did all the modelling I could do in London, and I did not show my pregnancy until about five and half months. I was so lucky that they were interested in me for for face or hair bookings. I have never looked so well, my hair so thick and glossy . . .'

'And the birth?'

'There was pain, yes, but when I took her into my arms—' she broke off, shaking her head.

'Why didn't you contact me when you visited Paris?'

'I thought it would upset you. I knew I needed to be alone.'

'And those British photographers? Don't tell me you didn't sleep with some?'

'Not one,' she laughed. 'Bailey's married to Catherine Deneuve, why would he want me? Anyway, they think I am very cold. Sex is the last thing a new mother thinks about. I used to flirt with men to test my attraction. But I was not a parent then.'

'And what are your plans, now?'

She leaned forward, holding his eyes.

'Gaby must get to know her father, that is extremely important. And, Christopher . . . I would like to get to know you, too.'

'So everything's OK?' he laughed. 'You ignore me for over a year and because Mademoiselle Sophie decides it is time, she wants to get to know me?'

'Yes.' She leaned towards him and softly kissed him on the mouth.

He resisted her kiss at first, a little sulkily, but there was undeniable proof that the magic he had always felt between them was still there. The child watched their kiss.

'What about you and Ghislaine?' she asked.

'That's over. And it was strictly business.'

'No, you loved the admiration. Still business partners?'

'Yes.'

'Are you sure it's all over with her? I can easily find out.'

'I'm sure.'

'I need a little time, Christopher. But if we start again—'

'I want my daughter,' he said firmly. 'She's half mine!'

'We must give it everything we've got,' she continued.

'One hundred per cent of ourselves!' he agreed.

Sophie looked as if she were about to cry. She took a sip of coffee, gazing into her cup.

A tear rolled down her cheek as she looked up. 'I was thinking of you so many times – didn't you feel it?'

He stared at her, reaching out to take her hand. 'Yes, I did,' he said. 'And it made me miserable.'

'Don't tell me *you* didn't have sex?'

He smiled. 'With Ghislaine and a few models. Hey, it's peace and love, remember! But it was more like peace and sex, not love.'

She kissed him again, deeper this time. A kiss, especially this particular one, could be so much more than two pairs of lips pressed together. A kiss could be sex. A kiss could be love. And this kiss: it was the most meaningful kiss they had ever shared, because she was giving something of herself in it.

They took the train back to Paris together, to give them more hours to talk, more time to be with their daughter.

She called the Antoines as soon as they got into her flat. She seemed to expect Christopher to stay with her. And, after fetching some clothes from his flat, that is what he did.

'Are we going to see our granddaughter?' Madame Antoine enquired when Sophie called. 'It's Saturday. Come for lunch. We have invited nobody . . . it will be just us!'

Nothing cut through the Antoines' formality better than a baby. They fussed and cooed and played with their granddaughter more than any parent could have dared hope. They gave her several expensive silver gifts, a set of teaspoons, a rattle, a picture frame.

'All family heirlooms . . .' Sophie murmured, trying not to sound ironic. Secretly, she felt flattered and touched that they were welcoming this baby as if it were their own blood grand-daughter.

'Our first grandchild!' Madame Antoine said at one point, flashing a look at her husband. She held her glass of wine high. 'I propose a toast to many more!'

After the usual perfect lunch, Laurent Antoine took Sophie and Gabrielle to play in the little garden. Madame Antoine poured some coffee for Christopher.

'So. You're together again?' she asked, her eyes sparkling.

He glanced out the window at Sophie. 'She's been the only woman for me since I first met her. That's the trouble.'

'Didn't Ghislaine de Rives rather get in the way?' She raised her eyebrows.

He nodded. 'Madame Antoine, that was unfortunate, but it's over. We're just business partners now.'

She watched him carefully for a moment, then took his hand and squeezed it, a rare moment of emotion from his future mother-in-law, for which he was suitably grateful.

'There's an adorable neighbourhood school near here that some of my friends send their little ones to,' Madame Antoine told Sophie when she joined her in the garden. 'You might enquire about putting down Gabrielle's name.'

The two women exchanged a glance. 'There is time for thinking about schools,' Sophie said. 'I haven't quite decided what we will do.'

Madame Antoine pulled Sophie aside, whispering urgently to her. 'You could start by deciding to marry the father of your child, Sophie. Christopher is a very decent man. You are humiliating him and your child if you do not marry him immediately.'

Sophie stared at her then burst into laughter. '*Maman*, times have changed since you had your children. This is nineteen seventy-one. Bourgoise society does not force me to marry. I need a little more time.'

Madame Antoine shook her head, disbelievingly. 'Still a rebel, Sophie?' she sighed.

'No, listen to me, Mother,' Sophie said urgently. 'I am deadly serious. I need just one small sign. Something to make the whole thing fall into place. And you could help me.'

'How?'

'By telling me who my real parents were.'

'What does that have to do with it?' Madame Antoine's eyes flashed.

'*Everything*,' Sophie cried. 'How can you not see that?'

Madame Antoine's face changed to a white mask, the blue eyes jewel hard.

'I have told you so many times,' she said. 'I don't know.'

Sophie stared at her. 'And I have thought many times that I don't believe you,' she replied.

Madame Antoine held Sophie's defiant stare for a long

moment. Then her eyes softened and she leaned forward to take Sophie's hand.

'Then, *please*, Sophie . . .' she pressed her hand, giving her the most meaningful look she could give. 'I beg of you, just accept that there are very good reasons for your not knowing.'

Sophie jumped to her feet. 'So you *do* know!' she cried.

She ran out to the garden and caught Christopher's arm.

'Will you please take us home,' she said calmly. 'Gaby needs her nap.'

Samantha rushed in and out of the studio with plans for presenting their new collection.

'There's a disused slaughterhouse a half-hour outside Paris,' she enthused one morning. 'All rusty metal . . . very *House and Garden*! We could fill it with dried flowers and rain down fake snow on the press?'

'Great.' Christopher nodded absently. Then he suddenly took in what she had said. 'Samantha, the locations must never overwhelm the clothes. Anyway, I just want to finish the collection. It's the hardest I've done.'

'You always say that.'

He was depressed, nervous, sleeping poorly, trying not to think of that lovely little girl who was his daughter. He hadn't even taken a photograph of her. He had made a mental list of the books he wished to read to her, the games he wanted to teach her, the colours he'd like to dress her in.

Dinners out with the new Face of Chanel attracted the press. They wanted to photograph and interview the new fashion couple. His HRRG clothes had collected a huge cliental and also a fashionable following of society women and their daughters. His name was getting known. He and Sophie had become gossip-column fodder.

'This journalist describes you as "dazed, withdrawn, somnambulist" . . .' Samantha read out.

He laughed. 'Women buy my clothes, not my personality.'

'They'll buy more if you project a positive image.'

Somehow, he got through the collection. The slaughterhouse presentation did prove a sensation, complete with a finale in an old train carriage pushed into the building with a bride spilling out of it. He was made to take a real bow while Ghislaine kept strictly behind the scenes. But the most extraordinary thing to him was that he and Sophie had not made love. Not once.

For a booking with London *Vogue*, Sophie insisted on taking Gaby with her. Christopher moved back to his own flat. But when Sophie returned after two days, she called him immediately.

'I need to see you,' Sophie's voice said. 'I'm with Gaby. I'm back.'

There was a silence. He needed to say something very cutting.

'And you want me to drop everything and rush round there?' he asked.

In a soft voice, she replied, 'I wish you would.'

'*Why?*' His voice betrayed him: it came out more as a cry than a casual question.

'Christopher,' she began hesitantly. He pressed the phone to his ear to hear. 'Remember last time when I told you I sought some magic sign – a kind of revelation – to show me what to do next? I found it in London, quite by accident. I must tell you about it. It involves our daughter. And you.'

An hour later, he held Gabrielle in his arms, sitting opposite Sophie at the window, open to the little balcony.

'I took her to feed the ducks in Kensington Gardens,' Sophie began as if continuing a conversation. 'Gabrielle loves that. When the bread runs out, she can watch them for hours. I was holding her tightly between my knees as a man led his little daughter to a paddling-pool with stepping-stones for children to walk across. If they fall, they only wet their feet, it's not deep—' she broke off, taking a sip of wine, her eyes holding his. He sensed how important this had been to her.

'The father held his daughter under the arms,' she went

320

on, 'lifting her from stone to stone, letting her believe it was under her own power, as if she were flying from stone to stone. She relaxed in his grip, completely trusting herself to him, knowing he would not let her fall.' She glanced at him. 'It was like a missing scene from my own childhood. Did my father ever do that for me? Did my father lift me? Did I relax in his grip? Did I ever learn how to trust a man?'

She gave him an intense, questioning look.

'In that moment I understood myself and my child. And I knew she must grow up with her father. It was the sign I had waited for . . . when everything clicks into place. I always loved you, but I never completely trusted you. I didn't know how to trust anyone. Now, I think I can.'

Twenty-eight

How do you make love to a stranger? A stranger with whom you have made love so many times before? A stranger who has given birth to your daughter without telling you? A stranger who displays her body to you regretfully, pointing out the marks and signs of ageing, in case you miss them?

As Christopher traced his fingers down her breast bone, Sophie lay, calm and accepting, on the bed watching him. The girl who first demanded sex in a transparent *cabine* had disappeared. This calmer person, this new mother, approached sex differently.

He removed his clothes to lay naked next to her. Ghislaine had always advised: '*L'appetite vien en mangeant*' – appetite comes as you eat; it was up to him to reawaken Sophie's appetite. Their child's presence in the next room changed the sex. Sex could turn to love; and love itself could be very, very sexy. This sex Christopher found the most exciting of his life. The most profound and the most risky. Sex with the most at stake.

As he inhaled the familiar perfume, his fingertips rediscovered the feel of her skin, the touch of her body. Now it was not just her body – it was the vessel which had borne his child, its whiteness like a shell or stone washed smooth by waves splashing against it. He pored over her, revisiting the nooks and crannies and hollows he had known, the curve inside her neck, the angular collarbones he could span with one hand, the long lines of her thighs which he massaged with strong thumbs as if moulding them, sculpting them, like the thick, spongy double-faced wools

322

he used for suits, steamed full of volume. The pert shape of her hard little buttocks when she lay on her front, the only part of her which could be called boyish. And when she turned to lay on her back, the large round dark nipples crowning the perfect breasts. The small white feet with their startling red lacquered toenails. And finally, the triangle of red hair, so provocative, as it outlined the most secret part of her. He was stiff with the desire to enjoy, slowly and pleasurably, this body he remembered so well that he could celebrate every little change.

'I've aged,' Sophie whispered as he examined her. She pointed out the stretch-marks. But her tight, compact body had not been pulled out of shape. The flat stomach and the skin stretched tautly over the hips. The secret entrance, as erotic as it had always been and as withholding of its secrets as ever, was the same. Until he touched his tongue to its saltiness and lapped at her. Sophie moved. *The appetite comes as you eat*, the French loved to say. He would awaken the sleeping beauty from her sleep. Was it possible that she had not experienced real sex since they had parted?

He massaged her for long minutes, her body moving almost resentfully as she arched her back and pushed herself up to him. His hands assured her that they would not flag, they would be there, moving firmly against her for as long as she wanted, needed. And his lips brushed her lips at the same time as his hands felt all over her body, like a blind man trying to recognise an old friend. A sigh escaped her. Sensing his patience and his desire, she began to respond. His hand caressed and caressed her and she was almost forced to accept the pleasure he offered. He moved a little faster. Another sigh. And soon, she pulled at his shoulders to make him lie full-length upon her, shoulders to shoulders, toes to toes, as he took the long plunge into her.

There was nothing mechanical about this, rather they worked together as if swimming in the sea or floating in the sky, existing in the pure blur of pleasure which enveloped them, growing and growing until it involved every part of the body, working up towards the final, fulfilling burst. The best sex of all is love. Love enhanced the pleasure, making them experience an almost spiritual meeting of their souls. A meeting of minds and bodies in what must be the ultimate bonding. It was wonderful, breathtaking, literally leaving them breathless.

As they floated down to earth minutes later, the cries she gave left no doubt that the magic was still there. They were better than ever. He held her closely as their wildly beating hearts slowed to resume a normal rhythm. He slipped from her bed and went into the living-room to find Gabrielle still asleep in her little cot. He gently gathered her in his arms and placed her on the bed between them. They snuggled up together, this new family, drawn into Sophie's spell a second, even more compelling, time. He turned to look into her eyes; a new warmth lent the green gaze a softer look, the wariness had gone.

'What are we going to design?' she murmured.

'The most beautiful clothes in the world . . .' he promised her.

Very few people were allowed to be this happy. It was so rare, one hardly dared recognise it. Could a happy ending really be possible? Christopher tried to relax, go with the feeling, enjoy it, but some little nag stopped him fully entering the reality of his dream. The nag was Chanel, he realised with a start. She was dead, but that did not mean her influence on fashion or on *people* was dead, too. Her influence on *them*. Something inside warned him that this was not quite 'happy ever after'. Not yet.

In her dream, Samantha presided over a Chanel Anonymous meeting. Camellias fell from the ceiling and she ferverishly gathered up the flowers which she knew were made from thousand-dollar bills, intricately folded like origami, affixed to waxy green leaves. She woke to find herself in the half-empty Marais apartment that Klaus was redecorating. Was her dream some kind of sign? Did it signify big money on the way? She stumbled to the fridge to find a huge chocolate éclair.

The three friends met at La Coupole one Friday evening to discuss their futures. There had been no mention of a bequeathment, a will, a bequest.

What about their positions in the house? This was something they should discuss, surely? They all wore Chanel. Monique still respectfully wore a black bouclé wool suit. Samantha was in a navy wool coat over a matching skirt and ivory blouse. And Sophie in the cream suit trimmed in navy braid.

'And Christopher?' Monique asked Sophie.

'With Gaby,' Sophie said. 'We don't like leaving her with babysitters.'

'I dreamed I inherited Chanel,' Samantha blurted out. 'Mademoiselle left the whole enterprise to *me*.' She took a gulp of her kir royale and sat up straighter in her chair, staring in surprise at them. 'There were all these camellias falling around me made out of thousand-dollar bills and—'

Sophie and Monique exchanged alarmed glances.

'Samantha, are you "on" anything?' Sophie asked.

'How could you inherit Chanel? You are not a designer, Samantha,' Monique gently pointed out.

'You are deceiving yourself, Samantha,' Sophie nodded.

Samantha looked affronted. 'I'm not a designer but I *could* be a director,' she said. 'I would like to think that maybe Mademoiselle left instructions for me to join the board of directors. We wouldn't need a designer. I could update Mademoiselle's designs each season with new fabrics, different skirt lengths, different details. You'd help me, wouldn't you, Monique?'

Monique swallowed her Scotch in a gulp, remembering Mademoiselle's words: 'I'm grooming you to take over . . .'

'Samantha,' she hesitated. 'You may be surprised at Mademoiselle's will. It is quite possible everything will remain the same.'

'They'll need *someone* to direct the design!' Samantha cried.

The three women shared a short silence. Sophie lit a cigarette and took a long drag. They watched her, fascinated.

She noticed them staring and said, 'She told nearly everyone that she would leave them something,' she blew out smoke. 'Old women sometimes do that to make sure that people are nice to them. I always had this feeling about Mademoiselle . . . that we were somehow connected. Related, even, imagine, she suggested adopting my baby, even though she was old enough to be its great-grandmother!'

'That would change nothing: she disowned her relations,'

Monique stated. 'She would not even receive her nieces. I had to tell them their aunt was indisposed. They only wanted to say hello to her, they were such nice girls.'

Sophie shrugged. 'I don't want either of you to be disappointed.'

'Oh, I expect nothing at all,' Monique signalled the waiter for another Scotch. 'I am just sad that she died alone, every unmarried woman dreads that.'

'You mean *you* dread that?' Samantha said.

'Yes, I do,' Monique agreed.

'Most women die alone because most women outlive their husbands,' Samantha shuddered. 'I only worry I might die not wearing Chanel!'

'Mademoiselle did not die alone: Jeanne was with her,' Sophie said.

'She was only a maid,' Monique said.

Samantha turned to her. 'Jeanne was more than a maid, Monique. She was a confidante. She knew all the secrets . . . that woman heard and saw *everything*.'

Sophie narrowed her eyes through her cigarette smoke.

'What kind of secrets?' she asked Samantha.

Samantha shrugged. 'How would I know? There were plenty. Why do you think all those writers pulled out of doing her "Autobiography"? Most writers' credits on the cover say, "As told to. . ." In Mademoiselle's case, it would have been, "As *lied* to". . .'

'She lied?' Monique asked.

'Are you kidding?' Samantha laughed. 'The dates, names and facts changed each time she told her story.'

'But why did she lie?' Monique insisted.

'Why would any woman lie about her life?' Samantha said. 'Because there's something to hide.'

'But,' Monique frowned, 'she achieved so much.'

Samantha nodded. 'That's the mystery.'

They ordered a second round of drinks and nobody noticed Sophie drifting off into a reverie.

Jeanne knew all the secrets. The words echoed in Sophie's

thoughts as she stared into her glass. The maid! Why hadn't she thought of that?

'Which one?' Samantha asked Klaus, holding up two Chanel suits, one pink, one baby blue.

'Neither,' he said. 'Black.'

She made a face, hanging them in her closet. 'I guess you're right.'

De Kousmine had invited Samantha, Monique and Sophie to his office to outline new plans now that Mademoiselle was no longer there.

The ten o'clock meeting was an event for which they would wear their best clothes. Samantha ended up borrowing a red suit from the boutique. She asked Klaus to accompany her.

On the following Monday, a small crowd of reporters and photographers waited around the Chanel front doors.

'Why are *they* here?' Sophie whispered to Samantha.

Samantha beamed, taking Klaus's hand. 'This is a news story, Sophie: *Who inherits the planet's top fashion house?*'

'*You* tipped them off?' Sophie stopped in the street. 'Samantha, of all the stupidest—I thought we'd agreed the other night that nobody will inherit anything?'

'Maybe, maybe not.' Samantha waggled her head. 'But I believe she may well have left *me* the house. Or at least a nice comfy chair at the directors' table. I contacted her on an Ouija board and she practically told me. And who are *you* kidding? You want it so much you can taste it.' She indicated Monique. 'So does she!'

'You are wrong, Samantha,' Monique protested. 'I don't want anything and I expect nothing.'

'You're freaking out, Samantha,' Sophie laughed. 'You've eaten one too many magic mushrooms. What are you giving her, Klaus?'

'Please, Sophie, good vibes only,' Klaus growled. 'Samantha's under a lot of stress.'

Samantha, her nose in the air, held onto Klaus's arm for support as she passed the photographers.

'You might get a scoop if you wait an hour,' she promised them as she entered the house.

'He cannot come in here.' An elegantly Chanel-ed arm barred Klaus from de Kousmine's office.

Samantha narrowed her eyes at de Kousmine's secretary, a rather snooty girl she had never liked.

'*Klaus est mon partenaire,*' she explained. '*Mon amant! Mon amour!*'

'There are only three people on my list . . .' the girl said.

'Oh, this is worse than Regine's!' Samantha exploded. 'Wait in the café downstairs.' She kissed Klaus, whispering: 'When you next see me, I may be worth a billion bucks.'

He shot her a disbelieving look. 'Don't be disappointed,' he warned. 'There is no such thing as a free lunch.'

'Free *lunch*?' she whispered fiercely. 'I expect a free couture house. I killed myself making sure that Mademoiselle wasn't lonely and she hinted a dozen times she'd leave me the house.'

'Samantha, darling,' Klaus began, 'please don't build yourself up to a big disappointment. You know what you are like. It's lovely to be full of illusions and fantasy, but . . .' He gave her a meaningful stare.

She pushed him away.

They waited in de Kousmine's office. He was late.

'Oops, he's here.' Samantha ran from the door to her seat just as Monsieur de Kousmine lumbered in. He sat at his desk, giving each of them an interrogative look from beneath those heavy black brows.

'Before I say anything, I want to make it very clear that I am not doing this in any official capacity. It is a courtesy to Mademoiselle who made me promise to speak to you in the event of her death. You were all special friends to her, not just employees.'

They nodded and Monique began to cry.

'First I would like to hear, from each of you, what you think fashion is. What it represents.' He stared pointedly at Sophie. 'Sophie?'

'Fashion is . . .' Sophie stared upwards, as if seeking the answer from her guardian angel. 'Sex,' she stated finally, 'a way of making women desirable.'

He nodded. 'Samantha?'

She got to her feet, 'If this house was mine, I would drag Chanel into the next century with publicity. I would . . .' She took some deep shuddering breaths, gasped and collapsed into her chair, clutching her throat.

Monsieur de Kousmine poured her a glass of water.

'This house is not going to be yours, Samantha,' he said, giving her the glass.

He glanced over at Monique who was shaking her head.

'Monique,' he said.

Monique looked up. 'Fashion is craft, Monsieur,' she stated. 'One must be absolutely dedicated to producing perfect work.'

Samantha held up a hand, gasping. 'OK, let me finish. Mademoiselle Chanel is not dead. We will keep her alive! And to answer your question: Fashion is . . .' She frowned. 'What was it her dad used to say? *It doesn't matter what you think! Tell men what they want to hear!* 'Fashion is . . . *money!*' she blurted out. 'A chic way to make loads of it!'

'I see.' Monsieur de Kousmine stroked his walrus moustache. He took a sip of water.

'You have all had your say,' he began. 'Because Mademoiselle was so fond of you, I feel you should be the first to know that the person chosen to take over from our late Mademoiselle as the most influential designer in the world will be . . .' He took a deep breath, had a coughing fit and took another long sip of water.

Samantha bit her lip hard to keep from screaming, eyes on her boss, digging her square-cut nails so hard into her palms that they almost drew blood. In one minute, she knew her life would change, never to be the same.

'From next season the house of Chanel's collections,' Monsieur de Kousmine began, 'will be designed by . . . Jean Phillipe.'

Samantha looked around as if someone was missing. 'Who the fuck is *he*?' she cried.

'Up until now, he has been an assistant at Dior,' de Kousmine explained.

'An *assistant*?' Samantha's voice rose. 'Are you kidding us?'

There was no reaction from the others. They sat there, silent.

'Who gets the house?' Samantha asked, getting to her feet. 'Who gets the house?' she repeated in a shriller tone.

De Kousmine stared dolefully at her.

'The house remains under the direction of the Wertheimer family, who have run things for the last fifteen years,' he said, closing a folder. 'The will can be dealt with by Mademoiselle's Swiss lawyers.'

'The *will*?' Samantha laughed, turning to the others. 'Don't hold your breath,' she advised.

'Samantha . . .' Monique reached out to take her arm because she looked as if she were about to attack de Kousmine. 'Sit down . . .'

'I called you here to clarify your positions in the house,' de Kousmine went on. 'Sophie, we want you to continue as the Face of Chanel. Mademoiselle Far, we hope you will continue your excellent workroom here.'

He folded his arms, as if finished.

'That is all,' he said.

'What about *me*?' Samantha squawked.

'Your services are no longer required,' de Kousmine told her.

Samantha stood in front of him, aiming her most killing look, '*You're* firing me? Mademoiselle *believed* in me! She wanted me to—'

'The directors feel that Chanel succeeds on its own merits. It does not need a publicist.'

'Doesn't need a publicist?' Samantha cried. 'Why, you arrogant French bastard!' She bent down to hiss at him. 'You could have helped me out on this. You could have put in a good word for me. I could have you *killed*! Forget seeing me again!'

'You may go,' de Kousmine told them.

Samantha stared at him for a moment before leaning very close. He flinched.

'From now on, you'll have to *pay* for your blow-jobs,' she growled in his ear. 'You won't be getting one from *me* again!'

Tossing her head, she walked out.

The others followed her out of the office.

'Never in my entire *life!*' Samantha exploded when they got to the street.

Christopher was waiting, Gaby in his arms. He kissed Sophie and the other two girls.

'I thought I should be here,' he said. 'Is everything all right? Klaus is waiting in the café.'

'Everything is fine,' Sophie told him.

'No, it isn't fine!' Samantha corrected her. 'I've been fired! *Again!*' she told Christopher, pushing through the photographers clustered on the pavement. 'Guys, gimme a little room to breathe, will ya?'

'You *told* us to be here,' a Jean-Paul Belmondo lookalike protested.

'I thought there'd be something to announce,' she glared at him. 'There isn't, so buzz off.'

They all followed Samantha into the café. She collapsed at the table Klaus was sitting at, bursting into tears. Klaus put his arm around her.

'Did I warn you?' he asked.

'Scotch!' Samantha gasped.

Monique touched her shoulder. 'Not this early in the day. Have hot chocolate,' she urged.

'I need a drink, goddammit!' Samantha cried.

Monique ordered Scotch as Samantha muttered about law suits. Christopher and Sophie ordered coffee. When the drinks arrived, Samantha tossed back her Scotch in a gulp and signalled for another.

'I never believed for one second—' she began.

'Samantha, I am sorry you are disappointed but she was very

lonely.' Monique said. 'She felt the need to offer rewards for our friendship.'

Samantha gulped back her second Scotch as if it were Coke.

'Firing me like that in front of everyone,' she muttered. 'I'll get even with him, I swear it,' she vowed. 'My father knows guys who kill people. Five thousand bucks. Worth every penny!'

'*Samantha!*' Monique cried, truly shocked.

'Calm down, now,' Klaus soothed her. 'You will find another position somewhere equally good.'

'Oh, where can you go after Chanel?' Samantha wailed.

'There are other houses,' Monique assured her. 'Guy is very happy at Saint Laurent.'

'Yeah, Saint Laurent, what has he come up with?' Samantha sneered. 'The safari suit? My entire life has been Chanel.' She grabbed a new drink. 'Even when I'm asleep, I run my treatment centre for Chanel-junkies. It sounds ridiculous, but—'

Sophie began to laugh. Klaus silenced her.

'She woke up yesterday convinced our bed was covered in camellias made from thousand-dollar bills. I had to switch on the light to prove it was a dream.'

Sophie shrugged.

'What do you think, Sophie?' Monique asked her.

Sophie regarded each of them gravely. 'My premonition,' she said, 'is that the story is not yet over.'

They were too busy to stay in the café for long. Klaus had a photo-session booked. Samantha wanted to supervise it. She also needed to see Ghislaine about the next collection presentation. Sophie and Christopher proposed to take Gaby home for lunch. And Monique had fittings to take in the Chanel *cabines*.

Samantha swallowed her third Scotch and stood up. They followed her to the street.

'You know what?' Samantha announced defiantly, swaying slightly. 'To *hell* with Chanel!' she cried out. 'Yeah. To hell with them!'

She ran the few steps back down Rue Cambon, stopped

outside the house and screamed: 'To hell with Chanel! Take your new designer and shove it! You'll *never* replace Mademoiselle! *Never!*'

The glass doors opened and the *directrice* of the boutique glared out of the doorway at her.

'That was borrowed from the boutique?' she said indicating the Chanel suit Samantha was wearing. 'May I have it back?'

'Here!' Samantha ripped off the jacket, and threw it at the woman's head. 'Stick it up your snooty French ass!'

She began to unzip her skirt but Klaus reached out and stopped her. As it was, a photographer managed to snap the jacket flying through the air at the manager.

'Come now, my little woman,' Klaus urged. He covered Samantha's shoulders with his black leather jacket and hailed a taxi. 'We will not make fools of ourselves. I have a session to shoot. I need your help.'

He opened the door and helped her into the back seat where she promptly fell asleep. Then he grabbed Christopher.

'C'mon, man, you've been kidding her along all this time, but we're a little more grown-up now, right? More real? She's going to be my wife. You gotta help me with her. This woman could die of Chanel! Offer her a fabulous permanent job, can't you? She'll do it well!'

'Of course!' Christopher patted Klaus on the back. 'She'll work full time for us. She's done a wonderful job so far . . . we love her!'

'Thanks, man,' Klaus said gruffly, patting his back. He joined Samantha in the taxi.

'Christopher, that was so sweet of you,' Sophie said as they walked up to the Boulevard de Capucines. 'She needs this new job before she does something really foolish. Funny, I have never realised before just how unbalanced that girl is.'

Samantha sat at her new desk at HRRG on the fourth morning of her new job. Suddenly she was overwhelmed and her eyes welled with tears.

'It's as if Chanel had never happened,' she whispered.

'She had a wonderful life.' Ghislaine hastened to her side. 'But now it is in the past. Fashion is the future, Samantha, remember?'

'I guess so.' Samantha sniffed. 'But you know something? I really loved that old lady. Her strength, her style! There'll never be another like her. Wherever she is, I hope they're wearing Chanel . . .'

Twenty-nine

Ten days after the funeral, Paris was dangerously quiet, as if stunned. Samantha was dangerously quiet, too. But not stunned.

She had begun to plan the most spectacular fashion presentation ever attempted in Paris, perhaps the world. The autumn 1971 collection would need a massive injection of cash into HRRG and she discussed this with Ghislaine, offering to squeeze the funds out of her father in return for his ownership of twenty-five per cent of the company. It was actually a vote of great confidence in a company she felt was bound to succeed.

'Couture is *over*, as everyone predicted,' she said. 'Without Balenciaga and Chanel, designers have no one to follow. Mademoiselle's death is just the nail in the coffin. Literally!'

For the HRRG showing, she had decided nothing less than an entire circus would do.

'And we could get married at the same time?' she suggested to Klaus when she got home that night. '*At* the circus! I'd get a sexy Ringmaster's outfit with fishnet tights, top hat and high heels. Very Josephine Baker!'

Klaus nodded, but he looked grave. 'Maybe we do this, darling, but right now, I have some news for you, and please stay calm and do not get too upset.'

'Never tell me to stay calm.' She clutched at Klaus. 'You know how excited that makes me! What is it?'

'Pack a suitcase,' he told her. 'We go now to Orly Airport for a plane to New York.'

'American *Vogue*?' Samantha guessed.

'No, it's your father. He has had a heart attack. He is in Intensive Care at Mount Sinai Hospital.'

'This plane trip is a guilt trip,' Samantha said a dozen times during the flight. 'This is what I get for wanting too much. It's my punishment.' She glanced across at Klaus who was trying to sleep. 'I was so sure I'd inherit Chanel and now God is showing me I was too—' she broke off, unable to complete the thought. 'If I lose my father, I don't know how I'll—' she wiped away a tear and tried to focus on a newspaper. Anything to take her mind off what awaited her. Klaus put an arm around her. 'Fathers have heart attacks. They recover. It is not your fault. Don't blame yourself. Just get there and hold his hand.' She stared at Klaus, as if seeing him for the first time.

'You know, you really are a very nice man, Klaus,' she said.

'Yes? What did you think I was, a fashion accessory?' he laughed.

She frowned, staring even harder at him. Yes, she thought, she *had* regarded him as something like that. An accessory and a sex object. Tall. With great marching rhythm.

'Well, if you *are* a fashion accessory, you're unique, the only one, and I am so glad I got you!' she declared.

'I don't think I want to carry on here . . .' The words, spoken in Madame Antoine's beautifully modulated tones, startled Monique.

'Oh, Madame Antoine, I never thought I would hear you say that,' she gasped. She was on her usual visit to Madame Antoine's office at the end of the week.

'Mademoiselle was the engine that powered this house,' Madame Antoine continued. 'I had no idea how empty it would feel without her. It doesn't feel the same and I know in my heart it never can. Perhaps it's time I stepped down?'

'Who could possibly do your job?' Monique whispered.

Madame Antoine regarded her seriously. 'I was thinking maybe *you* could?' she suggested.

Monique's mouth fell open. 'I'm a seamstress, Madame.'

The blue eyes appraised her. 'I've always thought of you as so much more than that, Monique,' Madame Antoine said thoughtfully. 'You earned your own atelier in record time, you have a wonderful way with the clients, you take fittings with the perfect mixture of advice, respect, tact . . .'

'But I'm from a humble doctor's family, Madame, with no society connections at all!'

'I'm not sure that you need those today, Monique.' Madame Antoine laughed a little bitterly. 'The women we dress no longer come from French society. Each season, we send sketches to the top Saudi Arabian households, with fabric swatches stapled to each sketch. The dresses are ordered, made to the measurements of each wife. They are beautifully wrapped and air-freighted, never to be heard of again. A sad fate for beautiful clothes made to be admired, isn't it?'

'Oh Madame . . .' Monique sighed.

'So you see, the whole situation has changed,' Madame Antoine said wistfully. 'You could handle it, Monique. This might be a wonderful new direction for you.'

Monique walked home slowly that night, not sure whether to be ecstatic or sad. She did not have to accept the position as Chanel *directrice*, but what an honour to be offered it. She had not come to Paris expecting to elevate her social status. *Directrice* of Chanel? It was impossible to imagine. Only reporting the news to Guy would make it real.

'Does Sophie have some kind of fetish for the Ritz?' Ghislaine asked Christopher at work. 'I keep running into her there. Are you keeping an eye on her?' Her eyes sparkled mischievously as she tried to make Christopher feel uneasy. That day she succeeded.

They were just leaving a small meeting about the 'Fashion Circus' Samantha proposed. It would launch HRRG as the most prestigious ready-to-wear clothing company in the world.

'The Ritz?' Christopher frowned, trying to take in what she was saying.

'Sophie's there every Saturday,' Ghislaine nodded.

'I can't imagine why,' he shrugged.

'*Try* to imagine?' she suggested, with a meaningful look. 'Why do women usually go to the Ritz?'

He refused to give her a reaction. He was still not completely sure of Sophie and perhaps Ghislaine sensed this. His jealousy could so easily be triggered, as it was now.

Sophie started to sketch children's clothes. She also proposed a line of 'classics' to be marketed under her name at HRRG. Ghislaine had decided that HRRG should stock basic classic items which every woman always needed and always sought. She agreed with Christopher that Sophie had talent and the two women now got on surprisingly well. As a top model Sophie now had a 'name'. Ghislaine saw her, commercially, as an asset. Twiggy was designing clothes under her own name in England, why shouldn't Sophie?

Sophie questioned her friends to find out which items they always sought – the perfect skirt, the perfect shirt, the perfect pair of straight slacks.

She was poring over a ninth version of 'the classic shirt', which was starting to drive her a little mad. She looked up as Christopher came home, one Saturday morning, laden with packets.

'Maybe it should just be a classic white cotton man's shirt, after all?' she asked.

'No!' He kissed her. 'It should be a little Bonnie Prince Charlie, as *if* it had lace cuffs . . .'

'Yet *not* have lace cuffs . . .'

'And a kind of smocking—'

'But without smocking?'

'What's wrong with smocking?'

'We'd have to find some little old ladies who can still do it. Smocking hasn't been seen in Paris for at least thirty years . . .' She jumped up. 'I'm going for a long walk,' she told him. 'I'll look at fabrics in the Rue de la Chaussee D'antin . . . or just *flâner dans la rue* . . .'

'Oh darling, will you take Gaby with you? I may have to go out . . .'

He knew what '*flâner dans la rue*' meant – to follow your nose.

'I thought you hated hysterical housewives tearing fabric out of your hands.' He tried hard not to sound suspicious.

'Today I shall tear it right back,' she called.

'Want me to come with you?'

'I may pop in to see Ines. She's having man problems: she won't confide in me if you're there.'

Sophie disappeared, and came back made up and dressed in a claret Chanel cardigan suit. She was far too smartly dressed for bargain-shopping.

'You look lovely. When will you be back?'

'I won't set a time, because you'll worry if I'm late. But not after five, surely. *Au revoir.*'

She leaned to kiss his forehead, swept Gaby into her arms and was out the door, the slam of it setting him into action. He leaped to his feet. What possible reason could a pretty girl have for visiting the Ritz? Damn Ghislaine for putting jealous thoughts in his head! He would have to follow her to see where Sophie's nose led her today. If her destination was the Ritz, he would catch her red-handed.

He was certain she did not know he was behind her. She walked rapidly down the left side of the Champs-Elysées, holding Gaby, surprising him by stopping at a bus-stop and waiting for a bus. Hiding in a doorway, he wondered if he could board the same bus without her seeing.

A crowd gathered around the stop as the bus approached. He hung back until the last person stepped on, then ran for it, jumping on the platform as the conductor rang the bell. Sophie was inside. He hung over the rail, face turned away. He would get off a stop before the Ritz and run the rest of the way. The bus rattled down the Champs-Elysées, sailed around Rond Point, and came into the Place de la Concorde. Sophie prepared to get off and he quickly turned his back to her. When she left, he hopped off the platform. She walked to the Place de la Madeleine, Gaby securely in her arms. At Fauchon's, where so many women liked to eat a pastry at the bar, Sophie waited to buy pastries. She did not like them so why was she in this shop?

He hung around in the Place, leaning against the old church, trying to spot Sophie through a window. She reappeared carrying a box tied with Fauchon ribbon: was it a gift for her lover? There was a sickening throb of jealousy in the pit of his stomach as he fell thirty paces behind her, nearing the Ritz.

Samantha sat by her father's bed in Mount Sinai's intensive care wing, flicking through the Style section of the *New York Times*. She had been sitting there for one entire day. Klaus relaxed in the armchair, reading a book.

Her first impression was that her father had shrunk! That the lumbering man who had been a big, somewhat clumsy guy, had suddenly aged and become a lot smaller. The figure outlined under the sheet seemed almost frail, and his face was thinner, although still dominated by his strong nose and shock of white hair. She could hardly look at him without crying. Was this really her big strong daddy who had always taken such care of her? He simply could not become an invalid.

'If he doesn't recover, I'm burning my Chanels,' she suddenly vowed. 'Even the camellias.'

'Why do you say this, Samantha?' Klaus looked up.

He rubbed his eyes. Neither of them had had much sleep.

She glanced at him. 'I can't get rid of the feeling that this is my punishment for being a Chanel freak.'

'A heart attack is nobody's fault,' Klaus said quietly. 'You must love your father very much to consider a Chanel bonfire.'

'He's the only family I have,' Samantha said quietly. 'Apart from some un-chic peasant cousins who wouldn't know a Chanel jacket from Macy's pyjamas.'

'Don't talk that way about your family,' a voice said.

'*What?*' she glared at Klaus: he hadn't spoken.

She bent to peer at her father. Sandor Lipstaadt's eyes blinked open.

'*Daddy?*' she screamed.

'You came all this way to see your poor sick father?' he said.

'Oh, Daddy, you know who I am!' Tears streamed down Samantha's face, carrying mascara with them. 'Do you know who *you* are?'

'Sure I know. I am a dying man.'

'Daddy, you are not dying. At least, not before you see my totally Chanel wardrobe. All genuine, not *one* knock-off! And I need you alive! To invest a lot of money in the firm of a talented friend of mine. Anyway, the doctors say you'll be just fine.' She knelt on the floor, taking his hand from the coverlet, pressing her lips against it.

'Oh Daddy, I've been so worried.' She beckoned to Klaus. 'Daddy, this is Klaus . . .'

A new face swum into the old man's range.

'How do you do, Mr Lipstaadt,' Klaus said, trying to click his heels softly. 'I would like to ask for your daughter's hand.'

'Her hand?' Lipstaadt frowned. 'What d'you need her hand for? If I give you her hand, will you get me out of here?'

Klaus nodded.

'Take her hand, take her foot, take anything you want. Just get me back to my own bed.'

'Klaus just bought an enormous apartment in Paris for us,' Samantha said proudly. 'There are three small rooms for nurseries but I'm turning them into walk-in closets . . .'

'Please, children . . .' The old man placed a hand on his heart. 'Make it two closets and one nursery. I want to see a grandchild!'

Samantha winked at Klaus. 'That's my Daddy!' she said.

*

341

Sophie chose the Ritz's back entrance, the one leading to the American Bar. Christopher watched as she passed through the revolving door, waiting a moment before following. He caught sight of her red suit at the end of the corridor, disappearing towards the foyer. He grabbed a *Herald Tribune* from an armchair to hold before his face in case she turned around. At the foyer, he caught a flash of red entering the lift. The door closed as he held the paper before his face. The pointer indicated the floor at which the lift stopped showed, 'One', 'Two', 'Three' and 'Four'. The fourth floor. The floor Chanel had lived on.

He sank into one of the Ritz's deep leather armchairs. Did she visit Chanel's empty suite? And if it was empty, why would she dress up? With her taste for fantasy, did she rent it, decorate it with transparent cubicles and entertain men as she had first entertained him? Each man who got into the lift underwent Christopher's scrutiny: each was a possible lover.

He buried his face in his hands, knowing that he would be unable to forgive her if she was unfaithful to him now. The lift returned to the ground floor. An older American couple stepped out into the foyer, a little befuddled, unsure which door to leave by. The wife pulled the husband towards the Rue Cambon exit. Christopher waited. He had forgotten Mademoiselle's room number. He could not very well knock on every fourth-floor door until he found Sophie. But if he waited here, he would see, when she came back down, whether she had just enjoyed sex. Her face would tell him.

He tried to focus on the *Herald Tribune* but the words swam before his eyes. He looked at his watch: Sophie had been up there for over twenty minutes.

The lift was called to the fourth floor. The indicator hovered some moments before the lift began its descent. It took so long. Finally, the doors slid open and Sophie stepped out, alone. Christopher studied her face. It was blank. No particular expression was on it, certainly not the fulfilled look of a woman who had just enjoyed sex. She stood in the foyer for a moment. Throwing down his paper, he ran up to her and grabbed her arm.

A jolt went through her. She gasped, her eyes widened and she regarded him with an amazed expression, looking around as if she had no idea where she was. He had never awakened a sleepwalker, but that is what he felt he'd done with Sophie. It is said to be dangerous, even fatal.

'What are you doing here?' he asked. Some faces turned in their direction. 'Who are you seeing? You come here every week, don't you? Ghislaine told me. She saw you! Didn't you realise people would see you?'

A series of expressions passed over Sophie's face, as her mind seemed to speed through excuses she knew he would not accept.

'Just tell me,' he urged. 'Is it some man? Let's have it out, and an end to it!'

She tottered backwards, holding onto his arm as if about to fall.

'And where's Gabrielle?' he asked. 'Don't tell me you leave her with *him*?'

'She's—' She tried to talk but could not get out words. Her anguished expression tore at his heart. He had woken her from some dream and she could not find her bearings. Instead, she held onto him, swaying. Finally, she broke away and regarded him.

'You think I have a lover?' she murmured.

'Why else would you be here?'

'Come. I'll show you,' she said.

She beckoned him into the lift, nodding to the operator. The doors slid to. The lift rose slowly, smoothly. The operator knew which floor was wanted. They stopped.

'Fourth floor,' the operator announced.

Sophie turned to her right, knowing the way. They passed a few doors. 408. 410. 412. Suddenly they were outside 414. He tried to swallow, producing only a dry gulp. Sophie looked at him closely with a direct, green stare. She indicated the door.

'Who's in there?' he asked.

Sophie knocked three times on the door, calling out, 'It's Sophie!'

There was some movement from behind the door. Shuffling. After a wait, it slowly opened a few inches. An icy shiver spread down the back of Christopher's neck as a face peered through the gap. He would have sworn that Mademoiselle Chanel, or her ghost, stood there in black cardigan and skirt. But as his eyes accustomed to the light coming from behind the figure, Christopher saw a fragile, small, old lady peering out doubtfully.

'I wanted you to meet Christopher,' Sophie began. 'May we come in?'

She took a step forward. The woman didn't move. She seemed to be thinking about it. Finally, she stood aside, opening the door wider. They walked in.

There were three rooms: sitting-room, bedroom and bathroom. They entered the sitting-room. It had the slightly shabby cosiness of the American Bar downstairs. Gaby was nestled in a leather armchair, which had aged gracefully. She smiled when she saw Christopher, holding her arms up to him. He lifted her and held her. One of Chanel's beautiful Chinese coromandel screens leaned against a wall. The room was austere, perfectly white and clean. But empty. Christopher hardly dared look around it: it felt wrong, somehow, to be in there. The presence of Mademoiselle was extremely strong and disapproving.

'Jeanne looked after Mademoiselle up until the very last day,' Sophie told him, smiling at the old woman.

'My name isn't really Jeanne,' the old woman blurted out. 'But Mademoiselle liked all her maids to be called Jeanne.'

'I didn't realise that,' Sophie said. 'What *is* your name?'

'Celeste, Mademoiselle.'

'From now on, I shall call you Celeste,' Sophie promised.

The woman inclined her head. '*Comme vous voulez,*' she murmured.

Christopher glanced around the room. 'So this is where she lived?' he said.

'*Oui, Monsieur.* For nearly eighteen years. She had very simple tastes. Would Monsieur care for some tea? I can order anything I like just by picking up the telephone.'

'Please don't bother, Celeste, thank you.'

She seemed disappointed.

'Christopher? Do you mind leaving us alone?' Sophie asked. She appeared to be drifting back into the waking dream. 'I only went down for a drink. I need a little time to be alone with Celeste.'

He stared, wondering why she wanted to be there.

'Why don't we all go down for some tea?' he suggested.

'No. I want to be here with Celeste. You'd prefer that, wouldn't you Celeste?'

The older woman smiled at Christopher. 'I do like tea,' she said.

'We'll order some,' Sophie said. 'Please, Christopher.' She looked at him almost pleadingly. 'I'll see you at home.'

'Should I take Gaby?'

'No, Celeste likes to play with her . . .'

He stared at them. Why was Chanel's maid suddenly so important to Sophie? And Jeanne/Celeste did not seem particularly interested in their daughter. She had put on some tiny reading spectacles and was ruffling through letters and notebooks in a red leather box. He wondered whether this was Chanel's property.

He glanced around at boxes of papers, at the letters and diaries everywhere. Something struck him as odd, but what harm could there be in Sophie visiting an old lady? He shrugged, kissed Sophie and said goodbye to Celeste.

Outside in the Place Vendôme, he spotted a taxi and was about to hail it when he again felt that Sophie's behaviour was odd. It was too puzzling. He must talk to someone about it. There was only one person he could consult. Realising this, he almost ran the short distance to 31 Rue Cambon.

Thirty

Madame Antoine sat at her desk, leafing through newspapers. Chanel had died during the final preparations for a new collection. The collection had been shown early and now a strange lull hung over the house. Chanel's death had paralysed it, her sudden absence had thrown it into a new mood where everyone was walking and acting slowly, in a dream. Had one very old lady's vitality and will and dream kept an entire enterprise going?

She had been asked to consult with the directors on who should take over from Mademoiselle. The very idea appeared absurd to her. Who *could* take over from Mademoiselle? The soul had gone out of Chanel & Co.

She looked up to see Christopher in the doorway. She smiled as he leaned down to kiss her white powdered cheek. She wore a no-nonsense black woollen dress. Against that, her vivid scarlet lips and perfect red nails showed up like bright red dots in a black-and-white movie. Her eyes glittered sapphire, as if grief had intensified their colour.

'What a lovely surprise. It is just about time for coffee, would you like some?'

He shook his head.

'Sophie took Gaby to the Ritz this morning,' he blurted out. 'I followed them.'

She frowned. 'Why on earth did she go there?'

'That's exactly what I wondered. She did not know I had followed her. I was watching as she went up in the lift.'

She held his eyes. 'To the fourth floor, I suppose?' she said faintly.

'Yes,' he said. 'I waited in the lobby until she came down later. When I approached her, it was like waking a sleepwalker. She took me back up with her. We walked down the corridor, she knocked on a door and for a weird moment I had the impression that Mademoiselle hadn't really died and was still in there.'

Madame Antoine's eyes were fixed on his. 'And?' she prompted.

'The maid opened the door,' he told her.

She nodded. 'Mademoiselle didn't want Jeanne thrown out on the street. Imagine, a maid living at the Ritz, with room service and everything.' She gave her amused gurgle. 'But *why* would Sophie visit her? Did you go inside the suite?'

'Yes, it was covered in boxes of letters and papers and diaries . . .'

Her eyes widened. 'Those are not supposed to be touched,' she said sharply. 'They were to remain locked in Mademoiselle's bedroom until the estate is settled. Where is Sophie now?'

'She wanted to stay there.'

'You left her there with Jeanne?' she asked.

Madame Antoine's hand went to her throat and her eyes darted around the room. Her skin, already powdered dead white, seemed to blanch even paler.

'Well, I did think it was odd,' Christopher explained. 'That's why I came to see you.'

She held up a warning hand, grabbed the telephone and quickly dialled a number.

'The Ritz?' she asked. 'Put me through to room four hundred and fourteen, please, it's urgent!' She shot him an anxious look. 'Jeanne? This is Madame Antoine. How are you, Jeanne?' She listened for a moment then asked. 'Is Sophie there? Oh? When did she leave? Did she say where she was going? I see. Thank you, Jeanne. I'll be by to see you very soon.'

347

She replaced the receiver, her eyes fixed on his. 'Christopher, this is extremely serious. Go home immediately. She may have learned something terribly upsetting from Jeanne, something I've always tried—' she looked down at her hands and swallowed, '—to keep from her.'

'*What?*' Christopher cried. 'Who her parents were?'

The sapphire eyes looked up to hold his for a long drawn-out moment. He had never stared into such an honest gaze, nor one so beautiful. As her thoughts succeeded one another, her eyes took on expression after expression, the blue turning different shades, colour after colour, as if he were looking into a kaleidoscope. He waited. Madame Antoine seemed to be making up her mind about something it had taken years to decide.

'Who her *father* was,' she said, finally.

Christopher nodded.

'Madame Antoine,' he said. 'Suppose you tell *me*?'

She hesitated a further long moment, then nodded and took a deep breath.

'Sophie's father was a Nazi general.' She gave a great sigh. 'Hans Von Dincklage,' she said quietly. 'He was younger than Mademoiselle Chanel. He was her lover for many years.'

Christopher nodded. 'And her mother?'

'Killed by the Nazis,' Madame Antoine said quietly. 'Because she was half-Jewish.'

There was a moment's silence as Christopher tried to take this in.

'You understand why we kept the facts from Sophie? Her father had to choose between his daughter and his wife. And he chose his daughter—' she broke off suddenly and hunched over, clutching Christopher's arm.

He held her as, eyes closed, she took some deep breaths. He poured a glass of water and held it out to her. She drank some.

Finally, she straightened.

'He was allowed to take Sophie with him to Paris only if he handed over his wife to the authorities. How could we ever tell her that? It may have damaged her if she knew,' she went on.

348

'She might have felt somehow responsible for her mother's death.'

'How did her mother die?' he asked.

Her eyes glittered. 'We don't know. Something quick, I hope, poor soul. Not something long and horrible—' she broke off. 'When Paris was liberated,' she resumed, sitting up straighter, 'Mademoiselle was arrested. Perhaps you know that Nazi collaborators had their heads shaved and were paraded in the streets? Mademoiselle was held for only two hours. Some very important people got her out of a tricky situation. She fled to Switzerland. Von Dincklage met her there. She stayed there eleven years until the Wertheimers reopened couture operations at Chanel and asked her to design again.'

'Is he still alive?'

She shook her head. 'Mademoiselle would have been with him.'

She sipped more water. When she looked up at him, her eyes had a new crystal-clear regard.

'He asked us to take care of his little girl so we legally adopted her,' she continued. 'You're English so perhaps you know Oscar Wilde's saying: "No good deed goes unpunished"?'

He nodded.

'But this was more than a good deed,' she shook her head. 'We found her enchanting. We renamed her Sophie and we really did love her as if she was ours, but . . .' she shook her head again. 'The shadow of her father seemed to hang over her. I never wanted her to find out. He was cultured, a reluctant Nazi. He did not torture people in concentration camps. He had to be a Nazi or be killed like his wife. He chose to live. And he did get Sophie to Paris.' She gave him a little push. 'Go to them, Christopher – quickly! If she has found out—'

'Jeanne told her!' he cried. 'I just know it!'

'Then *hurry*! The shock will be so great – she is liable to do *any*thing!'

He ran down the stairs to the front doors of Chanel, opened for him by the uniformed doorman. He ran up Rue Cambon to the Grands Boulevards, looking behind him for a free taxi. There was none in sight.

It was a cold sunny day and now there was a sickening dread in his stomach. The sun reflected off taxi windows causing him to wave frantically at many taxis before spotting someone on the back seat. Finally an off-duty taxi stopped to ask where he wanted to go. He was told to get in.

He hunched forward on the back seat, cursing every red light stopping them up until L'Etoile.

She is liable to do anything! Madame Antoine's words echoed in his head at Etoile as they stopped for yet another red light.

He threw some money at the driver, and leaped out of the taxi to run down the Avenue Kleber. The concierge was outside the building, polishing a doctor's brass plaque.

'Did Sophie just come home, Madame Claude?' he asked her.

'*Oui, monsieur . . .*'

He ran in and peered up the old-fashioned lift shaft, encased in its ornate metal grilles. The lift was at the top floor. He rang for it, waiting as it descended agonisingly slowly.

When it stopped, he wrenched the folding iron gates open.

His hands shook so badly that it took several tries to get his key in the lock. He ran into the flat. Sophie was silhouetted on the balcony railing. Gaby was on the floor watching her mother, a little puzzled. Only as he got nearer did he realise that Sophie's legs were dangling over the railing, facing outward.

'*Sophie!*' the name was torn from him.

She turned, giving him an agonised look.

'I am the daughter of a Nazi.' Her voice had a strangled high tone quite unlike her. 'A fucking Nazi. He killed my mother!'

'He was forced to choose between you. He chose you. You must not feel guilty.'

'This is why Mademoiselle chose me as her Face,' Sophie said. 'The face of a Nazi!'

'A very reluctant Nazi . . . why should *you* feel guilty?'

'Because it's in my blood, my genes! I don't want to live and I don't deserve to live!'

'You are innocent. Your father did not torture anyone. Madame Antoine says he was a cultured, charming man.'

'*No!*'

He began to approach her step by step, hoping she was too distraught to notice.

Gaby began to cry as if she did not like this game the grown-ups were playing.

He spoke soothingly. 'He didn't choose to be a Nazi, he was forced to. You must forgive your father.'

'Forgive a Nazi?' Sophie's eyes glared. 'For extracting their victims' gold teeth and using their skin? They made soap out of them! We learned that in school – it gave me nightmares. I have that blood in me.'

'You have your mother's genes, too . . .' He was advancing inch by inch. 'Your father loved you enough to bring you with him to Paris.'

'Betraying my mother!'

'Wouldn't you choose Gaby over me if you had to? Wouldn't any parent always choose their child?'

She stared agonisedly into his eyes. For a moment, they were both still. Then he made a sudden lunge for her, catching hold of her arm. Sophie struggled. She slipped off the rail, her legs dangling above the five-floor drop to the pavement. He held onto her but she was sliding from his fingers, which felt numb from clutching so tightly. But the fear of losing her gave him incredible strength and he managed to drag her backward off the balcony ledge. She fell to the floor as he reached for their daughter, now crying.

'I'll kill myself some other day!' Sophie cried, glaring up at him.

He knelt down on the floor next to her, holding her in one arm, taking the bawling baby in the other.

'No, you won't kill yourself,' he said very firmly. 'You won't, Sophie, because I love you. I haven't waited so long just to see you kill yourself, and for what? You would not deprive *your* daughter of her mother! You couldn't do that to our child. I'll get you through this. You have nothing to blame yourself for. I'll make you realise that.'

The expression in her eyes was agonised, but beneath it he saw that she *wanted* to believe him, she *wanted* to be convinced that she deserved to live, that she had nothing to feel guilty about. Life would be well worth living. And he knew he would be able to convince her. He gently stroked Sophie's head and soothed his daughter.

Thirty-one

'And for our *second* wedding, after the crappy City Hall one,' Samantha announced to everyone, 'we'll either rent the biggest chateau in Burgundy or fly in an entire planeload of New York fashion journalists for Christopher's new collection and get married in a circus tent in the middle of Paris! On a trapeze! It'll be the first time a Jewish girl gets married on a trapeze!'

It was spring and they were all sitting on the terrace outside La Coupole with Samantha holding court, newly arrived from New York, euphoric at her father's recovery.

'We will not be doing either of those things, Samantha,' Klaus said quietly.

'You're right,' Samantha agreed. 'They're not nearly spectacular enough. Maybe we could close off an entire Cannes beach and—'

'Not that either,' Klaus said firmly.

'What do you mean, Klaus? Where *can* we marry?' She looked around in exasperation.

'Somewhere quiet and small, with our friends Sophie, Christopher and Monique . . .' Klaus said. 'A little church no one knows, like the end of *Funny Face*, remember? Fred Astaire and Audrey Hepburn in a churchyard with white doves fluttering around? No fuss. Marry quietly. Isn't that best, Sophie?'

'It sounds charming.' Sophie smiled.

'*Ohhhh*,' Samantha looked as if she were about to swoon, clutching at her throat. 'I've never *heard* of anything so romantic. I would *never* have thought of that. You see?' she looked at them all. 'I gotta try thinking small sometimes. It's just like Mademoiselle told me: sometimes less is more! For my life, of course, *not* for your fashion shows, Christopher. Those must get more spectacular than ever.

On a July afternoon, with everyone close to fainting from the heat, the world of fashion gathered in a huge striped tent, decorated with flowers and trees and pulsating with rock music. The tent had been erected in an amusingly louche fairground near Montparnasse. The *fashionerazzi* had not even known the existence of this neighbourhood and were very impressed: low life always impressed them. For an hour or two, anyway.

HRRG's Autumn Collection was shown on the world's top models. Along with a few actresses and rock-stars, they paraded wools, velvet, silks, synthetics and jerseys such as had never been seen in Paris before. Outfits were shown in groups of six, in different colours and different skirt-lengths so that women could choose the lengths that most flattered them.

Clothes were sporty, wearable, wantable, saleable, buyable, but a funny thing had happened: the incredible hair-styles and wigs, the amazing hats, the over-the-top jewellery and the kabuki, geisha or Chinese opera make-up made every model mesmerising but also quite unrecognisable.

'Could anything be more throwaway chic than getting the world's top models and making them completely unrecognisable?' Samantha boasted.

The platform shoes were totteringly high and quite dangerous.

'They're so high the models are getting nosebleeds,' Samantha swore.

When they weren't being deafened by music or blinded by strobe lighting and flashing cameras, fashion folk were pelted with flower petals, artificial snow, and, at the end, shocking-pink goodie-bags, tied up in ribbon, full of the latest cosmetics and tiny bottles of champagne.

Finally, Samantha appeared in her 'Ringmaster' outfit: tight black satin tuxedo over long fishnet-stockinged legs and high,

high heels. She wore a silk top hat and carried a whip. Her red-lacquered lips beamed in a huge grin, her teeth dazzling.

'*Bienvenu à* HRRG!' she cried, cracking her whip and accidentally lashing the cheek of a middle-aged journalist from a Swedish knitting magazine with whom she later settled out of court.

But it was Klaus who provided the *pièce de résistance.* Out of nowhere he produced two trapezists dressed as a rabbi and a Catholic priest. Klaus ripped off his jeans to reveal black tights and climbed with Samantha up a very slippery rope ladder to the trapeze platform high above the ring.

There, he and Samantha were 'married' before the thousand chic onlookers.

'What happened to Audrey Hepburn's tiny sweet church with white doves?' she cried.

'This is more "you",' Klaus assured her. 'Fabulousness is part of your make-up, Samantha!' he cried over the din.

The 'rabbi' and the 'priest' were now performing gestures of blessings over them, trapezes swinging precariously alongside. 'I knew that dinky little City Hall wedding in New York meant nothing to you.'

'Oh Klaus, this is so damned romantic,' Samantha glowed, clinging to her rope ladder, bending one leg to show off its shapeliness. 'If only Mademoiselle was here, she'd be so proud, so thrilled.'

Klaus bit back an ironic comment. Surely nothing was less Chanel than this marriage ceremony? He doubted that Mademoiselle would approve of any of it.

The Antoines were down in the audience, Madame Antoine holding Gaby. Samantha's father was sitting next to them, flown in the day before by Klaus, looking up proudly from the front row, his pacemaker working perfectly.

The clowns were almost indistinguishable from the models, and an old-fashioned tango orchestra replaced the rock music for some welcome eardrum relief.

Ghislaine de Rives canoodled with Pierre, her handsome new

young lover, and Christopher and Sophie clapped their hands at the spectacle.

'Balenciaga said no designer should be afraid of vulgarity,' Monique whispered to Guy. 'But perhaps Samantha has gone a little too far?'

Mademoiselle would be turning in her Lausanne grave if she could see this explosion of opulence and, yes, vulgarity. There was a scrabble for the goodie-bags. Most journalists wanted two.

Guy hugged her. 'This is the future of fashion, Monique, now that Mademoiselle Chanel is dead. It is fashion no longer, it has become show business!'

She nodded, trying not to cry at the sudden surge of feeling. She would be the new *directrice* of Chanel. She had come to Paris expecting – what? Far less than this! And her sister Caterine was going to join them next month.

'Take me down, I'm getting giddy!' Samantha cried.

The pictures, taken by an over-eager paparazzo who stood beneath her as she clambered down the rope ladder, made many of the next day's front pages.

A few weeks later, they all sat on the terrace of a large café on the Boulevard St Germain on a sunny Sunday afternoon.

'Teh! We have learned to live without Chanel?' Samantha mused, admiring her wedding ring from different angles. 'But it sure wasn't easy.'

She sipped a huge, *café crème* and glanced down at her HRRG dress.

'Oh my God, everybody? Look! I'm not wearing Chanel! I'm wearing HRRG!' she cried. 'I've overcome my addiction! My name is Samantha and I am *not* a Chanel addict!'

'A small round of applause?' Klaus suggested.

They all politely applauded.

Sophie jiggled Gaby on her knee.

'Such a beautiful fashion baby,' Samantha said, studying her.

'When will you have one?' Sophie asked.

Samantha made a face. 'Chanel doesn't make maternity clothes.

It might be easier to adopt some sweet African orphans in various shades . . . from bitter chocolate to caramel?'

'But you don't choose children as if they're accessories!' Sophie said.

'Oh . . .' Samantha's face fell. 'But isn't it nice if they *match* your accessories?'

Sophie shook her head and sipped her *citron pressé*. She had found herself automatically defending the orphans Samantha had mentioned, because she still thought of herself as one. But she had not been an unwanted orphan, she reminded herself. Her parents had wanted her, loved her. Her father had loved her enough to choose her survival, to smuggle her out of Germany and to entrust her to the Antoines. She *had* been loved, and the realisation of this changed everything.

Christopher caught Sophie's eye and smiled as they exchanged a secret look. Her face was unrecognisable from the anguished expression of the woman who had contemplated suicide. Now she was seeing a therapist and learning about her father from Madame Antoine who had known him well. He watched, always keeping a careful eye on her, rejoicing that finally she accepted her life, her parentage, her future.

Monique sat next to Guy, drinking tea as he sipped his pastis. They were taking time off from looking at larger apartments, hoping to find something located halfway between Chanel and Yves Saint Laurent.

How strange, Monique thought. I came to Paris to learn how to be the best dressmaker in Angers. I've ended up as *Directrice* of Chanel and with a man I love. And I was probably the least ambitious of us all. There was a lesson there, somewhere.

She'd stopped having her recurrent dream of being held protectively in the arms of a loving, older man whose face was hidden. In the last dream, she had looked up to see it was Guy.

*

357

Watching the passing Parisians, they kept up a running commentary on the clothes being worn.

Christopher reached for Sophie's hand.

'We are fashion-addicts who incorporate fashion into our working lives,' he announced.

'Fashion-junkies who never need to go cold turkey?' Samantha said.

'We are professionals who earn our living from fashion,' Guy said. 'What is better than that?' There were murmurs of agreement.

Samantha took a long, slow look at her friends, one by one, as she finished her coffee.

'Teh . . .' she shook her head to herself. 'Everyone got a happy ending. Well, waddya know? And you know something else?' she asked them. 'I have this feeling that the seventies are gonna be even more fabulous than the sixties!'

Acknowledgements

Thank you to these people for their help, information, encouragement or for being wonderful sounding-boards:

Joan Marquès, Monique Hay, Jean Csaky, Shirley Kennedy, Susan Frend, Patricia Leckie, Barb Burg Schieffelin, Catalina Estarellas, Maria Antonia Llull, Elizabeth Suter, Joan Orlen and Bonnie Freeman.
And to:
Kate Mills for brilliant editing
And
Jane Turnbull for being the best agent.